Dear Mystery Reader,

The ever popular J.S. Borthwick returns with her eighth Sarah Deane mystery. J.S. has won acclaim from *The New York Times Book Review*, *Publishers Weekly* and her ever increasing number of loyal fans. For those of you yet to experience the wit and attitude of her cozies, *The Garden Plot* is the perfect opportunity to get hooked on this extraordinary writer.

This time out, nice-but-nosy English teacher Sarah Deane is off to Europe for a garden tour with her equestrian Aunt Julia. With free airline tickets and room and board, one would think nothing could go wrong. But with Sarah's luck, of course, it soon does. When the tour guide fails to show up and with the rest of the tour group acting weird, the trip suddenly takes a deadly turn. With murder lurking around every turn, Sarah's got to find out what's going on before she's pushing up the daisies herself.

The Garden Plot is Borthwick at her best. Once you've read this, you'll want to run out and pick up more DEAD LETTER titles. Until then, keep the pages turning and enjoy.

Yours in crime,

Joe Veltre
Associate Editor
St. Martin's Press DEAD LETTER Paperback Mysteries

Also by J.S. Borthwick

Dolly Is Dead
The Bridled Groom
Dude on Arrival
Bodies of Water
The Student Body
The Down East Murders
The Case of the Hook-Billed Kites

The
Garden Plot

J. S. BORTHWICK

St. Martin's Paperbacks

The village of High Roosting, Thalia Cottage, the inns, hotels, B & B's, the restaurants, the pubs, as well as the characters and events described in this book are fictitious.

THE GARDEN PLOT

Copyright © 1997 by J. S. Borthwick.

Text illustrations by Alec and Margaret Creighton.

All rights reserved. No part of this book may be used or reproduced in any manner whatsoever without written permission except in the case of brief quotations embodied in critical articles or reviews. For information address St. Martin's Press, 175 Fifth Avenue, New York, NY 10010.

Library of Congress Catalog Card Number: 96-30673

ISBN: 0-312-96291-6

Printed in the United States of America

St. Martin's Press hardcover edition / April 1997
St. Martin's Paperbacks edition / September 1998

10 9 8 7 6 5 4 3 2 1

For my daughter, Margaret,
without whose prodding I would never have trudged through
a hundred European gardens and to
my granddaughter, eight-year-old Louisa,
who cheerfully endured although she has now sworn
never to look at another flower.

Many thanks to Dr. Daryl Pelletier for suggestions, information, and a supply of periodicals on matters pertaining to the problems and solution of this mystery. To be more specific would be to give it all away. And a grateful nod to Snowshill Manor and to those wonderful gardens at Barnsley House, at Kiftsgate Court, Hidcote Manor Garden, the Cambridge University Botanical Garden, Sissinghurst Garden, Monet's garden at Giverny, and the gardens of the Villa Melzi. In all these nothing untoward took place; only cheerful help and hospitality.

A Gateway to Gardens

Whirlaway Tours and tour director Barbara Baxter are delighted to present a once-in-a-lifetime European tour for the Midcoast Garden Club of Maine. In addition, Lillian Garth, Garden Club president, has arranged for noted horticultural expert Dr. Ellen Trevino of Bowmouth College to travel with us and through informal on-site lectures to join us in celebrating the wonders of the chosen gardens.

SATURDAY, MAY 20, 7 P.M.: "Getting to Know You" dinner at the Surfway Restaurant in Rockport, Maine. Following dinner Barbara Baxter and Dr. Trevino will share with us some of the highlights of our trip.

TUESDAY, JUNE 6, Depart 8:10 P.M. from Boston's Logan Airport on British Airways. Please arrive at the international departure gate at least two hours before departure for passport and baggage check-in.

WEDNESDAY, JUNE 7, 7:35 A.M. Arrive London's Heathrow Airport, meet tour bus and drive to Ibis Hotel for refreshment and rest. Depart for Gloucestershire and the Shearing Inn.

JUNE 7–14: The Shearing Inn, High Roosting, Gloucestershire. A charming old inn will be our base for visiting many famous Cotswold gardens.

THURSDAY, JUNE 15: Depart High Roosting and visit a variety of cottage gardens in the Cambridge countryside. Overnight we are in the heart of Cambridge at Hotel Fatima.

FRIDAY, JUNE 16: To the weald of Kent and the fabled gardens of Sissinghurst created by novelist and poet Vita Sackville-West and her husband, historian and diplomat Harold Nicholson. In Kent we spend the night at the old world Hagglestone Arms in nearby Cranbrook.

SATURDAY, JUNE 17: We take le shuttle to France, meet our bus at Calais, and drive to Vernon to the Hotel Fontaine in time for dinner.

SUNDAY, JUNE 18: Giverny. A day to enjoy the world of Claude Monet: his house and studio, the *Clos Normand*, the water gardens. In the evening we drive to the outskirts of Paris to a delightful country inn, La Moustache Noire.

MONDAY, JUNE 19–22: Depart 10 A.M. Air France for Milan from Charles de Gaulle Airport and continue by bus to Lake Como and the picturesque town of Bellagio, where we stay at the Hotel Albergo Nuovo. Since ample time is provided for exploring the famous gardens of the Villa Melzi, the Villa Serbelloni, and the Villa Carlotta, we will also be able to visit Bellagio's many museums, shops, and restaurants.

THURSDAY, JUNE 22: Return by bus to Milan, spend the night at the Buonarroti Aeroporto Hotel and depart June 23, British Airways 11:40 A.M. Arriving Heathrow 12:35 P.M. Depart British Airways 3:50 P.M. Arriving Boston 6:10 P.M.

Cast of Principal Characters

The Midcoast Garden Club on Tour

Experts, Directors, and Tour Leaders
Barbara Baxter—Director, Whirlaway Tours
Ellen Trevino—Professor of Botany, Bowmouth College
Henry Ruggles—British garden expert

The Tour Group
Sarah Deane—Teaching Fellow, Bowmouth College, wife of Alex
    McKenzie
Julia Clancy—Aunt to Sarah
Edith Hopper—Sister to Margaret
Margaret Hopper—Sister to Edith
Doris Lermatov—Mother to Amy
Amy Lermatov—Fourteen-year-old daughter of Doris
Fred Ouellette—Undertaker
Sandi Ouellette—Fred's wife
Justin Rossi—Lawyer from Boston
Stacy Daniel—Publicity Director, Boston bank
Carter McClure—History professor, Bowmouth College
Portia McClure—Garden enthusiast, wife to Carter

And also:
Alex McKenzie—Physician and husband of Sarah
Gregory Baxter—Brother of Barbara
Mike Laaka—Deputy Sheriff Investigator
George Fitts—Sergeant, CID, Maine State Police

1

Lillies will languish; violets look ill;
Sickly the prim-rose; pale the daffadill;
That gallant tulip will hang down his head,
Like to a virgin newly ravished,
Pansies will weep; and marigolds will wither;
And keep a fast, and funerall together . . .

> —"The Sadness of Things,"
> *The Lyrical Poems of Robert Herrick.*

LILLIAN Garth couldn't concentrate. Everything was spinning around and there were these blank spots. Had she fallen over her own big feet? That's what her husband, Sam, seemed to think. Lillian did remember it had been the Midcoast Garden Club meeting at her house, and that new member, Sandi Ouellette, had asked a question about root cellars. After that, a gap, something about the stairs and everything going black. Then coming to with her head pounding like hell in the Intensive Care Unit of the Mary Starbox Memorial Hospital. And Sam hanging over the bed rails saying, "For God's sake, Lillian, what possessed you to go down into the cellar without turning on the lights?" Which wasn't very sympathetic of Sam, but she'd tripped down there only two months ago so his reaction wasn't surprising. That time she'd missed the last step and only cracked her elbow. But now her head was banging away, her leg—the right one—and her ankle—the left one—were both propped up encased in something rigid. Oh, God, she'd really done a job on herself this time.

Or had she? Something at the farthest edge of memory nagged at her, tried to take shape, and then faded. It was a feeling really. The feeling of something solid—something flat and hard, the heel of a hand maybe, hitting against her back. Shoving, that was it, shoving. And driving. Driving her forward into this awful whirling black emptiness. If only, she muttered to herself, I could remember.

But Lillian could not, and because she failed to give shape or definition to this wisp of memory, the hand would be free to push and strike again. And again. And again.

As Miss Austen might have written, it is a truth universally acknowledged that an expensive item offered free of charge will be accepted without thought to whether the item is desired or even useful. Thus, on a morning in late April it happened that one Julia Clancy, doyenne of the local equestrian world, found herself with the opportunity of visiting foreign parts during the month of June without the bother of paying for it.

It happened thus:

Saturday, April third began with what the French describe as a "blow of the telephone." Julia, who disliked telephone calls in general and early morning ones in particular, got stiffly to her feet, reached for her cane—her arthritis was very bad this spring—stumped over to the telephone, and barked hello.

"Julia?" queried the voice.

"Of course, it's Julia," said Julia. "That's who you were calling, wasn't it?"

"Julia," repeated the voice.

"Is that you, Adelaide? Well, I'm very busy in the barn so I can't talk now."

"You're not in the barn, Julia," said Adelaide—Adelaide Dempster, local stalwart of the Midcoast Garden Club. "I called there first and your stableman said you were at the house. Now do listen for once. I have an offer . . ."

". . . I can't refuse? Oh yes I can. If it's your summer garden tour, I'll buy two tickets and not go."

"Wait up," said Adelaide. She was Julia's second cousin and knew her ways and moods. "Not tickets. I mean, yes, it's a ticket—actually two tickets. A real tour. Not just around here. The UK, France, and Italy. The Cotswolds, Sissinghurst, and Giverny. Monet's lilies. And Bellagio. It's on Lake Como."

"I don't want to go away," said Julia in a cross voice. "I want to go down to the barn and check on my horses. It's past seven-thirty and Duffie cast a shoe last night. I've got to call the farrier.

"You must take the tickets. The Whirlaway Tours people have to be guaranteed a certain number of tickets or the whole trip will be canceled. Everything's paid for. I can't go, my back has gone completely flooey, and yesterday Lillian Garth fell down the cellar steps."

"What!"

"An accident. Well, I suppose it must have been an accident because poor Lillian is a little careless. You see, Lillian organized the whole tour and was going to help lead the trip. She's a real powerhouse when it comes to pulling things together . . ."

"Get on with it," growled Julia.

"Well, Lillian not only nailed another dynamo—Dr. Ellen Trevino (she wrote that book on English cottage gardens)—but she turned up this expert leader from Whirlaway Tours, Barbara Baxter, who's a sort of facilitator. Barbara's been terrific and she's already dug up two people to fill out the numbers. We needed four and you're the other two. A handsome man called Rossi and this other gorgeous blonde female . . ."

"For God's sake, Adelaide, I don't give a damn about handsome men and gorgeous blondes, so get to the point."

"Well, Lillian got the whole travel group together at her house—tea, coffee, cake, drinks, the whole bit—and Sandi Ouellette, who's a sort of bubblehead, asked about root cellars, and Lillian went to bring up some tubers she's been nursing along, and down she went. Not the first time, either, because it seems she slipped on the same stairs a while back. So, now she's got a concussion along with a broken right leg and a smashed left ankle. Totally out of action. So Barbara Baxter, along with Dr. Trevino, is going to handle the tour. So there you are. Two tickets. Mine and Lillian's. The whole thing on a platter—airfare, hotels, inns, B&Bs, and seats on the bus."

Julia, one of the world's non-gardeners, sat heavily on a kitchen stool and studied the roof of her stable, visible from her kitchen window. "There's so much to do on the farm," she said, but her voice betrayed a rising interest. The idea of going free to England and France and Italy in June had a definite attraction.

Adelaide persisted. "Not only the gardens, which are beautiful even if you know absolutely nothing about flowers, but you could hire a car and sneak off from time to time. Breeding farms, thoroughbreds, warmbloods," said Adelaide, who knew Julia's Achilles' heel.

"But I hardly know a poppy from a peony and my own garden is a mess. Besides, next month is such a busy time. The new foals. The show schedule and the dressage clinic. Riding lesson schedules."

"Julia, be quiet and listen. Your manager, the wonderful Patrick, can handle the farm nicely without you. And you have plenty of other help. Stablemen and those working students you starve to death. Give them all a break and go away."

"I'm on a cane," complained Julia. "My blasted knee hurts like hell."

"So keep your cane. It's an advantage. I'm sixty-three and I use a cane all the time. It empowers me. People give way. Get your family doctor—it's Alex McKenzie, isn't it, practically a relative—to plug you into some high-powered anti-inflammatory and go for it. You'll be fine. I'm just sorry I can't make it."

———

So it was that Julia Clancy dug out her passport, called her niece's husband, Alex, for a prescription, and began thinking of all-purpose washable garments. And a suitable companion. And who else but that selfsame niece, Sarah Douglas Deane, an adjunct on past assorted junkets and visits.

"No," said Sarah when called at her office in the Bowmouth College English Department. "I'll have just finished the spring teaching term and I'll be a wreck. Besides, I wanted to paint the living room. That leaves Alex to do it by himself. Or not do it which is more likely. And what about my dog, Patsy?"

"Patsy can come over to the farm. He loves my setters. And Alex did just fine for years without your help. Besides, I called his office because I want some killer drug for my arthritis. He just got word he has a Lyme Disease conference in Bologna the last week in June. We can be in the tour for the first part of the trip and later meet up with Alex in Italy. But I don't want to spend the whole time crammed in a bus with other people, so we'll hire our own car and duck out from time to time and go off on our own."

"So why not scrub the entire tour? Just fly over with them, then split and do our own thing?"

"Don't be foolish. Free meals at inns and hotels, free admissions to the gardens. Everything's paid for. Besides I thought you were getting into a garden mode. Those new peach trees."

"Eight feeble peach trees do not a garden make."

"Don't be a stick-in-the-mud. I need you."

"Who's this Barbara Baxter person?"

"Tour boss. She'll have to do the whole thing now that Lillian's laid up. And she doesn't have to know much about flowers because there'll be a real expert along. Dr. Ellen Trevino."

"Wait," said Sarah, her voice a shade more enthusiastic. "Did you say Ellen Trevino?"

"Yes, that's the name. I think she teaches at your college. Biology, botany. Something like that. Have you run into her?"

"Run into her?" Sarah exclaimed. "I grew up with her. Next door. In Carlisle. When my family was in its Massachusetts phase. Ellen was sweet but very shy and kept to herself. I was one of her few friends and we've known each other since sandbox days. I'm always amazed when I think about her lecturing, standing up in front of students. In grade school she used to freeze if the teacher so much as looked at her."

"Well, good. A friend on the trip. Besides old Julia."

"I haven't seen much of Ellen, really, for years. She's not a people person. She gives her lectures and goes into hiding. No time for lunch. Every now and then I go out and visit her—she lives way out in the country—and she's nice about it, but I can always tell she's itching to get back to her greenhouse."

"So why has she agreed to lead a group all the way to Europe? Be locked in with a bunch of strangers."

"Oh, I've heard she does that from time to time. Probably needs the money. Bowmouth salaries barely support life."

Julia returned to the matter at hand. "So Ellen Trevino is a plus. And I'm grateful she'll be along because I haven't time to read up on gardens. I'm much too busy with foaling."

Sarah's sigh was audible over the telephone. "And I'm too busy with exams."

"Not the same thing. Foaling is day and night work, very strenuous and quite nerve-racking. All you do is sit at a desk, ask questions, and scratch out answers with a red pencil."

Sarah ignored this thrust. "And I hate flying," she said. "A few hours is bad enough, but crossing the Atlantic wondering if the life jackets really float is my idea of torture."

"They have pills. Alex will prescribe for you. Something to knock you out. Now I've got to go. Work on your French and Italian. Useful phrases like *Aidez-moi* and *Où se trouve* the ladies room? In Italian it's *Dove sono i gabinetti?* And, Sarah, check your passport. Good-bye."

"Aunt Julia, wait," shouted Sarah, but the line was dead.

"Damn that woman," said Sarah aloud.

"So you're going on the garden tour," said her husband, Alex, when he made it home from the hospital that night. He threw himself down in one of the ancient wicker kitchen armchairs and grinned at her. "I know you're going even if you think you aren't. Aunt Julia has spoken."

Sarah looked up from a heap of student papers and rammed her red pencil down on the top sheet, breaking the point. "I am not," she said. "Never. Not on your life."

But somehow time went by, April turned into May and June stood on the horizon, and Sarah found herself, like Julia, checking her passport, taking out an international driver's license, and looking into wrinkle-proof clothing. And filling out the short "getting to know you" biographical questionnaire sent out by the Whirlaway Tours leader, Barbara Baxter—a waste of time in Sarah's opinion since most of the Garden Club members must be entirely too familiar with each other by this time.

But the final annoyance came when the energetic Ms. Baxter sent out announcements of a tour party in a back room of the Surfway Restaurant.

"I don't have time to go to some party," she told her aunt Julia when informed of the event. "Besides, I'll meet everyone on the plane and on the bus. At lunch and dinner. Why rush it?"

"We'll look like a pair of snobs if we don't go. Barbara Baxter has this idea that if we know each other ahead of time everything will run more smoothly. One happy family on tour."

"Gag. She didn't say that, did she?"

"No, I said it to get a rise out of you. Pick me up at six-thirty."

The tour group appeared to have been made up of a core from the local Midcoast Garden Club plus the two outside enthusiasts—the described handsome male and the gorgeous blonde—both from "away," as the people of Maine refer to those unfortunate enough to have been born beyond its borders. Barbara had waved vaguely in the direction of Massachusetts when introducing the apparently unrelated man and woman. "Both have been on our Whirlaway Tours before and we're so lucky they're free to go."

Sarah glanced around the table as she worked first through a daiquiri, then chicken Kiev and apple crisp. There was her old friend, Ellen Trevino, who, as the honored speaker, sat in the center of the table next to Barbara Baxter. Sarah had waved at her on entering the dining room, but had given up hope of conversation since Ellen, as the evening's ornament, had been from her arrival surrounded by garden enthusiasts.

Most of the club members were everyday types, she decided, the sort of people you could picture down on their knees with a trowel and a hand rake. Julia, of course, didn't fit the profile of persons devoted to slow nurture and silent growth. Her voice was too sharp, her gestures too abrupt. Only when dealing with horses did the patient side of her aunt become manifest; for the general run of humans, Julia had little tolerance. Now, having chugged two predinner whiskeys and gotten into a brisk argument about rotted manure, she was nodding over her coffee while Barbara Baxter made welcoming remarks.

This done, Barbara, armed with a map and a marker board, began drawing lines and triangles, listing dates and indicating inns, hotels, National Trust houses and gardens, periods of rest, and every now and again a stop for shopping and tea.

"And I hope to God the possibility of hard liquor," put in a fellow tour member, Carter McClure. Although many of the others were strangers, Sarah knew Carter by sight from Bowmouth College; he was one of pashas of the History Department and said by his colleagues to obsessed with his garden. He and his wife, Portia, were seated almost under Barbara Baxter's elbow, and Sarah found that they made a strange trio. Barbara had a pleasant freckled face, short-cropped sandy curls, and had a sturdy physique that suggested a former college soccer star. She had obviously dressed carefully for the occasion in a patterned navy skirt and a red blouse. Carter, on the other hand, was a tall, lean, hatchet-faced man with gray hair in a porcupine cut who, in contrast to other males present who wore jacket and tie, sported an in-your-face costume of black jacket, black shirt, and faded jeans and Nikes. Next to him sat Portia, a handsome African-American woman with sharp eyes, a firm chin. Portia wore an olive dress hung with several chains of colored beads and from time to time laid a firm hand on Carter's arm in an attempt to restrain her husband from offending the entire party.

"I mean," said Carter, "I won't belong to any tour that neglects opportunities for a stiff drink. We'll be stomping around gardens all day, so we'd better not be booked into some goddamn temperance inn. And I'll say right now, forget the shopping."

"Carter," said Portia. "Be quiet."

"Hear, hear," said Julia Clancy, waking up and blinking.

But Barbara Baxter was not one to be derailed by the likes of Carter McClure. She wound up her speech, suggested that they were all kindred souls—and then with an eye on Carter began detailing the greatness of English ale, the friendly pubs, the inns and hotels chosen for the tour. Not to mention the gardens themselves. The treasures of England. This was actually her very first garden tour, but she was doing her homework, boning up. And she certainly looked forward to visiting the cottage gardens of the Cotswolds.

"So exciting," gushed Sandi Ouelette. "I'm going right home and read up on cottage gardens." She paused. "What is a cottage garden, anyway?"

"An excellent question," said Barbara, "and one our experts, Dr. Trevino, will be glad to answer. She indicated the thin-faced woman sitting at her right hand.

Dr. Ellen Trevino, after the briefest of hesitations—Sarah was reminded of the shy, withdrawn schoolgirl she had known—stood up and in a low but clear voice began to extol the virtues of the English cottage garden, and as she went from the problems of various soils, peat and sand, and other useful particulate matter to the actual planting and dividing and massing of flowers, Sarah understood that here was a woman in love. In love with what she was doing with her life. And she remembered Ellen as a twelve-year-old running ahead of a small tractor her father was running and snatching blooming flowers out of his path—Ellen shouting, "You're killing them, you're a murderer, you're killing all the flowers."

But then Ellen's father himself was killed in an automobile accident, her mother remarried and moved, and the two girls lost sight of each other. Even so, Sarah through a trick of memory was able to superimpose the thin child Ellen with the fair skin, the taut mouth, the determined small pointed chin, onto the slender adult Ellen with her light brown hair in a braided knot on the back of her head, the chin still assertive, the skin still pale except for the two patches of color on her cheeks—color no doubt brought on by the excitement of lecturing.

And lecturing it was. Ellen was making few allowances for the uninformed likes of Julia and Sarah—or Fred and Sandi Ouellette, for that matter. But as Dr. Trevino's peroration became more and more larded with Latin tags—*Anemone pulsatilla, Campanula lactiflora, Syringa persica laciniata*—Julia slumped in her seat and Sarah found her attention moving away from Ellen to her fellow tour members. This examination was facilitated by a large mirror on a side wall that reflected the party. Sarah found that by twisting slightly in her chair she could account for almost the whole group.

The mirror, she thought, what with the flickering table candles and the angle of the reflection, the deep shadows in the background, turned, she thought, the table scene into a nineteenth-century period piece. She studied the reflection and then, having received the printout of every member's questionnaire, she decided to amuse herself by trying to fit the answers to the faces reflected in the mirror. First, of course, there was her aunt Julia, a terrier of a woman, fierce of eye, bristly gray hair on end, linen jacket rumpled. Julia had restricted her response to listing herself as the owner of High Hope Farm, a trainer of horses and riders, and one who knew absolutely nothing about gardens. Sarah, herself, had not been quite so honest. After noting her employment as a lecturer in English at Bowmouth College, she had put herself down as an amateur gardener, one whose special interest was peach trees, but was hoping to put in some peonies and perhaps a rose bush in the near future. Squinting at her own reflection in the mirror, Sarah decided that she was looking a little haunted tonight, what with her end-of-term pallor: her cheekbones prominent; her chin almost as sharp as Ellen's; her gray eyes, somehow exaggerated by the lighting, looking almost black; and her short dark hair standing unnaturally away from her head—static electricity perhaps.

Then there was Carter McClure, now hidden in the mirror by Ellen Trevino. Carter had noted on his information sheet that space did not permit the listing of his many botanical interests and areas of expertise, adding only that propagation of hardy variants of *Viburnum plicatum mariesii* was a new project. Portia McClure, now concealed by Barbara Baxter's torso, had written that she raised King Charles spaniels and loved herbal gardens, but that her real passion was developing superior compost.

Who was next of the Midcoast members? The resident feather-brain—Sandi Ouellette. Sitting there in a pink dress hung with bracelets, rings, and drippy earrings. A double row of twinkling buttons starting from her scoop neckline, traveling over her perky little breasts and disappearing waistward. Sandi, a person Sarah remembered from a previous encounter as being an enthusiast regardless of the event in progress. Even when the event had turned out to be sudden death, Sandi hadn't lost her friskiness. And her signature on the copied bio sheet showed a little circle over the "i" in her first name and a tiny happy face inside.

Sandi's partner in life was Fred Ouellette, a local undertaker, a tall bony dark-haired man who bore a slight resemblance to Abraham Lincoln. Fred thought Sandi was entrancing and Sandi thought Fred was a scream—this because Fred had a large stock of stories centered on lawyers and doctors in embarrassing situations. Fred himself had listed his profession as "mortician," one interested in the "burial practices of all nations," the good works of the Rotary, and especially in classic floral arrangements. For classic funerals, Sarah wondered. Or was it a joke?

She moved on to contemplation of the two Hoppers. Sisters, Margaret and Edith, who, having married cousins, shared the same last name. They were said to be staunch Garden Club loyalists. White-haired, they wore matching cable-stitch cardigans over their flowered silk dresses and carried Nantucket Lightship baskets. Margaret had declared herself a retired school librarian devoted to her grandchildren and the culture of Siberian Iris. Her sister Edith, retired from the management of a local bookstore, put in time with the Humane Society and enjoyed working in her rock garden. Both wore thick-lensed eyeglasses attached to beaded chains.

Then there were the four tour members seated at the end of the table who gave back interesting blurs of fuzzy heads and moving spoons and cups. Impossible to tell what they really looked like. The two other locals, Doris Lermatov and her daughter, Amy, sat together. Doris wrote that her interest was divided between "going to wonderful places to eat" and in raising different varieties of delphiniums. Amy, age fourteen, expressed an interest in British rock bands and in finding a really weird haunted castle.

Sarah moved on to the two outsiders. The man, last name Rossi—showing an indistinct but interesting reflection—looked familiar. The other woman, Stacy, a sort of blond lioness, appeared in the mirror only as a melting of pale blue into cream. But even at the distance she looked as if she had stepped straight from the pages of *Vogue*.

Sarah was about to refresh herself with the personal history of these two when she became aware of a switch of speakers. Ellen Trevino had sat down and Margaret Hopper held the floor. The injured Lillian Garth was the subject. Such a distressing accident. How much she would be missed. Her strong leadership, her enthusiasm for herbaceous borders, all the reading she had done about Vita Sackville West, Harold Nickelson, and Virginia Woolf and then to miss Sissinghurst. A real shame.

"Sissinghurt's not going away," said Carter McClure. "She can go next year."

Margaret Hopper ignored Carter. "Edith and I think we should send her something from a nursery. From all of us. Something Lillian can plant later. A hardy azalea perhaps."

There was a murmur of "Hear, hear," a vote was passed to send a suitable shrub to Lillian, and the table broke into little conversational groups, leaving Sarah to prod Julia and suggest home. But then Barbara Baxter was on her feet. "No oversized

suitcases, and for any of you who are unsteady on your feet"—
here she looked pointedly at Julia and then at the Hopper
sisters—"let poor Lillian's accident be a warning. Bring appropriate shoes because we will be doing a lot of walking. Remember traveler's checks or credit cards, and meet me at Logan
Airport on June sixth at the gates for international departures.
British Airways. Flight 214. Two hours ahead of departure time.
Your passports must be validated, your luggage ticketed, your
seats assigned." And your baggage searched for bombs, Sarah
said to herself, feeling a twinge in the bottom of her stomach.

The members of the Midcoast Garden Club and the extras
from "away" rose en masse, milled briefly, and then headed for
the coat room. Sarah tried vainly to reach Ellen Trevino for at
least a few words in honor of old friendships, but Ellen had
slipped away from the crowd of admirers and vanished into the
night. As she always does, thought Sarah, feeling rather cheated.
Privacy was all very well, but really. She picked up her handbag
and found herself joined by Sandi Ouellette.

"I just hope I can remember everything. Fred says I'm a real
fluff head when it comes to dates and places. And English names
for things. But I'm not such a fluff-head that I'd forget to turn on
the cellar lights. I'm very safety conscious."

"That's good," said Sarah absently, hunting ahead for Julia.

But Sandi had more to say. "And so is Lillian Garth. She's the
one who proposed me for a Garden Club member because we're
in the same yoga class, and I'm sure she turned on the cellar stair
lights that day. I know because I wanted to go down for her, and
she said I was to stay put and she'd go down herself and bring
up some roots she was storing, and, besides, she knew where
the light switch was. It was on the left side, not the right, because
the electrician had made a dumb mistake. So there. I think she
fell down because she's careless, not because she couldn't see."

Sarah frowned. "You mean the lights were *on* when she fell?"

"Well," said Sandi, "I went to see her in the hospital and she
can't remember what happened, but I say she couldn't have forgotten the lights because she talked about them. But, you know,
they were off when we found her. I think a fuse blew or some-

thing. Anyway, I'm sorry Lillian can't go because she's a real organizer and knew how to make everyone feel at home."

"And Barbara Baxter doesn't?"

"Oh, of course she does. Barbara's wonderful the way she's taken hold, but, anyway, it's a real shame," concluded Sandi, shaking her blond tangle of hair. And she scurried ahead to catch up with Fred, who stood by the door waiting with Julia Clancy.

Sarah was silent as she drove home with Julia but, as they neared the turn off to High Hope Farm, she could not resist saying, "Sandi Ouellette says Lillian Garth meant to turn on the cellar lights. She actually mentioned it to Sandi."

Julia turned in her seat. "Sarah Douglas Deane, stop that right now. You are asking for trouble. I swear you would stand at the heavenly gates and tell St. Peter that the gates are off their hinges and one of the angels is wearing a false nose. You have a diseased mind."

"Only a curious one," murmured Sarah. "It's sort of a habit."

"Well, go back to literature and stop bringing all those tangled webs and evil plots into our quiet everyday life."

"Your everyday life, my dear aunt," said Sarah firmly, "would choke a horse. And probably has."

"No unnatural harm has ever come to my horses," rejoined Julia.

"No," said Sarah, remembering only too vividly a summer of mayhem at High Hope Farm. "The horses have made out all right. It's the humans who haven't been so lucky."

2

IT was almost a week later when Sarah managed to catch sight of Ellen Trevino. It was after one o'clock on the last Friday in May and Sarah was heading for the faculty parking lot when she saw Ellen ahead, briefcase in hand, moving purposefully.

"Ellen," she called. "Ellen, wait up." Sarah hastened her steps and caught up with her friend. "Ellen, I'm so glad you're going to be on this garden thing. Maybe you can even teach a horticultural idiot like me a few things."

Ellen came to a stop and smiled. In the days when campus dress—even for faculty members—was casual to the extreme, she seemed to have stepped from a pre-Raphaelite painting with her long brown hair, her pale cream complexion, her long cotton skirt in a dark tapestry pattern, topped by a white ruffed-neck blouse held at the collar by a gold and jade brooch.

"Lunch," said Sarah, on sudden inspiration. "I've just finished the last of my student exams and I'm starving. We'll find some place quiet because I know you don't like crowds."

But Ellen shook her head. "Sarah, I just have too much to do. I'd love to sometime. Anyway, we'll all be having lunch together on this garden trip. I'm almost dreading the whole thing, and for two cents I'd cancel and let Barbara Baxter run it. She seems capable. Three weeks elbow to elbow, toe to toe. And Carter McClure can be such a pain in the neck; even Portia can't keep him civil all the time."

"Then why did you agree to do it?" demanded Sarah. "The money?"

Ellen gave a slight lift of her shoulders. "That, yes. I'm always short of cash and I'm still paying for that new all-season greenhouse I put in last year. Of course, it's a good chance to see English gardens in June. I'd have stuck to England, but the group wants France and Italy. Anyway," she added with more energy, "I'm afraid I've worked out a pretty rigorous schedule. It's not going to be a tourist trip—you know, with side trips to Harrods or Stratford, or going out of the way to eat at fancy restaurants."

"Not even a pub or a village churchyard?"

"At night they can all do what they want. But I think everyone will be tired after hiking around all day. It's to be a focused trip just as Lillian Garth planned it." Here Ellen paused and then brightened. "But I'm glad you found me. I need something to read on the trip. Nothing violent. English and nineteenth century and I've read all Jane Austen. What do you suggest?"

Sarah thought for a moment, discarded the Brontës and Dickens, and then said, "Try Trollope. Any of the novels, but if you haven't read him, start with *The Warden* and *Barchester Towers.*"

Ellen gave a little affirmative bob of the head. "Thanks, I'll do that. And now my greenhouse is calling. Time to finish thinning the perennial beds." She hesitated. "But it was nice of you, Sarah, to think of lunch. Only I almost never eat out." And Ellen turned and was lost among the cars in the parking lot.

Sarah watched the slim figure, her dark skirt billowing slightly in a slight gust of wind. So much for old times and gossip with childhood friends, she thought rather sadly. But then she shrugged and headed for her own car. Ellen was just being Ellen, her own private person. Focused on her own special piece of the world and steering carefully clear of the rest of it.

Sarah, at the beginning of the following week, tried once more to touch base with Ellen. Alex, hoping to see the last half of a Red Sox double header, had agreed to drive Julia and his wife to Boston's Logan Airport, and Sarah thought, Why not offer Ellen a ride? If she was short of money she might appreciate the lift.

But when Sarah phoned the offer was declined. "I think I'd rather drive myself," explained Ellen in her quiet voice. "I may stop here and there. Stop at a greenhouse. Look up someone. Or maybe not," she added vaguely. "But, anyway, thanks."

The departure date, Tuesday, June the sixth, came at last. Julia Clancy clutching two small phrase books sat in the back seat of Alex's Jeep and attempted to engage Sarah, in the front passenger seat, in what Julia considered to be essential French and Italian sentences. Alex, acting as chauffeur, let the two women get on with it while he listened to the Red Sox fumble their way through three innings against the Toronto Blue Jays.

"Je m'appelle Julia," said Julia to Sarah. *"Mi chiamo Julia,"* she repeated in Italian. *"Où se trouve le téléphone? Dov'è una cassetta postale, per favore?"*

"For heaven's sake," said Sarah. "Stick to one language. *Je m'appelle Sarah,* and shouldn't you be using *'tu'?* You're my aunt."

"Nitpicking," said Julia. *"Il fait beau aujourd'hui, n'est-ce pas?"*

"Il fait lousy," said Sarah. "The sky is dark gray, it's hot as Hades, and it's going to thunder and lightening and rain, which means wind shear and down drafts. And I don't like to fly even in good weather."

"In French," scolded Julia.

"Je n'aime pas les aeroplanes. J'aime seulement le chemin de fer ou l'autobus. Et peut-être a horse—un cheval."

"J'aime aussi les chevals," said Julia. "I mean, *les chevaux."*

"Hey," said Alex from the driver's seat. "A double to left field and two runs in. That ties it up. Okay, passengers, New Hampshire border ahead. And," as large raindrops splattered the windshield, "here comes the rain."

Sarah made an effort to put the flight out of her mind. "How is Lillian Garth? You said you'd been to see her this morning. Why? You don't do orthopedic stuff."

"She ran a little fever this morning. We were about to send her off to rehab but she began coughing. She's eaten up with jealousy about you all going off."

"Better not get on to the subject of Lillian," said Julia, "or Sarah will convince you that she was hurled down her cellar stairs by some alien assassin. It's too bad about Lillian, but the loose ends seem to be taken up by this Barbara Baxter. I think she could handle a platoon of teenagers with acute attention deficit disorder. And Ellen Trevino will make a good co-tour leader. She's very knowledgeable," said Julia, who had dozed through most of Ellen's talk. She tapped Sarah on the shoulder. *"Maintenant, je parle français. Je pense que les jardins d'angleterre sont très beaux, n'est-ce pas?"*

"Certainement," said Sarah, subsiding.

Meanwhile from assorted corners of the state in a variety of vehicles came the members of the Midcoast Garden Club. The Hopper sisters, Margaret and Edith, had chosen to join Sandi and Fred Ouellette in an airport limousine to the Portland Jetport and thence to Boston, and as Alex and his passengers crossed from Maine into New Hampshire, these four were busy discussing the necessaries for transatlantic flight. Margaret and Edith explained that in the interest of comfort they carried inflated pillows that fastened around their necks, and Sandi explained that she had bought an English novel—*The Shell Seekers*—because she wanted to soak up as much atmosphere as possible as this was her absolutely first trip out of the country. To this Fred added that he had brought a Patricia Cornwell mystery because the author featured the autopsy table, to which Margaret and Edith both exclaimed "Goodness" and then offered the fact that they never traveled without a folding photo album with pictures of their children and grandchildren and Edith's cat, Trixie, and Margaret's little Westie, Rob Roy.

It was generally believed by the Hoppers and the Ouellettes, as well as by the rest of the travelers, that Barbara Baxter would contrive to arrive early at the British Airways Terminal, ready to soothe, explain, and generally manage the departure of her flock, and that Dr. Ellen Trevino would stand at Barbara's right hand and make herself generally useful.

These surmises proved incorrect.

Sarah and Julia were the first of the party to arrive at the international terminal, partly because Julia always fussed about being late, but more importantly because Alex wanted to get to Fenway Park as soon as possible; he just hoped that the rain, which was still falling, wouldn't force a cancellation.

Sarah, in her usual state of knocking nerves, was able only to give her husband a quick kiss and a weak clasp around his neck and assure him that she did love him, even though by encouraging her to fly he was allowing her to die before her time. To which Alex laughed, hugged her, and said he'd see her in Italy in a couple of weeks.

Julia, distracted briefly by having to unearth her passport from a pouch hanging next to her bra, joined briefly in the farewell, and then led Sarah away in search of the other tour members. The international terminal was crowded with early summer travelers and already two lines had formed in the British Airways section—first class and economy.

"Economy, that's us," said Julia cheerfully. "This way. They'll want to see our passports and then they'll take our bags."

"I wish I'd only brought my shoulder bag," said Sarah, looking unhappily at her large canvas suitcase that was refusing to roll smoothly on its little black wheels. Pulling this object and clutching her shoulder bag and overseeing a large leather handbag was proving a chore.

"Well, Barbara did tell us to travel light. Everyone takes too much. I always travel with Tom's army duffel with the shoulder strap. Makes me think Tom is coming along on the trip."

Sarah nodded sympathetically. Irish Tom Clancy was Julia's long dead husband, never too far from Julia's thoughts. Together they had built High Hope Farm, together they had bred, trained, and shown their horses. It had been, Sarah knew, a most happy marriage founded firmly on a jointly held obsession for all things equine. "Uncle Tom," Sarah began, but Julia pointed to a door opening. "It's Fred Ouellette and Sandi. I don't have the energy to talk to Sandi. And Fred talks too much."

"Well, here come Edith and Margaret Hopper," said Sarah. "They're safe. They like to read and they won't rave about the wonders of flight the way Sandi will."

"And there are the McClures," said Julia, craning her neck. "I just hope Portia can keep a clamp on Carter's mouth."

"It's about time Barbara showed up," said Sarah. "All that talk about being early."

But, after a period of group restlessness, Justin Rossi, Stacy Daniel, the two Lermatovs, and Barbara arrived in their midst, Barbara pulling behind her a large wheeled suitcase.

"It's as big as mine," said Sarah. "So much for her advice."

"She probably has it stuffed with guidebooks and garden Cliff Notes," said Julia.

But now Barbara, explaining that their Delta 5:05 flight had been held up, began checking off names. All present and accounted for, she announced cheerily. Except . . .

Except for Ellen Trevino. Had anyone seen Dr. Trevino? Was she driving to Boston? Or flying? Did anyone know?

Sarah offered the information that she thought Ellen meant to drive, a remark contradicted by Doris Lermatov, who had seen her at the dentist's and thought Ellen mentioned a flight from Augusta. Or perhaps her dentist was the one flying from there. She wasn't sure, but then she hadn't been paying attention.

These remarks set up a buzz that ran round the Garden Club members. Sarah could hear exclamations of concern, surprise, and—from Carter McClure—annoyance. "Trust an academic," he said to the room at large. "They never know what time it is, let alone the day of the week. The Bowmouth Biology Department had Ellen Trevino for a couple of guest lectures and she was late at least once."

"Carter," said Portia, "everyone can hear you, and you're an academic, in case you've forgotten."

Carter drew himself up, his lean face turned into a sardonic smile. "Ah, I am the exception that proves the rule. Admit it, Portia. The Bowmouth faculty is filled with brainless hens and clucking chickens and mindless tomcats, and as for the English Department, they live on another planet entirely." Here Carter raised his eyebrows, looked directly at Sarah, and closed one eye in what looked like a provocative wink.

But before Sarah, who at times agreed with Dr. McClure, could think of how to defend the English Department, Barbara Baxter excused herself saying she was going to find a telephone and try to find out what was holding up Ellen. And she disappeared into the ever increasing swarm of overseas travelers.

Sarah, shuffling along toward the British Airways passport checkpoint, had now reached that state of preflight jitters where her mouth was dry and her palms were wet. Right now she didn't give a damn whether Ellen turned up or vanished for good into the stratosphere. She didn't care whether she lost her suitcase or whether the flight attendants were all vampires. She stuffed her sweaty hands in the pockets of her new camel hair jacket and gave her suitcase a vicious kick that sent it flat on its side, its little black wheels spinning.

At this juncture, Julia, who was usually oblivious to the moods of others, seemed to realize that all was not well with her niece. "For God's sake, take your pill," she ordered. "That's what it's for. Alex said an hour before we take off. It's nearly seven and we take off at eight. And you needn't fret, it's a Boeing 747 and big enough to carry elephants. Get a grip."

Sarah made an attempt to pull herself together. She pointed at Carter McClure, who had managed to insert himself and Portia ahead of the entire Garden Club entourage. "Carter fits the terrorist profile," she said. "That black shirt and the dark glasses. All he needs is a hand grenade."

"Oh, don't even say those words," squeaked someone in

back of her. It was Margaret Hopper. "We'll all be arrested or put into some sort of observation lounge. It happened to a friend of mine."

Sarah nodded and moved forward, submitted her passport, surrendered her suitcase, swung her shoulder bag across her neck, gripped her handbag, and followed her aunt into the main terminal. There, surrounded by the hundreds of noisy travelers, college students, families foreign and domestic, women in saris, Sikhs in turbans, Asian tour groups hung about with cameras, Sarah allowed her aunt to administer tea and then prod her forward through the metal detector, into the departure lounge, and on to the embarkation tunnel.

The tunnel, she always thought, was like some sort of mechanical intestine that by means of reverse peristalsis pulled its human fodder through its rectum and thence into the abdomen of the jumbo silver beast. It was a distressing image, and Sarah had never felt so disposable. Inching along, she had just reached that point where the passageway dips down into the plane entrance when Julia plummeted against her, sending her shoulder bag into orbit and knocking her forward and down in front of the welcoming flight attendant. She fell to her knees, turned, and reached for Julia and found Edith Hopper on top of her aunt. And Barbara Baxter athwart Edith and the man called Rossi bent double over a toppled Sandi Ouellette. And Fred Ouellette convulsed with laughter, hanging on to the beautiful Stacy, who seemed to be on all fours.

It was all like one of those turnpike pileups where one vehicle coming to grief causes a chain reaction. After cries of "I was pushed" and "You tripped me," everyone, no doubt on the crest of excitement, became cheerful. Bags, duffels, magazines, paperbacks, sections of the *Boston Globe* were retrieved, and amid a certain amount of hilarity, the boarders surged forward to be met by the laughing flight attendant who had assisted in the pickup and now welcomed them aboard Flight 214 and pointed out seats and aisles.

"She's got an English accent," exclaimed Sandi Ouellette as

she stored her new trench coat overhead. "Now I feel I'm really going somewhere foreign."

"You are," said Julia, sounding exactly like Carter McClure. Then finding that both their seats were in the middle aisle between the McClures on one side and the Hopper sisters on the other, she smiled at Sarah. "We lucked out," she announced, indicating Sandi and Fred settling in down two rows and across the aisle.

"Shhh, they'll hear you," said Sarah.

But Julia was engaged in stowing her possessions, thrusting the airline pillow behind her back, and producing to Sarah's surprise a square of needlepoint canvas on which the sketch of a horse flying over a timber fence could be made out. "I always do needlepoint when I travel. I don't want to feel I'm wasting time."

But Sarah had not heard her aunt. Her head was down and she was rummaging about in her shoulder bag. "I'm looking for my book," she explained. "I thought . . . ," but she never finished her sentence. Instead she held up a pair of black-rimmed sunglasses.

"These aren't mine," she exclaimed.

"You can't have too many sunglasses," said Julia. She was busily unfolding her needlepoint canvas and threading a needle with copper-colored wool.

"I already have a pair. These belong to someone else."

"They'll probably be useful," observed Julia, plunging her threaded needle into a horse's nostril.

"Read my lips," said Sarah. "My glasses are prescription. These are cheap and look like something a dope dealer might wear."

"Or someone with perfect vision who doesn't need to spend a lot of money."

"Well, I don't want them," said Sarah. "I have enough extra junk. But how do you suppose . . . ?"

The question was cut short by the insistent blinking of the seat belt light and the appearance of the no-smoking sign. Then the flight attendants took their seats, buckled up, and the 747's engine rumbled ominously, increased its volume, and the giant plane backed, turned and began its trundle toward the takeoff runway.

Sarah tightened her seat belt, wiped her wet hands again on the cloth of her travel jacket, leaned back, closed her eyes and began a recitation of a long ago learned poem she had commonly used when finding herself aboard a heavier than air machine. The poem fortunately went on forever and so could be employed for the entire take-off period. "There are strange things done in the midnight sun," she muttered, "By the men who moil for gold;

> The Arctic trails have their secret tales
> . . . . That would make your blood run cold;
> The Northern Lights have seen queer sights,
> But the queerest they ever did see
> Was the night on the marge of Lake Lebarge
> I cremated Sam McGee.

She had just reached that interesting point in the poem where "And before nightfall a corpse was all that was left of Sam McGee," when at exactly three minutes after eight o'clock eastern daylight time British Airways Flight 214 bound for London's Heathrow Airport mounted into the rain-filled air, climbed over Boston Harbor and turned northeast toward the coast of Maine.

"We go right over my house, I think," said Margaret Hopper to Sarah. "All the trouble of us getting to Boston and then we fly right back over where we came from."

"Maine?" said Sarah stupidly.

"Well, yes dear," said Margaret. "Check your map. Then it's on to Newfoundland and Iceland and so forth. What fun!"

"Fun?" said Sarah.

"Fun," repeated Margaret firmly. "At least I hope so because Edith and I are spending every penny we own on this trip. Even if it rains every minute." She pointed to the sunglasses on Sarah's lap. "You won't need those inside the plane. I think they turn the lights down later on."

This observation roused Sarah to greater verbal effort. "The glasses aren't mine. I just found them. In my shoulder bag."

Margaret nodded. "You can't have too many sunglasses, I always say. But you may not need them right away. It's raining in London. That's what the flight attendant told me."

At which point Julia put down her needlepoint. "I knew I'd need something waterproof so I brought my oilskin riding jacket. I can ride for hours in it and be almost dry."

"We're not going to be riding," Sarah reminded her. Again she indicated the glasses. "When we all fell into each other and everyone was grabbing books and magazines someone must have shoved these into my shoulder bag. It doesn't have a zipper, only leather straps and buckles. I should ask around."

But Sarah's plan was put on hold; it was dinnertime. Flight attendants, spruce in their tricolor scarves or ties, passed menus, took orders, delivered trays, and Sarah felt a slight relaxation in tension—the pill kicking in perhaps. Also, she had a fuddled idea that if the plane were in immediate danger of falling from the sky, the serving of dinner might take a backseat.

Unfortunately for post-dinner nerves, that other soother of the anxious—the evening movie—was canceled due to a malfunction of something electronic, leaving Sarah to wonder aloud that if the movie machinery was on the fritz, what about the plane itself?

"Sarah," said Aunt Julia, "shut up. Go around and ask about the sunglasses. It will do you good to move around. Then find your book. I, for one, am going to sew for fifteen minutes and then work out some breeding problems. I'm worried about repeating my Welsh–thoroughbred cross because I'm not getting the bone I wanted."

Sarah found no takers for the sunglasses. The only person interested was Portia McClure, who had forgotten her own, and Sarah presented them to her. Returning to her own seat, teeth brushed, face sluiced, she found her aunt and Margaret Hopper in conversation about perennial borders, her aunt contributing the opinion that the only flowers worth having were those that came up entirely on their own and Margaret shaking her head in disapproval.

"No takers," Sarah announced, "so I gave the glasses to Portia. She'd forgotten hers. And I'll take Aunt Julia's advice and read. I brought *Cranford* because nothing really happens in it."

She reached down into her shoulder bag for the second time and again came up with an alien object. This item proved to be a dark red and black patterned scarf, rather rumpled and knotted into a triangle. Sarah held it up before her aunt.

"Yours?" she queried.

Julia put her needlepoint aside and reached for the scarf. She held it up, turned it over, examined the label and handed it back. "Filene's," she announced. "Rather handsome. And the label says 'all silk.' Are you sure it isn't yours?"

"Quite sure," said Sarah. "It probably arrived with the sunglasses. It looks a little used. Anyway, I don't think I'll go hopping up and down the aisle asking if someone's missing a scarf as well as glasses. I can try later."

"They may not belong to the Garden Club group at all," Julia pointed out. "And now it's my bedtime." And she reached into the canvas case at her feet and produced an eye shade which she slipped over her head, stuffed the pillow under one cheek, and folded her hands in her lap.

It was so quiet now in the cabin that Sarah could hear the whoosh of the jet moving through the night sky. The overhead lights had dimmed, some passengers, like Julia, had put on sleeping masks, others had drawn blankets around their bodies and put pillows under their heads as if to imitate normal sleeping conditions. However, the large number of tightly packed passengers did not permit the seats from going back more than a few inches so Sarah thought that the entire scene resembled nothing so much as a strange necropolis in which vertical burying was the norm. She just managed to force this image out of her brain and had wriggled her head into a sidewise position, grateful that the pill was making her pleasantly groggy when she heard Margaret Hopper turn to her sister Edith and say in a hushed voice that it wasn't entirely a bad thing that Dr. Trevino had missed the flight. "She's a little bit intimidating, all that nomenclature," said Margaret. "Besides, I heard her say the night of the dinner that she didn't believe in any side trips."

To which Edith replied, "I agree. I felt quite stupid when I asked about late-blooming phlox. She was very polite but kept talking about subspecies. Perhaps Providence prevented her from making the flight. And now we must both try and get just a little sleep. Good night, dear."

And Margaret patted her sister's hand and said, "Good night to you, too," and leaned back against her seat and closed her eyes.

And Sarah opened hers and stared wide-eyed ahead of her seeing not the seat back, but Ellen Trevino standing up at the festive dinner and speaking in her clear, low voice of the wonders of English cottage gardens. Ellen Trevino, about whose company at least two of the Midcoast Garden Club were dubious. For several minutes Sarah stayed rigid, and then the sedative overwhelmed her brain, and she drifted into an uneasy sleep in which Ellen floated above her, face obscured by sunglasses, a red and black silk scarf tied tightly over her head, while a dark and ominous cloud labeled "Deadly Nightshade" hovered over her head.

3

NIGHTTIME overseas flights are not pools of peace. Sleeping upright in the presence of a multitude of strangers, the uneasy shiftings of cramped bodies, the tread no matter how tactful of the flight attendants, the sudden cry of a baby or the snore across the aisle, all are enough to ensure a disturbed night. Of the Midcoast Garden Club tour group only those two hard-headed characters, Julia Clancy and Carter McClure, got something resembling rest. The others turned and twitched and snuffled and finally sat up to be faced with a breakfast tray at what they considered rightly to be three in the morning.

Heavy-eyed and dry-mouthed from her disturbing dream of a levitating Ellen Trevino, Sarah woke to see that the black outside the cabin windows had given away to the gray light of morning. This was a relief because she was sure that the rescue of downed passengers was certainly easier on a daylight ocean.

"Sarah," said Julia. "We'll be landing in an hour and we don't want to join the others in one of those airport hotels where you waste half a day trying to catch up on sleep."

"You don't want to go anywhere and rest?" protested Sarah. "I mean jet lag is real. Five hours difference.

"I've hired a car," said Julia, "but an old woman like me shouldn't drive in morning rush-hour traffic, so I'm letting you handle it. It's not too far away. A B&B in the country."

Sarah interrupted. "You mean a horse farm?"

"I suppose they still have horses. Dodgeson Farm has a variety of animals. A very nice place. In Dinton. I stayed there a few years ago. We'll catch up to the others tomorrow night."

"Where," demanded Sarah, "on God's earth is Dinton?"

But Julia had turned and craned her neck toward the nearest window. The 747 had begun its descent and the buckled up passengers began closing their briefcases and checking on their passports. Sarah put aside the question of Dinton and herself as a sleep-deprived driver of a strange car. What was needed again was "The Cremation of Sam McGee" recited slowly with proper attention given to its singsong meter. Sarah closed her eyes and didn't open them until she felt the heaven-blest bumpty-bump of landing wheels touching down on tarmac. She turned to Aunt Julia and said with a sense of modest triumph, " 'The flames just soared, and the furnace roared—such a blaze you seldom see; / And I burrowed a hole in the glowing coal, and I stuffed in Sam McGee.' "

Lined up for passport inspection, Sarah had no time for further argument with her aunt. The passengers of Flight 214 broke ranks and headed toward their various destinations: the Midcoast Garden Club to the Ibis Hotel to rest, Sarah and Julia to change their traveler's checks for pounds and pence and then to the Europcar rental agency.

"We're off," said Julia when she had settled into the passenger seat of a blue Ford Escort. "And the rain's about stopped. I think we'll have a pleasant drive."

Sarah looked up from the automobile map. "Pleasant drive, my foot. We're surrounded by nine million cars, and I have to get us out of Heathrow and find the M40 without having a major wreck." She blinked and yawned. "Actually, I'm the major wreck.

Fasten your seat belt." And clinging to the left lane, Sarah slowly moved the Ford onto a secondary road, onto a tertiary gravel road filled with repair equipment, reversed into London-bound traffic, turned, and finally eighty minutes, five villages, three road blocks, two unnecessary roundabouts, and a construction detour later, left the M40, picked up the A418, and crawled to the edge of Dinton, found an opening into a promising hedgerow, and turned into Dodgeson Farm.

Julia, who had slumbered peacefully for the last half hour, opened her eyes and looked about with satisfaction.

"Well done, Sarah. I knew you could find your way."

Sarah, whose temper had been lost for good at the last roundabout, lifted her head and snapped. "I hate hedgerows, and passing on the right, and I think British drivers are worse than Boston drivers and that's going some."

To which Julia replied by patting her niece's shoulder, then led her into the farmhouse, accepted the management's welcome on behalf of both, climbed the stairs, pointed Sarah in the direction of the designated bedroom and pushed her through the door.

The rain had indeed ceased. The air was warm, a pleasant sixty-eight degrees, and five o'clock, after a tea featuring hot scones with currant jam, found Julia and her niece wandering the by-ways and lanes around the farm while Sarah explored the idea that the stuffing of a silk scarf and a pair of sunglasses in her shoulder bag had something of the untoward about it.

Julia, refreshed by her tea, was tolerant. "Neither item is in any sense either strange or lethal. Just someone picking up two odd items and finding the nearest open bag to tuck them into."

"And Ellen Trevino not turning up?"

"No possible connection. Ellen will no doubt surface at the Shearing Inn tomorrow."

"You think?" asked Sarah.

"Here's what's happened. She missed her flight and now she's scrambling for a seat on another airline."

Sarah, not entirely satisfied, nodded and turned, walked to

a gap in the hedgerow secured by a rail fence and a style. For several minutes she fixed her gaze on a pasture close to the Dodgeson Farm dotted with strange black and white sheep. Sheep which, with their arching horns, reminded her of those pictured in her grandmother's illustrated Bible.

"Those are Jacob sheep, a very old breed," said Julia, joining her. She peered over at an adjoining field. "And those horses, the heavy ones. Suffolk Punch. Handsome creatures, always chestnut. Makes a good animal when you cross it with a thoroughbred. Perhaps," she added in a dreamy voice, "I could diversify."

"Aunt Julia," began Sarah.

Julia reluctantly turned away from the grazing Suffolk Punch. "Sarah, the healing atmosphere will do you no good until you get rid of this burr in your brain. It's just after noon in the States. Go and call Alex. Or the state police. The FBI. The White House. Anyone." "No"—this as Sarah hesitated—"get it over with. I shall be right here wandering about in the lane and thinking about raising sheep and importing Suffolk Punch."

Fifteen minutes later, Sarah, after giving Alex her opinion on transatlantic air travel, unburdened herself.

And Alex, after proper expressions of love and loneliness without his spouse and complaints about her Irish Wolfhound, Patsy, rending the sleeve of a new sweater, reluctantly agreed to move on her request. "Okay, I'll call Mike Laaka and see if he can interest the Sheriff's Department in Ellen's no-show. And I hope you're not getting into a lather about a scarf and a pair of sunglasses."

"Not a lather. Just a little worried."

"Tell you what," said Alex. "I'll call around and get back to you in about an hour. After that my office will be stacked with patients."

Sarah breathed a sigh that sounded across the ocean waves. "Thanks. Aunt Julia's about to have me locked up, so if you can learn something reassuring I'd love to know it. Even hearing Ellen's fallen down Lillian Garth's cellar steps would be a relief."

"Any other news?" demanded Alex. "Something of a familiar and domestic nature beyond the fact that you love me even more than you love Anthony Hopkins, Robin Williams, and Patsy?"

"Nothing more than Aunt Julia is seriously looking at a kind of draught horse called a Suffolk Punch and some weird spotted sheep. She's thinking of spicing up High Hope Farm."

"Good God," said Alex, and signed off.

Fifty minutes later Sarah picked up the phone. Alex reporting. "Not much at this end. Ellen Trevino's nearest neighbor—a Mrs. Epple—is taking care of Ellen's dog while she's away. Ellen left the dog off on June fifth—the day before you all left from Logan. She said something about perhaps visiting a friend and then checking with someone about something. Perhaps the trip. Mrs. Epple says Ellen was quite vague about her plans, but Mike says Mrs. Epple is on the vague side herself.

"So Ellen was driving?" asked Sarah.

"She left in her car. A gray Subaru. Two-year-old wagon. She may have meant to leave it at the Portland airport, or at Logan, or anywhere else but she didn't say. Then I called Mike at home. He said the Sheriff's Department would give one big heehaw if he started yacking about a scarf and a pair of sunglasses."

"You're saying, Drop it?"

"I'm saying, my love, you're showing the classic signs of paranoia. Mike reminded me that it's tourist time in Maine, the police are busy and they won't budge until it's clear that Ellen is really missing, not waiting around as a standby in some airport."

"Maybe someone could check flights and passenger lists."

Alex groaned. "If she doesn't turn up soon, I'll call Mike again and see about checking flights out of Maine to Boston. But I've a full day at the hospital tomorrow, Mike's up to his ears with an arson case, so don't expect any great results."

Sarah, sitting on a stiff wooden chair at the Dodgeson Farm telephone table, felt an immense weariness creep over her limbs. "Okay, Alex. Thanks. I'm probably overreacting. Flying stimulated too many apprehension genes."

"Ellen Trevino could have changed her mind about the trip," said Alex. "Maybe she decided to stay home and make whoopee. Maybe she drinks and is having a lost weekend. Had a fever or an allergic reaction and checked into an ER somewhere between here and Boston."

"You could check hospital admissions," said Sarah, and then, hearing a louder groan at the end of the line, gave it up. Let it go. There were other things to be attended to. Other things like a quiet meal followed by bed, a pillow, a quilt, and Mrs. Gaskell's *Cranford*. "Okay, Alex," she said. "Good night. And I love you."

"And I love you, too. Wildly, madly, deeply. So try and keep Julia from shipping more than twenty horses back to New England."

Unlike Sarah, Alex McKenzie was not a man overly given to imagining the untoward in the world beyond his practice. His specialty of internal medicine, together with his occasional work as one of the local medical examiners, offered enough examples of human frailty and recklessness that, left to himself, he did not feel the need to look elsewhere. As he had often remarked, why look for trouble when eighty percent of the day he was hip-deep in the stuff. When he got home from a day's work he wanted a cold beer, the news of the Boston Red Sox—or in winter of the Boston Bruins. Or, weather permitting, the freedom to go bird-watching, sailing, hiking, skiing. And at night, if not on call, to hunker down with one of the naval novels of the incomparable Patrick O'Brian.

The problem, of course, was Sarah. Since she had entered his life—literally by force of homicide—the world had started to resemble a particularly active emergency room. Sarah tried to blame this on coincidence or, more realistically, on her overgrown bump of curiosity together with an urgent wish to get to the bottom of things. But Alex had begun to feel that something alien like Fate—Fate armed with a dagger and a cup of poison—hovered over any community Sarah was part of.

But now that his wife, this beloved but aggravating woman,

was an ocean away with her Aunt Julia—another female capable of attracting, in fact causing, mayhem—life in Midcoast Maine should be peacefully humming along on oiled wheels.

Except for this Ellen Trevino business. Despite his assurances that Ellen would turn up, Alex was uneasy. The day passed shadowed by all too many memories of when Sarah, sadly, had often been right. That night he couldn't settle down for a comfortable rest. The next morning couldn't read with complacency about the Red Sox annihilation of the Yankees, couldn't enjoy the soft June air as he ran Patsy down the road. Couldn't do anything without thinking about calling his old friend, Mike Laaka, Knox County Deputy Sheriff Investigator.

Which he did. Cutting Patsy's run down to twenty minutes, checking the time he was due in the hospital, he dialed Mike.

"Okay, Alex," said Mike. "I thought you'd call. Thought you—or is it Sarah—couldn't leave well enough alone. But there won't be any action unless someone files a Missing Persons. I've done what I could. Called the state police and kind of hinted at a stolen car, gave 'em the Subaru license number. So maybe in their spare time they'll take a look at cars that have been sitting around in parking areas."

"Like the ones on the Maine Turnpike," said Alex. "Ellen was supposed to be on her way to Boston one way or another."

"That leaves a hell of a lot of room, but unless something solid . . ."

"You mean a body?"

"Yeah, a body, a hank of hair, a bloody bra, or some relative saying Ellen was screaming help over the phone, so I'm not going to blister my butt until I have to." Here Mike paused and listened to a disapproving silence on the other end of the line.

"Listen," said Mike, "I'm up to my ears in this arson case and it looks like the owner burned down his own frigging barn first and the fire spread. I mean, Christ, what someone won't do for a few thousand lousy dollars."

"Ellen's family?" put in Alex.

"All right, all right. I did touch base with that neighbor, Mrs. Epple, who said she thought Ellen Trevino only had a stepfather somewhere in Vancouver. And"—Alex could hear a note of weary resignation in Mike's voice—"I'll do this. I'll get a photo of her from the college and pass it around. Listen, she's probably got amnesia. That's always popular. Or she's absconded with the tour funds. That's popular, too."

"Mike, shut up," said Alex, and replaced the receiver.

Mike Laaka's speculations were not unique. Julia Clancy and Sarah drove up to the Shearing Inn in the village of High Roosting in central Gloucestershire in time for tea and in time to join in the ongoing speculations about the missing Ellen Trevino.

The rain of the previous morning was a thing of the past, the sun had come out gloriously, and the temperature had stayed in the high-sixties. In celebration of these favorable omens the Midcoast Garden Club had assembled on a back terrace of the inn, a pleasant place which featured tables with umbrellas, a ring of terra-cotta pots filled with a mix of petunias and geraniums. There Sarah and Julia had joined the others in the attack on a handsome spread of cakes, biscuits, sandwiches, and little tarts.

"It's flying that makes you hungry," said Barbara Baxter to her flock. She reached for a second slice of lemon sponge cake.

"Oh, yes." Doris Lermatov sighed, biting into a miniature gooseberry tart.

Margaret Hopper nodded her agreement. "It's all that anxiety about getting to the airport and worrying about the weather and having jet lag. And wondering where Ellen is."

There followed a period of relative quiet devoted to munching and sipping, then, appetites having been subdued, Margaret's last comment became the cue to return to Topic A and what in the bustle of the airport departure had just been aroused puzzlement and random comment now assumed a more anxious character.

"A bug," suggested Portia McClure. "One of those sudden stomach bugs. They can knock you absolutely flat."

"A family emergency," said Margaret Hopper. "You know, where you have to drop everything and just get there."

"Wouldn't she have called? Or faxed us here?" asked Sandi.

Barbara Baxter summed it up. "We'd have heard if anything

had gone wrong. My office has our itinerary and so does Dr. Trevino. Poor thing, she's probably trapped in Berlin or Rome waiting for a flight."

This was followed by further expressions of concern and then Barbara turned to Julia and Sarah. "I wish you and Mrs. Clancy hadn't gone off the way you did. We had such a good day. After our naps, we all went in and spent the day in London. I said to the others, why just drive for hours in our bus and get to the Shearing in the middle of the night. I knew this nice little family hotel on Ebury Street, and they managed to find rooms for us. After all, it does pay to be in the travel business."

"Such fun," exclaimed Sandi. "Fred and I were so excited. We went to Westminster Abbey and Harrods and the Tower."

"And Kew Gardens," Barbara reminded her. "Because, after all, we're on a garden tour."

"Terrific food," put in Doris Lermatov. "A pub—a place called the Bulldog for lunch and a wonderful dinner."

Here her daughter looked up. Amy Lermatov, the red-haired fourteen-year-old, had been looking morosely off into space—contemplating, Sarah decided, three weeks spent in the company of her elders dragging her steps through garden after garden.

"The food," said Amy, "sucked."

"Amy liked the Tower," said her mother, giving her daughter a warning frown. "And she'll get used to the food."

"Don't bet on it," said Amy. Then, seeing the maternal eye still fixed on her, added that the Tower was okay. "You could see where they beheaded people."

At which Margaret Hopper rose to her feet. "Edith and I need a walk. All this food and sitting down. There's a church down the next lane. Some of these English village churches are fascinating and I'm told this one has a Norman tower." And the two white-haired women—twins almost in their wrinkle-proof navy skirts and white cable-stitch cardigans—set out.

Sarah also felt the need to stand upright and move her limbs. She jumped up and pulled Julia to her feet. "You, too, Aunt Julia. Your arthritis will freeze you into position if you don't move."

The two were joined by Portia McClure, who expressed a desire to look around the village, and husband, Carter McClure.

Sarah, looking him over, taking in his rumpled seersucker jacket and askew tie—donned no doubt to give a professorial appearance for the Shearing staff—saw that Carter was in a temper. It was the London visit. London hadn't been on the tour schedule. "Was this a garden trip or was it a sight-seeing expedition? Kew Gardens for only a little more than an hour? And that Barbara Baxter doesn't know a rosebush from an oak tree. Ask her a serious question about fertilizer and she comes up empty."

"She wasn't hired for her horticultural knowledge," Portia reminded him. "Lillian wanted her for the nitty-gritty tour details, reservations, timetables. That sort of thing."

"So let her stick to counting luggage," said Carter, "because I have someone up my sleeve."

"Oh?" said Sarah.

"What are you up to, Carter?" demanded Julia, who knew Carter from other days, and had tangled with him on past occasions.

Carter smiled a satisfied smile. "Since the Baxter woman is not up to snuff, I have Henry Ruggles. An old friend of ours. Lives in Moreton-in-Marsh. I'm going to call him to come and fill the gap left by Lillian."

"We've stayed at his house," Portia explained. "He has a wonderful garden. Quite a showplace."

"Right," said Carter. "He'll keep the Baxter in line. And he'll be a good foil for Ellen Trevino when she does turn up. She's much too serious and Henry's disgustingly jolly. Can charm the knickers off you."

"Hardly," put in Portia. "Henry's affections do not that way tend. But he knows his stuff. Writes articles, gives lectures, and, best of all, Henry will pay his own room and board, which is no trouble since he's simply loaded. He's like a character out of Dickens."

Julia scowled. "I'm not sure we want a character out of Dickens foisted on us. Which one did you have in mind?"

"Mr. Pickwick," said Portia. "Henry is very Pickwickian. And now I'm going off by myself to explore. Carter, you behave yourself or Julia will chop you up into liver bits."

With which Portia turned off in the direction of a small dirt path that led up a shaded hill, and Sarah, looking back over her shoulder, discovered that they were now being followed at short distance by the Massachusetts couple, Justin Rossi and Stacy Daniel. Although, thought Sarah, after a quick glance, if they are really a couple, they're certainly not working at it, the man striding ahead, the woman, falling behind.

Stacy was a tall, elegant woman, whom Sarah had privately decided was some sort of high-profile female executive trapped accidentally in a tour of garden enthusiasts. A travel agent mistake, perhaps. She had the sort of presence that spoke of expensive massage, French cosmetics, and couturier clothing. Her cheeks were high, her shoulders broad, her eyes a velvety dark blue, and her flax-colored hair swirled into a fashionable topknot. Her skin, which looked as if someone had tipped a bottle of maple syrup over it, suggested a winter spent beside pools or power walking on the beach. Sarah, watching her closely, saw that she exhibited an almost bored air that did not encourage companionship.

The reverse was true of Justin Rossi. He left Stacy behind and joined Julia and Sarah at the turn leading to the churchyard lane.

"We haven't really met," he announced. "Saw you both at that dinner and on the plane but, God, overseas flights are no places to make friends. I'm more concerned with whether the wings are holding up and if the landing gear is in working order."

"Sarah," announced Julia, "you've got a kindred spirit."

"You don't like to fly?" Justin turned to Sarah and smiled down at her. And Sarah felt a strange crawling sensation. A buzzing in her head. The pitch of Justin's voice, the angle of his chin, his dark hair, the way his shoulders swung when he walked, all of him in some uncanny way was Alex. Her husband Alex. She remembered that at the restaurant dinner there had been something familiar about him. Now, on closer inspection, this man was thinner, not quite up to Alex's six feet. The black hair cut shorter. And his eyes were lighter, a pale blue gray. A lesser Alex. But the resemblance was still was unnerving.

". . . not like to fly?" Justin was repeating the question.

Sarah shook herself and said something incoherent about hating to be more than eight feet above the ground. This seemed to satisfy Justin, who began a tale of an engine failure episode at Miami International.

At which juncture Carter McClure turned to Julia and began to remind her that one of his graduate assistants had broken a leg during a riding lesson at Julia's High Hope Farm and this had caused great inconvenience to the History Department. Julia, who remembered the incident only too well, rose like a trout to a dry fly and began a condemnation of the carelessness of this same student. At which both fell into argument, raising their voices and slowing their steps.

And Sarah was left with Justin, who pointed out the little churchyard and suggested an inspection. "I don't think there's much in a botanical sense, just common roses and probably some not very interesting annuals."

"I wouldn't know an interesting annual if it bit me," Sarah admitted. "But then I don't even rank as an amateur gardener. I'm below beginner."

"Perhaps your mind is on something else. For instance, on Ellen Trevino being missing?"

"Concerned. Wondering, that's all."

"I suppose we're all concerned, particularly that very talkative Sandi Ouellette. I suppose enthusiasm has its points, but she's a bit much. As for her husband, that undertaker . . ."

And Sarah, much to her own surprise, found something warm inside her rising in support of Sandi. And Fred.

"Sandi's not so bad. Her heart's in the right place. And enthusiasm isn't the worst quality in the world. And Fred, well, he's just Fred. Everyone's used to Fred. He overdoes the story-telling sometimes, but he's a good citizen. I've heard he drives for Meals-on-Wheels."

Justin looked down at her quizzically. "In a hearse?"

The idea, mildly amusing, forced Sarah into a grin. "All right, maybe the Ouellettes aren't the most exciting people in the world, but that's okay by me. I've had my fill of excitement."

"I'll say you have," remarked Justin.

Sarah jerked her head up. "What's that supposed to mean?"

"I got it from your friend Sandi. She was full of some Audubon thing she went on with you. Something about a body found by the birdfeeder, and how you got in your car and chased the murderer all the way to L.L. Bean's. Sandi was a little fuzzy on the details."

"Oh, God," said Sarah.

"So I thought if you've fooled around with local Maine crime you must be mildly interested in Ellen Trevino's no-show."

Sarah took a deep breath. "I'm just sorry she's not here yet, but beyond that I haven't any ghoulish ideas." She said this, making an attempt to sound both sympathetic and totally uninterested at the same time.

"You don't think the lady is curled up in an airport locker or whirling around inside a suitcase at the luggage claim place?"

"No, I don't," snapped Sarah. "And please drop it. Ellen Trevino is an old friend of mine."

Justin grimaced. "I'm sorry. A bad joke. I didn't know."

"And I'm sorry. I didn't mean to bark. Call it jet lag."

"As good an excuse as anything," said Justin cheerfully. "Let's look at the tombstones and see if we can spot some mute inglorious Milton." And then, taking her arm he turned her toward a small wooden gate and quoted in rhythm with their steps:

"Beneath those rugged elms, that yew-tree's shade,
Where heaves the turf in many a mould'ring heap,
Each in his narrow cell for ever laid,
The rude Forefathers of the hamlet sleep."

And Sarah found herself simultaneously beguiled by someone who could recite the fourth verse of that nineteenth-century chestnut and irritated by Justin's supporting her arm. It was hardly a matter for a scene, but she firmly slid her arm free when they reached the churchyard gate and moved a step away.

"I like churchyards," she said. "I think they're at least as interesting as roses."

They wandered about, peering at moss- and lichen-covered stones, finding a family called Hemstich which featured three little Eliza's, three stone lozenges on which some childish hand had laid an untidy wilting handful of primroses.

"I suppose," Sarah mused, "the second Eliza was named after the first, then she died, then came the third and she died. Some epidemic, smallpox, diphtheria. Old graveyards are very sobering."

"*Cursor mundi,*" said Justin, kneeling down and scraping grass away from an inscription. "See this. Lost at sea. Lieutenant Nichols. During action of the Nile. Was there action on the Nile?"

"I think it had something to do with Nelson," said Sarah vaguely. "Not Trafalgar but earlier." Suddenly she shivered. Partly from cold, but partly from a sense that Justin was entirely too companionable. Too familiar—not in the physical sense, he hadn't touched her again—but in a different way what with the literary references and his deep voice. And looking like Alex.

"I think I'll go back," she announced. "Regroup. Unpack. Put my feet up."

"Good idea," said Justin pleasantly. "Enough of worms and epitaphs." He waited for Sarah's reaction, but she closed her lips. "That's Richard II, isn't it? When he's feeling very very sorry for himself."

Sarah sighed. Impossible to dislike someone who came up with the proper quotation at the proper time. "Yes, Richard was rolling over and playing dead, practically handing it all over to Bolingbroke." And together they sauntered back toward the inn, pausing only for Justin to identify two chaffinches in a hedgerow and a blue tit in a tree.

Arriving in her bedroom, Sarah gave a token kick to her hated suitcase. He even birdwatches, she told herself. Maybe he's Alex's brother. Born out of wedlock and given up for adoption and now he's turned up. She considered Alex's mother, Elspeth, noted artist and loyal wife of Alex's father, and tried to picture her having some grand affair with a dark-haired stranger.

"What are you staring at," said Julia, knocking and marching into the room at the same time.

Sarah started. "Nothing. My mind is a blank."

Julia sank down in a chair and began unlacing her new walking shoes. She stretched out her feet, wiggled her toes, and then regarded her niece. "It's that Justin Rizzi or Rossini. Looks enough like Alex to be his brother. He headed straight for you."

"No," corrected Sarah, "Justin happened to be there and his name is Rossi. We hit the graveyard and he quoted Gray."

" 'The ploughman homeward plows his weary way and leaves the world to darkness and to me,' " announced Julia unexpectedly. "My generation had a proper education. Forty lines each Friday. Anyway, Carter was becoming positively obnoxious about his damn student when that Stacy woman came twinkling up and joined us."

"Twinkling? She's about as twinkly as a bath towel. I think her ticket was mixed up and she's supposed to be on the Executive Woman's Tour of British Industries."

"Perfectly friendly," said Julia. "Wanted us to help identify the roses, which I couldn't, but Carter went on about grafting and hybrids and Stacy said she adored gardens. Adored—her very words. Has been looking forward to the tour, thinks Barbara Baxter is, to quote, a perfectly marvelous organizer."

"Barbara Baxter reminds me of my eighth-grade basketball coach. All she needs is a sweatshirt and a whistle around her neck. Hustling and bustling everyone around."

"Sarah, you're beginning to sound like me, and there's only room for one Julia Clancy on this trip."

4

BUT before Julia could elaborate on the dangers of two Julia Clancys, a knock sounded on the bedroom door and a muffled voice called, "Telephone for Sarah Deane. She can take it down in the front hall."

The Shearing Inn was one of those hostelries built in the seventeenth century and added on to thereafter in a haphazard fashion. "Down in the front hall" meant Sarah followed a short series of steps that wound up and down under low beams and ended in a small entrance space. The table holding a guest register and a telephone was midway between the front door and the Shearing pub room door, thus ensuring that a good deal of telephone conversation would consist of "What?" and "I can't hear you."

"What," said Sarah. "Alex? I can't hear you."

Alex, sounding like a seal calling from a distant harbor, repeated something and then in an interval of silence, Sarah heard, ". . . the car was pretty clear of stuff. No suitcases or briefcases."

"Car!" squeaked Sarah. "What car?"

"Aren't you listening?"

"I can't really hear you. The pub door is right next to the phone and everyone's in there chatting it up and . . ."

"Listen again." Alex raised his voice and spoke very deliberately. "A car, a Buick, driven by an elderly woman."

"A Buick?"

"Listen, will you? By an elderly woman who whammed into Ellen Trevino's Subaru."

"Ellen! She's had an accident."

"Christ, Sarah. Wait up. Ellen wasn't in the car. The car was empty. At the Kennebunk exit on the Maine Turnpike. In the parking area near the end of the picnic benches. You know that exit, it's the southbound pit stop with the Burger King restaurant."

"Yes, I know," said Sarah impatiently. "But Ellen wasn't anywhere around?"

Here followed a period of noise and door openings and then Sarah exclaimed, "This is impossible." Then, "Okay, speak up."

"Ellen's car was slightly damaged. The woman in the Buick reported the accident, the police have traced the license, couldn't locate Ellen, decided it may have been stolen, and have hauled it off to give it the once-over."

"But it hasn't been reported stolen? Not by Ellen anyway."

"No, but the police are figuring Ellen doesn't know it's stolen. That maybe she took a plane from Portland to Boston and the car was taken from the airport parking garage and dumped at the Kennebunk exit."

"If she took a plane to Boston, then where is she?"

"No one has yet filed a Missing Persons on Ellen. You have to wait forty-eight hours."

Sarah drew a deep breath. "Back to square one. Shit."

"Not entirely. The police need Ellen to claim the car, so they are doing some looking around. Checking Delta and U.S. Air flights. Commuter planes and airport limousine passenger lists for June sixth to Logan."

"Well, that's something," said Sarah. "Are you absolutely sure there was nothing left in Ellen's car?"

"Mike—he's the one who called me—got the list from the state police and told me. Jumper cables, gardening tools in the rear. A road map, car registration stuff, five or six cassettes—classical and folk music, and two paperbacks. *The Warden* and *Barchester Towers*."

"I suggested those books. Why did she leave them in the car?"

"So she forgot. You forget things like that all the time. So do I. *Homo imperfectus.*"

"I'm getting a queasy feeling."

There was a pause on the line, the clinking sounds from the pub room, a burst of laughter, and then Alex again. "Mike says keep a lid on this car business. Right now it doesn't affect the tour group. Ellen may turn up tomorrow."

"All right."

"And, just for the record, says Mike, would you send him a list of the tour members with any personal bits, details of Ellen's travel plans if anyone knew about them. Nothing official. The police don't want to approach Whirlaway Tours. No point in stirring people up for no reason. Mike thinks maybe it's time to lay some groundwork in case the Missing Persons thing is filed."

"Am I supposed to mail this stuff? Or telephone?"

Behind Sarah a man in a suede jacket hovered, his gaze fixed on the telephone. "Do you mind? It's rather important. A call home," he said.

"Sarah?" said Alex. "Mike says fax it, okay?"

"Damn. Yes, I'll try."

"Thanks. And you can tell Julia—only Julia—about this because she'll screw it out of you anyway."

"Isn't faxing sort of public?" said Sarah.

"Get away from everyone. Okay? Good-bye."

"Thank you," said the man reaching for the telephone.

Sarah returned to her room—a narrow chamber connecting to Julia's slightly larger one, both rooms brave in flowered chintz, and welcoming trays supporting an electric teapot, teacups, and bags of Typhoo Tea. After washing and changing into her all-purpose blue shirtdress, she and Julia—in red paisley cotton—joined the rest for a drink in the pub room, and then dinner in the Shearing Inn dining room. This was a rectangular space dominated by heavy hewn beams and featuring uneven floors, bubble-glass windows, and, at each table, a potted geranium. Clutches of diners were already in place plying knives and forks and a soft babble of German and—was it Japanese?—rose from two tables at the darker end of the dining room. Sarah, eyeing them, thought that the elderly headwaiter—possibly a World War II veteran—may have decided that these two nationalities had something unsuitable in common and should be relegated to a space away from the light.

She took her place at an extended table with a view of the garden, and decided that the five-hour time difference combined with a strong and evil-tasting rum and Orangina had loosened her mind in a way that transformed the whole Midcoast Garden Tour. Transformed it from a benign group of persons whose interests centered on the wholesome growing of flowers to something altogether different.

It was as though each of them, Sarah and Aunt Julia included, had stepped out of their mundane personae and had been wafted onto a stage set or a movie screen. What was that movie, Sarah asked herself, as a dish called Chicken Bombay was placed in front of her—a dish she couldn't remember ordering. Oh, yes, Woody Allen. *The Purple Rose of Cairo*, where Mia Farrow had left her theater seat and had joined the screen characters on a glamorous set of the thirties: cocktail shakers, furniture made out of glass and aluminum tubes, Van Johnson in a white dinner jacket, and . . .

"The chutney, Sarah," said Aunt Julia. "I've asked twice. You're asleep at the switch."

Sarah shook herself. "Sorry. I was just out of it."

"You mean 'out of the loop,'" said Sandi Ouellette, who sat across the table and had dressed for this first festive occasion in a low-cut lavender outfit. She leaned across the table exposing the upper reaches of her breasts. "I just love that expression. You know when all those senators and President Bush said they were out of it."

"Sandi," said Fred Ouellette, "loves Senate hearings. Watergate, Iran-Contra. Special investigators and taking the Fifth and sexual harassment charges."

"Better than sitcoms any day," said Sandi.

There's more perhaps to Sandi's brain than had been apparent from her everyday conversation, Sarah told herself. And then she realized how little she knew about the woman. Did she work or sit all day watching Senate hearings on CNN? Then, in the minutes that followed as everyone chattered and plied fork and knife, Sarah returned to the task of assembling her cast of characters for Mike. And the movie, titled for the moment: *Ellen Is Missing*.

First, put Sandi Ouellette on hold since Sandi might reveal hidden depths that would complicate the casting process. Fred, however, seemed simplicity itself. The contented undertaker. Or mortician. Whatever they called themselves now. Sarah had heard that a new favored title was "morticle surgeon." Fred, two places down the table, was finishing one of his jokes, the plot of which seemed to involve a New York judge adrift on an ice floe. Sarah, after assigning Fred a place in the supporting cast, moved on to contemplate Doris Lermatov and her daughter, Amy.

She had neglected these two. Doris Lermatov had sat a short distance from Sarah on the British Airways flight. Doris was built on the classic lines of the old-style Coke bottle, usually wore the sort of garment known as a float, had a crown of puffed hair of ash blonde—a favorite choice for those going gray. But Sarah knew very little of her beyond the undeniable fact that she seemed upbeat and was fond of food. On the plane Sarah had seen her help herself to her daughter Amy's chocolate pudding, and now, sitting slantwise across the dinner table, she bent over her roast beef, a study in concentration.

And of Doris herself, her interests? Her job? Sarah, thinking back remembered someone saying that Doris wrote a garden column for one of the smaller local papers.

And then there was Amy at Sarah's left elbow—a slender young person with a head of frizzy red hair, a round face, and the white skin and freckles that often goes with such hair. Right now Amy had the same sulky look Sarah had seen before. And she wasn't eating, simply pushing a heap of pasta around her plate.

Sarah, catching her eye, smiled. "Are you a garden fan? Or along for a change of scene."

"Gardens," said Amy, "suck."

"All gardens?"

"Any I've seen. Probably the ones I haven't seen."

Sarah, hardened early by work in secondary schools before she picked up a Bowmouth College fellowship, was not put off. "I know you're Amy Lermatov and my name is Sarah," she said. "And maybe we'll hit a garden that isn't too bad. Some of them are amazing. Mazes you can get lost in. Or again we might have a chance to look at something else. Old graveyards and castles." This producing no response, Sarah asked what sort of music she liked, expecting to hear of some punk rock group with a name like "The Barf." She was not disappointed.

"Well," said Amy, her expression becoming slightly more animated, "I like a group called 'The Decomposers.' Back in Maine my Uncle Nick plays the lead guitar. But what I'm going to be is a writer. I'm keeping a journal and making notes about the trip."

"And your mother brought you along so you could do research?"

Amy looked down the table where her mother, Doris Lermatov, was lifting a second slice of Yorkshire pudding onto her plate.

"Mother," Amy said with a heavy sigh, "made me come. Like it's her turn for me this June and July. In August I'll stay with my father on Cape Cod. He's a biologist, but I think biology is an incredibly boring subject." Amy paused and then added, "Except for the DNA part. If I'm going to be a writer I have to know about things like that."

"Are you going to write about science? Or medicine?"

"I want to write novels. Not romance junk, but real ones with meaning."

"With DNA as a base?"

"You're making fun of me." And Amy returned to her pasta and gave it an awkward swirl with her fork.

"No, honestly," said Sarah. "I'm just curious about how DNA fits in."

Amy looked at her suspiciously and then relaxed. "Well, for the book I'm doing about this trip I'll need some scientific information because it's going to be a mystery. That's where the psychological comes in. The murderer's going to have this weird motive. He—or maybe she, I haven't made up my mind yet—is going to be very mentally disturbed."

Sarah sat up and stared at her. "You mean you're going to use *this* Garden Club tour?"

Amy gave a slight giggle. "It's the only tour I'm on." She pushed her plate to one side. "This is lousy spaghetti," she observed. And then, "Yeah, a murder mystery. The garden tour will be raw material. I thought with Dr. Trevino missing I could use that and then figure out why someone wouldn't want her to be here."

"Dr. Trevino," Sarah began.

"Yeah, I know she might turn up by tomorrow, but I've got to start somewhere. I thought I could make notes and start working on my cast of characters." Here Amy looked up and circled a finger taking up the entire table.

"Do you know any of these people well enough to turn them into characters?" asked Sarah.

Amy regarded her with something close to contempt. "In fiction you don't have to use *real* personalities. You use your imagination. I thought you were an English teacher. Do you make your students do everything true to life? I mean I'm going to *create* people and maybe use the way they dress or talk."

Here Amy paused for breath and Sarah, feeling suitably

squelched, thought if Mike were here investigating Ellen's non-appearance, he would have cat fits. Sarah *and* Amy bumbling around asking unsuitable questions.

". . . your imagination," finished Amy.

Sarah, suddenly aware that Amy had been talking at some length, came to and said, "Uh, yes, the imagination."

"It's where writers aren't like other people," persisted Amy. "A lot of teachers aren't into imagination. They're grammar freaks and just about destroy you if a semicolon doesn't go where it should, and they go yacking on about proper paragraphs."

Sarah, who believed strongly in proper paragraphs, was just about to temporize in the matter when Amy shook her fuzzy head and held up a rather grubby hand.

"Let me finish about imagination. I think it's really more true than things that are supposed to be true, if you know what I mean. But I guess you only think I should use real facts about people and just pay attention to the grammar."

Sarah turned on Amy and fixed the girl with a look. " 'I am certain,' " she said, " 'of nothing but of the holiness of the Heart's affections and the truth of the Imagination.' "

Amy's eyes widened. "Huh?"

" 'The Imagination may be compared to Adam's dream—he awoke and found it truth,' " said Sarah crisply, and she returned to her chicken curry.

Amy's face crumpled, rather as if some hand had grabbed it and squeezed. "You really are making fun of me," she said resentfully.

Sarah relented. "John Keats. One of his letters boosting the imagination. You're right, Amy. Up with imagination."

Amy looked relieved. "I like Keats. That 'Nightingale' poem and the one about a woman's head planted in a flowerpot. So what do you think about me writing a murder mystery about the tour?"

Sarah decided to derail this aspect of the idea if possible. "It doesn't have to be a murder mystery. How about a novel full of love-hate relationships. Co-dependents. People fighting over an adopted child on the tour. Then you could use your DNA material."

"You think?" said Amy doubtfully, but at this juncture a waiter's hand removed her dish of pasta and the remains of Sarah's curry and almost immediately two glass dishes supporting pyramidal lumps of crème caramel made their appearance.

Sarah, who had ordered baked apple, found that it really didn't matter. Dessert was dessert. It could have been sugared cardboard for all she cared. She was suddenly extraordinarily tired. Amy, fortunately, had lost interest in the conversation and attacked her caramel custard with the greed of a hungry adolescent, and Sarah was free to sink into a mild coma. Tomorrow would be time enough to pursue Mike's request and find out about some of the strangers in the party, their life's work, their travel routes to Logan. About Amy, she felt, she had already found out more than she wanted to know.

Julia, on Sarah's right, who had been in animated conversation with Fred Ouellette on the need to "put down" people as was properly done with ailing horses, now subsided and half-closed her eyes, so that when a general shuffling of chairs indicated that dinner was over, Julia, with Sarah close on her heels, were the first to hustle out and up the winding stairs toward room and bed.

"I'm too old to lose five hours just like that," Julia complained. "That Rossi man and Fred are going to hit the pub for a nightcap but they're in the prime of life. I'm just an old biddy and I need bed. Good night, Sarah. You look done in. As old as I feel." And with this encouraging remark, Julia pushed her key into her door, turned the knob, and disappeared.

As Julia's door snapped closed, Sarah remembered that she had intended to tell her aunt about the finding of Ellen Trevino's empty car at the Kennebunk exit. She hesitated, took a step toward Julia's closed door, and then stopped. She would tell her tomorrow when they were prowling around the tour's first scheduled garden visit, a place called Barnsley House. Large English gardens, she seemed to remember, were noted for their high hedges, little green nooks, and shaded walkways. Perfect for private exchanges. Or perfect for overheard conversations and sinister encounters. For meeting the evil suitor in the maze. Perfect for fatal trysts, for ambush. For sudden death.

Stop it, she told herself irritably. You sound like Amy. She shook herself and began to prepare for bed, grateful that Europeans install washbasins in hotel bedrooms. She could at least sponge away the travel dust. Next, deciding to do penance for untoward thoughts, she turned to a wholesome—in fact, positively symbolic, activity. Washing out her underpants, her bra. Her shirt. Her cotton socks—too long encased in rubber-soled Nikes.

She loaded these items in the sink, added soap powder from her travel supply, pumped them up and down, rinsed and draped them over the towel rack. Then she remembered. The scarf. The scarf that had turned up with those sunglasses. The one with the Filene's label. Well, if someone was going to force a scarf on her and there were no claimers, she wasn't going to refuse a freebie.

Sarah returned to her open shoulder bag and extracted the scarf with its crumpled swirls of red and black. She turned it over in her hand. Underneath the Filene label was a smaller one: "All Silk." She ran the lukewarm water into the sink—you had to be very careful about silk—added the soap powder, dunked the scarf gently, then pulled out the drain. Rather surprised, she noticed that the color had run. A muddy rusty red. Perplexed, she ran the tepid rinse water and dropped the scarf in. Less color this time, a fainter brown-red.

Well, so much for Filene's and color-fast days. But perhaps the scarf was a fake from Hong Kong or Taiwan and using the Filene label. Sarah ran a second rinse and this time was rewarded with only slightly tinged water. A last rinse, this time using only the cold tap, and now the water ran almost clear.

Enough. She could repeat the operation tomorrow and then, since it was a rather handsome object, she would probably wear it.

Sarah settled into bed, closed her eyes, and was almost immediately asleep. It wasn't until the first dawn light, which came as a pale shaft through a crack in the curtained window opening, that Sarah, with a start, sat up and reached an entirely new conclusion about the Filene scarf.

5

SARAH pushed away her pillow, sat upright, and stared at the silk scarf now hanging on the towel rack over the bedroom sink. Her sensation was similar to that of someone finding a coiled cobra within striking distance.

That damn scarf. The thing appearing—along with those cheap sun glasses—in her shoulder bag. No, not "appearing," planted. Planted by some hand. A bloody hand. Then she stopped and began scolding herself. All I can think about is Ellen missing and maybe being kidnapped from her car at the Kennebunk exit and a bloody scarf—belonging to God knows who. Aunt Julia is right. I need to wash my brain out with soap. And with this bracing thought, Sarah swung out of bed and planted her feet squarely on the floor.

By the time Sarah had taken a shower, scrubbed herself with unnecessary vigor with a rough towel, she had made several resolutions, the first being to buy some self-help paperbacks at the nearest village bookstore. Books about getting in touch with your center, finding peace in nature's own biorhythms. The second resolution was to have earnest conversations with the most reliable tour members—the Hopper sisters, for instance—and so learn about planting her own summer garden back home in Maine. And next, above all, to avoid Ms. Amy Lermatov and all discussions of her projected mystery novel. That scarf simply ran rusty red because red is a color that runs and not because the thing is soaked in blood. Here Sarah paused and glared at herself in the bedroom mirror. "You fool," she told the face. "Look at you. A scruffy secondhand person with a head full of unfounded suspicious and abnormal inklings.

It was not a scruffy face, but there were signs of travel fatigue on Sarah's thin face. The gray eyes looked darker than usual; the dark brown hair, disordered by her shower, stood up on her skull; and her high cheekbones and chin reminded her unpleasantly of her third-grade teacher, Miss Edith Brackett.

Sarah turned from the mirror, pulled on her new travel-proof blue linen jumper and denim jacket, and, with shoulders braced and head erect, marched down the stairs and into the dining room for breakfast.

It was a fine English breakfast heavy with eggs, fried tomatoes, finnan haddie, kippers, toast, pots of Cooper's Oxford marmalade, and Fortnum & Mason's strawberry jam. Aunt Julia, busy with kippers, waved a fork in her direction and called out that she hoped Sarah had "settled down." Julia, an early riser, had been up it seemed for hours. Hair tangled, a speck of mud on her cheek, she had been regaling the table with a description of her walk to a nearby farm at which she had had a gratifying conversation on the subject of fodder with a gentleman leading a pair of Cleveland Bays—a type of horse, she kindly explained to her listeners.

Sarah moved away from her aunt and found a safe place between Portia McClure and Margaret Hopper, and listened gratefully to conversation that centered about the upcoming visit to Barnsley House, the wonders of the Laburnum Walk, the golden balm, the *Allium aflatunense*. The talk drifted pleasantly between problems of seed dormancy and methods of dealing with caterpillars.

Sarah, thus soothed, returned in to her room in an uplifted

frame of mind to confront the suspected scarf hanging over the towel rack. She looked at the object with disdain and then folded it—now quite dry—into a toilet paper nest and shoved it into the bottom of her suitcase. She felt that she could be entirely garden-minded if it were not for those notes about the group to be faxed to Alex in some clandestine manner yet to be devised.

Returning to the lower regions, she was met by Julia Clancy armed with a walking stick and straw hat. "I hope you've calmed down, Sarah," she said. "Looking at gardens demands a peaceful personality. As for me, I've had my horse fix and now I'm prepared to be entirely amiable and admire everything I see."

Sarah hesitated, looked over her shoulder scanned the front hall. Then, taking a deep breath, she told Julia about Ellen Trevino's car turning up at the Kennebunk exit of the Maine Turnpike, the scarf running rusty red, and Mike's request to come up with a few remarks about the various tour members.

Julia listened, for once not interrupting, and then frowned. "That scarf was probably made in India and everything I've ever had from India ran like crazy. However," she added, "if you need any tidbits, gossip about our group, I'll be glad to help. I have a very good eye . . ."

"For horses," put in Sarah.

"It's the same thing. One develops an eye for the abnormal, the cowhock, the goose rump, the parrot mouth, the slew foot. The tendency to spook, to bolt. It's exactly the same with humans. I consider myself an expert in assessing humans. After all, I've been in the business of matching humans with horses for years."

"I guess so," said Sarah doubtfully.

"Trust your old Aunt Julia. Bring something to write on. Everyone will think you're taking garden notes."

"Well, I really *would* like to take garden notes," said Sarah.

"Fine," said Julia. "Mix and match. Now hurry up, we're taking off in ten minutes."

Travel by bus, Sarah decided, had certain advantages for the foreign visitor, not the least of which was the driver—an amiable Londoner named Joseph—knowing where he was going and so not taking wrong turns and spinning like a top in round-abouts.

And the bus wasn't one of those Leviathans that roared along the big motorways, but a smaller green Ford Club Car able to take the small country roads and slip from hedgerow to hedgerow without a major confrontation with some other vehicle. And it was a lovely day, the sun had come out, and from time to time shifting clouds sent long shadows across rolling meadows and pastures dotted with sheep. And always there was a small village or town, its buildings of honey-colored stone hidden away in the folds of hills or huddled on the edge of a dark copse.

Unfortunately for Sarah, who would have preferred gazing at the landscape, she had a job to do. But the small size of the bus had one disadvantage. Armed with her notebook and ballpoint, she decided that making notes was a rather public affair, particularly when seated next to Sandi Ouellette on one side and Margaret Hopper across the way.

Sandi applauded the appearance of the notebook. "I should take notes, too. About everything. Even the vocabulary. All the words are so different. Did you know that your backside is a bum in England? Think of the mistakes you could make talking about bums. And I'm sure the whole Cotswold scene is absolutely going to swamp me. I mean, look at the cottages with those thatched roofs. They look like doll houses. Not real at all. And the gardens, all those Latin names. But I'm having the best time, and you know what Fred said to me this morning, he said he wants to start having an English breakfast when we get home; but I told him, Fred, you just forget that, I'm not about to cook kippers when you've been perfectly happy eating Cheerios all your life."

When Sandi stopped for breath, Margaret Hopper took over. Leaning toward Sarah, she said with approval, "You're quite right to be taking notes. I always jot down a few memories before I go to bed. We're so lucky to be going to Barnsley House.

You know I wouldn't be at all surprised to find Ellen Trevino meeting us there. She's the one who insisted on the Barnsley House gardens."

But Sarah, thus reminded of her promise to Alex, found that Barnsley House had to get along without her complete attention. She clutched her notebook tightly and followed the group down a path to a bed of vivid blue iris. Here the party halted only briefly and then broke into units of twos and threes. In vain, Barbara Baxter asserted her leadership. She flourished her guide map and tried to regroup her flock in order to move everyone into an orderly progression down one garden path, up the next.

Barbara, thought Sarah, straggling in the rear, was another person about whom she knew little. What was clear, though, was that the tour leader knew next to nothing about handling garden enthusiasts because the party having been hustled down the fabled Laburnum Walk, rebelled and divided abruptly at a sundial. Sarah and Julia retreated, Carter McClure and Portia branched off announcing a desire to inspect the bronze irises, Justin Rossi sauntered in the direction of a walk featuring delphiniums and Oriental poppies, and the beautiful Stacy Daniel announced the intention of looking for a bench and getting some sun. Barbara, looking confused, found herself left with only the Hopper sisters, Doris Lermatov and daughter Amy to oversee.

Sarah, with Julia behind her, having dodged a side path, reflected that gardens aren't like museums where a brief lecture in front of a Matisse or a Rembrandt satisfies the visitor's need. Garden people have their own pet interests, their own agendas; they like to hang fondly over certain plantings, bypass others. Perennial fans make for the perennial beds and the lovers of annuals, of herbal displays, of roses, wisteria, of pastoral prospects, go elsewhere.

Aunt Julia, never one to withhold criticism, put it bluntly. "That young woman should stop trying to herd us around." She turned to a small bench and sat down heavily.

"Barbara is trying to do Lillian Garth's *and* Ellen Trevino's job," Sarah reminded her.

Julia snorted. "Then she'd better start reading up and stop trying to organize everyone."

"Hello, Mrs. Clancy," said a voice. Amy. Amy Lermatov. "Hello, Sarah. Can I call you Sarah or should I say Mrs. McKenzie?"

Sarah shook her head. "Sarah will do fine, but I'm not Mrs. McKenzie. I use my own name. It's Sarah Deane."

"I should hope you use your own name," said Amy. "Catch me using my husband's name."

Julia gave her a look. "You have a husband?"

"Are you kidding?" said Amy. "But if I had I wouldn't use his name. I suppose your husband's name was Clancy because in your day women just gave up their identity."

Julia drew herself up to her full five foot three inches. "I did not give up my identity, I made a conscious choice, and I am extremely proud to have Tom Clancy's name."

"But he's dead now, isn't he?" said Amy. "So you could go back to whoever you were."

At this point Sarah, foreseeing a major storm, interrupted. Said the first thing that came out of her head. "So how's your story coming? Amy"—she explained to a purple-faced Julia— "is writing a mystery based on this trip."

Amy grinned. "I'm taking notes on everyone. I found out that Stacy Daniel used to be a fabulous model. I mean she's been in magazines and on TV, and now she works for a bank doing public relations. But I don't think she likes gardens all that much."

Sarah, having brought the subject out, tried to shut the barn door. "Where's your mother, Amy? Should you try to find her? It's easy to get lost in all these paths."

Amy assumed a look of extreme scorn. "My mother . . . ," she began, but Julia broke in. "Why, tell me, have you chosen a mystery that features the tour group?"

"Oh, that's easy," said Amy. "Because I'm not really into gardens, so I brought a notebook. Like yours, Sarah." Amy pointed to Sarah's small spiral model. And then when Dr. Trevino didn't show up it seemed like a great idea to write a mystery. Dr. Trevino would make a good murder victim because she's what my teacher calls an interesting character. Like Jane Eyre. Of course, it will be a real bummer if she *does* show up because I'll have to rewrite the whole thing." Amy hesitated and then brightened. "I could say she had amnesia like Agatha Christie. She'd been hit over the head on the way to Logan Airport."

Julia gave Amy the famous "Clancy eye," a look long familiar to her beginning riders. "You should not go sneaking about taking notes on people."

Amy looked offended. "I'd just take an interest in each person and find out about their life and hobbies and how everyone got to the airport. Stuff like that."

Sarah decided it was time to move Amy on. And use the girl for her own purposes. "Okay, Amy, why don't you go back to Stacy Daniel and find out why she doesn't like gardens?"

"I can tell when I'm being got rid of," said Amy. "But that's okay. I'll take notes about you both later on. Sandi Ouellette says she knows all about you, Sarah, but if I quote Sandi I'll say she's an unidentified source."

"Amy," said Julia in a grating voice. "No one wants a junior spy in the middle of a tour."

"How about a senior spy?" asked Sarah when Amy had taken herself back down the Laburnum Walk and disappeared from sight.

"One senior spy and one antiquated spy," retorted Julia. She rose stiffly from the bench and strode off in the direction of a thicker growth of evergreen.

Sarah, following, found Julia had herself produced a small spiral pad from the recesses of her denim skirt. "We need to split assignments. You take the Hoppers and Justin Rossi, because he's interested in you . . ."

"No, he's not," said Sarah, rather too hastily.

"Don't interrupt. He looks like Alex and he may act like Alex, so you may be his type. And you're the unattached younger female."

"I'm attached and Stacy Daniel is the younger female."

"Forget Stacy. You have caught his eye. Now time is running short so we've got to mingle and be full of feigned interest and the milk of human kindness of which I have very little. Beside the Hoppers and Rossi, take the Ouellettes—you know them anyway—and I'll do Barbara Baxter and Stacy. You can have Amy and Doris Lermatov, and I'll take Carter McClure and Portia since I already know them. We'll compare notes after lunch."

"And then we'll have to find a place to fax the stuff."

"We can do it in town because I heard Barbara Baxter say we're going into Cirencester for lunch and will have an hour for looking around, for shopping—whatever—before we hit the next garden."

Sarah looked puzzled. "I checked the itinerary after breakfast and it said something about a country lunch. Near something called Lavender Cottage. Cirencester is a big town, not country."

"I heard you," said a voice behind them. Margaret Hopper and a step to the rear, Portia Mcclure. Margaret explained. "Sandi Ouellette and Doris were just begging to be allowed off the leash and Barbara gave in. Barbara's very accommodating."

"Well, Carter is fuming," put in Portia.

"There are interesting Roman remains in Cirencester," said Margaret. "The town was built on the ruins of Corinium, and there are sixteenth-century houses and a Woolgather's House. And many specialty shops. Sandi Ouellette is so pleased. She wants to buy a teapot. She's gone very British and talks about lorries and the bonnet and boot. Anyway, we'll eat at twelve-thirty and be on the road by two-thirty. Plenty of time to see Lavender Cottage."

"All right, all right," said Julia in a rather cross voice. "But what else is Barbara going to change? Sarah and I are driving and if the tour's changing its route it will be great nuisance. I hope this will take care of this lust to shop, goggling at store windows. Shopping is what anyone can do back home." Julia, by no stretch of the imagination, could ever be called a shopper, unless one considered time spent in tack shops fingering blankets and turnout rugs and varieties of liniment and wormers, and all the wonderful equine merchandise so dear to the horse lover.

"Never mind about Aunt Julia," said Sarah, seeing Margaret looking slightly offended. She plucked at her aunt's sleeve. "Aunt Julia, I think Cirencester's a good idea. Remember we wanted to look for"—here Sarah hesitated because what they wanted to look for was a place from which to send a fax—"we wanted to look for gloves," she said. "The Cotswolds are famous for gloves."

"They are?" said Margaret. "I've never heard that."

"Wonderful leather," said Sarah, because after all it seemed safe to guess that leather goods could be found in large towns.

"Gloves?" said Julia. "I don't want gloves. After all, I have perfectly . . ." Here she paused as Sarah's toe, hidden by a garden growth marked "Bowles' Golden Grass," came into sharp contact with her ankle.

"Yarn," said Julia. "Not gloves. I need yarn for my needlepoint."

Ten minutes later, safely separated from the main body of retreating Garden Club members, Julia turned to Sarah. "You don't have to kick me. And in the Cotswolds I'm sure it's wool, but I do see that Cirencester works out for sending the fax."

"It might be easier," said Sarah peering ahead to a clump of delphiniums, and seeing Amy Lermatov with her notebook, "to fax Amy. I'll bet she knows more than we do about the group."

"Knows more dirt," said Julia darkly. "She's probably got a list of violence, molestation, drug use by our friends, and what she doesn't have, she'll make up."

"So let's go to work," said Sarah. "We'll be interested garden lovers who want to get to know everyone better."

"Like Justin Rossi? Watch your step there, Sarah."

"I can handle the likes of Justin Rossi. Most men have a healthy interest in themselves and that'll make it easy."

"As I said," Julia reminded her, "en garde." And Julia settled her straw hat firmly on her gray tufted head and marched off on a path in the direction of a small temple.

Sarah, as she had promised, "went to work" on her chosen tour members. This was made somewhat difficult by the increasing number of visitors. It was Friday, for tourists the beginning of the weekend, and Barnsley House, as one of the National Garden scheme properties, was deservedly popular.

As a result of the thickening crowds, Sarah found it almost impossible to take notes in privacy and had to start and stop a number of conversations, skipping back and forth from subjects like past interests, place of business, the trip to Logan, to exclamations of delight over the herb borders, the purple lunaria, and the fascination of a pink fuzzy asterlike growth labeled *Thalictrum aquilegiifolium*.

Feeling she had a fair grip on the Lermatov pair and already knew a lot about the Ouellettes, she concentrated on the Hopper sisters, and then caught up with Justin Rossi, who stood staring fixedly at a mix of scarlet poppies and blue delphinium.

She took a deep breath. "So, hello. Are you as good at garden quotations as you are at graveyard ones?"

Justin swiveled about and brightened. "Hey, there. I was wondering where everyone was."

"Gone every which way. Barbara Baxter's going to have her hands full if she expects us to . . ."

"To be led up the garden path," finished Justin.

A little too apt, Sarah decided, but she acknowledged the remark with a small smile and then launched on her program of discovery.

It was fairly easy going. After a brisk exchange of rather tired garden quotes, the identification of several common birds including the greenfinch and a yellowhammer—"I call it the yellow bunting," said Rossi—Sarah, prompted by a sense that time was slipping by, came out and asked what had prompted Mr. Rossi . . .

"Please. Justin."

"Justin. To decide to come on the trip?"

"You first. Why did you decide?" asked Justin looking at her with a quizzical expression.

"I adore gardens," said Sarah firmly. "I just don't know much about starting them. My husband and I"—it was time to reassert her married state—"have just settled into an old farmhouse and

I've planted peach trees, but no flowers yet. Except for the stuff that comes up by itself."

"Stuff? And you call yourself a gardener? Besides, some of the best flowers are wild ones. Pearly everlasting, wild phlox, bouncing betty, marsh mallow. Lupine."

Sarah made a humble noise and submitted to a lecture on wild versus cultivated flowers. Then, when the flower stream had dried, Justin was moved to describe his life and works and egged on by encouraging murmurs from his companion, launched into biography. His college in Vermont, law school at Boston University, and finally the glory of a well-known, and most staid, solid, and conservative law firm in Boston, an outfit called Philips, Follett, Follett, Crashhow, and Rossi—Rossi being the newest star in their legal firmament. Trusts, corporate affairs, insurance suits, some criminal cases, a smattering of family law.

"I'm family law," stated Justin.

"You mean divorces, custody fights, child support, all that?"

"You've got it. Trusts, too, of course. Wills, contests, settlements. Even domestic strife, although if that gets too hot we turn it over to our criminal team."

"Well, well," said Sarah. Then, without much originality, added, "It must be fascinating."

"That's one word for it," said Justin cryptically. "There are others."

But now Barbara Baxter hove into sight and called out that it was time to leave for lunch.

Julia, however, was lingering at the end of the retreating group. She beckoned to Sarah and whispered loudly, "I've hit pay dirt."

And the two hurried forward to the car park.

6

"HOW do you mean, pay dirt," Sarah demanded as the two women hustled along the gravel path. "Is it about Barbara?"

"Keep your voice down. As an investigator you lack even the most elementary skills. Not Barbara. Stacy."

Sarah lifted her eyes in surprise.

"Yes," hissed Julia. "The beauty queen, or whatever she is, doesn't know the first thing about gardens."

"That's what Amy said." Sarah considered for a moment and then added, "Not exactly what I call 'pay dirt.' After all, I don't know the first thing about gardens myself."

"But you have a fairly intelligent interest. Stacy's like a mechanical doll. Wind her up and she'll make a few appropriate remarks about mulch or acid soil or how she just loves magnolia trees while she's pointing at wisteria. The woman's a fraud."

"You mean," said Sarah with a grin, "a plant."

"It's no joking matter. And that child, Amy, is right. Stacy has worked as a model and now is doing PR for a Boston banking outfit. Gardens are no part in her life; she lives in an apartment. So why pretend an interest? I've spent an extremely boring twenty minutes with the woman and an equally boring time with Barbara Baxter. I've been down the Laburnum Walk five times. As for Barbara, I think it's a case of what you see is what you get. A tour leader who doesn't know squat about flowers."

"Because there was no reason for her to," said Sarah.

They had now reached the car park and Julia paused and turned on Sarah. "The only thing I am absolutely sure of is that I have sacrificed my own pleasure in the Barnsley House garden in the interests of faxing a tedious collection of gossip."

"We're doing what the powers at home have asked us to do."

"Those dim bulbs in the police department probably have Ellen Trevino locked up for a traffic violation and they don't know it."

"What's that about Ellen Trevino? Have you heard from her?"

It was Edith Hopper, scraps of her usually neat white hair poking out of its net and all flushed from her perambulations around Barnsley House.

"Oh, no," said Sarah quickly. "We were saying we missed her."

"She would have been so happy," said Edith. "Such a wonderful morning, the sun out, and the garden, absolutely incredible."

But here Barbara Baxter appeared and gestured toward the bus. "Hurry up," she called. "A new restaurant, The Grimalkin Arms in Cirencester. I looked it up in the guide and it's supposed to have lots of atmosphere."

The Grimalkin Arms, once an ordinary eighteenth-century structure of the buff-colored Cotswold stone, had been transformed by its new owners, lovers of the Elizabethan look, into a gloomy space with stained-glass windows, heavy tables of dark wood, highbacked chairs, and along the wall a number of heraldic devices featuring the head of a gray cat. Waitresses in ruffs and farthingales scurried back and forth with loaded trays.

Barbara Baxter, however, seemed pleased with the ambiance, and Sandi Ouellette, enchanted by what she called "a real English look," explained to all who would listen that "grimalkin" meant an old cat and had they seen the cats on those shields on the walls? The others suffered the dimly lit atmosphere in the interest of eating as soon as possible. However, when lunch proper was over and dessert had arrived—large helpings of sweetened starch in various shapes and flavors—Barbara tapped lightly on her goblet with a spoon and called for attention.

She knew that some people might be wondering why the trip plans deviated—ever so slightly—from the original schedule. But many had expressed interest in seeing more of Britain, availing themselves of the cultural opportunities. Here Barbara looked meaningfully at Sandi and Fred, Doris Lermatov and Stacy Daniel, all of whom nodded vigorously while Justin Rossi looked up and added a "Hear, hear."

"Fortunately," Barbara went on, "I found some unscheduled time in our schedule, so I've felt I could tinker a little with our itinerary."

Sarah looked over at Carter McClure. Judging from his expression he was about to reach over and strangle Barbara.

"So now," said Barbara, now well into her pep talk, "I've arranged a trip to Cambridge. We can visit some of the colleges, the chapels, the bookstores. And especially, the Cambridge Botanic Garden. I'm surprised neither Lillian Garth nor Ellen Trevino didn't include it."

"Because," growled Carter McClure, shaking off Portia's arm, "that's an institutional garden. We're doing private gardens, cottage gardens, not goddamn city university gardens."

"Oh, do hush, Carter," said Portia. "Cambridge might be fun."

Carter's opinion of Cambridge was shared by the Hopper sisters, who mentioned that cities—even ancient university ones—are often hot and crowded, a view seconded by Julia. However, the others made approving noises, and even Sarah thought it might be a nice change of pace.

And then it was time for shopping. Freedom to wander about Cirencester and then meet back at The Grimalkin Arms at two-thirty for the trip to the Lavender Cottage garden, a site which lay to the north, outside of Little Barrington.

"Free," said Sarah as she and Julia stepped off in the direction of the high street. "Free to dig up a fax machine."

"A nuisance, writing out everything," complained Julia.

"There's a stationers across the way," said Sarah. "I saw it when we came out. Paper, pens, and probably a place to sit down."

Not only paper and pens, but a fax machine, the stationers being one of those all-purpose shops that catered to many needs.

"There," said Julia when they returned to the street fifty minutes later. "We've just time to look for gloves for you and wool for me. We have to be authentic."

"You mean cover our tracks," said Sarah. And then she started. Amy. Amy Lermatov, looming just behind her shoulder.

"What tracks?" demanded Amy. "Are you on an assignment? Or is it just PI stuff?"

Julia, who had whirled around at the sight of Amy, recovered first. "PI? Whatever are you talking about?"

Amy smiled broadly, showing a large stretch of tooth hardware. "Private Investigator. Like Kinsey Millhone and V. I. Warshawsky. Because PIs are the only people who cover their tracks except for hard-core criminals or spies."

"We are looking for leather goods," said Julia. "And wool."

"For needlepoint and gloves," said Sarah.

Amy's grin grew wider. "Yeah, right. You bet."

"Why," demanded Julia, "are you floating around Cirencester by yourself?"

"Honestly, Mrs. Clancy," said Amy, "I'll be fifteen next month and I'm allowed to explore. I've very cultural. Do you see that art gallery?" She pointed across the street. "I followed the Hopper ladies into it. To get a line on them. They didn't even see me. And I've almost finished the notes for my first chapter."

"Good grief," said Julia. "Sarah, I think I see a leather shop down that side street. Good-bye, Amy. There's nothing of cultural interest in a leather shop."

"Oh, don't mind me," said Amy. "I should visit the boring places as well as the good ones. I'll just tag along. Writers need atmosphere."

❧

In an entirely too real atmosphere in the late afternoon, Alex McKenzie sat in the claustrophobic space that Deputy Sheriff Investigator Mike Laaka called his office. This small rectangle, more closet than workspace, crouched in the lower reaches of the Knox County Sheriff's building and accommodated one scarred metal desk, a number of gray file cabinets, three elderly wooden office chairs and a calendar featuring Cigar, recent Horse of the Year. Mike was a diehard race fan, and the fact that the State of Maine had no thoroughbred racing never deterred him from putting together Byzantine betting combinations through unidentified off-track betting establishments.

"Lot of silly garbage," announced Mike, pushing the thin sheets of fax paper to the back of his desk. "Have you read it?"

Alex shrugged. "I've stuck my neck out having the fax sent to my office. My nurse, that's Betty Bartlett, gave me a very fishy look when it came in. She knows some of those people. And, what do you expect, an FBI report? An Interpol workup? This is from two women trying to put some random information on paper without anyone knowing what they were up to."

Mike pulled a sheet toward him. "Listen. 'Stacy Daniel. Model, PR bank executive. Doesn't know about gardens, jogs, member of health club, done modeling. Classy dresser. Lives in Lexington, Mass. No friends in group except maybe B. Baxter, leader pro tem.' That's signed by Julia. You see, worthless."

"Okay, so it's not very meaty," agreed Alex. "What's next?"

"Nothing we couldn't figure out about the Ouellettes or the two Hoppers. And Doris Lermatov is eating her way through Britain and loves treacle tarts, trifle, spotted dick—what in hell is that? Daughter Amy says she's writing a mystery based on the idea that Ellen Trevino didn't show up because she's been murdered."

"Christ," said Alex.

"Carter McClure is another bad-tempered academic kept on track by wife Portia. Justin Rossi looks like you, quotes poetry and knows birds. Lawyer, family law, and seems to know flowers—the common names anyway."

Alex stood up. "I'm glad Sarah's found a replacement for me. I've looked over the rest. Except the Barbara Baxter blurb."

Mike pushed the fax papers into a neat pile. "Acting leader and to quote Julia, she's 'overorganized.' "

"Not a bad quality in a tour leader," observed Alex.

Mike nodded. "Actually, the state police did a little checking for us. Last job done by Baxter for Whirlaway Tours was a six-city art thing in the U.S.: Boston, Chicago, Philly, Santa Fe, LA. Before that a southern tour: Louisiana, Mississippi, Alabama, the Carolinas. Historic houses, old plantations. Last year Hawaii."

"I suppose," said Alex, "at some point you'll have to be checking departure times. Who flew in from Maine, who drove."

"Yeah, I suppose," said Mike in a tired voice, "and that'll take . . . ," but the telephone rang and the sentence hung in the air. Mike held up his hand to keep Alex from leaving and picked up the receiver. And then.

"Jesus H. Christ. I mean Jesus. Where? Well, sure. Yeah, I'll come right away. Sure. Okay. I mean, Christ Almighty."

"You're repeating yourself," said Alex. Then, "What's up."

"What's up is Ellen. Ellen Trevino. Or rather she's down. Along the Maine Turnpike. Off the Scarborough exit.

Alex stared at him. "What do you mean 'along the turnpike?' "

"What I said. Along it. Off the exit ramp. In one of those sections with trees and bushes."

"You mean an accident? A hit-and-run."

Mike shook his head. "No accident. The lady was rolled up in a plastic sheet. Like a sausage. I'm on my way down now. The state police need a positive ID because there wasn't any found on the body. Dental records take too long."

"So why do they think it's Ellen?"

"We haven't got any other missing females who fit her general description. Maine isn't Chicago or LA with fifty women reported missing every day. So there's a fair chance it's Ellen."

"You know her well enough to identify her?"

"No, but I'm bringing you. You're not on call, are you?"

"No, not tonight."

"We'll take your car. Mine's in the shop and the cruisers are out. At least you won't have to do the medical examiner bit. She was found out of Knox County. We'll drive straight to Augusta and see the body there. They'll do the post sometime late tonight—or tomorrow morning. Johnny Cuzak will meet us. You remember Johnny, assistant state medical examiner. Nice guy, but he hates bodies turning up on weekends. Anyway, if you make a positive ID we can try to get in touch with her family."

Alex walked to the office door and held it open, Mike following. "This'll be some gruesome scene from what the dispatcher said. Lady's a mess. Jesus Christ, and to think I've been saying Dr. Trevino must have missed her plane and telling everyone to stop making a fuss."

It was Ellen Trevino. Or what was left of her. Even Alex, familiar as he was to death in various shapes and conditions, felt a wave of horror as he studied the swollen and barely recognizable features of the woman now stretched out on the autopsy table, still partially wrapped in the full-length plastic sheet in which she had been found. And unbidden in his mind rose the picture of the Ellen Trevino as he had heard giving a lecture on need for stricter state environmental controls. Her voice had been low, but she brought a certain intensity to her remarks. And she had had that appealing otherworldly appearance, right out of an antique illustrated book. He also remembered Sarah saying that as a child she had been painfully shy and this fitted with the diffidence he remembered when the lecture was over and the audience had crowded about her for questions. And now this.

Johnny Cuzak, the assistant state medical examiner from Augusta, shook his head in disgust. "She was wrapped up like some goddamn piece of meat," he complained. "Killed inside that sheet maybe or lying on it. Like whoever did it wanted to keep everything tidy, didn't want to get splattered with blood. Which from his point of view is a smart move."

"Stabbed?" said Mike Laaka, pointing to a dark and sodden perforation in Ellen's blue print dress just below her sternum.

"Murderer was right on target," said Johnny. "But the guy tried to kill her twice. Maybe three times. Maybe a karate chop to knock her out. And a plastic bag over her head. Must have been a race between asphyxia and hemorrhage. If I had to lay money on it I'd go for exsanguination. But it's a guess. Temperature's been in the seventies the last few days so we've got putrefaction to deal with."

"Doesn't look like a knife wound," observed Mike.

"Nope," agreed Johnny. "Entry's too large—but we'll know more later. Now we'll have to take the photographs, with and without that damn plastic bag, with and without clothes, get an X-ray, check her for sexual assault, all the usual. I'll schedule the autopsy for tomorrow, eight o'clock. Talk about a loused-up weekend, why does it always happen?"

"How about time of death?" asked Mike.

"Don't be impatient. Stomach contents, degree of lividity, tissue dissolution, the whole picture. I keep telling you guys that we can't fix the time down to the last minute unless the victim's wearing a smashed wristwatch.

Alex, foreseeing a lecture on forensics, stepped in. "Where exactly was the body? And who found her?"

"This guy in a pickup pulled off on the Scarborough exit road to take a leak. There's a bunch of bushes and trees in there and since he was kind of modest he went way in. Found the body. Wrapped in the plastic sheet with a few old branches pulled over it. Not a real job of hiding, but I guess from a car driving out the exit you wouldn't have seen it. Forensic team is there now sifting through the place. So far the usual crap mostly along the road edge. You know, plastic cups, beer cans, cigarette butts."

"Weapon?" asked Alex.

"Nothing so far. Meanwhile we'll let the state police know

we've had an ID. You two go home and get your beauty sleep while poor old Johnny Cuzak spends the night fooling around with body fluids and leaving his family alone for the nine-hundredth consecutive weekend."

"God, what a lousy scene that was," said Alex as he turned his Jeep into Route 17 out of Augusta and headed toward the coast. "That poor woman. Sarah told me Ellen Trevino was a very quiet private person."

"And now," said Mike, "she's as public as all hell."

Alex nodded. "Ironic, isn't it? Okay, what's next? Ellen's family, I suppose. Who and where?"

"The state police CID will take that on," said Mike. "I'm just a handyman. Still only that stepfather in Vancouver as far as we can tell. But I know what's next. That tour group has to be shaken up and interrogated. What they knew about Ellen, when she was last seen, and so forth. They'll have to go to some cute little English village police station and give depositions."

Alex shook his head. "I keep asking myself, For God's sake why? Why would any one hurt such an entirely harmless woman who lectures on horticulture and specializes in English country gardens?"

"Freak accident, maybe. Wrong place at the wrong time. She got out of her car at the Kennebunk exit and then, wham. Some fucking maniac nailed her. Raped her, maybe. Robbed her, maybe, because her handbag, luggage, everything's missing. Stabbed her, wrapped up the body, and toted it out to the Scarborough exit and dumped it. And got the hell out. Okay, I suppose you want to call Sarah and the others, but don't."

"Because I'm not allowed to?"

"Our old friend George Fitts will want to do it kosher. Not let the sheriff's department or you handle anything so tricky."

This proved the case. The redoubtable Sergeant George Fitts, Maine State Police CID, human refrigerator and specialist in the analytical approach to crime, did indeed want to follow proper procedures through proper channels. And these involved communication with one Inspector Defoe of High Roosting Police Department in the County of Gloucestershire, and the setting up of the machinery for the taking of statements followed by the faxing of same. Notification of what was in store for the Midcoast Garden Club of Knox County, Maine, USA, to take place the next morning, Saturday, June the tenth.

"We'll let them get their beauty sleep," said Inspector Defoe, echoing as if by transatlantic telepathy Johnny Cuzak's words.

7

AN innkeeper does not take kindly to finding the constabulary on his doorstep. This is especially true at seven-thirty in the morning, a time when guests are coming down for breakfast or returning from early morning walks.

But at least, thought Mr. Thomas Gage, the Shearing innkeeper, he's not driving one of those great bloody white police cars with its horizontal orange stripe for all the neighborhood to gawk at. And he's not in uniform, so I suppose I should be thankful for small mercies. Thomas made attempt to fix his face into a neutral frame and told him to come in.

Inspector Defoe stepped over the threshold. He was indeed a low-key presence. Gray suit, maroon tie, blue shirt. Polished black shoes. Quite respectable, except, of course, no one with half a glance would take him for a tourist.

"Come out of the front hall, please, and go into my office," said Thomas Gage, after he had scowled at the identity card produced by the inspector—an unnecessary gesture since High Roosting was a small village and everyone knew the man by sight, but Defoe liked to do things by the book.

"Now," said Mr. Gage, when the inspector had joined him in the tiny office off the front hall. "What's this all about? I can't have our guests upset. The inn is full. We've had no trouble since those two Albanians with the motorbikes left."

"Thomas, please," said Defoe, who knew Mr. Gage as a fellow supporter of the High Roosting Football Club. The inspector was a sturdy, gray-haired, heavy browed man with a square jaw who bore the burden of the first name of Daniel and was forever fending off cries of "Have you found Crusoe yet, Defoe?"

"There'll be no fuss," continued Daniel Defoe, helping himself to the one comfortable office chair. "You won't even know I've been here. I will tread very softly. All I want to do is talk to the American tour group. Nothing to do with the increasing crime rate of High Roosting. I'll be wanting to see the whole lot of them in your front parlor, everything quiet and private. Then their tour bus can bring them over to the station for statements."

"I still don't know what on earth you're going on about, Daniel," said Mr. Gage, becoming informal in his exasperation.

"Homicide. In the States. New England. Or Maine, to be exact. Some woman who was supposed to be with the group and missed her flight. Missed it, apparently, because she was dead. Or kidnapped and then died. Not alive, anyway."

"Why do you want statements then if it's a murder in the States?" demanded Mr. Gage.

"I don't want them. The Maine State Police CID want them. They're working through Interpol and we cooperate. It's not as if we're dealing with Iran or China. The Maine State Police want certain information and we'll supervise the statements and send the information along. And there's the end to it with not a bit of bother to you and the Shearing. Now, when do they have breakfast?"

"I expect some of them are down now," said Mr. Gage in an unhappy voice. "I heard the tour driver—he's got a room over the old stables—say they were due to leave at nine. Going to a couple of special gardens north of Chipping Camden."

"The best-laid plans," said Inspector Defoe. "Please ask each of them to step along to the parlor after breakfast."

"The parlor is open to *all* our guests," said Mr. Gage. "It's where we put the papers. The periodicals."

"And for about an hour or so this morning it won't be open to all your guests. I'll meet them there."

"Damn the police," said Mr. Gage to Mrs. Hosmer, the Shearing secretary, when Inspector Defoe was out of hearing. "If he lets on about this affair, even if it happened in the States, it may put people off."

The secretary looked up from her computer keyboard on which she was tapping out the evening's dinner menu specials. "None of our guests is going to be put off by a murder in the States. Everyone expects murder in the States. That's what they do over there. Kill each other. It's a perfectly normal everyday thing."

However, it fell to Mrs. Hosmer to speak to each member of the garden tour, urging them to come directly after breakfast to the parlor. That someone wanted to meet them. All of them. Together.

"What someone?" demanded Julia Clancy, looking up from her poached egg.

"Oh, I can't rightly say," said Mrs. Hosmer, avoiding the Clancy eye. The secretary had been instructed to keep quiet about the nature of the meeting.

"I'm sure you can rightly say," returned Carter McClure, who sat next to Julia. "So say it. Otherwise, we have no reason to go to the parlor. We all know each other, the plan for the day is set, and we're due on the bus by nine."

"And we have just time after breakfast to write postcards," said Doris Lermatov. "I haven't sent a single one and three days have gone by."

"In the parlor," said Mrs. Hosmer with greater firmness. "It's the small room leading off the front hall. The gentleman will meet you there and explain."

"Gentleman!" exclaimed Julia. "What gentleman?"

But Mrs. Hosmer was on the move, only turning at the door and calling across two tables, "His name is Defoe. Daniel Defoe."

"Robinson Crusoe," said Carter McClure. "How jolly. The author himself."

"Moll Flanders, Journal of the Plague Year," added Sarah, who had used both books in her English class the past year. She had been listening to Mrs. Hosmer's request, and now decided that this must be part of some High Roosting village affair going on in the village which needed tourist money. A church fête or a white elephant sale—what did they call it here, a jumble sale?

Sarah bent again over her thickening porridge. She had chosen oatmeal out of a sense that a day spent slogging over two of the United Kingdom's major gardens demanded serious fortification. On her right side Justin Rossi was finishing his second cup of coffee and ignoring Barbara Baxter's descriptions of the wonders of the Kiftsgate and Hidcote Manor gardens. Barbara, Sarah decided, must have spent a large portion of the previous evening boning up because she was now regurgitating what sounded like an entire guidebook of information. But if Justin Rossi appeared uninterested, then Stacy Daniel went him one better. She yawned, shifted in her seat, wondered out loud if there were any good movies around.

In fact, only Sandi and Fred Ouellette listened to Barbara with anything like attention. Portia concentrated on her muffins, Doris Lermatov sorted postcards, Carter McClure dissected his trout, while young Amy Lermatov spent the time between large bites of toast with writing in her notebook.

Sarah looked down the table, taking in the still unfinished breakfasts, the second cups of coffee and tea now being poured, and then rolled up her napkin and stood up. "Please excuse me," she said. "I need fifteen minutes of fresh air before the meeting. I'm going out and check out the garden right here. We've been neglecting what's right on our doorstep.

The Shearing Inn garden was rich in early summer flowers, red and white valerian, hanging wisteria, and trellised roses. After rambling aimlessly about for several minutes, Sarah, hearing agitated female voices, moved away toward a grassy terrace that overlooked a pasture dotted with sheep. There she remained for some ten minutes in a sort of post-breakfast trance watching the sheep moving separately and by twos and threes, the ewes followed by their now partly grown lambs. Then, with a guilty start, she remembered the parlor meeting, turned and started back.

And came upon the Hopper sisters, whom she realized had not been at breakfast. Both were in some disrepair. Red eyes, trembling lips, Edith holding a handkerchief, Margaret swallowing hard.

Sarah hesitated. Was this a private moment of grief or did they want help? Or comfort?

She settled for comfort.

"I'm sorry, I don't mean to interrupt, but is there anything wrong. Something I can do? Have you had bad news?"

Margaret snuffled and then shook her head. "No, Sarah dear. Nothing at all. Just a little shock. Something we'd forgotten . . ."

"Or didn't know about," said Edith.

"About our passport, a sort of mixup," said Margaret, but with such lack of conviction even Edith looked puzzled.

"I'm sure that it can be straightened out," said Sarah, who wasn't in the least sure; she had a horror of losing documents.

"Oh, I'm sure it can," said Edith. "Only we, well, we didn't know at first. Just a mistake."

"There you are." It was Barbara Baxter standing at the garden gate. "We're wanted right now. Mrs. Hosmer sent me to find you."

"Are you sure you're both all right?" asked Sarah, "because I'm sure this Mr. Defoe will excuse you if you're ill."

"No, I mean yes," said Margaret. "Quite all right. Just an upset. Unexpected. But nothing we can't deal with."

"Never mind us, Sarah," said Edith. "We'll be right there. I just have to put my hair to rights."

Your face to rights is what you should do, thought Sarah looking at Edith's cheeks where tears had streaked lines through the light face powder. She left the two sisters to recover from whatever calamity had overwhelmed them and climbed to the stone steps to the Shearing Inn entrance. And walked into Amy Lermatov, who stood by the door with her notebook.

"I'm making a sketch of the outside," said Amy. "Setting is important, and I have to remember where the doors and windows are. Old inns are good places for mysteries because they have those twisty staircases and the high bushes outside to hide in."

"We're supposed to be meeting in the parlor," said Sarah. She had about had it with Amy as a private investigator.

"I know," said Amy. "That's where I'm having my characters meet the chief inspector. That's what they call them in England, chief inspector. My chief inspector's going to meet the group and tell them this body's been discovered . . ." Here Amy paused and Sarah could see that she hadn't decided where the body was to be found. But Amy wasn't blocked for long.

"The body was in the graveyard. That old church. Saint something or other. Under a bush, so it wasn't found right away. Maybe the body is Dr. Trevino's sister. I haven't decided."

Sarah took Amy by the elbow, and pointed the girl toward the front door. "Right now we're supposed to be in the parlor. And I think you should keep your story ideas to yourself. People like Edith and Margaret Hopper don't want to hear all the gruesome details about some dead body."

"People love gruesome details," announced Amy, but she opened the door and followed by Sarah walked into the parlor.

The room was a cheerful little space overlooking a side garden. It had comfortable chintz-covered chairs, a fireplace, a bookcase filled with a number of elderly looking novels, and low tables on which were scattered recent editions of the less strident British newspapers: *The Observer, The Times, The Daily Telegraph,* and *The Guardian.* Sarah settled herself on a window seat next to Julia who had chosen a wingchair. Amy Lermatov stationed herself on a stiff chair by the door, the better, perhaps, to study her cast of characters. Then, just as the brass mantel clock struck nine, the Hopper sisters appeared, hesitated, and then joined Sarah on the window seat. A wise choice, she thought, since the light would be at their backs and not illuminating their red-eyed, puffy faces.

There was a moment's pause after the clock had finished its nine chimes, a pause in which Carter McClure tapped his foot with impatience and Stacy Daniel gazed at the ceiling, and then Daniel Defoe appeared on the threshold, nodded to no one in particular, and took a chair directly in front of the bookcase.

He went directly to the point. "Good morning. I am Inspector Defoe of the High Roosting District Police." He paused and looked about the room, allowing this piece of information to sink in. Then he said, "I'm very sorry to be the bearer of bad news, but we've received word from the States—actually from the Maine police—that there has been an accident to one of your members."

Here Inspector Defoe paused again and then, by some sort of intuition he settled on Barbara Baxter as his focus and went on. "Dr. Ellen Trevino—I believe she was to have joined you on your tour—has died. To be accurate, the state police believe, because of the circumstances in which she was found, that her death must be considered a homicide." Another pause and Sarah felt the whole room begin to wobble and for a second put her head down, then choking back a gasp, she turned away from the inspector and so found herself staring at Amy Lermatov. Amy, with her mouth gaping, her eyes wide, had let her notebook and pen slip to the floor. Otherwise, except for small choking sounds from Margaret and Edith Hopper, and an audible gulp from Sandi Ouellette, there was silence. A general holding of breath, and then slowly, as if a large balloon had been punctured, a slow exhalation. And then, only then, exclamations.

"Ellen!"

"Not Ellen! Our Ellen?"

"Ellen Trevino? Oh, my God."

"But we thought she just missed her plane."

"What do you mean how she was found?

"Homicide? You're saying Ellen was murdered?"

"Holy shit!" Amy Lermatov had found her voice.

"You mean someone actually killed her?" demanded Stacy Daniel, alert and awake for the first time that Sarah had seen her.

Stacy shook her head back and forth. "God, is this some sort of bad joke? I mean, aren't you putting us on? One of those mystery weekends they do for tourists?"

"Be quiet all of you and listen to what Inspector Defoe has to say." This was Carter McClure in his academic mode.

Seconded by Julia. "Carter's right. Wait and see what the man wants."

Broken into by Barbara Baxter, "This is terrible, horrible news. I don't believe it. Not Ellen Trevino. Are you sure?"

"Holy shit!" repeated Amy, who seemed to be stuck on that single response. Then Doris Lermatov, suddenly awake to the fact that her daughter had been making unsuitable comments, turned and said loudly, "Amy, you be quiet and pay attention."

And now the two Hopper sisters, already upset by whatever private grief had hit them earlier, began to sob in a muffled way. And to Sarah, unbidden, rose the image of Ellen Trevino standing at the dinner table, heard her thanking the Garden Club and saying how she was looking forward to the trip, how she hoped it would be a memorable one because English gardens in June were as close to heaven as anyone was likely to get. And then Sarah heard, as if from a long way away, the voice of the twelve-year-old Ellen calling after her father, "You're killing them, you're a murderer, you're killing all the flowers." And now someone had killed Ellen.

Inspector Defoe, having allowed a small space of time for the news to sink in, gathered the reins in his hands. "I regret having to give you this sad news, but now you must all do what you can to help your police. Miss Baxter, ah yes, over there. I understand that you are in charge of the tour details? Good. What the Maine State Police want are voluntary statements from each of you. Just a few simple questions to answer, so the sooner you can arrange for your driver to bring your people down to the station to make those statements under our supervision, the sooner you can return to your tour schedule."

Here Inspector Defoe, a grave expression on his broad face, looked slowly about the room, catching those eyes that were lifted to his, and then he rose from his chair, thanked them for their attention, and strode out of the room.

Again a collective silence except for the soft moist sounds from Edith and Margaret Hopper and a sort of whistling noise from Justin Rossi. And then Barbara Baxter stood up, seemed to brace herself for something heroic, and announced that she would warn their driver, Joseph, of the change in plan, and that they must all be ready in fifteen minutes. And that she, herself, was horribly shocked, she still couldn't believe it, it was awful, but they must help the police in any way they could.

At this there was a general rising and movement toward the door, a returning to rooms for handbags and passports—there seemed to be an unspoken agreement that passports might be required—and then an anxious clustering outside of the front door.

"That poor Ellen Trevino, oh dear, oh dear," repeated Edith Hopper. This, like some sort of responsive reading was repeated in theme and variations throughout the group. Only Justin Rossi and Stacy Daniel, who after all had only met Dr. Trevino at the pre-tour dinner, seemed by their silence immune to the general sorrow.

"Look at them," said Sandi Ouellette. "Cold fish. They don't care." She peered at Julia. "And I don't think you do, either."

"Never mind me," said Julia Clancy, "but I think that if Mr. Rossi and Ms. Daniel went into paroxysms of sorrow I'd have handcuffs on them in a second."

"What?" said Sandi. "You mean you think . . ."

"I don't think, I know that Dr. Trevino was more or less a stranger to both of them, and so the best thing they can do is keep quiet and not make inappropriate noises.

"You," said Sandi, "are a mean old woman. There, I've said what I've thought and I'm sorry but it's true."

Julia smiled. "Correct. I'm a mean old woman, but I'm a sensible old woman, and I'm not going to loose any sleep over two of our group who aren't sprinkling ashes over their heads. As for me, everyone deals with grief in their own way. I'll deal with mine in my own way, thank you."

At which Sandi, head high, moved away, and Sarah, pulled her aunt's sleeve. "Aunt Julia, ease up."

"Well, I'm extremely sorry about Ellen Trevino, it's a terrible thing, but I'm not going to start a public keening."

"You're too hard on Sandi. I think there's more to her than meets the eye. She's perfectly intelligent, but that fact gets lost in the delivery."

"All right," grumbled Julia. "I'll make it up to her."

"We certainly won't be going to Hidcote and Kiftsgate this Saturday," said Doris Lermatov, joining the two. "It wouldn't be a very nice thing to go off and look at gardens when poor Ellen Trevino is dead."

But this observation was cut short by the arrival of their tour bus, and hardly had the group settled in their seats but they found themselves decanted into the police visitors' car park, and led into a spartanly furnished room with a desk, several wooden chairs, a file cabinet, two long tables, and a framed photograph of Her Majesty, Queen Elizabeth II.

"Interrogation room," announced Amy, who seemed to have recovered something of her equilibrium. And then, looking around, saw a tall man in a dark suit standing by the file cabinet. "Are you a constable in plainclothes," she asked. "Or a sergeant? And isn't this an awfully big police station for High Roosting, because it's such a dinky little village?"

The man looked down at Amy much in the way one might examine an unexpected earwig. Not a very large one, but nevertheless an earwig. "I'm Chief Inspector Wingate," he said. "And the police station here serves more than High Roosting. We're responsible for what goes on in the surrounding area: Nether Roosting, Lower Roosting, Little Swinecote, and Swinecote. And to answer your question, young woman, we have uniformed constables and sergeants and plainclothes detectives, just as you do in the States."

Then Chief Inspector Wingate turned and addressed the now assembled group, told them that the questions were simple ones intended to fix for the Maine State Police the times and places when they had last seen or heard from Dr. Trevino. "And thank you very much for your cooperation. Sorry for the unhappy occasion. Inspector Defoe will take you one at a time in the next office."

"The questions were certainly simple-minded," remarked Julia when she, Sarah, and the tour group emerged blinking into the noonday June sun.

Sarah shook her head. "I can't believe this is happening. I can't do a thing about Ellen and I feel sick and totally useless. The trouble is that I've been worried about her since Boston."

At which point they were joined by Doris Lermatov and her daughter. Amy, still somewhat subdued by her immersion in the real world of police and homicide, was on the receiving end of a lecture. "I hope," her mother was saying, "that poor Ellen Trevino's death will put a stop to your turning our trip into some cheap mystery novel."

For a moment the girl's lip trembled and then the old Amy returned. "I wouldn't write a 'cheap' novel," she said. "I'd make it all true to life because my English teacher wants us to keep notes no matter what happens."

But then up came Sandi and Fred Ouellette and pointed out that the bus was loading. "Barbara," announced Sandi, "says there won't be time to make it all the way to see those two gardens, you know Hidcote and the other one, but she'll arrange for us to go somewhere. She says Ellen would want us to, and if we keep busy we won't have so much time to be upset."

"Being busy," said Julia sharply, "does not prevent me from being upset. I'm not that easily distracted."

And here Portia came up and defended Sandi. "It does make sense, Julia. What's the point of us staying at the inn and stewing. We can feel awful about Ellen and still look at gardens. Because, honestly, there's nothing on earth we can do. Except what we've done. Help the police at home with our statements and cross our fingers they can hurry up and nail whoever did it. So a garden might just be the thing. A garden keeps Ellen in our mind and gardens are hopeful places."

"There's nothing hopeful about Ellen being murdered," complained Julia. "But I see your point. You can go and look at gardens if Barbara Baxter has another one up her sleeve."

"I remember," said Sandi in reminiscent voice, "how after we found the body of that woman by the bird feeder, and after we'd given statements, we all went out and had dinner together. To be with each other. It helped us get through the rest of the day."

You see, Sarah wanted to tell Julia, Sandi has a perfectly normal brain. But then these kindly thoughts were interrupted by the necessity of climbing back on the bus and returning to the Shearing Inn. As the bus rolled to a stop in the car park, Barbara Baxter stood up by the driver. "I've the very place. That nice constable at the police station suggested it. A National Trust house called Snowshill Manor. It has a collection of toys, musical instruments and antiques and even a very lovely garden."

Here Carter McClure, sitting in the rear of the bus, exploded. *"Even* has a garden she says. We didn't come to Gloucestershire to see antiques and toys and musical instruments. I'm extremely sorry about Ellen Trevino. A real loss to the college and everyone who cared about gardens. But the fact is that she's gone, so I have a proposal. I'm going to call my friend Henry Ruggles. He's very knowledgeable about gardens. Lectures all over the place. Henry lives in Moreton-in-Marsh. Retired. He'll probably eat up the invitation to come down and take charge."

Barbara Baxter looked aghast. "Really Dr. McClure, we can't just add people to the tour."

"Don't give it a thought," said Carter, climbing past her and pausing at the bus door. "You've done very well, I'm sure, with all the tour details so far, but we need a garden leader. Henry will fill the bill nicely. Right, Portia?"

"Carter, I think you could have waited before mentioning Henry," said Portia. "It's as if you're rushing someone into Ellen's place, which isn't tactful." She smiled at the group at large. "But Carter, for once, is right. Henry Ruggles is a real expert. And a very agreeable person."

"I don't think," began Barbara, but the others, possibly thinking of luncheon—it was past one—rose soberly from their bus seats and one by one headed for the Shearing Inn.

But just as the dining room was reached, Margaret Hopper stopped cold. "I know it's lunchtime, but I couldn't touch a bite." She looked over at her sister, who nodded vehemently. "After all, poor Ellen Trevino has been murdered," went on Margaret, her voice taking on a tinge of hysteria. "Murdered and now she's a body somewhere waiting on some table and we're about to go into the dining room, and I think that it's . . . it's almost obscene to sit down and enjoy lunch." Here Margaret took hold of Edith's arm, and moved her sister away from the dining room entrance.

Sarah, who was not feeling much like eating herself, watched the retreat of the two sisters with sympathy, but, as the troop stepped into the dining room, she came reluctantly to the conclusion that whatever was blighting their appetite was not entirely due to answering police questions about Ellen Trevino. Their faces still held traces of the early morning's anguish and Margaret had developed a noticeable facial twitch.

8

"THE Hoppers must feel very badly about Dr. Trevino," said Sandi Ouellette, who was working her way through a substantial helping of Cotswold pie—Sandi being determined to sample all the regional dishes, her appetite not being diminished by grief.

"Edith and Margaret Hopper have always struck me as being on a very even keel," said Sarah, who sat on Sandi's left.

"But they must be super-sensitive because I heard on the plane that they hardly knew her. Only met her a few times at lectures. In fact, they said she frightened them a little because she knew so much. I know what they meant because after I'd met Dr. Trevino at that get-acquainted dinner I thought, Whoa, Sandi, better keep your lips buttoned and so had Fred. Because we are such beginners."

"Yes," said Fred. "Ellen Trevino in her quiet way could be intimidating. Some funeral directors are like that. Perfect gentlemen, but at our conventions they can make the younger directors feel, well, inadequate. Of course, in our profession there's no substitute for years of hands-on training."

"I suppose," said Sarah, beating a retreat from the embalming table, "that it isn't so much Ellen Trevino by herself—since they didn't really know her—who upset Edith and Margaret, as it was the horror of someone being murdered."

"They're probably not as used to violence as the rest of us," remarked Justin Rossi. "A sheltered life, small town, nothing more terrible happening than the minister's daughter running away with the town drunk or a teenager driving off a dock."

"Really, Mr. Rossi," said Julia Clancy, spearing a prawn, "small towns have their share of misery. Besides, I think that Edith and Margaret were upset before we heard about Ellen. They both looked as if they'd been crying when they came into the parlor."

"What I want to know," said Doris Lermatov, "is whether we're suspects? All those questions about how we got to the airport? When did we last see Ellen? Did we notice anything unusual?"

"What was unusual," said Carter, "is this tampering with our schedule. Going into London and mooning about in Westminster Abbey and Harrods. Scheduling Cambridge."

Barbara Baxter, at the end of the table, leaned forward and said in a patient and much tried voice, "I'm doing my best without Dr. Trevino's help. Several people on the tour wanted very much to see a bit of London and we did go to the Kew Gardens. And quite a few of you seem to be in favor of Cambridge. Since Dr. Trevino wasn't here I had to make some decisions. Broaden the base of the trip, so to speak." Barbara paused and looked up and down the table, and smiled, a rather wistful smile. "What do you all think? Can we live with the changes? How about you, Stacy?"

Stacy shrugged. "It's okay by me, I guess. This Snowshill place today, Cambridge later. Fine. Great. Go for it." And Stacy returned to her salad.

Justin Rossi seconded this opinion—if so offhand a response could be called support. "Sure, I'm agreeable. Someone has to run this thing, and Barbara seems to be doing a good job."

"Well, thank you," said Barbara. "And I'd like to say that no one could be sorrier about Ellen's death than I am. Such a nice person. Before we left I drove out to her house—it's at the end of nowhere, only one farm around—to go over plans. Three days before the trip. Ellen said she'd really worked on her lectures."

"There you are, Carter," said Portia, the peacemaker, "and," she added, "when Henry Ruggles comes . . ."

Sandi looked up. "He's *really* coming?"

"Carter says yes. And I'm sure Henry—though never a replacement for Ellen—will fit right in and add a great deal."

"I called before lunch," said Carter complacently. "Henry's delighted. He'll be here after dinner ready to take over."

"Take over?" Barbara's voice rose.

"Don't worry," said Portia. "I've made Carter promise that he'll make it perfectly clear to Henry that you're the tour chief. He'll just do the garden lectures."

"Well," said Barbara, "then we'll do our best to welcome him."

And the group returned to the matter of lunch, breaking naturally into small conversational segments.

And Sarah, whose mind had been busy with something closer to the bone than the arrival of Henry Ruggles, turned to her aunt. "I didn't put it on my questionnaire, but I think maybe something unusual did happen at the airport. Logan, I mean. Those sunglasses and the scarf that turned up in my shoulder bag."

Julia raised her eyebrows. "I thought we had disposed of those questions. I don't think either item could qualify as a murder weapon . . . no, listen to me. Not that scarf. Thin cotton and hardly big enough."

"You're an expert on scarves used for throttling people?"

"I've read enough mysteries to know that you need strong material and a piece large enough to get a grip on the ends of the scarf and twist. And plastic sunglasses couldn't hurt a flea."

"And the fact that the scarf ran a sort of reddish color."

Julia regarded her niece with exasperation. "Sarah, just what do you want to do? Tote the scarf and glasses to New Scotland Yard and demand a forensic exam?"

Sarah sighed. "Relax, Aunt Julia, I'm not going to annoy the British police. But those two things bother me. Particularly after all of us being knocked down—maybe deliberately—just before boarding. So I'm going to mail the scarf to Alex, and he can turn it over to the police. I want to get rid of the thing."

"Splendid," said Julia, folding her napkin. "Now, while everyone is off to look at toys and musical instruments, I've decided to take the car—Sarah, you're welcome to come—and go for a drive in the countryside. I know of nothing so soothing after a shock than seeing fields and pastures and farms."

Sarah shook her head. "I'm going to stay local. I haven't even started to come to terms with Ellen's being dead. Killed like that. I feel as if I've swallowed a stone. I need to be alone, be quiet, and think about her, so I'll just wander around the village and the footpaths."

🦋

Johnny Cuzak peeled off his surgical gloves, untied his protective apron, and briefly ran his eye over the body of Ellen Trevino, her body now slit, probed, gutted, suctioned, hosed; her stomach contents, samples of hair, fingernails, blood, brain, other organs, fluids, tissues, extirpated, withdrawn, weighed, examined and photographed. Then he placed these items in appropriate envelopes, flasks, and tubes, sealed and dated and stored.

"So far, so bad," said Johnny. "We're fixing the time of death sometime on June sixth. For now we can't make it closer. Too bad a gun didn't do the job because we'd have ballistics to go on. Now we're stuck with a monster chest wound and whatever made it."

"Not asphyxia," said Alex, who standing behind Johnny, had watched the proceedings and, as was usual with him, trying to detach his professional observing self from the human one that had known and admired Dr. Ellen Trevino.

"That plastic bag tied over the head didn't do it. Someone trying to make double sure. Well, yeah, it would have done the trick, providing the victim stayed unconscious. That conk on the head was probably meant to keep her quiet, not to kill her."

"Which it didn't. The conk, I mean."

"Nope." Johnny pointed at the chest cavity. "Peculiar wound. Narrow at the base, wide at the entry point. Did the job though. Rupture right through the descending parts of the thoracic aorta." Johnny turned to his assistant. "Okay, take her away. I'm done. For now." He turned to Alex. "No sign of rape, no pregnancy, no long-standing pathology. Organs, tissues all look pretty healthy."

"Being healthy won't protect you from having a hole punched in your chest," said Alex. "Lab tests to follow, right?"

"Yeah. And the police can start sniffing around for the weapon. Probably something the shape of an elongated ice cream cone. One with real heft. The thing went in more or less straight with a very slight upward thrust. Suggests the victim was lying down when she got the blow. If she'd been standing face to face with the murderer the line of the entry wouldn't be so on target. Just try and direct a heavy blow like that without bouncing off the sternum, going a little down, or sideways."

"Why not up?"

"Slightly up, okay. But up would have been awkward. Try it yourself. You lose force by striking underhand and up. I'd say it was well aimed for doing what it did."

"A railroad spike?"

"Something like. But more tapered. Sharper point."

"What about that plastic tarp she was wrapped in?"

"Lab's working on it. So far only one blood type present. Ellen's. DNA testing to follow. They're going over it for fibers and hairs and other crud. But that plastic tarp looked pretty new. No evidence to show it'd been used to cover a lawn mower or a greasy motorcycle."

"Possibly bought for the purpose," Alex said grimly. He turned and, followed by Johnny, walked out into a small office off the autopsy room.

"Tarps like that are sold everywhere," said Johnny, sitting down at a desk and switching on the monitor of his PC. "Tell Mike it's time the police came up with some family. Then we can think about releasing the body for burial."

"They're looking. Ellen's neighbor—Mrs. Epple—thinks the stepfather may be hiking somewhere out west. They're putting the park rangers on it. Her own parents are dead. No kids, no husband. No signs of a lover of either sex. Looks like Ellen Trevino was going through life solo. I gather Bowmouth College will be having some sort of memorial service for her in the chapel this week."

Johnny scowled at his monitor and moved the mouse pointer to "File," then said, "Okay, Alex, get out of here. I've got to write my report. And tell Mike and his buddies in the state police to leave me alone next weekend. Both my kids have Little League and Jennifer's pitching her first game."

"Like a heavy-duty ice cream cone," said Alex to Mike Laaka when the two met at the Mary Starbox Hospital cafeteria for dinner; Alex having just admitted a patient and Mike checking on an uncle with a broken hip. Mike, Alex thought, looked incongruously healthy in the hospital setting with his fair almost white hair and his deep summer tan. But he looked worried. "You're kidding about an ice cream cone, aren't you?"

Alex shook his head. "Sorry, I'm not."

"Okay, you're not. Well, the field lab team hasn't come up with anything close to a weapon like that. Actually, except for an area of depressed grass and pine needles where the body was, they've come up with zip. Besides the crap I told you about, they've picked up a dead groundhog, two hubcaps, and a pair of boxer shorts. There was a lot of blood on that tarp, but so far none seems to have leaked out onto the ground."

"Footprints?"

"Only after the fact—from that truck driver who found her body. She was dumped before it started raining—the earth was dry under the tarp. With the ground hard and dry like that footprints wouldn't have made much of an impression. Of course, later in the day it rained like hell. So the only marks that survived the rain were some old sharp deer hoofprints."

"Johnny says it's up to you to dig up the weapon. He's never seen a wound quite like this one, and Johnny always claims he's seen everything." And here Alex addressed himself to a slice of meatloaf while Mike worked his way through macaroni and cheese.

Then, Mike put down his fork and said, "Okay, okay. So the weapon is weird. Let's give it a rest. Don't you want to know about the questions and answers we got from the High Roosting police? God, what a name. High Roosting, Jesus."

"You like Slippery Rock or Kalamazoo or Scraggly Pond better? No, don't answer. Just tell me in three short sentences.

"Right. Nothing much to tell. The only people of the Garden Club to go by car to Boston were Sarah, Julia—driven by you—and Fred and Sandi Ouellette with the Hopper sisters, who took an airport limousine all the way. The rest drove, got a ride, or took a taxi to Portland and left from the Jetport to Logan. US AIR and Delta. Different departure times. Ellen Trevino was found at Scarborough exit 4, northbound. Her car was at Kennebunk exit 3 South."

"And her car was clean?"

"Absolutely. Her own dog's hair, her hair, plus the stuff I've told you about. The car was pretty tidy. No sign of a struggle or blood. As for prints, hers and about three other sets. Her car went in for a tune-up last week so maybe the prints belong to the mechanics who worked on her car. The lab's working on a match."

"But no heavy ice cream cones."

"No. There was a weeder—sharp devil with a V notch at the end. And a heavy folding shovel, but no blood. Ellen's prints on those. We're guessing she left the car voluntarily. It was locked and the keys were gone. Mrs. Epple says Ellen was careful of her car, so it doesn't seem likely she'd go off on her trip and leave it in a turnpike parking lot. So maybe she went in to buy some food at the restaurant, or to use the ladies' room, and expected to come back to her car. But she ran into someone who changed her plans."

"Changed them for good," said Alex. "But isn't a rest stop a very public place in which to stab someone to death."

"Yeah. No one can figure out how Ellen could have been hit, stabbed, and had her head bagged at a pit stop that was swarming with tourists. By June first the state is alive with the buggers. But who said it was done there? Say she was kidnapped. Gun or knife in her face. 'Get in my car and don't say a word or I'll blow your head off.' Someone trying for cash. Because where is her handbag, her suitcase, all her travel gear?"

"You're betting on robbery? Homicide cum robbery?"

"Could be. Anyway, according to Barbara Baxter's deposition, she met with Ellen three days before departure to talk about the tour, and Ellen was all set for the trip but never mentioned when and how she was getting there. Sarah and the neighbor, Mrs. Epple, are the only ones who heard Ellen say she intended to drive."

Alex brought his chosen apple crisp front and center and considered the application of whipped cream. Rejected it and returned to the subject at hand. "Have you thought that Ellen meant to meet someone at the Kennebunk exit and drive to Boston with them—or him—or her? What was that Mrs. Epple said about visiting a friend and then checking with someone— possibly about the trip?"

"Aaarr," said Mike thickly, his mouth full. He was now well into pecan pie with a frosted brownie on the side. Mike had the digestion of an alligator and had inherited from his Finnish ancestors a physiology that seemed to be unaffected by food or lack of it. "Forget about Mrs. Epple. She doesn't know any more than she first told us."

"Maybe Ellen made arrangements for her car to be picked up and stored. At a friend's house. Or a garage."

"We've checked with garages in the area and come up with zip. As for seeing a friend, meeting someone? Who? When? That'll take a hell of a lot of sweat and pavement pounding to find out."

Alex pushed back his chair and threw his napkin on the table. "So if it's robbery and murder, it goes like this: Ellen with a gun at her head, gets in the other car—murderer's vehicle—is driven off to a cozy corner and is killed and her body dumped at the Scarborough exit. The murderer first heads south, then changes directions and gets off at a north–south interchange. But why? Why not keep going south, find a side road and real woods to hide the body?"

"You only turn around and head north if you have a plane to catch," said Mike, adding with a knowing look, "A plane that flies from Portland Jetport to Logan. And then on to Heathrow."

"Or you live north of Kennebunk. You kill Ellen, dump the body, and head home. Wherever home is."

"But I keep saying, where the hell's her luggage? The police all along the pike are starting to hit town dumps—not many left anymore. And trash bins, refuse containers. Landfills. Airport dumpsters. Fields and marshes by the edge of the road."

Alex stood up. "Well, keep after it. Me, I've got to be off. Serious poker tonight. A chance to lose a few bucks."

Mike grinned. "Glad someone's got leisure time. I'm supposed to meet Sergeant Tightass Fitts and reread the questionnaires the UK police sent on. George wants to correlate Sarah and Julia's profiles with those answers. Trouble is that except for Julia, and maybe Carter McClure, it's a pretty ordinary bunch of people."

"Add Sarah Douglas Deane to the oddballs. Her bumps of curiosity exceed that of the dromedary. I'm sorry I'm not there to throw safety nets over her head or pull her away from the edge of a cliff. I can only hope she sticks with the tour and doesn't try any solos while there's even the faintest chance that someone in the group may be tainted."

❦

Sarah, being unable to read transatlantic warnings, spent, as she promised, a solitary Saturday afternoon in High Roosting. Julia, joined by Carter McClure, took off by car to check out the

96

local farm scene, but otherwise most of the faithful climbed into the bus and went off to view the wonders of Snowshill Manor.

High Roosting was a small Cotswold settlement which in the past had boasted little more than the usual village collection of churches, a school, two pubs, a post office, a chemist, and a limited number of shops selling food. However, with the ever-burgeoning tourist trade, High Roosting had become swollen with a number of new gift shops, tea shops, a new pub, a wool shop, and several emporiums displaying antiques and works of art.

Sarah, after posting her suspect scarf airmail and wandering for several hours about the streets and paths of the village with no particular purpose other than to think and mourn the death of Ellen Trevino, heard the town hall clock strike four. The air had turned chilly and she stepped into a wool shop and purchased a raspberry-colored cardigan and then betook herself down Market Street to Mrs. Jellicoe's Tea Shoppe.

The soft warmth of the new sweater and the hot tea did much to soothe Sarah's mind. Ellen's death moved a little distance away, and, in fact, the absence of chatter about homicide made her almost wish that she might never return to the Shearing Inn. Seated near a geranium-crowded window, she made an effort to imagine that she, and she alone, was on a voyage through Britain with nothing untoward having happened, no timetable, no scheduled visits, no need to do, see, or say anything to anyone.

She began to think where she might travel and then in her mind began a tour which involved owning an ancient two-seater Triumph and a large bank account. Perhaps down to Dorset and the Hardy country. Then off to Cornwall—Daphne du Maurier—swing around east to Lyme Regis—Jane Austen and *Persuasion*. Then perhaps Canterbury, Brighton, and the Pavilion. Or should she reread *Northanger Abbey* and begin with Bath? Then north to Yorkshire, Haworth, and the Brontës? Later meet Alex in Scotland and they could do the Highlands together. The Great

Glen. Climb Ben Nevis. Alex had said he'd always wanted to climb Ben Nevis.

From these musings, Sarah was aroused by finding a woman of comfortable proportions—perhaps Mrs. Jellicoe herself—standing by her table and pointing reproachfully to the clock. Five-thirty and closing. "We're only a tea shoppe, miss, and we don't do dinners. There's the Shearing Inn down across the way if you're looking for something more solid."

And Sarah paid for her tea, took her departure, and walked slowly back to the inn on a winding route that took her over a curved stone bridge and past a reed-edged stream inhabited by a family of mallard ducks. Like Cranford or a hundred other fictitious villages, she told herself, still lost in a literary tour of the British Isles. And in this detached and tranquil frame of mind she arrived at her room, opened the door. And stared.

Ransacked.

Suitcase open. Bureau drawers pulled wide, clothes spilling out. Her toilet article bag on the floor, unzipped and upended. Her shoulder bag open on the bed, its contents dribbled on the counterpane.

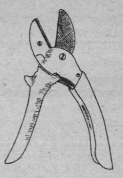

9

SARAH stood for a moment absolutely still, turned to cement, her mouth open, her hands curled into fists. Then reaction. Rage. Fury. She stormed into her room, slammed the door closed behind her, and snatched at her empty suitcase and hurled it against the chintz chair. Kicked angrily at her toilet article kit, which lay disemboweled on the floor, little bottles and tubes scattered about it. Then swore loudly. A spate of serious four-letter words.

And then stopped and ordered herself to cool it. She was out of control, her rage at Ellen's death spilling out over this mess. But random hurlings and kickings would get her nowhere. But what now? She was torn in two directions.

One direction: Sarah the enraged tourist should fling herself down to the office of the Shearing Inn and raise holy hell. Drag the manager by the scruff of his neck to the room and point and exclaim and generally foam at the mouth.

Other direction: Sarah of the long nose, Sarah, whose friend Ellen had been murdered, might want to hold it. Look around.

Check for missing things. See which members of the garden tour were back from their various sight-seeing toots, from Snowshill Manor and country driving. Check on those two over-wrought women who had retired to their room. She walked purposefully over to the washbasin and splashed cold water over her face—her invariable remedy for an overwrought emotional state.

Drying her face, she found herself prey to the awful possibility that she had forgotten to lock her room before she went out. But, no, she had just used her key to unlock it. So perhaps one of the maids had rifled her room or had carelessly left the door unlocked when she finished her tidy-up work. Or—this was also possible—someone had come in through Aunt Julia's room since there was an unlocked door between the two rooms. And that meant that Julia may have forgotten to lock her bedroom door.

Well, she couldn't go screeching into the office if there had been free access somehow to one or both bedrooms. She was sure there would be one of those ubiquitous signs at the front desk reminding guests to not keep valuables in their room and that they were responsible for keeping their doors locked AT ALL TIMES.

But why her room? Or Aunt Julia's? Or both? Nothing about either of them suggested women of great wealth. Was it just a random hit, or had other rooms been torn apart? But even as Sarah asked herself these questions, the small, sickening seed of doubt grew, bore leaves, flowered, and resolved itself into the answer. Or one answer.

That goddamned scarf. Never mind what Julia had said. The scarf had certainly shed any claim to being an innocent piece of wearing apparel and by now had taken on the sanguinary quality of Lady Macbeth's hands. Blood, blood. The miserable scarf that all the perfumes of Arabia would not sweeten.

But, for God's sake, she had just mailed the thing. And another wave of anger swept over her and she had to keep herself from shouting. So cool down, count to ten, recite the alphabet backwards. In French. And then breath deeply and slowly.

Okay. First, check calmly and carefully through all her things to see what, if anything, was missing, then see if Aunt Julia was in her bedroom and ask about unlocked doors. Next, find out who of the Garden Club had returned. Last, see if anyone else had found his or her room in disarray. Shake these answers around and if nothing useful emerges, go to the manager and report the disturbance.

Nothing was missing in her own room. It seemed that the visiting vandal had simply rummaged about, opened and closed, pitched and tossed, and departed.

Sarah knocked on the door connecting Julia's room with her own. No answer. She knocked louder, rapped, drummed, and then opened. The room was empty. The counterpane on the bed was smooth, and everything else was in its place. Julia, though not a notable housekeeper, always kept an orderly stable: Saddles, bridles, buckets, blankets, all in place. And here, in her own "stall," shoes were lined up, toilet article bag was zipped, and suitcase closed. Certainly not the scene of a search. But her bedroom door into the hall was unlocked. Careless Aunt Julia. Or careless maid. And lucky intruder who could have slipped through Julia's room into Sarah's and exited the same way. An intruder who knew Julia was off on a pastoral adventure with Carter McClure.

Sarah opened the door into the hall and was instantly rewarded by the appearance of Sandi Ouellette, swaddled in terry cloth. "There's still hot water," said Sandi, "but you'd better hurry. Everyone will want a shower. We walked and walked. All over Snowshill Manor and then took a hike. The footpath between Nether Roosting and Little Roosting."

"How long have you been home," demanded Sarah, getting to the point.

"We had tea here at the inn, so I guess we've been home an hour. Or a little more. Does it matter? Were you looking for someone? I don't think Julia's back yet. She and Carter McClure drove off together, so maybe they've eloped."

Here Sandi giggled and then added, "At least it gives Portia a free day. She spends so much time trying to keep Carter from yelling at Barbara Baxter. And I think Barbara's been wonderful to have found Snowshill Manor. It was great. I mean we were still all terribly sad about Dr. Trevino, but Snowshill was a terrific distraction. You wouldn't believe the stuff like Japanese warrior masks mixed up with toys and doll's houses and ship's things. I mean it was the sort of place someone might go totally mad in."

"Sandi," said Sarah, breaking the flow with greater urgency, "did everyone have tea with you here? After you got back from Snowshill? Or did some go back to their rooms and not come down?"

Sandi frowned. "What's the matter? Is someone sick? One of the Hoppers, because they certainly looked awful."

"No, no. I just have a personal reason for wanting to know, something to do with my room and Aunt Julia's. I found a message but it wasn't signed," said Sarah, not entirely untruthfully.

"I'll bet it's because your room has a view of the garden and some of the others—like ours—look out on the parking lot. Maybe someone wanted to switch rooms and went in to look your room over. Anyway, it's a fact, isn't it, that you and Julia and Barbara Baxter and the McClures and the Lermatovs have the best rooms?"

"Maybe you're right," said Sarah. "I just wondered who went upstairs after your bus came back. I thought maybe the maid let someone in my room. Or Aunt Julia's."

"I think we all went upstairs to wash before tea. Change our clothes, shoes. The footpath was pretty dusty. Of course, Edith and Margaret Hopper didn't have to wash up because they stayed right in their room. But they did turn up for tea, only they hardly said a word. They just sat there looking like they'd swallowed something that tasted awful."

Sarah thanked Sandi, told her that she and Julia didn't want to trade rooms with anyone, and returned to her bedroom to regroup.

And there in the middle of the rumpled clothing and scattered shoes and toilet articles stood Amy Lermatov, notebook in hand.

"What do you think you're doing here?" Sarah almost shouted, her rage boiling up again.

"Wait, hold it. It's okay." Amy backed up stammering, looking genuinely frightened. "I just came in to ask a few questions about my book. Because you're an English teacher."

"And," said Sarah fiercely.

"I knocked and there wasn't an answer and your door was open a little so I went in to see if you hadn't heard me and then I saw all this stuff. And I didn't think even if you were as messy as I am you'd start throwing your stuff around the room unless . . ."

"Unless what?"

"Unless you were sick or having some sort of a seizure and then I thought you might be under the bed because of the seizure and maybe I need to call for help but then I decided . . ."

"Go on."

"That you probably weren't having a seizure but that someone came into your room looking for something valuable and searched it and threw the stuff around and that you'd been robbed. Or something. And then you came in," Amy finished lamely.

Sarah blew a long-winded breath through her cheeks and subsided into a chair, a chair now covered with her uprooted underwear, shirts, and jeans. "Oh damnation, Amy. What am I going to do with you?" she said in exasperation.

Amy showed her braces producing something halfway between a grimace and a grin. "You could look at my mystery story. I've put someone in it who's searching the rooms for clues."

Sarah stifled the impulse to shake Amy until the braces flew off her teeth. But no, she told herself, I can't pretend nothing happened. "Look, Amy. You're here so you certainly can see someone's been looking around. But I'd appreciate your not mentioning the incident. I'm not going to make it a secret, but I'd like to check with Aunt Julia to see if she's missing anything before I go to the office."

"How about other rooms being messed up? Our room wasn't, but maybe some other people's were?"

Sarah hesitated. How far to trust this girl. Just so far, she decided. But perhaps Amy might be given a small role to play.

"Okay, Amy. If, just if, you hear of other rooms being disturbed, being entered, well, come quietly and tell me. Don't worry, I'm planning to tell the Shearing Inn people about this."

Amy nodded. "You know in the beginning when Mom told me about this garden tour I thought, boy, how totally boring. A bunch of people going around smelling roses and yacking about compost. But after Dr. Trevino and now this, it's like I'm on the actual site of something gruesome happening."

"Amy," said Sarah in a severe tone, feeling when she spoke to the girl that she always sounded like her own grandmother. "Go on and write your story, but don't run away with the idea that you're living real-life crime just because someone came in here and threw my underwear around."

"But what about Dr. Trevino?"

"A horrible accident. Probably one of those awful random attacks. Nothing to do with this tour. So please don't consider our group just a mass of raw material. Dr. Trevino's death is much too sad and too serious." Good, thought Sarah, seeing the light die in Amy's eyes, that might just put a damper on teenage journalism for a while.

Amy turned to leave, then hesitated at the door, and Sarah was sorry to see that the girl was beginning to bounce back. "Look, I'll turn Dr. Trevino into someone else—a man maybe. But I want to keep in some of the other details like your finding those sunglasses in your bag and like the two Hopper sisters being upset. I mean one minute they're having a good time and the next they're totally unglued. But, off course, I'll change all the names. Everyone is staying at the Black Sheep Inn, which is a pretty good name, and I'm having two Asians and two African Americans in the story and also one Latino, which makes it more real. After all, Dr. Trevino was the only Hispanic person we had and she's dead, and Mrs. McClure is the only black person and that doesn't . . ."

"Amy," said Sarah in a dangerous voice. "Go away. Now."

"But you want me to listen around to see if anyone's room

has been busted into, don't you?" said Amy in a plaintive voice.

"If," said Sarah, "you can do it without inciting a riot, accusing anyone of breaking and entering."

Amy took one step back into the room. "But someone did break and enter. Right into your room."

"OUT!" shouted Sarah. "OUT. BEGONE. SCRAM. BEAT IT."

Amy beat it and Sarah turned to find Aunt Julia, returned from her drive and coming to report. The expedition had been restful; she and Carter McClure having been shown around a large breeding facility, visited a pasture of mares and foals, and had a useful discussion with the farm owner on the management of strangles.

But Julia's contentment evaporated at the sight of Sarah's room. "You think," Sarah told her, "that I have an overheated imagination, that I look for trouble, but believe me, trouble has walked right in the door and made itself at home. And my door was locked and yours was open."

"But I always lock," began Julia and then stopped. "I came back for my jacket and I might have, well, I could have left it unlocked."

"And everything in your room is in order?"

Julia nodded. "Yes. Just as I left it. But I don't bring anything valuable with me. Did you," she began accusingly, "bring some jewelry, leave money in a drawer?"

"No, I did not," said Sarah, biting off each word. "The only item of any interest that I possessed was that blasted blood-soaked scarf someone stuffed in my shoulder bag."

"You don't know it was blood-soaked," said Julia. "Was it taken? Was anything taken?"

"I mailed the scarf this morning. And, from what I can tell nothing is missing."

"Jealousy," announced Julia. "Someone wants our rooms. I've heard rumblings. A maid or a guest with sticky fingers. Or it's a terrorist group hitting the tourist scene."

"Sure, you name it. The Mafia is busy and the Pink Panther is loose. Well, what I want to know is if mine is the only room hit."

Julia settled herself in the pink-and-green–flowered chintz chair. "I haven't heard any outcries." And then, she sat up straight. "I know. That's what's wrong with Margaret and Edith Hopper. Their rooms were entered and they've lost something valuable, some jewelry, and they're too ashamed to admit they didn't put the things in the office safe."

Sarah looked up. "Maybe you're right. There's a thief on the loose and the sisters were the first hit. Well, damn, it's time I went down to the office and made a scene. And, Aunt Julia, why not go over to Edith and Margaret's room and see if that's why they're in such a stew. But, please, be tactful."

And Sarah, fire in her eyes, strode out of the room while Julia, who, as a woman of direct and sometimes abrasive action, never liked the role of the psychologist, walked with reluctant steps down the hall and tapped on the door of Margaret and Edith Hopper.

Twenty minutes later Sarah met Julia in her still-disordered bedroom, Sarah having raised suitable Cain in the office and been appropriately reminded about unlocked doors, the propensity for crime among American citizens who made up a large number of the inn's guest population, and an offer—a lukewarm offer—to bring in the police. But this, Sarah was told, was rather pointless since she had found nothing missing. And no other guest had yet reported a similar intrusion. Innkeeper Thomas Gage and his assistant, Mrs. Hosmer, both suggested gently that Sarah ask her fellow tour members whether someone in their party had, for some personal and, they hinted, some unsavory reason, a motive for the search.

"All a bunch of bullshit," Sarah told her aunt, "but they're right. I'm not missing anything. And no one else has reported trouble. So how about Edith and Margaret?"

"I struck out. Well, in a way. Their room was a miracle of order. I told them about your room, and they said they were appalled. They always lock, they make a special point of it, and nothing was out of place. But, I'd say your little scene didn't occupy more than a fraction of their minds. What they're really upset about didn't come out. Some secret sorrow. They're past the age of menopause or I'd have thought they were both unstrung by a simultaneous hormonal breakdown. They've obviously been crying again and weren't sure about coming down to dinner."

"Not the Hoppers' room then," said Sarah, slowly sinking down on the bed among the crumpled pieces of clothing.

"No, but if you're hell-bent on mystery you might find out what's eating those two women. They're perfectly miserable and won't say why. I probed, then asked directly, but they just shook their heads. I think Barbara Baxter should talk to them. Isn't that one of her jobs? She knows little enough about gardens, so let's hope she can at least handle a little social work."

And, as if on cue, a knock on the door sounded, the knocker was admitted, and Barbara Baxter walked into the room. She took one quick look around at the debris and exclaimed. "You, too!"

Sarah jumped to her feet. "You mean the room? You've been broken into?"

Barbara nodded. "Someone came in and opened drawers and tossed my clothes around. Out of the closet. All over the place."

"Was your room unlocked?" Sarah demanded.

Barbara's freckled face took on a rueful expression. "I must not have," she said. "I'm usually so careful, but I went back to get the directions to Snowshill Manor for the driver—he's from London and not sure about driving around Gloucestershire—and I must have forgotten to lock. Wouldn't you know. Here I am a tour director and I do something stupid like that."

"Did you go to the office," Julia put in.

"I thought about it, but nothing was missing and it was all my own fault. And I thought we've already had enough of the police because of poor Dr. Trevino, so, anyway, I decided not to."

"I did," announced Sarah. "I made a fuss but it was the same with me. Julia's door was open and we have connecting inner doors. So it's on our head's if someone came in."

"Come and see my room," urged Barbara. "I'm right down at the end of the hall."

"That's not necessary," said Julia. "We'll take your word."

"But you might see if you think it's the same sort of mess. If it looks like the same person hit both rooms."

"Well, I'd certainly hate to think that there were two room destroyers at large," said Sarah. And then, "Barbara has a point. Let's take a look."

Barbara's room did indeed mirror the disorder of Sarah's. Shoes, clothes, toilet articles, drawers spilled open. Even, in Barbara's case, the bedding rumpled, the mattress askew.

"As if I'd hidden jewelry or something," said Barbara.

"As long as nothing is missing," said Julia, "you'll both just have to count it as vandalism. But I have something else on my mind. I think, Barbara, you need to find out what's eating Margaret and Edith Hopper. If some tragedy has befallen them or if one of them has come down with an incurable disease. I think it would help if they talked to someone. Or went home to deal with it. They shouldn't be dragging around all over Europe if they're utterly miserable."

Barbara nodded her agreement and seemed to square her shoulders as if to bear this new burden. "I hoped they'd get over whatever was bothering them, but apparently not. I'll go now and see them before dinner."

And Sarah and Julia watched Barbara Baxter head out down the hall ready to offer a sympathetic ear.

But before the sound of her footsteps on the creaking boards of the upper hall had faded, Amy Lermatov had taken her place.

"Amy," said Sarah sternly, "I thought I told you to get lost."

Amy grinned, her spirits obviously revived. "But it's what you told me to find out about. There weren't any more room searches. Everyone seemed okay except the Hoppers and they don't count because they're a wreck anyway. I was very subtle. I went around asking when was dinner and so I saw into all the rooms and no one was yelling about being searched."

"Except Barbara Baxter," said Julia in a low voice.

"Hey, really?" Amy looked positively pleased. "That's sort of exciting. She didn't answer when I knocked, but then I saw her come out of your room and take you both into hers."

"So," said Julia in a stern voice, "please leave us in peace and thank you for your information. And don't talk about this to anyone."

"Hey, no sweat," said Amy. "And I'll keep my eyes open. Tonight I'm watching Justin Rossi. I think he wears a wig."

"God help that girl," said Julia when Amy had departed.

"A wig," said Sarah slowly. "Do you think?" She let the question hang in the air.

"And God help you, too," snapped Julia.

10

BARBARA Baxter apparently had counseled to some effect because the Hopper sisters made it to dinner, where it was generally felt that they seemed to have taken a turn for the better. Both had taken trouble with dress: blue silk with lace collar (Edith), red print with navy buttons (Margaret). Across each shoulder a soft white shawl, on their feet low-heeled navy pumps suitable for formal dining or gentle evening walks. They were of the generation, Sarah decided, who used proper dress as armor against the world.

Thus, as dinner progressed from soup to entrée and on to the sweet and the savory, although no one could have thought them lively, Margaret and Edith from time to time put in a small word whenever the subject matter took a horticultural turn.

As for the rest, the trip to Snowshill Manor seemed to have provided not only an escape from the dark cloud of Ellen Trevino's death, but it also provided a common subject for discussion.

Only Carter McClure complained. An unnecessary trip. Not

even a very distinguished garden. Fortunately, Henry Ruggles would be arriving that evening and a proper focus would be reestablished.

At which Portia McClure turned to her husband and pointed out that he, Carter, hadn't even visited Snowshill Manor; he had been gadding about the countryside with Julia Clancy. And if he'd been so wild to see superior gardens, why hadn't he gone and found one. There were plenty in Gloucestershire. So be quiet.

And then Stacy Daniel took up the torch for Snowshill. Sarah, looking up from her lamb chop, saw Stacy, her color heightened by the task of making a public appeal, hold forth on the attractions of Snowshill. It was almost, Sarah decided, as if she had taken notes for some class.

"Do you remember the French sedan chair?" prompted Stacy. She ticked off the items of interest: the ship models, the Japanese Samurai armor, the banners, the Sicilian cart, the old bicycles.

This recitation and the responses were good enough to carry the group all the way to the Stilton, coffee, and brandy.

And then, just as the attractions of Snowshill Manor began to fade, Justin Rossi took up the cause. His was the humorous, semi-scholarly approach. The great enjoyment to be had from viewing such a truly idiosyncratic collection, the amazing diversity of artifacts. The Indian oxcart, the Balinese and Javanese dancing masks, the mangle, the baby tether.

Justin's enthusiasm resulted in almost universal support for Barbara's choice of Snowshill Manor, even by the Hopper sisters who had not been there. As to future changes in the tour plan, they would all leave it in Barbara's capable hands. "And," declared Sandi Ouellette boldly, "we can't let this Mr. Henry Ruggles interfere with Barbara. He can stick to talks in the gardens."

"We want what everyone wants," said Margaret and Edith Hopper almost in unison, although in tremulous voices, proof that emotional recovery was not complete.

"So, okay," said Stacy Daniel, "that's settled. Barbara is chief.

It's easier that way. We don't need a lot of hassle every morning about who goes where."

Sarah, who was essentially neutral in the matter, helped herself to an after-dinner mint and let it melt slowly in her mouth. She had reached two conclusions during the recent scene. First, Barbara Baxter, cheerful and energetic as she was, must have leadership qualities that she, Sarah, was as yet unable to fathom.

Her second conclusion was that Justin Rossi, despite Amy's suggestion, was surely not wearing a wig. Several times, while speaking, he had absently reached up and run his hands through his short-cropped black hair—a gesture unnervingly reminiscent of Alexander McKenzie's, although Alex wore his hair longer. And Justin's scalp and facial skin seemed natural, no signs of an artificial attachment. Of course, today they could do wonders with hairpieces. However, Sarah put the idea for the moment on the shelf and returned her attention to Barbara.

Flushed by the wave of approbation, Barbara beamed on the assembled group, and then suggested that a small contribution in Ellen Trevino's name be made to the National Trust. She had picked up a pamphlet at Snowshill Manor and began a lengthy explanation of the Trust's almost hundred years of protecting the British countryside, its historic buildings, its coastline.

Sarah, finishing her coffee, decided that the whole tenor of the table was becoming entirely too high-minded and decided to seek fresh air, so, followed by Julia, she slipped away from the table and headed for the garden.

"Really," said Julia. "Barbara Baxter is power-mad. It's not like we're an Elderhostel on the hoof or a collection of dentists and bank clerks from Terre Haute who don't mind being jerked around because they've never been in Britain before.

Sarah objected. "Barbara is organized, not power-mad. And everyone seemed to love Snowshill Manor. And I don't think the Cambridge Botanic Garden sounds like a bad idea. Besides, we're still going to all the gardens that Ellen planned. And you, Aunt Julia, are beginning to sound just like Carter yourself."

Julia plunked herself down on a stone bench overlooking a series of rosebushes in full creamy bloom and Sarah joined her.

It was quite dark by now, but a lamp shone distantly from the back of the inn and the narrow paths and flowers were just visible as forms of light and dark while the scent of the roses, the bordering sweet alyssum, and the wisteria hanging on nearby trellis was almost overpowering.

And Julia softened and became sympathetic. "Oh, I suppose Barbara means well. She's always cheerful, and she seems to be popular, not just with Sandi who would probably love Dracula, but with the others, too, even Rossi and Stacy Daniel, who seem to have minds of their own. But I do not understand the Hopper sisters chiming in like a secondhand chorus. They were quite critical of the Cambridge plan but now they're all for it. Though," she added, "I'm truly glad they're pulling themselves together. When they're cheerful they're a great asset, and we must all try to get along with each other."

"You *are* mellowing."

"It's this garden. It's taking me back. Tom and I rented a little house—Holly Cottage it was called—in the Cotswolds. It was our last trip together because Tom died the next spring." Julia gave a heavy sigh and reached for her cane. "Anyway, for at least ten minutes I'm in charity even with the likes of Stacy Daniel, whom I suspect is as hard as a rock, and Justin Rossi, who reminds me of a slightly tame pirate."

"Because he looks like Alex?"

"Yes. Both the piratical types, though naturally I prefer Alex. And it's a funny thing. I don't mind the Ouellettes as much as I did. Sandi and Fred seem genuinely devoted to each other, which is quite remarkable in a married couple. And Fred has been kind enough to tell me in detail about the funeral practices in the Congo. He's an absolute mine of mortuary information."

Julia pushed her cane into the ground and, clutching it with both hands, rose to her feet. "Before I become entirely mush-headed I'm going in and settle down with Dick Francis. A stolen horse and skullduggery at Newmarket."

And Sarah was left alone.

But not for long.

"I suppose," said a voice behind her, "you're still mad at me."

Amy.

Sarah swallowed hard, but the wisteria and the garden lit by the now rising moon had softened her as well as Julia.

"Sit down, Amy," she said. "I'm not mad at you. And I will look at your story sometime. But not tonight. Okay?"

"Okay," said Amy, plunking herself down on the bench beside Sarah. "It's neat out here. The moonlight. You can just see the edges of things, the garden and the pond, and those bushes clipped into shapes. And everything smells wonderful. What is it?"

"The wisteria, the roses. And those white flowers along the borders, I forget the name. And the bushes are box. I do know that much. You can clip them into shapes—rabbits and urns and swans. Topiary. You'll see a lot of it before we're through."

"England is really different." Amy sighed. "It's so tidy with all those little cottages and villages and footpaths. Like a stage set in one of those old romance movies. Or a *Star Trek* show when the crew is blasted back into the past and everyone is wearing top hats and hoop skirts." For a moment Amy was quiet apparently considering. Then, "I suppose I could write a romance instead of a mystery, but my English teacher says my strong point is realistic description. Besides," she added, "I think our garden tour group is too weird to put into a romance, don't you?"

"I think," said Sarah, lapsing reluctantly into her teacher mode, "that any group all with a particular hobby would seem a little weird. They have one interest in common and not much else."

"But that's not what I'm saying," cried Amy. "What I mean is this great interest in gardens isn't so great. Only a few people are really into it. But Stacy Daniel and Mr. Rossi and Mrs. Clancy and you aren't. Like you look at the flowers and you don't know any of the names."

Sarah wanted to interrupt and say that she and Julia were there through the accident of free tickets and lodging, not because of any horticultural passion, but suddenly it seemed of no importance. Instead she rose from the bench. "What I think is that we're wasting time on speculation and it's a beautiful night. Let's walk around the garden and then go in. It's getting late."

"Okay," said Amy agreeably. She stood up and shook her mane of hair. "I'll save weird for my novel."

And so they walked, slowly moving from one moonlit path to the next, the fragrant air, the faint night breeze, the moving shadows all acting for Sarah as an anodyne to the day's events. Even the terrible fact of Ellen Trevino's death lost some of its immediate resonance. And the attack on her bedroom faded from being a personal assault to the sort of annoyance one might expect when traveling in alien places. Certainly irritating but not overwhelming, and, after all, Barbara had had the same thing happen.

Amy walked by her side with that easy careless movement of the young, and Sarah found herself humming the "Music of the Night," which was the sort of melody once begun cannot be easily shaken loose.

"Hey," said Amy, "I know that, I played the Phantom in our eighth-grade production. We had a really creepy set. And I've been thinking, maybe I need a mysterious person or a phantom in my story. Like that woman last night who was sitting in the garden."

"Woman?" said Sarah. "Have you seen a phantom woman?"

"I don't know. It's just that last night I had to go to the bathroom in the middle of the night because of all that Orangina I drank, and my bed is next to the window, and so when I got back I looked out of it and there was this woman walking up and down out in the garden. Because of the moon I could see her pretty well. She had white hair and wore this long silvery gray dress, and I thought, What is she doing out there?"

"But not from our group?" Sarah asked, in spite of her intention to squash any more of Amy's flights into fiction.

"I don't think so. She looked pretty tall, but maybe the angle from my window made her look that way."

"Well, there's no law against walking in the garden at night. And the air is marvelous. No bugs, mosquitoes, or black flies. It was probably someone who couldn't sleep."

But Amy shook her head. "It was two in the morning. I know because my mother has one of those travel clocks that glow in the dark. And don't laugh, but when I was looking at the woman, I thought, Hey this is England, and I could be looking right out at a ghost because isn't that one of the specialties in this country? In Europe. Ghosts, I mean."

Sarah laughed. "Maybe you're right. A friendly ghost taking the night air."

"Or a vampire," said Amy. "Or are those just in Transylvania and Louisiana? Anyway, I thought maybe I could put a ghost in my story. Some woman who'd been abused or raped or strangled a hundred years ago and she walks in the garden until someone avenges her. It happened in the garden, you see. The rape or the strangling. What do you think?"

"What I think," said Sarah firmly, "is that it's after ten-thirty, which is past my bedtime. Maybe even past yours."

"Yeah. Okay, I suppose it is. Mother's probably having a fit wondering where I am. Anyhow, I'll think about putting a ghost into my mystery, though it might make it too complicated."

"Much too complicated," said Sarah. "I'd say scrap the ghost. But, you know, suddenly I feel as if I could sleep for sixty hours."

But she couldn't.

Whether it was the moonlight, or a reviving distress over Ellen's death, she couldn't settle down. Finally, as the luminous hands of her wristwatch hit eleven, she climbed out of bed, reached for her jeans and a sweatshirt, and headed back to the garden. It was one of those nights, she told herself, that are meant to send people outside. And where better to go than a sweet-smelling moonlit garden.

But Sarah was not alone in her sleeplessness. It was as if a spell had settled on the Shearing Inn—or at least on the members of the garden tour.

Julia Clancy, a light sleeper at best, put Dick Francis aside and settled herself by her bedroom window. Here, looking out but not really seeing the nighttime garden, she fell into a reverie over past times. Tom and that last visit to the Cotswolds. Tea with farm families talking over new foals and promising yearlings. A visit to the bird sanctuary in Bourton-on-Water, an overnight in a seventeenth-century hotel in Lower Slaughter, a picnic by the River Windrush. "Tom, Tom," Julia whispered aloud, "damn it, Tom, you old Irishman, I do miss you."

Barbara Baxter was awake, not from a surfeit of nostalgia, but from a lively sense that she had homework to do. Seated at a small writing desk, surrounded by pamphlets and maps of the Cotswolds, she tried to chart the next few days for the Garden Club so that the dissenters—Carter McClure in particular— would be mollified. But, although Ellen Trevino's blueprint called for almost every hour of the day to be spent at a garden of note, unlike hotels and inns, reservations for these had not been necessary, and so some shuffling was possible. And, furthermore, she, Barbara, would show them that the details of English gardens were not beyond her. To this end, she reached for a handbook on British wildflowers purchased in haste during the London expedition. Not that wildflowers would be the feature of the tour, but one had to start somewhere, and Barbara, at the outset of the trip, had not been aware that there was much difference between wildflowers and the tame ones in gardens, except that the tame ones seemed to be bigger. She opened the book and with great determination began reading the details of the *Ranunculaceae:* the buttercup family.

The two Hopper sisters were also awake. The improvement in their spirits noted during the dinner hour had not been sustained. Wearing white lawn nightgowns covered by a crêpe-de-chine bedjackets, they sat, each on a twin bed and faced one another. But now instead of choked-back tears they turned to lamentation and blame. "If only you hadn't started it," said Edith to Margaret, "then I wouldn't have and none of this would have happened."

"How can you say that," said Margaret to Edith. "You went right along with me. You even thought it would be fun. You agreed it would make a difference. And it did. It really did."

Edith gave a heavy sniff. "But I'm younger than you are and I've always looked up to you from the very beginning. And so I just followed along. Your idea from the start."

"You have to admit we did it very well," said Margaret with a certain tearful complacency.

"Until Friday, we did it very well. And now, only a day later, we've lost everything."

"But I repeat, we needed to. Otherwise we might not have managed." And, Margaret went on, gathering steam, "It's always been a matter of discipline. Of self-control. And you've never had much. You get excited. And now look at us."

"Perhaps," said Edith in a hesitant voice, "it won't be quite as bad as we think. At least there's an alternative."

A long moment of silence. A sob. Then breakdown.

At last Margaret swallowed hard, reached for a tissue, blew loudly, stood up from the bed, walked to the window and put her forehead against the glass. "The end of everything," she repeated.

But Edith had recovered. She joined Margaret at the window and put her arm around her sister's waist. "We can't argue. We're together in this and we'll get out of it someday. We can live with it because what choice have we? Look out there because it's such a lovely night. You can see way across the car park. The houses and the garden gates and the beginning of the footpath. Later on I'll mix some Ovaltine. I packed a supply."

Margaret with one final gulp, one notable sigh, pressed her sister's hand, and the two women stood together at the window.

Amy Lermatov, too, was wide awake. Excited by the idea of inserting a female specter into her mystery story, she sat hunched in a chair by a standing lamp and sucked on the end of her ballpoint pen. Should the specter or ghost have unearthly powers or perhaps be simply the manifestation of some spurned or tortured highborn lady. Could ghosts be lowborn? A serving maid, a peasant? Should the ghost be headless? Or visible to only a chosen few? Or, even in the face of Sarah's objections, should the specter take the form of the late Dr. Ellen Trevino?

Amy's mother, Doris Lermatov, after halfheartedly urging her daughter to go to sleep, gave it up herself. She shouldn't have had that second helping of pudding and now she was wide awake. She turned on the bedside light, pulled out a copy of *Gourmet* and settled down to read.

Unlike the two Lermatovs, Sandi and Fred Ouellette had no literary interests to engage them. Instead, moved likewise by the moonlight and the excitement of being in a foreign place for the third night of their lives, they decided to see more of it.

"Such a beautiful night," said Sandi. "Not a bit cold or damp. Whoever said it always rains in England? Let's just walk around the village."

To which Fred agreed, adding that if time permitted he would like to visit the local undertaker. He had been eager to discuss embalming problems and techniques in the United Kingdom.

"Not tonight," protested Sandi. "It's past eleven."

"Might be the best time. I often do my best cosmetic work in the middle of the night. No distractions. I'll check the telephone book for the location of the funeral home and then if we see a light on we can make a call. Professional courtesy."

"You can call," said Sandi with unusual vigor, "but I'm going walking. I don't think they have muggers in little English towns."

"Now you just be careful," said Fred. Then he leaned over and kissed the back of Sandi's neck and together they prepared for an evening expedition.

Stacy Daniel and Justin Rossi also had nocturnal plans. Without consulting the other, each decided to check out the local pubs. Each had noted these establishments on their trips first to the police station and then on the round trip to Snowshill Manor. To the north on the same road as the Shearing Inn sat the Hound and Hare, to the west on a street off from the churchyard was the Black Badger, beyond that The Jolly Blacksmith. Stacy planned to make the rounds, but Justin hadn't made up his mind. However, for each the evening plan entailed a change of costume.

Stacy shucked her dinner outfit of gray knit trousers and long gray silk blouse to something more striking, more suitable for the night prowl. To this end she chose a tight short skirt of tangerine, black heels, and a loose black jacket over a low-cut cotton tank top. In other words, Stacy dressed up.

And Justin Rossi in the next room dressed down. He wrenched off his necktie without bothering to untie it, pulled off his trousers, his blue-striped shirt, and began searching around in his suitcase for looser and more comfortable garments. Garments that would not immediately identify him as a tourist attached to an American garden club group.

As for the others, Portia McClure, like Sarah, opted for a garden stroll, while her husband, Carter, said he'd look in at the Shearing pub for a last pint before bedtime—or take a walk, look around the village.

Portia, who had been settling a light wool jacket over her shoulders, turned toward her husband. "Please don't get into an argument with anyone because when you put your mind to it you can be an absolute monster." She shook a token fist at her husband, opened the door, and stepped into the hall. Followed by Carter.

And within the hour, Henry Ruggles, Esquire, garden lecturer designate, arrived, signed the register, received his room key, and took possession of the single room which had been reserved for the late Dr. Ellen Trevino. By eleven-thirty Henry was in bed and so became the only person connected with the garden tour who fell asleep before midnight and slept without stirring until morning.

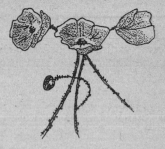

11

SARAH, wandering at the foot of the garden, found herself falling increasingly under the potent spell of the soft nocturnal breeze freighted with flowery scents. And now, somewhere below her, she heard the distant rustling of something moving through the underbrush. Perhaps a fox or a weasel. Or a badger. Sarah had never come across a badger except in the pages of *The Wind and the Willows*. Walking along the extreme verge of the lower garden she found a small worn path that descended for about thirty yards into a bordering pasture. Well, why not? The sight of a badger would be worth much. And then, as if she had entered into a different kingdom, close to a low stone wall the rustling again, then a soft moaning ooo-ooo-ooo. And from a great distance a rising and falling long drawn out churrr—churr.

Birds as well as the possible badger. She needed Alex— Alex the birdwatcher. Was she hearing owls and what was that other night-flying bird? She frowned thinking of nineteenth-century poets and came up with nightjar. Not a poetic name. Back home they were called whip-poor-wills because that was what they called, over and over. And how about a nightingale?

She would gladly give up the badger for a nightingale even if she hadn't the least idea what they sounded like. But she was sure the song would ravish her because it had for centuries ravished poets without number. Keats had certainly been ravished, going on about light-winged Dryad of the trees and thoughts of easeful Death.

But high-flown thoughts often end, as another poet has warned, in the muck, and Sarah's next steps through a small gap in the stone wall took her into a boggy patch of meadow and forced her into several squelching steps before she worked her way back to higher ground. There she found the length of a fallen tree and sat down, the more comfortably to contemplate the possibility of a nightingale.

What she got was a cow. Several in fact, their tan hides almost colorless in the moonlight, creatures who, as restless as the other species of the area, had wandered up close to the fence.

"Good girl," said Sarah tentatively, withdrawing her legs from a large moist breath that blew on her bare ankles.

And suddenly far behind her a human noise. It sounded—though at the distance she couldn't be sure—like a low chuckle and felt as if an icy finger had drawn itself down her back. She twisted around at first seeing nothing but low-growing bushes. But then, looking ahead some fifty yards on the footpath she made out the figure of a woman. A tall white-haired woman in a long silvery gray dress. She was standing quite still, her head turned toward Sarah. A specter? Or, to be exact, Amy Lermatov's ghost! This idea no sooner came into her head than Sarah dismissed it. Statuesque, yes, unearthly, no. Sarah could see now that the woman had tied a light shawl over her shoulders, and this suggested a very human desire to keep out the night chill. Then, just as Sarah was thinking about calling out, the woman raised her arm in greeting and continued her way up the footpath toward the village, her layered skirt billowing gently behind her.

Almost, Sarah thought, as if a Greek statue had stepped down from her pedestal for an evening's stroll. Artemis, perhaps.

Wasn't she the one worshipped very early as an earth goddess who concerned herself with wildlife and growth of the field? And human birth. Later on, of course, the virgin huntress who watched over all living species. One of the more positive goddesses. But why had the woman laughed like that? That low chuckle had certainly had an eerie quality. But then, Sarah reminded herself, the sight of a lone woman beset by cows was probably mildly amusing.

From these thoughts, she was diverted by the more insistent attentions of one of the cows which began pushing against her knees, and just as she was trying to think of how to rid herself of the animal, a voice sounded behind her.

"Hello, Sarah. Beautiful night, isn't it?" Portia McClure.

"I couldn't sleep," explained Portia, "so I thought I'd take a walk. There's a footpath here that goes by the edge of the pasture and leads to the village. I walked along it yesterday. Shoo, shoo," she called to one of the cows who was now pushing its head into Sarah's lap. Apparently offended by this lack of welcome, the animal turned and with its companions made a leisurely departure.

"One of those nights," said Portia, settling down on the tree trunk beside Sarah. "Everyone's out and about. Half the people from the village. I saw the vicar on the road—still in his collar—and the two people from the cottage across the way from the inn and then I met Fred and Sandi Ouellette heading out somewhere. As well as Stacy Daniel at the door. Said she was going pub crawling. Had had quite enough of gardens."

"Then why in heaven's name is she on the tour?" demanded Sarah. "It's hardly gotten off the ground and she's had enough?"

"Oh, I think she's one of those self-loving beauties who wouldn't be happy wherever she went. Or she's a special friend of Barbara Baxter's. Perhaps they're a couple. You never know why some people come together. Anyway, it's one of those nights. 'The moon shines bright. In such a night as this . . .

> When the sweet wind did gently kiss the trees
> And they did make no noise, in such a night

Troilus methinks mounted the Troyan walls . . .
And sighed his soul toward the Grecian tents,
Where Cressid lay that night.' "

She broke off. "I was named for the Portia in the play. My parents made me learn great gobs of it because they thought it might turn me into a lawyer, but I fooled them."

For a moment they sat in companionable silence, and then Portia said thoughtfully, "You know, Ellen Trevino cared deeply about her gardens, her research. She wouldn't have wasted time slipping into poetry, and she certainly didn't have much patience for uninformed raptures. To her, gardens were wonderful and intricate arrangements of botanical items. They offered contrast and mass and pattern and color, and they presented problems in growth and propagation, and fertilization. Gardens were marvelous as living and manageable facts and they deserved our full and passionate attention." Here Portia paused and gave a small sigh. "I guess what I'm saying is, that if Ellen had been here, it would have behooved us all to have been entirely serious about our trip."

"You're saying," Sarah began.

"What I'm *not* saying is that I'm relieved Ellen isn't here. I admired her tremendously and I'm striken by her death. But without Ellen in charge, there's a certain ease. Carter would have been a royal pain, argued with her every inch of the way, and I can't be pulling on his leash every minute. And I intend—or did intend—to enjoy myself. June in the Cotswolds is an absolute gift."

"But," Sarah protested, "if Ellen had been here, then Barbara wouldn't have made any changes. She would have stuck to the schedule and not done any freelancing."

"Maybe, maybe not. Two generals pulling two different ways. General Ellen and General Barbara."

"And Field Commander Carter McClure."

Portia laughed. "Right. Anyway, I hope Henry Ruggles will work out. Carter's very own choice, so he'll shut up. And Henry has a rather courtly way about him. He won't defer to Barbara but it will look like he does."

"That sounds hopeful."

"Carter has no idea of how annoying he can be. He does a lot of barking, but he hasn't any fangs. Those were pulled long ago."

"By you?" asked Sarah, wondering if this was too personal a question. But the night, the air, all seemed to encourage intimacy.

"Perhaps. He was a sort of enragé when I met him. I was a graduate student, and he was the wild and woolly instructor of the History Department. Our marriage was part chemistry and part a sort of in-your-face to our objecting parents. Mine called him a reactionary redneck and his thought I was out to ignite the entire black population of New England. And I think the idea of racially mixed grandchildren made them queasy. But the grandparents have come round, our children were spoiled rotten by both sides, and the marriage has worked, heaven knows why. Carter will behave if you stand up to him. I think I'll give Sandi Ouellette a tip because she's cowed by him. She's not half as fluff-headed and ingenuous as she seems. Well, there you are. Thumbnail bio. But I don't need yours. Sandi had told all."

Sarah groaned. "Oh, God, I wish she wouldn't do that. But I'm glad you're here without Carter. And I am glad he's found Aunt Julia. They can work off their spleen on each other."

"Let's hope," said Portia. "And now I feel like a short walk down the footpath toward the village. Want to join me?"

Sarah did, and for some fifteen or so minutes they followed the path that wound around the pasture's edge, turned back on itself, offered a stile, a brook, another pasture, and then rose in an inviting way toward the village center. For a moment the two women came to a halt by a small brook and stood bathed in moonlight.

"Peace," said Sarah. "Perfect peace. All these little Cotswold towns and those names—High Roosting, Nether Roosting, Bourton-on-Water, Chipping Camden, Moreton-in-Marsh—make me expect toadstools and elves and dairy maids sweeping hearths with brooms made of twigs. And the houses—the cottages—like honeypots or illustrations for Mother Goose."

"I know what you mean," said Portia. "Not the inner city, is it? Or rural backyard America. I haven't seen any wrecked cars in front yards or tripped over disposable diapers on the path. But, cheer up, maybe inside one of these cottages something is brewing. Jack the Ripper is preparing for an evening stroll."

Sarah agreed. "You almost want to see blinking lights and hear a siren to make the whole place seem real."

At these words they were immediately rewarded with a siren. A distant siren rising and falling, coming closer, going away.

"So much," said Portia briskly, "for Mother Goose."

"The police," said Sarah, pointing up toward the village as two white cars, one after the other, whizzed past, and turned toward the village center.

"Well, shall we go on to the village and gawk like tourists or go on back?" asked Portia.

Sarah hesitated. "I did want to just reach the rise and see the whole village spread out in the moonlight. We can ignore the police cars. It's probably just a rumble at one of the pubs."

They climbed the footpath and reached the juncture of the main road, which indeed offered a nighttime panorama of the village.

"And we can't even see the police cars," said Portia with satisfaction. "It's a wonderful view: church steeples, town hall, the market square, the high street, the whole bit."

"And the population going to bed," added Sarah, pointing. And indeed from several village streets emerged small clusters of persons on foot. Persons who seemed to be hastening toward some destination, not walking with the evening languor that she had noticed earlier.

"Time for the hot milk or a last brandy and soda," said Portia. "Or even a nice refreshing cup of hot water. Did you know Carter's parents—they're Scottish—have a cup of hot water every night before going to bed. They claim it cleans the bowels."

But before Sarah could say what she thought of hot water as a nightcap, she caught sight of a slender woman's figure coming at a run from a small side street. The woman plunged across the main road and was about to gallop on down the footpath when she saw Sarah and Portia and skidded to a halt.

"Sandi!" exclaimed Portia. "Whoa up."

"Oh thank goodness, people I know," panted Sandi. "I was going to run all the way to the inn, but now I can walk with you. Get my breath. Pull myself together."

And indeed Sandi seemed to need pulling together. Her clothes were in disarray, and she seemed to be clutching at her bodice to hold it together while her flowered skirt had swiveled around so that its belt hung down on one hip.

"Whoa, take it easy. Everything's all right. You're all right," said Portia in a soothing but firm voice, sounding to Sarah's ears like a sort of archetypal Everymother.

For a moment Sandi stood and trembled. Then she bobbed her head. "Yes, I am all right. I think I am, anyway. In fact, I'm not sure anything's wrong. Except my blouse. Torn or slit right down my front. I mean it's made to crisscross and then tie in back and now it's completely open unless I hold it together. I don't know if it was an accident or it's like what happened to that other woman. The police are still talking to her."

"Sandi, take it easy," commanded Sarah.

"We'll walk back down to the inn together," said Portia, "and you can tell us what happened."

"If anything really did," said Sandi. "I mean to me."

"Begin at the beginning," said Portia. "We'll take it easy and the moonlight makes the path perfectly clear."

"I know," said Sandi. "I came up that way. After I split off from Fred because he wanted to see the local undertaker, and I wasn't really up for dead bodies on a beautiful night."

"And so?" prompted Sarah.

"So I came back to the inn and picked up the footpath at the end of the garden. I said to myself, Sandi, you're in England so why not get the flavor, the feel of the place. Why just do gardens, why not make every minute count?"

"Where did you go to make every minute count?" asked Sarah, and Sandi gave a sort of giggle that had the slightest touch of hysteria at the top of it.

"All over the map, into the village, down the high street, but the shops are closed late Saturday night just like they are in little Maine towns. Not like Miami and Atlantic City and Vegas. Fred and I go to mortuary conventions and those places really move at night. Anyway, I walked up and down all the side streets and half the townspeople—or maybe they were tourists, too—were walking around. It was so bright we didn't even need the street lamps to see. And then I thought for real atmosphere I should try and see if a pub was open. I asked someone and they told me there were three pubs in town, and that I was lucky because right past the Wool Gathering Book Shop was a pub called the Hound and Hare. So I marched right in and the place was absolutely packed, but I found a seat near the wall and ordered up a pint of Guinness because that was about the only name I could think of."

"But what *happened?*" insisted Sarah impatiently.

"Wait up," said Sandi, who now seemed to be enjoying the role of narrator. "I've got to get this in sequence because maybe nothing would have happened if that football club hadn't come in and everyone got more jammed in than ever. Well, after I'd finished two drinks of this ale or stout—whatever it was, and boy was it strong—I thought I'd watch the darts or this really stupid game called shove ha'penny. You know, get all the local color. So I got up and moved over to the edge of a bunch of people watching the dart throwing and then it happened."

"WHAT HAPPENED?" demanded Portia in something like a shout, proving to Sarah that her companion was not endlessly patient.

"Don't rush me," said Sandi. "What I'm saying is that there we were, all in there like sardines and what happened was this screech. Pretty close to the pub room, although how close was kind of hard to judge because everyone was making a lot of noise, talking and calling. And the smoke, you wouldn't believe. Forget about no-smoking rules, the place was blue. Anyhow, the first thing I saw was this big hunk of a red-haired guy being almost thrown out from the place where the toilets are. You know the restrooms. Only here they call restrooms the WC or the loo."

"I know," said Sarah through her teeth. She wondered if it would be ruled just cause if she murdered Sandi for drawn-out narration. This was as bad as the wedding guest and the Ancient Mariner. But that at least had a moral. She doubted if Sandi's tale would.

"Go on," said Portia.

"Well, this big red-haired guy landed in the middle of all the people and everyone started yelling, and then there was the woman screaming. She was standing in the doorway of the hall where the restrooms are, and her dress was slit right down the front. I mean there she was hanging out of her bra with one strap loose. Totally out in the open." Here Sandi giggled again and the hysteria was closer to the surface.

"Calm down, Sandi," said Sarah. "You're okay."

"Yeah, I know I am, but this woman—her hair was all messed up too, like she'd been in a sort of struggle—was half crying and said she'd been molested. Or groped. In the WC. By this red-haired guy, and she pointed to the man who was still sitting on the floor and the woman said that was who attacked her. And then the bartender, or whatever he's called in England, shouted and told everyone to stay where they were, and that he was calling the police. And for someone to sit on the red-haired man, and that's what happened. Except the woman—and she's sort of crying and screaming, said she'd been saved—or rescued by this woman who had been in one of the toilet stalls."

Here Sandi paused for breath. "Well, that's about it. So there we all were, packed in together, and I think everyone was kind of sweating—especially those football club guys—and a waitress took the woman with the torn blouse into the ladies' room and before you could count to ten the police turned up. Two of them. They took names and addresses and said they'd be in touch if they needed extra identification for this guy. The police were taking him off. Then one of the policemen turned to me and asked could I identify the man who did it to me, I didn't know what he was talking about. And then he looked a little embarrassed and pointed to my blouse and asked if I wanted to go into the WC, and I looked down and, shit, it was torn from top to bottom and my bra and me were there for everyone to look at. But I hadn't even noticed what with the crowd bumping into each other and no one feeling any pain. But I just pulled my blouse together and said I was fine, that I must have caught it on a nail or something."

"But you hadn't?" said Sarah as Sandi paused for breath.

"I don't know really. But I wasn't hurt. Not scratched or anything. I mean if someone had used a knife to slit my blouse he was pretty good at it. I suppose it was something sexual, you know, the man got kicks from slicing off clothes. I'm sorry about that other woman because she looked scared to death, but she was lucky. Saved in the nick of time. Anyway, one of the other policemen or constables—he was in a blue uniform—was making a circle around my name in his notebook and told me they might ask me to come down to the station for a statement. Then I beat it out of there. Enough is enough. I've had it with local color, and England isn't so different after all. Except no one shot anyone like they do in Vegas or Miami."

"Are you sure, Sandi," said Portia in measured tones, "that you are perfectly all right?"

"I guess so. Maybe I'd better get used to things like this. I've heard that women get their bottoms pinched in Italy. Just for walking down the street. Even people like Mrs. Clancy."

"Who pinches Aunt Julia's bottom does so at his peril," said Sarah.

"You know something," said Sandi, "maybe I've met up with a real English hero. Jack the Ripper. Only he ripped throats didn't he? Not blouses."

Here Portia—the mother born—took charge. She took off her jacket and put it about Sandi's shoulders. "You're shivering," she said. "Put this on and I'll get you a nice warm drink when ve get back. The air is turning much cooler and you've had a little shock . . . no, don't interrupt. Not a big shock, a little one, and a warm drink will be just the thing."

And the trio made its way down the descending and winding path, now being joined by an increasing number of moonlight walkers, many of whom Sarah recognized as guests of the Shearing Inn. There were two from the German group who sat in the back of the dining room and several Americans from another bus tour. Then, walking by herself, the same woman in a flowing silver gray dress, the one who had laughed at Sarah's encounter with the cows. Seen more closely, Sarah found her a handsome woman. In fact, as she overtook them, she looked very like Alex's redoubtable mother, Elspeth McKenzie. Tall, with the slightly beaked nose, the long thin mouth, the firm chin. The same white hair fastened in the back, as Elspeth often did—with a heavy clasp.

The resemblance was marked enough for Sarah to slow her steps, but then as the woman came abreast of Portia, Sarah saw that the eyes weren't right—Elspeth had the hooded eyes of a hawk. The woman merely nodded, smiled slightly, and in a husky voice remarked that it was such a lovely night and then walked past the three, down the path and out of sight.

And Sandi erupted again with that same high-pitched giggle. That woman. The one in the silver dress. The one who passed us. She was in the garden last night. I think she's dead and has come back to haunt us."

"And I think," said Portia firmly. "The ale has gone to your head and you need Fred and that warm drink as soon as possible."

12

THOUGHTS of Jack the Ripper do not make for sound repose, and after climbing into bed Sarah lay awake for the better part of an hour. She wished Portia McClure hadn't mentioned Jack preparing for an evening stroll. It was as if the simple evocation of his name had sent some man abroad to slit blouses and molest women. But at long last she fell into a jumble of dreams in which Alex tried to explain to her that his mother often wandered about the Cotswolds impersonating a ghost.

Sunday morning, coming too soon, brought a slight headache and a strong sense of reality. It might have brought Mr. Henry Ruggles, newly arrived garden expert, to the fore, if Sandi, arriving for breakfast, hadn't taken center stage with her tale of the night's molester. Or Jack the Slitter, as she called him.

"It's like this," said Sandi, putting down her toast and observing that everyone, even the moist-eyed Hopper sisters, were listening with attention. And Sandi launched into the disconnected saga of last night's event. "And," she added, "the maid on our floor knows the woman—it's her cousin's best friend, her name is Margery. They call her Marge. Anyway, she was at the pub and had to go to the ladies' room—the loo—and when she got in there she's grabbed by this red-haired man who starts tearing her blouse."

"Why did he do that?" demanded Amy Lermatov. But Amy's voice has alerted the others to the fact that a fourteen-year-old girl was hanging on every word, although Sarah, listening, reasoned that most teenagers have such a wide knowledge of the seamy side of life that the tale of a blouse demolition would seem rather dull.

Sandi must have thought the same because, after a brief pause she went on with only slight modifications, substituting front for breast. "He reached for her front," repeated Sandi, "and before anything really happened this other woman who had been in one of the toilet places came bursting out and picked the man up and tossed him into the pub room. Like she was some of sort weightlifter. Then a policeman came and told me my blouse was ripped down the front, so I was taken to the police station early this morning, but I told them I didn't know how it happened and I'd never met the red-haired man or the woman who'd saved Marge."

Sandi subsided and the wave of outcries and questions rippled up and down the breakfast table, and it wasn't until the second round of coffee that attention was directed to the presence of Henry Ruggles.

Henry, during Sandi's recitative, had remained quietly busy with his poached egg. Sarah, examining the newcomer from across the table, couldn't decide whether his focus on food was related to hunger or simple diplomacy.

One thing was certain: Henry most certainly wore a wig. She remembered Amy's speculations on wigs and decided that here was the real thing. Henry was somewhere between sixty and seventy with a round ruddy face, bristling eyebrows, and fluffy gray-rust colored sideburns which ended suddenly at the line of a mop-shaped wig of mixed hues. A tweed wig, Sarah decided. A gray-brown-heather mix. And not quite straight. But the whole effect of the ancient corduroy Norfolk jacket, the old school tie (or was it a regimental stripe?), the horn-rimmed glasses hanging from a black string around his neck, was rather fetching. Somewhat Dickensian, as Portia had suggested. Perhaps he wore spats. Or gaiters. And knickerbockers with great clumping brogues.

But, more important, was the question of his ability to get along with Barbara Baxter and her support team and at the same time take his place as the new garden arbitrator. After all, only the McClures vouched for the man; they had produced Henry without any general vote of approval. Now it was up to Henry.

No problem.

Henry proved to be a charmer. When the murmurs over Sandi's tale had died down, Henry went to work. He was seated between Portia McClure and Barbara and it was to Barbara he turned. Wisely, Sarah concluded, since Portia was already in his camp.

Barbara, at first, was restrained. Defensive about the side trips taken, the Snowshill Manor trip, the proposed visit to the Cambridge Botanic Garden, pointing out that many had been in favor of the changes. But Henry poured it on. He had sometimes a curious way of emphasizing certain words as if to give them extra weight. NEVER miss a chance to see Kew Gardens. What a happy thought. He LOVED Kew. How he wished he could have been with them. She must know those old lines of Alfred Noyes, "Go down to Kew in lilac time." Of course the lilacs would have gone by, but the ROSES! The iris, the lilies, the peonies. As for Snowshill Manor, the perfect distraction after the tragic news. That HORRIBLE accident. Will the violence never end. He'd read with such interest Dr. Trevino's pamphlet on *Pedicularis lapponica*—the Lapland lousewort, as you know, he added tactfully to Barbara.

By this time, Sarah, observing from over her teacup, felt that Barbara was actually purring. Even Julia, who usually devoted all her attention to her breakfast, had her head up and finally whispered loudly to Sarah that Henry Ruggles was really laying it on with a trowel. "But a good idea. That's the way to peace.

Carter may have actually known what he was doing when he brought the man in. Now let's hope he knows a rosebush from a thistle."

Henry Ruggles wound up with stating his enthusiasm for Hidcote and Kiftsgate. "DEAR Kiftsgate, a miracle of planning, a perfect tapestry of color. The home of *Rosa filipes 'Kiftsgate.'* And even the swimming pool, which I deplored at first, does not detract." And then only then, when Barbara was at her beaming best, did he throw a small pebble into her pool of happiness. "Perhaps not the WHOLE day in Cambridge. All those NOISY undergraduates. Perhaps a morning at the gardens and then out, out, and away."

"But I promised everyone a bit of shopping," murmured Barbara, not sounding entirely mollified. "And to see the colleges. King's College, Trinity, the Samuel Pepys Library, punting on the Cam"—Barbara had obviously studied her Cambridge guide— "And, I think," she went on, "many of our group are enthusiastic about the *whole* day. You were, weren't you?" Here Barbara swept the table and found the two Hoppers, Sandi and Fred, Justin Rossi, Stacy Daniel—all of whom nodded their support.

"Bunch of trained seals," grumbled Julia Clancy a bit thickly, her mouth being full of toast. "And who wants to be trapped in a city." And Julia returned to her toast and marmalade.

"Cambridge *would* be fun," said Sarah.

Doris Lermatov nodded agreement. "I've only been there once, years ago, and Amy should like it. The whole university scene."

"Amy," said Amy, "thinks Cambridge sounds incredibly boring. Rancid old churches, old buildings, old streets, and people bicycling around in black gowns. I've seen pictures."

"Not a bad setting for a mystery," said her mother. She turned to Sarah. "Amy is keeping a journal and is working on a mystery. It's to be set in England."

"I know," said Sarah, her spirits sinking.

"And," said Amy, "I've got a new chapter. About one of the characters being molested. Her, what do they call it, her bodice being ripped—or maybe all her clothes being pulled off so she has to run away into the woods. Totally naked."

Sarah gave up. Squashing Amy took more energy than she had available. "And which character is the bodice ripper?"

"Easy," said Amy. "This new guy. Henry Ruggles. Did you see he wears a wig? I was hoping that someone would turn up wearing one. They're so sinister, especially if they don't fit."

But before Army could elaborate, Henry Ruggles raised his voice and looked up and down, now embracing the entire breakfast table. "Such a KIND reception. Miss Baxter so HELPFUL. How she had stepped in when needed. Later, when they all had got acquainted, the Cambridge stay could be discussed. Perhaps if a particularly fine cottage garden could be found close to Cambridge, well, Miss Baxter and the the others, might yield. On the other hand, a day in an ancient university town had its attractions."

And so forth. Henry Ruggles was doing everything to ingratiate himself with all parties and keep Barbara from having her feathers ruffled.

Sarah, wearied of Henry, decided that it was a toss-up whether Barbara and company were to be charmed out of an entire day's worth of Cambridge, only half a day, or Henry was going to give in. As for Sarah herself, well, damn it, she *would* like a whole day in Cambridge. Look around, visit the bookshops, prowl around some of the colleges.

But now Henry Ruggles and Barbara Baxter were on their feet, the bus would be at the door in fifteen minutes, and then it was off to Brookside Cottage, then lunch back at the Shearing, followed by Upper Thatching Farm and Lavender Cottage in the afternoon. Tomorrow, Monday, the morning devoted to the Rococo Garden at Painswick House. In the afternoon a very special treat, Thalia Cottage, a name Henry Ruggles pronounced with modest pride. A splendid small garden tended by two old schoolmates with whom he still exchanged Christmas cards and paid an annual visit.

"So be it," Sarah said to her Aunt Julia as they made their way to the bus. "I'm up for a totally flower-oriented few days. No more blouse ripping or ghosts of my mother-in-law."

"Right," said Julia. "And I'm ready for little botanical tidbits. As you said I'm turning mellow in my old age. I keep seeing Tom around every farm fence corner. You may be haunted by Elspeth McKenzie, but I've got Tom on this trip. It's rather comforting."

Returned for lunch from Brookside Cottage gardens—an entirely peaceful visit—Sarah had barely finished her cold salmon mousse when she was called to the telephone. She made her way to the tiny front hall, thinking again how badly this space served anyone wanting to converse on the subject of murder.

It was Alex. Greetings, expressions of love were exchanged, and then Sarah described how Elspeth McKenzie's look-alike had suddenly appeared in the midnight garden and was assured by Alex that he had seen his mother in person only an hour ago. "I hope," he said severely, "that you're not beginning to see things. Now listen, because I do have news."

Sarah gripped the telephone receiver a shade tighter. "Yes?"

"Police think they've found the weapon. Something that qualifies, anyway."

"Not the ice cream cone thing?

"Yes, but it's called a dibble. Sometimes a dibber. It's for planting bulbs. This one has a wooden handle and tapered metal shaft ending in a point. It was found in a drainage ditch about a mile from the body site. Probably thrown out of the car. It looked perfectly clean but the lab is working on it and we ought to know by tonight if any blood turns up."

"A dibble," repeated Sarah. "What a funny name."

"You wouldn't think it was funny if you could see it. It's a wonder more damage hasn't been done by dibbles. They're lethal."

"So are lots of garden tools. Weeders, scythes, pitchforks."

"The dibble is in a class by itself. Anyway that's it. I'll call again if something else breaks. Nothing yet on Ellen Trevino's stepfather. He seems to have vanished into space."

"Wait up," said Sarah suddenly, remembering. "I've airmailed you that scarf, the one I told you about that turned up with the sunglasses. I thought it might have bloodstains on it or the dye may have run. And if it is blood, well draw your own conclusions."

A pause on the line, Alex undoubtedly rolling his eyes, frowning. Then, "I'll keep an eye out for it. And, my dearest beloved, for God's sake don't go around talking about bloody scarves and lost sunglasses. Only to Julia. Okay?"

"Alex, come on. Give me some credit. You seem to think I haven't a cautionary hair on my head."

"You are correct," said Alex, and the line went dead.

Sarah returned to the luncheon table to find the garden tour members pushing back chairs. To judge from anticipatory chatter, Ellen Trevino—alive or dead—had receded further from the general mind, and thoughts were now focused on the upcoming gardens.

Sarah and Julia kept to their resolutions and became compliant—even docile—members of the garden tour. And in actuality, the rest of the group—even the subdued Hopper sisters—seemed to have entered a new phase. Argument about the schedule ceased, individual tastes and interests bowed to the greater need of grappling with horticultural details presented in the procession of cottage gardens.

It was as if Ellen Trevino's death and the midnight incident at the Hound and Hare had brought a sobriety and purpose to the group. A sense of everyday reality so that there were fewer comments about the "quaintness" of the Cotswold villages and the idyllic beauty of each view. Instead, conversations now centered on how to remember the Latin names, how to identify variants of veronica, the optimal size of the peony blossom, the use of lady's mantel as a border, and problems of pruning. And even for that fan of the dinner table, Doris Lermatov, food yielded pride of place to the garden. Make that THE GARDEN, as Henry Ruggles might stress it. As he did stress it.

Henry Ruggles proved a miracle of information, guiding couples, singles, trios, the whole troop, up and down the paths, from this plot to that thicket, to the rockery, to the pond, to the marsh, from the climbing roses to the knot garden. Wearing an ancient topi, hands in constant motion, he expounded with boundless good nature and energy. Barbara Baxter, relegated to second fiddle, remained determinedly cheerful, collecting explanatory pamphlets at the entrance gates, and making notes as she trailed the others.

Amy Lermatov was the only holdout from the collective garden mania, but since she remained occupied with her pencil and notebook as garden after garden unfolded, no one took much notice of her. Only, when Amy aimed her pocket Olympus not at flowers but at members of the tour did she excite any comment.

"Take that thing out of my face," commanded Julia. "I don't allow pictures. Who wants to see a close-up of a seventy-year-old woman."

"Damn it, Amy, get away," said Carter McClure, caught leaning over a planting of salvia, his shirt detached from his trousers, a layer of white dorsal skin exposed.

"Oh, please, not us. We're just not up for a photograph," pleaded Margaret Hopper.

"Maybe later," said Edith. "The whole group together." At which thought she gave a gulp and turned away.

Thus, Sunday and Monday morning passed and now it was Monday afternoon and the tour had arrived at the last garden of the day. Thalia Cottage, south of Moreton-in-Marsh, featured a cheerful, crowded garden, bright with purples, blues, and yellows and overseen by two retired theatrical gentlemen, Harold and Leslie, former schoolmates of Henry Ruggles. Harold's special care was the perennial beds and Leslie supervised the roses, the wisteria, the clematis.

"I do the climbing things," said Leslie.

"And very well you do," said Harold. He appealed to the visitors. "Isn't the wisteria magnificent? Leslie has such a way with wisteria. It doesn't dare not do well."

"But have you seen the delphinium?" said Leslie, returning

the compliment. "Harold has it bewitched. Twice as many blossoms this year."

"It's only a matter of proper composting," said Harold modestly.

It was past three and other visitors had gone, the shadows were lengthening, and only the dedicated Midcoast Garden Club members remained, frowning at species labels, puzzling over a bank of pale yellow poppies. Henry Ruggles, knowing that his party might soon encroach on the sacred hour of tea, approached his two friends with an eye to saying thank you and good-bye.

But Harold had time for old schooldays. He clapped Henry on the shoulder. "Toad," he said—"we called him Toad then," he explained to the others. "Toad, do you remember that fifth-form school play we were in together? *Julius Caesar.* I was Caesar and Leslie here was Brutus. And Toad, you played Caesar's wife, Calpurnia. Absolutely fetching in a bedsheet."

"I remember," said Henry. "My God, what a long time ago that was. You were both very good. And I was pretty awful."

"Well, you got through it, dear boy. But Leslie and I never looked back. Bitten by the theater bug. The whole business. Music halls, Birmingham Rep, the Old Vic. Carrying spears and bringing messages to the king. Then later a spate of cinema. Nothing too tremendous."

"Well, we did move up the ladder," Leslie reminded him. "Me in that flick with Wendy Hiller. And Harold did *The Charge of the Light Brigade* with Trevor, and then all those charity stunts with Larry and Hermione."

"What I remember," said Henry Ruggles, a/k/a Toad, "was that the night of the play we lost the wooden dagger that Leslie was supposed to use to murder Caesar—you had a bag full of jam under your toga—and I came up with this absolutely lethal tool. I'd found it in the potting shed behind one of the playing fields—we used to go in there to smoke—and I ran to get it. The murder scene was a great success."

"Of course," said Leslie, "I had to be frightfully careful. It was a heavy devil. A gardening tool. I'll show you, there's one right in our greenhouse." And Leslie turned, disappeared, returned holding up an ice cream cone–shaped implement. Wooden handle, tapered metal shaft, sharp point.

Sarah felt a cold hand clench itself in the center of her stomach.

"A dibble," said Henry Ruggles with satisfaction. "Probably what pushed me into gardening."

"At least not into murder," said Leslie, laughing. He reached for it, held it in the air, raised his chin, frowned, stared into middle distance, and in a trained and anguished baritone cried out, "Is this a dibble which I see before me, the handle toward my hand? Come, let me clutch thee."

And then Toad Ruggles stepped forward. Opening his hands in a pleading gesture he called in a pathetic falsetto, " 'What mean you, Caesar? Think you to walk forth? You shall not walk out of your house today.' "

Harold braced his shoulders, folded his arms, and confronted his wife.

> How foolish do your fears seem now, Calpurnia!
> I am ashamed I did yield to them.
> Give me my robe, for I will go.

And then, rolling his eyes at Leslie, staggering backwards while clutching his chest, he whispered, " 'Et tu, Brute.' "

And Sarah, overcome by a wave of nausea, turned away and stumbled toward the exit gate.

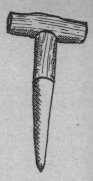

13

SARAH sat in the returning bus, looking out the window and taking in nothing of the passing scene: The snug village with its church spire, the rolling meadow, the copse, the hillside. But for all she saw or cared these could have been scenes of Pittsburgh mills or the mean streets of Detroit.

The dibble. She knew it now. The tool that had been struck into Ellen Trevino's chest had become real. The heft and length, the sharp point of it. On the telephone, as described by Alex, Sarah had not been able to visualize the thing. Descriptions in newspapers of (in police jargon) "the weapon used to perpetrate the crime" were usually the familiar automatic, the Beretta, the Smith and Wesson, perhaps the knife or the hatchet. Or the ax. Sometimes a sport's item: the oar, the baseball bat. Or the workman's choice: the shovel, the rope, the acetylene torch. Those agents found on household shelves: cyanide, arsenic, strychnine. From the garden, from the woodland: foxglove, monkshood, the deadly amanitas. All these Sarah had read or heard of, could imagine in use.

But she had never quite believed in the dibble. A childish

name related to dribble and scribble and nibble. Described by Alex as partly resembling an ice cream cone. Another childish image.

But not anymore. The dibble had become the dibble-as-weapon. It had always seemed to her that there was something particularly horrible about using a domestic object for killing. Something designed for a benevolent purpose become lethal: the knitting needle that pierces, the stocking that strangles, the cocoa that poisons. And now the dibble. A tool for planting those lovely spring bulbs, the daffodil, the narcissus, the tulip, the hyacinth.

Had it all happened by chance? A fellow garden fan en route to Boston spots Ellen Trevino on the turnpike, sees her Subaru turn into the Kennebunk exit and follows her to the chosen parking place. Makes friendly overtures. "What a coincidence!" Urges her to team up for the trip to Logan. "Leave your car here, we can arrange to have it picked up. No point in two cars making the trip. Here, let me help you with your luggage. Have you got your passport, your handbag? Give me your car keys and let me just check and see. It's so easy to forget something."

And in checking the Subaru the dibble comes to light. Such a suitable object sitting there saying, take me, use me! Grab it quickly and slip it under your raincoat, your jacket. Then under the driver's seat of your own car.

Or had everything been planned ahead? What had Alex told her about Ellen meeting a friend or checking on something? If it were all premeditated, the killer brings a gun ready for action. Then the dibble comes to light so the gun is canceled—guns are so easily traced. She could see it. Ellen unconscious in the killer's car—that blow on the temple—courtesy of the dibble's handle, perhaps. Ellen slumped on the plastic sheet—the sheet carefully provided so that blood, hairs, fibers, and other alien particles would not contaminate the car upholstery. But now the dibble is gripped by a gloved hand, is suspended for a moment above Ellen's chest. Then down comes the ugly metal point thrusting through the epidermis, the dermis, through subcutaneous tissue. It splinters cartilage and bone, splits blood vessels, the aorta itself. Blood wells. The heart gives up. And the dibble, its work finished, is pulled up, out. Wrenched free. Wiped, washed perhaps. A restroom at a gas station somewhere. Then thrown away.

And today a dibble is brought forth for a demonstration at Thalia Cottage. How Brutus struck down Caesar. Or how Leslie could reenact murder on his friend, Harold. And by their skill—these men were professionals—Sarah saw the murder taking place.

"Sarah, you look awful. White as cream cheese." It was Julia.

Sarah jumped in her seat as if some inner spring had been released. "What?"

"What on earth is the matter? Are you carsick? The bus driver can pull over. There's a lay-by coming up."

Sarah shook herself. "No, no. It's all right. Just something bothering me. Something I thought of."

Julia eyed her suspiciously. "Something that makes you look as if you're going to lose your lunch?"

"No, I'm all right. I can handle it."

"Now don't go morbid on me."

"It's just that something got to me. Well, if you must know it was that scene with Caesar and Brutus."

"You can't be serious. Just two old hams hamming it up."

"It wasn't the hams," said Sarah. "It was the whole scene."

"You mean *Macbeth* and *Julius Caesar?* You're such a literary purist, Shakespeare is so sacred that you can't stand a little foolishness."

"No," said Sarah crossly. "It isn't that at all. It has nothing to do with Shakespeare. I'll explain later. Back in my room. This bus isn't the place."

And Julia, for once, forbore to push the matter and the two rode in silence back to the inn.

Back in her aunt's room, Julia soaking her tired feet in a basin of warm water, Sarah told her about the dibble. "Alex described some of the forensic details and then, at that murder pantomime when Leslie held up the dibble, I could see the other dibble, too. I could picture the whole business, the thing going right into Ellen Trevino's chest and it turned my stomach."

144

Julia nodded soberly. "Yes, I can understand that. How awful. And a dibble is certainly a deadly object."

Sarah was silent for a minute. Then turned toward the door. "I'm not going to join the others for tea. I need space. I'll take a walk around town. It isn't quite five so if the shops are still open maybe I can buy something for Alex. A McKenzie tartan tie."

"We're not in Scotland," Julia reminded her.

"Tartan ties are everywhere," said Sarah. "Like locusts. Tourist items. Do you want to come?"

"No," said Julia firmly. "I'll stay here and soak my feet, but if you see a nice woven green tie for Patrick—he needn't know that I bought it in England—then buy it for me."

"Gladly," said Sarah. "It gives me a mission. I think Patrick certainly deserves a tie. Holding the farm and the horses together while you're tooting around here."

Her first stop at Maud's Wool and Linen Shop was entirely successful. A tie for Alex in the ancient McKenzie tartan, a silk scarf printed with entwined thistles for Elspeth, and a shamrock-green tie for Patrick. She was just puzzling over a set of linen place mats for her mother when she felt a tap on her shoulder.

"You're skipping the Mad Hatter's tea party," said an accusing voice. Justin Rossi.

"I wanted to be off by myself," said Sarah firmly.

"Far from the madding crowd," said Justin, adding before Sarah could open her mouth, "but this is the wrong country for Hardy. And I don't mean to start quoting the minute I see you. It's that literary aura you carry about you."

"The aura and I are about to take ourselves off," said Sarah.

"Don't go. I need your help. A woman's eye. If there is such a thing. Something for my mother. She's seventy-three and quite conservative in her tastes. What do you think? A scarf or a luncheon set? And something for my sister. A silk shirt perhaps. Size sixteen and she likes blue. Or perhaps a shawl."

Few people can resist a chance to spend another person's money. Sarah gave in. After all, she had nothing against Justin except for the fact that he looked like Alex. And knew birds and could come up with appropriate quotes at the drop of a hat.

Twenty-five minutes later found Sarah and Justin having tea and plum cake and cucumber sandwiches at The Tea Cozy.

"Usually I'd head for a pub, but the nearest one is the Hound and Hare and it's pretty smoke filled," said Justin. "So how do you like the gardens so far? Pretty spectacular, don't you think? But all that work, hoeing, edging, replanting. Digging up lilies, cutting down roses, dividing the iris. Makes my back ache to think of it. The trouble is that once you have a sensational garden you have to keep it up. Letting it go to seed would be a crime against the state."

Sarah, who was trying to keep cucumber slices from slipping out of her sandwich, managed a noncommittal nod.

"I think I like the little ones best. Thalia Cottage, for instance. Thalia, the muse of comedy or merry poetry. Seems appropriate. Harold and Leslie are enjoying their retirement. Especially if there's an audience. All those little references to Larry and Hermione. And doing scenes at the drop of a hat."

"Yes," said Sarah shortly. She did not want to review the dibble scene.

"But the scales have fallen from our eyes," said Justin, vigorously stirring a large quantity of sugar into his tea.

"What do you mean?"

"All the ooing and ahing over the idyllic Cotswold village which isn't so idyllic if women aren't safe in the ladies' loo."

"Oh, that," said Sarah. Another distasteful subject.

But Justin hadn't finished. "How on earth in that crowded pub—Sandi Ouellette said the place was a madhouse—how on earth did a man hide away in the ladies' loo when half the women probably had to pee at the same time. You'd have thought he'd have been nailed right off the bat. Anyway, Sandi, who's our greatest Anglo fan, must think that this England she's so crazy about isn't quite up to snuff."

"One incident shouldn't disillusion her for life," said Sarah. "I heard her chatting away happily today. She apparently loved Harold and Leslie."

"As did we all," said Justin. He helped himself to a third sandwich, bit down, and then looked at his watch. "Good Lord, it's getting late. Do you think there'll be any hot water left? Stacy Daniel spent a good fifty minutes in the shower yesterday. And Amy, our budding Agatha Christie, I thought she'd drowned in the tub. An hour if it was a minute."

Sarah, in her turn, suddenly yearned for a shower, a very hot shower, put down her teacup and stood up. "Right," she said. "Shall we flip to see who gets it first?"

"There are two showers," Justin reminded her. "One at the far end of the hall. We can each try to nab one."

And on these amiable terms the two paid for their tea and headed for the inn.

"So," said Julia when they met on the way down to dinner. "Did you find peace and quiet?"

"I found Justin Rossi and discovered he's as much of a gossip as the rest of the garden tribe. Wonders how a man inserted himself into the ladies' room in the middle of pub rush hour."

"It *is* a bit of a puzzle," admitted Julia. "But maybe he's envious. Wanted to be the molester himself. Vicarious enjoyment."

"What a horrid mind you have. He was perfectly civilized."

"That's what you say because he's your type."

"Wrong," said Sarah lightly. "On this trip I thought I'd look for short, fair, and stout. A complete change."

They went into the dining room together, and Sarah saw that Justin Rossi was in place expending his charm on Edith and Margaret Hopper, who sat on either side. And the Hopper sisters weren't buying it. Pale and rarely speaking, they kept their eyes down, twisted their water goblets, and moved restlessly in their chairs.

However, it was obvious during dinner that many of the garden tour were beginning to bond, to coalesce. Shared experiences, in-jokes, *sotto voce* references to "Toad" Ruggles and "Jack the Slitter," all these acted as integrating forces. The tragic fact of Ellen Trevino had moved yet another step into the background and talk was light and good-humored. Sarah, along with Carter McClure, Julia Clancy, and the Hopper sisters, remained holdouts from the general cheer; Julia choosing to attack Carter on the subject of academic tenure, the Hoppers picking at their food, and Sarah silently enduring several reenactments with a dinner knife of "Is this a dibble I see before me?"

She had reached the point of deciding that there had to be some strand of crazy logic connecting Ellen Trevino, the Kennebunk exit, Logan Airport, the scarf, the sunglasses, the search of Barbara Baxter's and her own bedroom. And the end of this strand must surely be tied to a member, or even several members of the Garden Club. A scary thought. But even more scary, there might be secondary filaments leading to Jack the Slitter, to the breakdown of the Hopper sisters, to the changes in the tour schedule. Even lead—and this was a longshot—to Carter McClure's pulling Henry "Toad" Ruggles out of his hat, as if Carter knew in advance that there would be a vacancy. And Henry himself, so available, so eager to fill Ellen's place. To volunteer his time and money. Henry in his ill-fitting wig.

Sarah, turning these things over and over in her mind, found that an apple tart had appeared as if by magic in front of her. She reached for her fork and picked up a morsel of apple, but before the first mouthful had been swallowed she returned to Henry Ruggles, who sat two seats down, across from her.

Well, the wig aside, Toad Ruggles appeared to be the genuine article. He seemed to know his stuff, his little lectures were larded with the scientific names, he identified plants without recourse to labels, and was able to come up with whether certain plants did well with sun or partial shade, acid or an alkaline soil. Of course, she, Sarah, couldn't have possibly told whether Henry was faking it, but surely some of the garden hotshots in the group would have caught him out if he hadn't known his facts.

In truth, all Henry's reviews had been favorable. Not only his knowledge but his upbeat personality. Not condescending either, because he included the garden beginners such as herself in his discussions. Of course, he was a little clumsy, stumbling hither and yon, but perhaps this was because he was so preoccupied.

Which thought immediately reminded Sarah of Lillian Garth and her plunge down the darkened stairway, but fortunately all the tour excursions took place in broad daylight and a descent into a cellar seemed unlikely. Sarah firmly shoved the problem of Lillian to one side; she hadn't finished with Toad Ruggles.

Returning her attention to Henry, she found him addressing his dinner partners on the subject of the Cotswolds annexation by the powerful Hwicce tribe in early Saxon times. Henry was humorous but unrelenting in the matter of dates and places, and Sarah saw that his listeners had grown heavy-eyed and silent. After all, it had been a long day and the tour members clearly wanted to depart for their rooms.

Doris Lermatov started the exodus. She scraped her chair back, put down her napkin, and said clearly—in the middle of Henry's description of the Hwicce melding into the kingdom of Mercia—"This is all so interesting, Mr. Ruggles, but I'm behind with my postcards. I really must write at least three tonight and then it's to bed. Come on, Amy."

The word "postcards" acted as stimulus and the group rose almost as one murmuring, "Yes, postcards, a letter to finish, my travel diary, good gracious, why it's almost bedtime."

And Henry was left to an audience of Portia McClure and his sponsor, Carter McClure.

"Toad Ruggles," said Sarah to Julia as they reached the top of the staircase, "seems to be the real thing."

"Well, what did you think he was?" demanded Julia.

"I was trying to connect the oddball things that have happened, but I can't fit Henry into the picture."

"Because Henry doesn't fit into any lurid plot you're trying to hatch. He's a last-minute fill-in. If I were you I'd keep an eye on Justin Rossi. I saw him with Barbara Baxter before dinner, and she was giving him quite a piece of her mind. I couldn't hear what she said but it sounded very sharp, and I'm an expert on sharp."

"He was almost fifteen minutes late getting on the bus this morning. Enough to make any tour leader see red."

Julia shrugged. "Perhaps. He does seem rather casual. Now I have my needlepoint to attend to and a book to finish, so I'll say good night. And, if you take my advice, you'll stop—at least for tonight—worrying about, as you put it, oddball things. The only oddballs on this tour are you and I. We're the ones who have no valid reason to be on the trip. The others are probably as suspicious of us as you are of them." And Julia walked away down the hall to her bedroom door, inserted her key in the lock, opened the door and disappeared.

14

THE next day, Tuesday the thirteenth, garden visiting was put on hold. The skies opened, the thunder clapped, the lightening zigzagged, rain and hail spanked against the window, and Henry Ruggles, by permission from Innkeeper Thomas Gage, usurped the parlor for readings from horticultural works, including his own. These were sparsely attended, a fact that did not appear to discomfort the always ebullient Henry.

However, on Wednesday, the fourteenth of June, travel became possible. Uncomfortable but possible. The air was still moist, the sky heavy with intermittent showers and swept by sharp gusts of wind. But, grateful to be out and about, the Garden Club members, protected by Mackintosh, poncho, and cape, clambered aboard their bus. And with the exception of Edith and Margaret Hopper—both with clear plastic boots over their shoes and muffled in plastic coveralls—the group seemed full of cheer and ready to appreciate—no matter how doubtful the weather—those two National Trust treasures, Hidcote Manor Garden in the morning and Kiftsgate Court Gardens in the afternoon.

The trip took them along the A424, and by the time they swung northwest good humor was so rife that song had actually broken out. In French. It had all begun because the irrepressible Henry Ruggles reminded them that they would be in France soon and they should celebrate by singing "The Marseillaise." Unfortunately, only four of the group could handle this request, Henry himself, Julia, and the other two being, to everyone's surprise, Sandi and Fred Ouellette, who ended with a triumphant *"Abreuve nos sillons."*

"I'm not completely illiterate," Sandi announced to the listeners. "Fred and I do speak French. Where do you think the name 'Ouellette' came from? Montréal, that's where."

"Chalk one up for Sandi," Sarah told her aunt after the singing had subsided.

"She may have her uses after all," replied Julia. "Five days from now we'll be in France and I haven't stuck to my homework."

"Et bien," said Sarah, pointing to the rainstreaked bus window, *"ce vent et cette pluie sont très miserables, n'est-ce pas?"* And then with no reply, she added, *"Est-ce que vous écoutez?"*

"Yes, I'm listening," said Julia, "but the wind is going down—*le vent est tombé.* We'll start tomorrow. Everything in French. Or Italian. *Quand nous arriverons à Cambridge,* because," she added, "I expect the Cambridge Botanic Garden to be rather dull. A good chance to practice."

❦

"Pull them in, that's what I say," announced Mike Laaka. "They'll be heading for France in a few days and then, for God's sake, Italy. All over the blessed map. And where they need to be is where we can lay a finger on them. Or handcuffs." Mike thumped the desk in front of him for emphasis.

Mike, like some sort of Nordic warrior, fair hair ruffled, cheeks red, paced the narrow confines of Sergeant George Fitt's office—a gray cell in the CID annex of the Maine State Police barracks in Thomaston. Alex McKenzie, a more contained character, sat listening on one of George's folding metal chairs.

"Mike has a point," said George, who did not often concede that Mike had anything in his head beyond misbegotten froth. George was the by-the-book sort of a detective gifted with a fishy glance—this enhanced by thick rimless glasses—and a steel trap for a mouth; a man who, even if dressed in tiger skin or a clown suit, would not be mistaken for anything but a criminal investigator.

Mike pressed his advantage. "Those birds, the ones on the tour, are tied up with Ellen Trevino like no one else is. Everything she did in May had to do with getting ready for the trip. I've asked around the university, around the town, and everyone says the same thing. Not what you'd call a social or a sexy type. Everyone liked her, but no one seemed to have known her that well. She was, what's the expression, 'very respected.' "

"A real professional," Alex put in. "Lived for her job."

Mike nodded. "Yeah, that's what I'm saying. And her job this spring was all tied up with this goddamn Garden Club."

"Yes," said George. "We would like them in the flesh," a remark that made Alex think of cannibals. George tipped his chair back and put the tips of his fingers together and frowned. "But as of today we haven't any solid evidence to link anyone to the murder. Just the connection of the trip itself. I've talked to the investigating team in the Kennebunk area, and they're scrambling to come up with something tangible. The dibble, for instance. They've made a positive ID for Dr. Trevino's blood on that. Which we expected since a quick washing couldn't eliminate every blood cell. And we're working on the soap."

Alex, who had been staring at a wall calendar depicting a sunset view of the Maine State Prison, jerked his head up. "Soap?"

"The dibble," explained George patiently, "was washed. Soap and water. Not detergent, soap. So, unless the murderer was carrying around a jug of water and a bar of soap, we think that he—or she—stopped off at some restroom facility. Gas station or one of the turnpike rest stops. The lab's working on identifying the soap, and when they do we've a chance of nailing down the washroom it came from. And if it's a gas station, there's a chance someone remembered a person whose clothes may have been a mess. Stained. Most stations keep their rest rooms locked up so you have to ask for the key. The killer must have wanted to wash up, maybe change his clothes, his shoes. Get rid of the works. Well, the CID down in Kennebunk will hit the entire area on and around the pike. Just as soon as the make of soap is nailed down.

"Don't count on bloodstained clothes," put in Mike. "Anyone careful enough to wrap the body in a plastic tarp may be in a coverall, a raincoat, a slicker, or a whole rainsuit."

"A rainsuit would be pretty conspicuous," said Alex.

"Remember," said Mike, "it was raining that day. You ought to know. You drove in it."

Alex shifted in his seat, frowned, trying to remember. The metal chair didn't encourage thought, and the small desk fan was only circulating warm, dusty air. "It wasn't raining the whole way," he said. "It'd been overcast earlier, but I don't think it started until around the time we hit the New Hampshire border."

"But," persisted Mike, "someone in a raincoat wouldn't look funny if it was about to rain."

Alex looked dubious. "I don't know many people—except Sarah's grandmother—who put on rain clothes in advance of the rain."

"Let it go," said George. "In the meantime"—here he looked at Alex reprovingly—"there's that head scarf that someone did wash. Too often. One washing wouldn't have been so bad. But all that sudsing and rinsing. Well, the lab hasn't found blood yet, but their people are practically unweaving the thing to try and come up with anything—fibers, hairs, dirt. Unfortunately, it was kicking around at the airport, in the plane, in Sarah's pocket or her luggage until it was mailed."

"You'd think," put in Mike, "that after all this time, all the things Sarah has been mixed up with, she'd have learned something about evidence. Not to mess with it."

Alex rose in defense of his absent wife. "She wasn't thinking about evidence when she first found it."

George looked from a series of doodles, squares and triangles he'd drawn on a file card. He pointed his pen at Alex and clicked it. "We'll wait and see what the evidence team turns up. For now, ask Sarah to try to retrieve those sunglasses as soon as possible. Since they turned up with the scarf they may prove useful."

Alex nodded and decided to change the subject. "Can you tell from what you've got so far who could have gone through the whole process of trailing Ellen?—she must have been trailed. Or had set up a meeting place? Who then had the time to kill her, leave the Kennebunk exit, reverse directions, and dump the body at the Scarborough exit, find a washroom, clean the dibble, wash his hands, change clothes, and somewhere dump Ellen's luggage. God, that takes a hell of a lot of time, and if you happen to be a member of the garden tour, you have to make that British Airways flight at Logan, getting there two hours in advance for passport and baggage checking. Driving there would be dicey what with the summer traffic gridlock, construction areas, so flying to Logan is a must. From Portland, most likely, because the other airports are too far away from the body dumping site."

George held up his hand. "Think about charter planes, small airports—which we're checking."

"Back to the car," said Mike. "The killer's car. The killer didn't arrive at the Kennebunk exit on foot. Where is it? Was it a private car, a rental, or maybe stolen?"

George sighed, a small squeezed sort of sigh, the sort of exhalation that told Mike to shut up and stop pushing things.

"We're working on it. Now let's back up and look at what we're sure of."

"Like Ellen Trevino being dead," Mike put in.

George gave him a sour look. "Yes. The lab is fixing the time she was killed sometime between about nine A.M. the morning of June sixth to about two-thirty of that afternoon. For what it's worth, the stomach contents show she had breakfast but no lunch. The rain began on the southern section of the Maine pike sometime between three and three-thirty. Since the ground under the body was dry, it means Ellen Trevino was killed before it began raining."

"Okay," said Alex, "but the murderer has to dump his own car, switch to a limo or a rental or have a friend drive him to the airport. Or he—or she, I'm neglecting the possibility of a lady murderer—may have done in Ellen in a rental. Then turned in the rental minus, of course, that plastic sheet."

George turned a page on his notebook and then frowned at Alex. "Don't rush me. You're acting like Mike. Let's take the whole day of June sixth. Start with you, Alex, Sarah, and Julia Clancy."

"Some day," said Mike, "we can hope to find Sarah as the chief suspect. It'll make a nice change. But we've got some others off the hook. The Hopper sisters and the Ouellettes."

George nodded. "Right. We've got Alex making rounds at the hospital, Sarah at the English office, Julia on her farm. The Hoppers spent the morning with family members. Sandi had her hair done in the A.M., lunch with a friend; Fred spent the morning with a casket salesman, then worked preparing a body. His assistant vouches for him. The Hoppers and Ouellettes took the US AIR 4:05 to Logan."

Alex stood up, stretched, looked out the window at the bumper-to-bumper Route 1 traffic into Thomaston and sat down again. "Were all the rest of the tour racing loose around Maine?"

"More or less," said George. "Here you are, one by one. Stacy Daniel had a rental Buick Century from Avis. She'd flown into Portland from Boston on Sunday for a bank branch meeting on Monday. On Tuesday the sixth she claims to have driven north from Portland to Freeport to do some last-minute shopping. Said she paid cash for a pair of walking shoes at some outlet, put them on, and threw away the box. And the receipt. Then drove the car back to the Portland Jetport, turned it in, and caught the 5:05 Delta to Logan."

"And her car?" prompted Alex.

"The next person to rent the Buick was a family of four driving to northern Québec for a three-week tour. We're trying to trace it, but nothing so far. We've a problem with rental cars. After they're turned in, the vehicle is completely cleaned, deodorized, vacuumed, washed, which makes it hard on the lab."

"And get this," said Mike. "Justin Rossi—he lives in Concord, Mass—gave a talk on family law to a U. Maine law school class Friday. Flew into Portland that A.M. and picked up a Hertz Ford Sable. After the lecture he spent the weekend plus Monday at the Samoset Resort in Rockland. Started south on Tuesday the sixth and turned in the car at Logan at around five-fifteen. And, wouldn't you know, the next renter was a mother with a sick kid who puked all over the seats and floor, so not only has it had the usual cleaning but it's been practically sterilized."

"What about the morning and noon hours for Rossi," said Alex impatiently. He had decided that if there had to be a villain, it might as well be Rossi, the man Sarah claimed looked like him and seemed to be so agreeably literary and companionable.

Mike looked cheered. "Some holes there. Rossi said he drove down from Rockland in the A.M. and stopped at a diner near Portsmouth for lunch—doesn't remember the name of the place—and said that he had time to kill . . ."

"Or Ellen Trevino to kill," said Alex.

"Yeah, or that. Anyway, after he made it to Massachusetts he left the freeway and drove around. Stopped to watch a high school girls softball game. In Amesbury, I think it was. So what I say, is that Rossi doesn't have any kids or a wife or a girlfriend . . ."

"As far as we know," said George.

"So maybe he likes high-school girls. Maybe Ellen Trevino reminded him of a high-school girl. She was pretty young looking." He looked about at two disapproving faces. "Well, it's just an idea," he added.

George scowled. "Mike, watch your mouth and don't go throwing those ideas around. Rossi's a lawyer and there's something called defamation of character.

"Get on with it," said Alex, always irritated by the often acrimonious Mike Laaka–George Fitts dynamics.

"The Lermatovs," said George, "Amy and the mother, spent the early morning packing—the only confirmation is for each other. Then Mrs. Lermatov's sister, Elsie, drove them to Portland. Sister got out at the Portland Museum of Art and Mrs. Lermatov borrowed her car to do—and I'm quoting—some looking around with her daughter. Picked up sister Elsie about three who drove them to the airport in time to catch the 5:05 Delta to Boston. To think that mother and daughter zipped back to the Kennebunk exit and killed Ellen is stretching it beyond belief."

"Next," said Mike, "is our eager-beaver tour director, Barbara Baxter. She spent the very early A.M. at her agency—Whirlaway Tours in Yarmouth—picked up a Budget Ford Taurus there and met a client for coffee around nine-forty-five in Brunswick—an art tour being arranged—left saying she wanted to hit Freeport. God, just try to track someone in that town knee-deep in people looking for outlet bargains. Did she get there? Well, she claims she got a new big suitcase for the trip—the kind with wheels. Paid cash. Natch. Why can't we have a suspect who uses a credit card?"

"Not a suspect yet," observed George.

"Anyway," Mike went on, "Barbara claims she went from Freeport to the jetport in time to catch her late afternoon Delta flight along with the Lermatovs, Stacy Daniel, and Rossi. And no one has remarked that any of the tour group on that flight looked anxious, disheveled, or hurried as if they'd scrambled to make the flight."

"The 5:05," said Alex trying to keep the details straight in his head."

"Yeah," said Mike. "And you'll love this. Baxter's Budget rental has been rented twice since she turned it in. First was a one-day by a man with two Samoyed dogs who shed white fur all over—the Budget people went crazy cleaning it. The second rental was a man driving to New Jersey who got himself drunk and totaled the thing near Trenton. Hit a tree. A one-person accident with no personal property damage, so no legal case impending, and the car was cannibalized for parts and is being sold as junk—God knows where."

"What we have," said George, who liked neat summaries, "is the fact that the Lermatovs—who are very doubtful—Justin Rossi, Stacy Daniel, and Barbara Baxter were all loose in the area, had the time, maybe the opportunity, to pull off a late-morning or early-afternoon murder."

"Wait up," said Alex. "You've forgotten the tour grouch, Carter McClure. And his wife, Portia, who is not a grouch—though being married to Carter must be wearing her down."

George consulted his notebook. "Portia McClure seems to be in the clear. A long dentist appointment and a luncheon meeting. The History Department people remember Carter throwing his weight around in the early morning. But he left around ten. He met Portia at two in Wiscasset—driving his own car. They left the car at a garage and took an airport limousine all the way to Logan. The McClure car is being checked and so far is clean."

Mike shook his head. "Carter would have to have sprouted wings to get to Kennebunk and nail Ellen. And get back to meet Portia. But he could just have done it."

"Bad temper doesn't always add up to murder," said George. "I've uncovered a lot about Carter McClure. He's crotchety and difficult but he gives a lot of time helping students. Tutoring in the summer. Helping them with scholarship applications."

"Don't spoil it," said Mike. "I love to hate people like that. Especially the snooty Bowmouth College types."

Alex stood up. "Okay, so you'll leave the garden tour in peace unless some direct evidence from the tour members turns up. Or a clear set of strange prints turn up in Ellen's Subaru."

"Guess what," said George. He raised his eyebrows and peered at the two men through his rimless glasses.

"I'll bite," said Alex.

"Prints from Barbara Baxter. All over the Subaru window—passenger side—and the dash, and the passenger seat. Also hairs that match some we picked up at Barbara Baxter's Whirl-away Tour office."

"Whoa up," shouted Mike. "What are you doing sitting there? Bring her in. Put a net over her head. Call up the Brits and nail her down. Christ, George, all this crap about rental cars and flight times and Baxter's prints are in the Subaru. Hey, case over. Let me outta here."

"Except," said George smoothly, his expression benign, "we know that Barbara Baxter visited Ellen Trevino three days before the trip to go over the trip details. Not only that but Ellen drove Barbara out to lunch and to visit a greenhouse. In her Subaru." And George reached for the telephone and began hitting numbers.

"Jeezus, I hate that guy," said Mike as he and Alex left the office. "Boy, did I ever bite."

"And you're always saying George has no sense of humor," observed Alex. "Actually, I think he's quite funny."

15

HENRY Ruggles stood in the entrance courtyard of Hidcote Manor Garden, his umbrella unfurled against the spattering rain, his voice raised against the rustle of raincoats. He was never one to shorten a lecture because of foul weather and he was now launched into a consideration of the vines that decorated the courtyard walls. He extolled the wisteria, "Such a PROFUSION of growth," lauded the scarlet Cape figwort *(Phygelius capensis)*, examined the potato vine *(Solanum crispum* 'Glasnevin'), while all the members of the Midcoast Garden Club listened, took notes, and admired.

All the members, that is, but Julia Clancy, who made two restless tours of the courtyard, pulled her olive-drab riding slicker closer around her shoulders, and moved off impatiently in the direction of the garden and toward a great stretch of lawn.

Her niece, Sarah, remained a damp physical presence on the fringe of the group. But her mind was elsewhere, fixed on the dubious party with whom she was associated. No, not associated, trapped, chained to them. Eyes only for them. I suppose, she told herself grimly, that from stewing on the edge of events, I'm focused. Completely focused on Ellen Trevino and her death by that most horrible of gardening implements, the dibble.

The morning progressed, the rain eased and then ceased altogether and a certain brightening in the sky promised future sun. Even to this favorable omen Sarah remained oblivious. Still tightly buttoned into her raincoat, she squelched along on the sodden grass and pebble paths from one splendid planting to the next, from the Pine Garden, along the Rose Borders through Camellia Corner, and down the Long Walk and back through paths and avenues and corners of banked floral color and saw nothing of the periwinkles, the day lilies, the polygonums, the poppies, the phloxes, the roses.

Instead, she considered the homicidal personality, the violent opportunist, the psychopath, the impulse killer, the revenge seeker. The gold digger, the drug-crazed. The defender of some dark and gloomy secret. The hater of Ellen Trevino.

Be impartial, she ordered herself. Everyone guilty unless proved otherwise. She wished, almost for the first time of her life, to talk to Sergeant George Fitts. He would, by now, know which persons had spent a harmless day in the company of reliable witnesses. Well, she couldn't call Alex now from the middle of a garden so she would have to rehash all those odd and unaccountable events of the last few days and see what came bubbling to the surface. So, after setting aside only Alex, Aunt Julia, and herself as innocent, she tried to fit the cloak of murderer over the shoulders of her other companions.

In many cases it was a terrible fit. Take Amy Lermatov. Sarah eyed the girl, standing, notebook in hand, ahead on the path next to a clump of ornamental grass. There she was in her worn bluejeans, her rumpled wind parka tied around her waist. And hadn't she been wearing that Decomposers rock band t-shirt for days? But as a suspect? Forget it. Scratch Amy. Scratch her mother. If the two of them made up a murder team, then she, Sarah, would jump into the nearest and thorniest rosebush.

How about Portia McClure? Sensible, kind, expert on herbal gardens and compost. Not a murdering type, but was she the protector of a hot-tempered husband? Well, you never could tell about the loyalty of wives, so put Portia on hold along with Carter.

Here her ruminations were broken by a call for her from Henry Ruggles to come and admire the topiary doves in the White Garden.

He stood in the center of his group, exactly as Portia had described him, a benevolent Pickwick—not quite wearing gaiters but with a corduroy hat which perched on top of his wig. He aimed the point of his umbrella directly at Sarah and then moved it to indicate the closely clipped green doves.

"Miss Deane, isn't it? I've been watching you because I do have eyes in the back of my head. I've had the feeling that perhaps flowers aren't the CLOSEST things to your heart. Perhaps you are a shrubbery person. You like the formality of green walls and verges. Or trees, a STRUCTURED wilderness? A creative tangle?"

Sarah, coming to with a start, told Henry that she admired the topiary and the garden walks and all the flowers, but she was such a beginner that she had no specialty.

"A generalist," said Henry. "The very BEST way to begin. Then choose. But these topiary doves are charming." He flourished his umbrella a second time at them, and Sarah decided that Henry must have concluded that she was a complete fool and must be appealed to on the simplest level: bird shapes. However, she managed a smile, and Henry, with the satisfied air of a teacher of the horticulturaly challenged, returned to the campanulas and the phlox.

Left again to herself she considered Edith and/or Margaret Hopper. An *Arsenic and Old Lace* duo, but more lethal than those two old biddies because the dibble was on a different scale than poisoned elderberry wine. Certainly something was eating away at the two. From being quietly moist-eyed, they now seemed to have entered into an almost manic state, interrupting Henry Ruggles in the Poppy Garden in the middle of his explanation of *Hydrangea aspera villosa*, and giving in to sudden bursts of high-pitched laughter. Okay, say one or both had done in Ellen (whom they hardly knew) for some arcane purpose, would there have been a period of fulfillment, of disassociation, and then, whoosh, when remembrance and guilty conscience kicked in—wouldn't they have started to come apart at the seams? After all, Margaret and Edith belonged to that stern generation whose upbringing included a heavy dose of conscience.

And now Sarah, following the McClures into the Bathing Pool Garden, tilted her head to one side and assumed a thoughtful look in an effort to seem as if she were listening to Henry Ruggles. He had relaxed into his raconteur mode and was relating how pools and fountains—all bodies of water—made him TERRIBLY nervous because he had been tossed into the Severn as a child and told to swim. "I was never Frog Ruggles." He laughed.

Sarah joined in the amused response, but then sternly returned to what she thought of as top-rank suspects. Stacy Daniel, the lion woman, beautiful and bored; Barbara Baxter, dethroned tour leader; and last, the family lawyer, the Alex McKenzie lookalike, Justin Rossi.

And here Sarah stopped being objective. If it had to be someone, why not Stacy? Stacy had made only the faintest attempts to meld with the group, to chat it up, to even look interested. She could almost picture the lovely Stacy swathed in protective plastic, her hand closed around the dibble.

"Sarah, I might as well be traveling with a lamp post."

Aunt Julia. Where had she come from?

"For heaven's sake," scolded her aunt, "take that look off your face. You look as if you've been tasting vinegar."

"Vinegar? Well, something like it." Sarah looked about in confusion at surrounding walls of a courtyard. "Where are we?"

"We are leaving. This is where we came in. And the rain has stopped so you can unbutton your raincoat. We're going to have the sandwiches the inn packed for us and then go on to Kiftsgate. Too much of a good thing, I'm beginning to think."

Fortunately for Sarah's state of mind she was abandoned after lunch by Julia, who declared that today she wanted to be left alone to do the gardens by herself. She would see Kiftsgate

Court in her own way. There were times when the elderly need space.

This was a relief. Today Julia reminded her niece of a yellow jacket—a lot of buzz and a nasty bite. Now she could pace unnoticed behind the group while Henry exclaimed over the *Salvia candelabra*, and *Rodgersia pinnata* "Superba"; while Doris Lermatov hung over the peonies, while Sandi Ouellette took pictures of the White Sunk Garden, its fountain, its hydrangeas; while the rest, invigorated by lunch, exclaimed and pointed.

For the first few gardens Sarah kept her brain in neutral and then returned to the hunt. And to Justin Rossi.

It was hard to accept him as the murderer. Men who looked like Alex didn't drive dibbles into women's chests. Did they? And today Justin wore a tweed cap and was good-looking enough to carry it off. The hat suggested to Sarah a rather engaging eccentricity. Not many Americans could have worn such a thing without hearing a British snicker behind their backs. But Justin could. Of course, there was no rule that said murderers couldn't be personable. Sarah remembered once flinging herself on the broad chest of one and crying out something like, "Thank heavens you're here!" Okay, so Mr. Rossi could be charming and Ellen Trevino was probably not totally immune to charm. Put Rossi on the doubtful list.

Ditto Barbara Baxter. Double that for Stacy Daniel.

Sarah came to a halt above a steep zigzag path that led down to a lower level through rockery and ground plants. She needed a moment to herself to consider Suspect Number One. Stacy Daniel fitted the new and popular type of murderer because wherever you looked—fiction, the tube, the movies—beautiful women who power walk and appear on magazine covers and work for banks seemed to be much in demand as killers. Yes, Stacy had all the requirements. Now all that was needed was to discover motive and opportunity.

"He's such a stumblebum, a real klutz," said a voice. Stacy Daniel. "He's going to be hurt and really he's quite a nice old guy."

Sarah gave a start and found her first choice for homicide

165

standing at her side. Stacy. Looking today particularly lovely in a peach linen shirt and a fawn cotton skirt, a rust-colored rain coat open and hanging off her shoulders.

"Who's a klutz?" Sarah asked, trying to rearrange her thoughts. It was hard to banish the scenario of Stacy she was working on—Stacy standing by Ellen Trevino's Subaru, leaning into the driver's window, asking Ellen to join her for the ride to Logan.

"Henry. Toad Ruggles," explained Stacy. "He falls over his own feet, going down steps. God, he even stumbles going *up-hill.* I'm glad he's not showing us the White Cliffs of Dover or we'd be scraping him off the beach."

Sarah made an effort to be responsive, which was difficult because she'd really put a lot of feeling into sticking Stacy with Ellen's death. And now here she was acting human, even sympathetic. Liking Henry and wanting to help him keep on his feet.

"Henry is a little on the clumsy side," she murmured.

"Clumsy!" exclaimed Stacy. "Why he needs a walker. Or better shoes. Something. But does he know his stuff. I mean, I guess he does, although you couldn't prove it by me, but that old crank Carter McClure shuts up when he talks and everyone else seems to be wowed by him."

"Henry Ruggles does put on quite a show," agreed Sarah. "Ellen wouldn't have been so dramatic but," she added loyally, "I think she was the real expert. Henry may be more flash and talk."

"Well, I never thought Ellen Trevino came off as a really warm personality," said Stacy.

Look who's talking, thought Sarah. Aloud, she said, "Ellen was very, very serious and very shy."

"If you say so. But anyhow, I sort of like this old coot Toad Ruggles and I hope . . ."

"What do you hope?" It was Barbara Baxter, wearing a sort of waterproof running suit which, judging from her heightened color and wet brow, must have turned into a sweat box. She shook her head at the two women. "I've been looking for you both. I've just tracked Mrs. Clancy down and here you are. It's getting late and everyone wants to have tea here at the Kiftsgate tea room. But Mr. Ruggles thought we should all see the lower garden first. He particularly asked for you, Sarah, because he thinks you'd like the Scotch firs and the Mother and Child statue because you weren't really a garden person. So, if you could . . ."

But Barbara's sentence was drowned by a sudden cry from below. A sort of surprised yelp. A pause. And then muffled shout. "Help, help!"

Stacy and Sarah and Barbara—like some sort of relay team sprang into action, Barbara running first, then Stacy, followed by Sarah. Down the zigzag path, down along a wide flight of stone steps and to the edge of a clump of people. Sarah falling at the lower step and skinning her knee on a particularly unforgiving rock. She climbed painfully to her feet, ran ahead, and charged into a melee of people surrounding a swimming pool. Familiar people most of them. Her own tour group plus a small array of strangers all brought together by the cries and a joined sense of consternation.

Sarah grabbed Margaret Hopper by the arm. "Who? What's happened?" she shouted.

Margaret gestured frantically. "Henry Ruggles. In the pool. He fell in. They're trying to get him out. Sandi Ouellette and Mr. Rossi. And I don't think Henry can swim. He keeps going down. Sandi's diving."

Sarah pushed past her impatiently. Three figures in the pool. No, two figures and a head. A head that kept bobbing up and down like a large smooth soccer ball. Henry? No, it couldn't be. But it was Sandi Ouellette and Justin both hanging on to a pair of arms. Sarah without thinking of what she meant to do kicked off her shoes and threw off her raincoat.

And felt a restraining hand. "It's okay. They've got him. They're swimming him in," said Doris Lermatov, appearing at Sarah's side. "We were all looking at the Ha-ha and we heard a splash."

"Henry?" said Sarah puzzled. "But that's not Henry."

"Without his wig," said Doris. "There, he's out. Good for Sandi. I'll never say another word about her. She just dove in and had hold of him before any of us made a move. Justin Rossi dove in, too, but Sandi really saved him."

Sarah, feeling useless, watched the aftermath of Henry Ruggles's immersion. He sat, wigless, on the edge of the pool, and coughed and choked and gasped but in a remarkably short time pronounced himself able to stand, to walk, and to look forward to tea. He even managed a wan smile when presented with a dripping wig, which looked for all the world like a small drowned fur-bearing animal.

In no time, towels appeared, blankets were produced, the ladies of the National Trust having enlisted the help of the Kiftsgate housekeeper. Then bundled up, the trio, disappeared into the area marked toilets, reappeared somewhat drier and the Garden Club clambered on their bus, having agreed that tea back at the Shearing would be the wisest choice. Barbara, with Henry temporarily out of action, took charge of the loading, the thanking, and promising the return of the towels and blankets.

But just as the bus was about to make the turn out of the car park, Portia McClure called stop. "Has anyone seen my sunglasses? I've lost them. Somewhere by the pool. I had them before that. The ones Sarah gave me on the plane."

"No," said Barbara firmly. "We must get Mr. Ruggles back. He'll need a hot bath and we can't go looking around for the glasses. They weren't prescription, were they?"

"No," admitted Portia. "And you're quite right, Barbara. I'll pick up another pair tomorrow."

And the bus rumbled into life, turned the corner, and headed south in the direction of High Roosting.

And Sarah was left to contemplate the shambles of her murder scenario. Stacy Daniel had not pushed Henry Ruggles into the pool. Nor had Barbara Baxter. And that left who? Carter McClure, but he had sponsored Henry. Why try to drown him? No, who it really left—face it—was Justin Rossi. Justin, whose rescue efforts did not come into play until Sandi Ouellette had Henry almost in her grasp. Sarah felt almost actively ill.

Because if she had ever been sure of something, she was sure that Henry Ruggles, never too sure on his feet, had been pushed. Tipped, shoved, nudged into the Kiftsgate swimming pool. As Lillian Garth must have been pushed down the cellar steps. And Ellen had been stabbed. It was so simple. Henry had just made his fear of pools and rivers and ponds only too clear. Opportunity offered and Justin Rossi had struck.

It was a subdued group of garden fans who began the return trip to the Shearing Inn. After all, Sarah reflected, it had been a near miss with Henry. Now, in a seat ahead of Sarah and Julia, he sat, blanketed, a sodden wig on his knees, his hands clutching a thermos of tea. Next to him sat Portia McClure. Sarah, listening to her reassuring murmurs, decided that if anyone could restore Henry to his usual cheerful self it was Portia.

Across the way, also wrapped, sat Sandi Ouellette next to her Fred. Fred, beaming, was explaining to all who could listen that Sandi had a job teaching Red Cross Lifesaving at the Y and how lucky it was that Sandi was so alert. With a number of other visitors around chattering their heads off, no one heard Henry fall in. He hadn't, apparently, made much of a splash, and beyond crying out for help he hadn't struggled. Panic, Fred supposed. Well, Sandi beat them all to it, did a flat dive right into the pool—you know the kind of dive where you keep the victim in sight—they teach it in lifesaving.

Here Sandi interrupted, saying that no one wanted to know every little detail, but she was overruled. Everyone did want to hear it all again. And so Fred described the whole rescue operation and concluded with a few words on drowning victims—victims he had, most sadly, to deal with in the line of his profession.

"Cosmetic problems like you wouldn't believe. The skin tone has to be completely restored. Petechial hemorrhages, cyanosis are real challenges, and it takes a real craftsman and endless patience, but when you see the family's faces, how relieved they are when they see their loved one, well, it's worth every extra minute spent."

This sobering thought brought an end to the general desire for details and the listeners subsided.

"I think," said Julia in a low voice to Sarah, "that I'm going to have to apologize on two scores."

Sarah looked at her aunt with surprise. Apologies did not usually play a part in Julia Clancy's repertoire.

"First," said Julia, "I'm sorry that I suggested Sandi was a lightweight. She may not be an intellectual, but she went into action like a pro. She would have made a good rider."

Sarah nodded. Julia had just paid Sandi the highest of compliments. "Maybe she does ride," she said. "Anything's possible, and if we wait long enough, we'll probably find out that Sandi has won the Pulitzer Prize for history."

"My second apology," said Julia, "has to do with your suspicions about our traveling friends. They may have some merit. It's as if there's a plot to eliminate all the tour directors. Except Barbara. Leave the whole tour to her direction. Though I can't for the life of me imagine why."

Sarah shook her head. "Barbara was on the upper-level garden with me when Henry went in the water. And Stacy Daniel was there, too, talking about how clumsy he was. Stacy apparently has a sneaking fondness for Henry."

"Oh dear," said Julia. "That shoots my Barbara theory."

"And my Stacy theory. I'd just settled it in my head that she was a cold, calculating bitch with no interest in the trip or in anyone here and then she turns up and goes all warm and fuzzy."

"Which leaves . . ."

"I know. Justin Rossi. And he dove in when he saw Sandi in the water. Had to cover himself."

For a while both women were silent, and Sarah turned for relief to the window to view the passing scene: sheep, sheep, and more sheep, moving slowly along a rolling pasture, their woolly backs showing almost pure yellow from the light of the low sun. Sarah glared at them. She was sick of sheep. Cows, too. And she was sick of gardens. She turned back to Julia. "Of course, it's possible that Henry fell in the pool all by himself. Heaven knows he's been stumbling all over his feet since he arrived."

"Yes, I know it's possible."

"But not probable?"

"Probable if it hadn't been for Lillian. And Ellen."

Another period of silence. For Sarah another stare out the bus window. Stupid little houses with thatched roofs. Unreal. Too cute. Too clean. Altogether too perfect. She thought that today she'd rather look at the slums of Liverpool and Birmingham. Or backcountry Maine farms, ramshackle buildings, tire swings, old cars rusting under laundry lines.

Then, as the bus entered the outer layers of High Roosting, Julia clutched Sarah's knee.

"Ouch," said Sarah. "I fell on it. Talk about being clumsy. I'll be the next one to fall down something."

"Never mind your knee," said Julia with a noticeable lack of sympathy. "I think I figured out what's wrong with Margaret and Edith. It came in sort of a flash. I have these insights sometimes. Like suddenly knowing exactly why a horse has gone lame. Anyway, it's all perfectly simple and accounts for all the Hopper symptoms."

"You have my full attention," said Sarah.

"Income tax," said Julia triumphantly.

"What!"

"Income tax. They forgot to file their quarterly return. Or had word that they owed from last year. Took improper deductions. Or hid some little bit of income. Something like that. So they got a nasty call or letter from the IRS. No, wait," as Sarah began to protest. "Listen, to me. The IRS can be absolutely brutal. Those two women are probably frightened to death by monsters like the IRS. And maybe they have fudged a little on their returns for years. A sort of game. And they've been caught."

Sarah looked doubtful.

"It fits," said Julia. "Think about it. They won't say why they're upset. They'd have told us if it had been a family tragedy."

"You know," said Sarah thoughtfully, "you may have a point. And they're pretty conservative, so I have another idea. Maybe some loved grandson or granddaughter has come out of the closet. Or been caught with drugs. Picked up as a hooker."

"I like the IRS idea because they seem to be recovering."

"Overdoing it I'd say. They were babbling back at Kiftsgate."

"Just listen. At first they were upset, couldn't eat, wouldn't join in. Then they pull themselves together. Realize they can't do anything right now and that they have to go on with the tour. But can't tell anyone because they're so ashamed. Sarah, those two are my generation, and, believe me, half my friends live in mortal fear of the IRS. It's the twentieth-century bogie man."

"You mean they might have been audited?"

"Exactly. And found wanting. And threatened. Picturing themselves in some minimum security prison. Poor dears. We must try and have more sympathy but not let on we've found out."

"If we have. I still think some family member may have done something unmentionable—in their eyes."

"Trust your old Aunt Julia. Now, here we are. I'll get in line for the bathrooms and save you a place while you're calling Alex to find out what's going on at home."

Sarah got up from her seat, offered her aunt a hand as she rose creakily to her feet.

"Damn arthritis," said Julia. "I feel like a rusty machine."

"Get in a hot bath," said Sarah. "I'll go and call Alex. I almost dread it. Everytime I've called he's had worse news. All we need to hear right now is that we're in the middle of a giant consortium of horticultural racketeers."

16

ALEX answered on the second ring.

"Are you sitting next to it," said Sarah.

"I'm living next to it," said Alex. His voice came loud and clear, almost in the next room. "It's a mix of worrying about you and covering for a couple of other internists, and then being on tap for Mike whenever he feels like unloading on me."

"I want to unload on you, too," said Sarah. "I miss our intimate little pillow talks about blood types and fingerprints and those nice details about lividity."

"You're not getting yourself out on a limb, are you?" Alex sounded anxious. And with good reason. To his certain knowledge, Sarah had spent a fair amount of time out on a number of limbs.

"To make it short, I'm centered. Focused. I feel right down to my fingertips that someone in our friendly little garden tour killed Ellen. Maybe pushed Lillian Garth into the cellar."

"Have you just come to a boil or has something happened?"

"You could say that." And Sarah gave Alex a thumbnail

sketch of Henry Ruggles dip in the Kiftsgate swimming pool and ended by saying that Aunt Julia had become a believer.

"So, if you do find that Ellen was killed by some insane vagrant on the Maine Turnpike, let me know right away. Otherwise what Julia and I want to know is who's safe? Who we should sit next to in the bus. Who we should share a sandwich with."

"It's not a joke."

Sarah relented. "No, I know it isn't. But tell me, hasn't George figured out who *couldn't* have killed Ellen that day? And Alex, please hurry. I've got the front hall to myself now because everyone's scrambling for the bathrooms. But any minute I'll have someone breathing over my shoulder."

Alex became businesslike. "Okay. Here it is. Accounted for are Sandi and Fred Ouellette, Portia McClure, Margaret and Edith Hopper, and most probably the two Lermatovs."

"What about Carter McClure?

"A very tight squeeze if he did it. He'd have had to drive well over the speed limit both ways and spend almost no time on body disposal and washing up."

For a moment Sarah was silent and then, bracing herself, she said, "Thanks. That's helpful. And now, I want to know a couple of things. Have you got a pencil?"

"I always have a pencil. Do you love me or do you just say so because I can come up with these exciting details?"

"I love you and exciting details. And I'm mad as hell about Ellen. Also I'm blessed—or is it cursed—with a nose like an aardvark when it comes to weird things like these garden tour experts being done in?"

"Don't you mean a nose like an anteater? And Lillian Garth's doing well, and Henry Ruggles is okay, isn't he? He's just wet."

"Thanks to Sandi Ouellette he's just wet. Anyway, listen. First, find out, or squeeze it out of Mike, if there's anything nasty in anyone's background. Anything. Has anyone got a record, been out on parole, got caught selling pot? Had violent scenes? Run a shady business? Barbara Baxter's travel bureau, for instance?"

"You don't want much do you?"

"And," Sarah persisted, "see if there's anything odd in Margaret or Edith Hopper's background."

"But they've been cleared for Ellen's murder."

"Yes, I know," said Sarah impatiently. "But something's going on with them. Aunt Julia thinks they're tax dodgers."

"You're not serious?"

"She is. Thinks they've had word that they're being audited. Me, I think someone in the family's done something they can't handle. Listen, I've got to go. Someone wants the phone. I'll call you tomorrow. We're going to be somewhere around Cambridge."

Alex had just time to call, "Be careful," before Sarah was confronted by the man behind her.

"Some people," said a man with a German accent who stood tapping his finger on the telephone table, "do not have any idea that they take so much time when other people wait."

"And a good evening to you," said Sarah, hanging up the receiver and heading for the stairs.

An hour later found Aunt Julia knocking on Sarah's door. Which was opened, revealing Julia dressed for dinner in her all-purpose paisley, a conspiratorial expression on her face.

"I think," said Julia, "I had the last of the hot water. The tap ran quite cold at the end."

"It ran entirely cold for me," said Sarah, who, shivering, had added a cardigan to her green silk jumper.

"Never mind. I have a plan. And I've memorized everyone's room number. So whatever I do at dinner, go along with it."

"Does it involve missing dinner?"

"Part of dinner. But the cause is just."

"If you're thinking about searching rooms . . ."

"Shhh. The walls have ears."

"I'm for searching, too. Especially tonight because Portia has lost those sunglasses I gave her, and I'm wondering if they've been stashed somewhere, dumped in a wastebasket. But how are we going to do it? Everyone locks his bedroom door. Particularly since Barbara's and my rooms were pulled apart."

Julia smiled and plunged a hand in her pocket and produced

a brass key with a wooden tag. "Master key. I borrowed it from Mary. You know, our maid. Said I'd lost mine and my arthritis was acting up and I hated to climb all the way downstairs and would she? She said yes, as I promised to return it tomorrow morning. She was going off duty."

Sarah was incredulous. "She *gave* you the key."

"You should never neglect human relations," said Julia complacently. "Always show an interest. Mary Fiske lives on a farm outside of High Roosting and her father has a team of Shires. He uses them to plow with because he doesn't believe in mechanical things like tractors. And Mary used to do Pony Club and still rides when she's home. We've become quite good friends."

"Good God," said Sarah.

"Exactly. God helps those who help themselves. Now shall we go down? I'd hate to miss the cocktail hour."

Sarah sat through cocktails and through the soup course all the while keeping a watchful eye on her fellow diners, particularly Henry Ruggles. She wondered if he would show any sign of resentment, appropriate certainly if he thought he had been pushed into the Kiftsgate pool.

But Henry showed no such thing. In fact, he seemed to be doing his best to keep up appearances with lively chat, but a certain weariness was noticeable and from time to time his lip turned down and his eyes drooped. And his wig, now thoroughly dry, had not entirely recovered from its dunking. It looked more like a thatched roof than a hairpiece. And he had twice sloshed his consommé over the rim of his bouillon cup. Henry, she decided, being no spring chicken, needed bed.

As for the others, the early days of distress and the recovering good cheer seemed to now have subsided into low-key conversations that centered on the gardens visited. Henry's "accident" and Ellen's death were studiously avoided. As was the issue of the Cambridge Botanic Garden. But the details of that visit, Sarah decided, must somehow have been resolved since the tour was set to take off for Cambridge in the morning.

Dinner had advanced to the main course, for which Julia and Sarah had both ordered the lemon sole, when suddenly Sarah was aroused by a fork clattering on a plate. She swiveled about and saw her aunt lean forward, recover, pass a hand over her brow, and then give an audible gasp.

Sandi, sitting opposite, looked up with concern. "Aunt Julia, what's the matter? Are you all right?"

"It's nothing," said Julia. "A little faint, that's all. Too much sun today, perhaps."

"But it was raining and then mostly overcast. Not much sun at all," Sandi—always literal—reminded her.

"The humidity," said Julia. "The sun about to come out. Just a little faintness, but I'll be all right. I'm sure I will." This last sentence being accompanied by Julia's right hand nailing Sarah on her sore knee.

"Ow," squeaked Sarah. "I mean, oh. Oh, Aunt Julia. You do look pale."

"I don't think I can eat my fish," said Julia. "I'll just stay here quietly." She looked around the table with a brave smile.

Barbara Baxter pushed back her chair. "Let me take you upstairs to your room, where you can lie down quietly, and then if you don't feel any better soon I think I should call a doctor."

"Quite right," said Fred Ouellette. "You must never neglect a sudden faintness. You have no idea where it might lead. I've had loved ones on my table . . ."

"Oh no," said Julia with a slightly stronger voice. "I'm quite used to these little spells. A fall I had once from my horse. An injured nerve. It sometimes comes over me. But yes, I think I will go and lie down. And Sarah—she's quite used to my little episodes—she'll take me up. Your hand, Sarah. And, all of you, please go right on with your dinner."

"I think you overdid it," said Sarah in her aunt's ear as they slowly climbed the stairs to their bedroom floor.

"Just your arm, dear," said Julia in a penetrating voice. "Whisper." She added, "Some good Samaritan may be tagging along behind us. Then louder, "Into my room so I can put my feet up."

Sarah steered her aunt into her bedroom and carefully closed the door. "Now what?"

"It's your turn. I'm the planner, you're the experienced snoop into other people's business. We don't have much time. Some of the group may skip dessert. And there'll be other guests prowling around."

"Okay," said Sarah. "Alex said the police have cleared the the the Ouellettes, the Hoppers, and the Lermatovs. We'll skip those rooms."

"We should do everyone," insisted Julia. "But start if you want with number one suspect, Justin Rossi. Room seventeen. I'll stand by the door and check out the hall for intruders."

"You mean legitimate owners of bedrooms."

"Right. Just whisk through and try not to make a mess."

"And if I'm caught?"

"That's negative thinking. Here's the key. I'll stand watch."

Justin Rossi's room was a miracle of order. Sarah poked about in the clothes closet, opened an empty suitcase, examined a washstand collection of toothpaste, brush, and deodorant, noted on the bureau a camera with a long lens, a birdwatcher's guide to British birds, a Penguin paperback mystery, and arrived at last to a number of packages and boxes that had been piled on a chair.

"What are those?" said Julia from her station by the door.

"He's been shopping. Actually, I was with him when he bought some of this. Things for his mother and his sister."

"Or his girlfriend."

"And for all I know his wife. Or daughter."

"What's in them?"

Sarah cautiously lifted a cardboard lid. "Blue silk blouse, stockings, a skirt or a slip. The next one, a white knitted shawl." She slipped her hand into the third box. "Feels like a sweater. A wool one. Soft. Probably damn expensive. And the bottom, those placemats for his mother. An attentive son and brother, I'd say.

"Don't jump to conclusions. You can use stockings to strangle."

Sarah made a face at her aunt and then went over to the bureau and surveyed neatly stacked boxer shorts, polo shirts, and rolled socks. Zip," she announced. "And no sign of those sunglasses."

"So move on," commanded Julia, her voice anxious, and Sarah, glancing back saw her aunt's gray hair tousled, her face red, looking, as she did when agitated, like a worried terrier in search of a rat.

The McClure quarters only proved that Portia was orderly and Carter was not. And that Carter had a taste for police procedurals and Portia was reading an Eleanor Roosevelt paperback biography.

Barbara Baxter's room contained only a sheaf of notes to and from Whirlaway Tours, showing that Barbara had kept in touch with home base.

"Nothing but travel dates and reservation stuff," said Sarah, leafing through them. "And writing paper and stamps." She poked a finger at a little leather case that sat beside the notebook. "Expensive paper," she remarked. "Crane yet, with blue monogram and blue lined envelopes. Very posh. Barbara's a stationery snob. And that big suitcase like mine." She reached down and unzipped the cover. "Empty," she announced. "We should both dump them."

"Trivia," said Julia. "And hurry up," she added. "I think I hear someone on the stairs.

She heard correctly. Two female members of the Japanese contingent, both hurrying down the hall and arguing. "Or it sounds like arguing," Sarah said to Julia when the two had disappeared. "But since we don't know Japanese, they could be proclaiming eternal love."

"Stacy Daniel, next," said Julia. "Put a nickel into it."

"Don't rush me," said Sarah sharply. "I'm the one sticking out my neck. You can just collapse against the wall pretending to be faint or say you're walking in your sleep."

Stacy Daniel's room was a major disappointment, and Sarah came out of it shaking her head. "An expensive-looking camera. No sunglasses, and underwear that would make Victoria's Secret blush. Beyond that, nothing."

"Sexy underwear isn't helpful?"

"You tell me. Okay, we've just time for the Hoppers."

The shared room of Edith and Margaret Hopper yielded one

interesting document—or aborted document. Sarah rummaging in the wastebasket came up with a crumpled piece of Shearing Inn writing paper on which a firm called Warneke, Lewis, and Dubois, Attorneys-at-Law. Sarah smoothed the paper and brought it over for Julia to see. "It's just the beginning of a letter," she explained. "Addressed to Sam. Samuel Lewis. I've heard of him. He practices in Rockland with that firm."

"I can read," snapped Julia, whose job as door guard was beginning to take its toll. She snatched the paper and read in a low voice. "Dear Sam. To go straight to the point, Margaret and I find ourselves in a rather distressing predicament. What we need is advice, but it's awkward at this distance, and for all we know, our situation may be affected by some unsympathetic British laws, or rules that might make us decide to go home sooner than we planned. Anyway, Sam, we both wonder . . ."

Julia rolled the paper back into its original crumple and returned the paper to the wastebasket. "I think that supports my IRS theory."

But Sarah had tilted her head. "Someone's coming." She pushed Julia into the hall, turned and closed the door. "There's a lavatory next door. Duck in there."

Facing Sarah across the toilet bowl, the air humid and thick with a floral deodorant, Julia looked pleased. "I'm right. Margaret and Edith have gotten themselves into some financial mud." Then, listening, "Whoever it was has gone by."

Sarah looked at her watch. "We've run out of time. Skip the Ouellettes. They're safe." She opened the lavatory door and listened. "Okay, go on back to your room, Aunt Julia. I've got to go to the toilet. This is all too much for my bladder. I'll meet you in your room."

But she didn't.

Returning from the lavatory, she turned at the bend of the hall and fumbled in her skirt pocket for her own room key. And remembered she'd left her door slightly ajar in case she and Julia needed instant refuge. She withdrew her hand and shook her head at her forgetfulness.

And as she did, an alien arm bent around her neck, her head

was violently jerked back, the arm clamped around her throat in a crushing choke hold. And the pressure against her throat increased so relentlessly that Sarah had no chance to duck her chin down to protect against the throttling grip. And no chance to swivel about and see her attacker. No chance to do anything but give a strangled gasp for breath and flay her arms about in a desperate effort at self-defense.

And with the first wild circle of Sarah's right arm the attacker increased the throat hold and with the other hand delivered a sharp chop to Sarah's elbow, and then cranked Sarah's left arm behind her back and gave it a sharp upward thrust.

Streaks of pain radiated from Sarah's shoulder to her pinioned arm and simultaneously knifed through her stricken elbow. She opened her mouth to scream, but could only give out with a strangled gurgle.

And then a knee thrust itself into her back and she was propelled forward, down the hall, pushed into a room—her own room she saw, her tilted head taking in blurred details of curtains and pictures. Then she was kneed to the edge of her own bed, twisted about, heard a rustling of the bedcovers, the stranglehold eased for a second, and a pillowcase was yanked over her head, and the arm tightened again about her throat.

"On the floor," said a low, hoarse voice. And with the command came a kick at the back of Sarah's knees and she toppled to the floor, her head in its bag striking first.

Her attacker released the neck hold and at the same time Sarah's right arm was again cranked around to her back and given another upward excrutiating shove.

And then the hoarse voice. "What in hell do you think you're doing sticking your nose where it doesn't belong. Listen to me. Cut it out. You and that old aunt of yours." And one hand took hold of the pillowcase over Sarah's head, raised it, and then slammed it back on the floor.

"Got that? You understand?" said the voice. "Will you kindly lay the fuck off? Don't ever try going into other people's rooms again. Forget this spy business or I will blow the whistle for every fucking policeman in Britain to haul you and Julia Clancy

in for breaking and entering. There are laws in this country."
Here Sarah's head was lifted and given another bounce off the
floor.

"So," repeated the voice, "you understand? Say it."

"I understand," Sarah managed in a strangled voice through
the pillowcase cloth.

"And listen. We'll have a deal. I won't report you pulling a
room search—and God help you if anything's missing. And you
won't mention that I was a little rough on you, which I had every
goddamn right to be. I'll be generous and pretend like the whole
thing never happened. So don't move. Don't lift your head. Don't
open your eyes. Don't even breathe. Stay here and count to one
thousand. And then you're on your own. Understand? Answer
me, you understand?"

"Okay," mumbled Sarah into the pillowcase.

"I'm watching you so stay put. When you finish counting
you can go and give Julia Clancy my message. If she steps out
of line, if you do, you will be in very deep shit. The kind of shit
you don't get out of. Okay? Okay? Say it, okay?"

"Okay," choked Sarah.

"Better be," said the voice, and the grip on her arm released,
soft footsteps retreated, and a door was slammed shut.

17

SARAH—as instructed—lay prone, not moving. Her eyes closed. Her body stiff, her nose pressed into the pillowcase. But she was not counting to a thousand; her brain was otherwise occupied, whirring around, a maelstrom of rage, indignation, and self-accusation.

Shit, shit, shit, she said to herself. Sarah, you goddamn fool. Then, as the pain receded and the tension eased, she moved her head to one side. Something wet slipped down her chin and she stuck out her tongue and tasted salt. Her nose was bleeding. Her lip, too. A tooth must have cut right into it. And her head felt hollow with a sort of buzzing going on inside. Of course—her head had been slammed into the carpet. Was that how boxers felt when they'd been decked by a good left jab?

Well, what did she expect? To feel good? Happy and satisfied after a rewarding evening of sneaking into other people's rooms? Cautiously her tongue explored her swollen and bloody lip and then she took a deep and unhappy breath, and unbidden into her mind came her father's voice saying a hundred years ago about some childish scrape she'd gotten into: "You can't make an omelet without breaking eggs."

So she'd broken a whole carton of eggs. A baker's dozen at least. Oh, stupid, stupid, stupid.

Because just look at this not so brilliant idea. She and Julia hadn't even discussed the possibility of failure; they had just gone for it, never considering that the chances were very good that someone from their corridor would come up from dinner. Someone who needed a Tylenol, a sweater, an emergency visit to the toilet. A fix. Whatever. Or a someone who hadn't bought Julia's fainting act. And there they were, Sarah and Julia, ripe for the finding, two dumb females dipping in and out of bedrooms.

She pulled off the now blood-smeared pillowcase, lifted her head like a turtle emerging from its shell, then stopped and lowered it, aware that if someone was really watching from the door, she was breaking the agreement.

What agreement? Hell, she hadn't agreed to anything. She'd been slammed down on the floor and told to say okay. It was extortion or blackmail or felonious assault. At least.

But there was the other side of coin: being caught breaking and entering. How would her fellow tourists feel about that? Margaret and Edith Hopper, those two polite, gently nurtured elderly ladies? Shock and horror would be the least of it. Carter and Portia? She could almost hear Carter if he'd caught her looking through his bureau drawers. The others? No one would feel forgiving. She and Julia would be damn lucky if they were not turned over to that Inspector Daniel Defoe and shipped home.

Shit. A hundred times shit.

For a few moments she lay there on the floor feeling sick and violated, aware that her nosebleed had made the lower half of her face sticky with blood. And that the buzzing in her head had settled down into the heavy bang, bang of a major headache.

Then, cautiously, she rolled over and sat up.

Safe in her own bedroom. The bedroom with the door she herself had left so conveniently open. A smart move bringing her here because if she'd been hauled off to some other room the identity of her escort would have been blown. No, her own room was the perfect place to make sure she got the message about future behavior.

Sarah pushed herself into a sitting position, her head, feeling like an overripe squash, pulsing and thumping while the walls of the room wavered and lurched.

She squinted and then slowly, holding her head steady, looked around. She was alone. The room looked its usual cozy chintzy inviting self, her afternoon jeans and shirt hung over a chair, her copy of *Cranford* on the bedside table. But where was Aunt Julia? Her trusted co-enterer and breaker? Why wasn't she here hanging over her beloved niece with wet sponges and towels?

Or had she been nailed, too? And Julia—no matter how tough an item—was still a seventy-year-old woman and might not be able to recover easily from having her head bounced off the floor.

Sarah rose shakily to her feet, reached for the back of a chair to steady herself, and walked to the bedroom door, pushed it closed. And snapped the lock. So much for visitors. The last thing she—and Julia—needed was someone like Amy Lermatov skipping into the room all bright-eyed and filled with homicidal interest.

Next she walked, more steadily, and confronted the door connecting to Julia's. Knocked. Waited. No answer. Knocked again. No answer.

Hell. A wave of dizziness hit her and for a moment she hung onto the doorknob. Then a new and terrible fear. Aunt Julia assaulted, floored, helpless. Bones cracked or broken. Perhaps unconscious. Or worse. Oh, the poor old thing.

At that very moment, when Sarah's sympathy had reared up a mental picture of Julia trussed, bloodied, maybe dying or already deceased, the "poor old thing" was snuggled into her eiderdown, taking a short snooze after the rigors of garden visiting and room searching. Julia always slept soundly. In fact, her family and neighbors always said that once asleep that the only thing that could wake her was the restlessness of a sick horse, the sound of a mare going down in the straw ready to foal, the neigh and snort of an aroused stallion. Not the mere noise of a disturbed human.

After ducking back into her room, Julia, not daring to reenter the hall, had paced her floor waiting for Sarah's return. Then excitement subsiding and fatigue getting the better of impatience, she had pushed aside the counterpane of her bed, pulled up the eiderdown in its flowered duvet cover, and, telling herself that it was just for five minutes, had drifted off. She was just floating into a dream of sunny pastures when a harsh whisper close to her ear broke the spell.

"Aunt Julia. Aunt Julia, are you all right?"

Here the comforter was tweaked back and Julia opened her eyes, frowned, and then sat up. She blinked, then focused on Sarah's still-blooded face and swollen lip. "Sarah! Oh my God!"

"Oh my God is right," said Sarah. "I'm okay, but how about you? Are you all right?"

"I'm fine but you're not. You look horrible."

"It's been a tough fifteen minutes. Or ten minutes. I've no idea how long the whole thing lasted. It seemed like hours."

"What are you talking about," demanded Julia. "And your poor face! You didn't fall down stairs, did you?"

"I wish I had," said Sarah with feeling. "It would have been easier. Listen, and if you feel up to it, please make some tea. We're both going to need it. With a slug of your travel whiskey. Thank heavens for electric kettles in every room. I'll wash up and examine the damage and then I'll tell you what's going on—or what went on."

"But," Julia fumbled, "your face. You need a doctor. Let me call down to the office."

"No call, no doctor. In fact, don't answer the telephone or let anyone in the door. Not until I explain. Tea and then maybe we can order sandwiches from the grille room. After all, we've missed dinner. But right now I need soap, water, and a serious dose of whatever pills you have for bad heads."

Settled ten minutes later, Julia arranged herself on the edge of her bed, and Sarah sank into the armchair. She had changed her bloodied shirt, brushed her hair, and washed her face—a face disfigured by a swollen nose and an enlarged lip. Each woman clutched a cup of Typhoo tea laced with Julia's whiskey.

Sarah took a deep breath, fixed her eyes on a framed colored print featuring a woman in a straw bonnet, two children clinging to her long gingham skirts. She was welcoming a man in a smock and gaiters holding a crook and followed by a collie. The little woman had probably just taken a cottage loaf from the oven, while a mug of home brew and a Cotswold pie stood ready on their rough-hewn table. Later, after supper, little Fanny and Theobald would recite the Twenty-third Psalm to dear Papa. The simple life, Sarah told herself; we should all try it.

"For the Lord's sake," exclaimed Julia. "Don't just stand there staring. Get on with it."

Sarah dragged herself back to the world of breaking and entering. "It's like this," she began and took Julia step by step by grab and grasp and shove through the events of the last hour.

"So you see," said Sarah, finishing her tale and her second cup of tea-cum-whiskey at the same time, "you see, we've just been caught red-handed and we can't do a thing about it."

Julia nodded slowly. "All right. You can't complain about being mugged. I see that. But now we know, don't we?"

"That we've got Ellen's murderer along on the tour? I was sure before being mugged. The trouble is I'm not one hundred percent certain the person who attacked me is connected to the murder. Say he or she found us sneaking in and out of bedrooms and lost it. Blew up. What the hell do Sarah and Julia think they're doing. Well, I'll show them they can't get away with that kind of stuff. Nothing about Ellen—her being killed—was even hinted at when I was on the floor."

"But still . . ."

"Okay, the attack probably was connected, but that's just my gut feeling. But who in hell was it? No accent, but then no one on this trip is from the south or west or a Brit except for Henry. All from New England and they use everyday northeast American diction. Except whoever it was sounded like a tough—or someone trying to sound tough."

"Male or female?"

"I couldn't tell. A hoarse voice, the kind anyone can fake. But I was grabbed so fast—I couldn't turn with my head in that strangulation hold—and then shoved into my room and slammed into the floor. With all that going on I wasn't exactly concentrating on identifying the voice. Just on the message."

"To lay off snooping and keep your mouth shut."

"Right."

"How about the strength factor? I don't see Edith and Margaret strong-arming you."

"No," said Sarah thoughtfully, "but most of the others could handle it. The attack depended on surprise, getting that arm around my throat. Even Amy could probably beat me in arm wrestling."

Julia rose from her perch on the end of the bed. "Listen. You stay put and I'll go down and collect some sandwiches."

"You're supposed to be feeling faint."

"But now I'm better. And you're . . . well, you're tired out. And while I'm down I'll see if I can find out who didn't stay through dinner."

"I should have thought of that," said Sarah. "Of course, anyone who slithered away during dinner is the snake who grabbed me."

"Snakes don't grab, they wrap. Or strike," said Julia who was always factual about animals. "Besides," she added, "it may not have been a snake."

"An honest person acting from righteous anger," said Sarah. "Okay, we're the villains. But, Aunt Julia, take it easy. Don't go stomping into the dining room and ask for a head count."

"Trust me," said Julia. "An *eminence grise, c'est moi.*"

But, as it proved, there was no need for Julia to put on her diplomatic robes. A soft double knock sounded at the door, and Julia opened it a bare two inches. Then wider.

Doris Lermatov. Followed by Amy.

They had come to check on Julia. Faintness, claimed Doris,

as they both stepped into the room, shouldn't be neglected. She, Doris, had been worried.

Then they saw Sarah. Sarah's nose. Sarah's lip.

"Wow!" said Amy. "What hit you?" Amy pushed her electric red hair out of her eyes and peered at Sarah.

"She slipped," said Julia quickly. "Hit the end of the bed."

"But," objected Amy, "the beds don't have bedposts on the beds. Only a headboard."

"The edge," said Julia. "The bed frame. A nasty fall."

"I'm all right, really," said Sarah, taking charge. "A nosebleed and I cut my lip. And Aunt Julia's feeling much better."

"Just fine. A tiny faint spell. I'm quite used to them. It's nothing. Absolutely nothing, But," said Julia, eyeing the open door, "but thank you so much for coming."

But Doris had settled on a straightbacked chair by the bed. "We would have come earlier, but it's been wild. Absolutely wild. We missed dessert completely."

"Mother's favorite," said Amy. "The sweet trolley. Went completely off the rail."

"It isn't on a rail," corrected Doris. "They just call it a trolley. But Amy's right. I think it got loose somehow. It was being wheeled over to that Japanese party, and I was turning around because the trolley went right by our table, and I was absolutely torn between the chocolate torte and the trifle, which is out of this world because I had it last night . . ."

"Mo-ther," said Amy.

"Yes. Well, the trolley was going by and then the waitress pushing it tripped—or at least I guess she tripped. Anyway, she fell into the trolley and it tipped over and the wheels must have caught on an extension cord from the sideboard because the lights went out in that part of the dining room. You know these old inns are absolute firetraps. They're probably hung together by extension cords."

"Mother," said Amy again.

"Well, the waitress is on the floor and there's chocolate torte and trifle and pudding and everything all over the place—the

sponge cake—it has a lemon frosting, absolutely wonderful—
ended up in Edith Hopper's lap—and then the lights went out.
In the whole dining room. A short or something."

"And," giggled Amy, "one of those big German women began
shouting about lights—at least I think that's what she said.
'Lichte,' which must mean light."

"Then," said Doris," the manager, Mr. Gage, came in with a
flashlight . . ."

"They call it a 'torch' in England," put in Amy.

"Don't interrupt. With a flashlight and began poking around
by the outlet in the wall, and then Edith Hopper stood up because she was all sticky with sponge cake, and she tripped over
the sweet trolley, which was still on its side—you know Edith
and Margaret have those thick glasses and neither can see very
well and it was dark. Anyway, Margaret went to help her, and
stepped into something—I think it was the bowl of trifle—and
began crying. It was just like a Marx Brothers movie, only a lot
worse."

"Or the Three Stooges," said Amy. "I couldn't stop laughing."

"Very funny," said Julia in a repressed voice.

"How long," asked Sarah, "did this whole scene go on?"

Doris smiled. "Who knows. It was a complete circus. It
seemed like forever because the waiters and then the chef—
well, someone in a white jacket and a hat showed up and began
trying to help."

"You see," said Amy, "like first there's this trolley mess and
the two Hoppers trying help each other out of the dining room
and people with flashlights or torches are trying to replug everything in and no one can really see what they're doing. I'm going
to use the scene in my mystery because while everyone's falling
over everything, I can have someone stabbed with a carving
knife."

"Stop it, Amy," said her mother.

Sarah, in desperation, tried once more. "When the lights
came on, did you see who was still in the dining room?"

Doris shook her head. "I don't really know. As soon as we
saw that it was going to take a while to get the place cleaned up

we left. Amy and I did, anyway. And the Hoppers left before we did. We went to the parlor and looked at magazines. Perhaps the others just went to the bar. You'd have to ask. Does it matter?"

"No," said Sarah hastily. "I just wondered."

"No you didn't," said Amy. "I'll bet you're on to something. Because that was such a neat scene for something to happen in. You didn't go and push the waitress with the trolley and turn the lights off yourself, did you?" Amy's voice was hopeful.

"No," said Sarah rather too loudly. "We were upstairs."

"I was having my little lie-down," said Julia. "Because of feeling faint. Sarah was so helpful."

"That," said Sarah, when the door had closed behind the two Lermatovs, "is that. Groucho and Harpo and Zeppo downstairs, Julia and Sarah upstairs. Not much difference."

"Window of opportunity, you think?" said Julia.

"Who knows. Scenes like that do happen."

"Or can be made to happen. If need be."

Sarah made a face. "I'm afraid so. Well, is the whole evening a total loss? What did we find out? If anything."

"No sunglasses anywhere," said Julia.

"Barbara uses Crane writing paper, Stacy has an expensive camera, Justin has a cheaper one and buys his mother and sister presents."

"Sandi Ouellette has a camera," added Julia. "And Carter McClure has binoculars. And a camera? I can't remember."

"All these people seem to be trusting that no one breaks in and steals their things. But, after Barbara's and my room were ransacked, you'd think they'd be more careful."

"That day those two doors were unlocked. Tonight every door was locked tight."

"And look how easy it is to find a key," Sarah reminded her.

"Not everyone has my skill in obtaining keys," said Julia.

18

SARAH and Julia spent the remainder of that Wednesday evening enduring a number of condolence calls. Tentative knocks at the door, anxious faces peering in: How *are* you, Julia? No, don't get up. You're doing too much. You know, Julia, at our age we must learn to take it easy. (This from Margaret Hopper.) When did you have your blood pressure checked? (from Portia). You really look like death (from Fred Ouellette, who found this coming out of his mouth before he could check it).

And for Sarah, exclamations over her damaged nose and swollen lip: Oh my goodness, look at you. You stumbled? Well, it's the floors in these old inns. So uneven. I watch *every* step. Have you tried ice/aspirin/a heating pad/called the doctor?

Julia and Sarah, each in her own way dealt with the visitors, some bearing welcome sandwiches, fruit, digestive biscuits, or in one case Pepto-Bismal and a bottle of mineral water. Together both women found the easiest way to divert attention from Julia's faintness (and recovery from) and Sarah's damaged face was to direct the conversation to another retelling of the absolutely hilarious sweet trolley incident and the amazing similarity of the scene to cinema comedy of the thirties.

This ploy was successful and Fred Ouellette claimed he had been convulsed and completely lost it, groping about in the dark and ending up almost in the lap of an indignant German fraulein. The whole scene had reminded him of a funeral in which one of the pallbearers had been overcome by a fit of coughing—"a chain smoker," said Fred in a disapproving voice—and lost his grip on the coffin, lurched forward, upset the next pallbearer, and the coffin had slipped to the ground, slid down the snow-covered walkway of the Proffit Point Methodist Church. "Right out into the road," said Fred, chuckling at the memory. "Lucky for us a car wasn't coming."

"Hahaha," said Julia, giving Fred a dark look.

"Oh well," said Fred in an apologetic voice, "at the time it seemed hilarious. Even the family laughed and, after all, it was great-grandfather's funeral. He was ninety-two and a real tyrant."

"Tomorrow," said Sarah to Julia when the last comforter had departed, "we shall be clear of the lot of them. At least for a day. Our own car, right? Colleges and bookstores. Gives us time to sort things out. What to do."

Julia nodded her agreement, adding that indeed it had been a day from hell but tomorrow was another day.

"I've heard that one before," said Sarah glumly. "Okay, lock all doors and take a sharp instrument to bed with you."

"I knew I should have brought my hunting crop," said Julia as she closed her bedroom door.

Breakfast, the Thursday morning of June the fifteenth, was a hasty affair. The sun was shining, a mild breeze had risen, the highway beckoned, and it was good-bye to the Shearing Inn. Luggage piled up in the tiny front hall, tips were disputed and translated from dollars to pounds, and Barbara Baxter and Henry Ruggles joined forces in harrying the Garden Club members into the bus. The length of the Cambridge visit had been resolved in Barbara's favor, and Henry was left urging everyone to

"At LEAST make the best of the Botanic Garden." Sarah, however, had made it clear that she and her aunt might not be seeing the rest until they met that evening at an establishment called Hotel Fatima—a hostelry Barbara had described in the tour itinerary as being in the "heart of Cambridge."

"I suppose," said Sarah as she and Julia climbed into their Ford Escort, "it wouldn't hurt to drop in on the Cambridge Botanic Garden at some point in the day."

"From horticultural or investigative interest," asked Julia.

"Both," said Sarah. "I'm not letting some thug dictate my day."

"We could give it an hour of our time," said Julia. She refolded the driving map and smoothed the center section. "Head northwest on the A424 and pick up the A44 after Stow-in-the-Wold."

"North? Let me guess. We're going to Yorkshire and visit the Brontës. Or a side trip into Wales."

"Sunglasses. The ones Portia said she dropped. We can go back to Kiftsgate and ask. They probably have a Lost-and-Found."

"Good idea," said Sarah, "I'd like to know whether they've been picked up on some path or if they were deliberately dumped in some trash bin."

"You read my mind," said Julia.

Sarah's second guess proved correct. Fortunately, the rubbish of the day before had been bundled but not yet hauled away, and she and Julia were graciously permitted a tour through four large bags of tourist detritus. Reward in the shape of a familiar pair of sunglasses came at the top of bag three. But the glasses—although identifiable—were broken as to lens and bent as to eyepiece.

"They've been wrecked," said Sarah, holding them up and removing a clinging piece of banana peel.

"Someone stomped on the glass . . ."

"More than that. They're all twisted."

"Which means?"

"Which means that the glasses were wrecked past the point of anyone wanting to put them in a Lost-and-Found."

"Oh, dear me," said a voice. A stout National Trust woman wrapped in a coverall frowned at the glasses in Sarah's hand. "You'll not be wanting to keep those. They're no use at all. Even the frames. And quite filthy." She reached out a hand to relieve Sarah of the distasteful objects.

Sarah retracted her hand. "Sentimental value," she told the woman. "They were my mother's." And she and Julia beat a retreat, Sarah holding the glasses between thumb and forefinger.

"My sainted mother," said Sarah, when they had regained the safety of their car. "Mother set great store by these glasses." She turned the ignition, shoved the car in gear, and shot out into the access road. She turned to Julia. "I'm going to stick the blessed things in an envelope and leave them at the High Roosting police station with a note asking that they be forwarded to the Maine State Police. Care of George Fitts."

"Just like that. If you hand in an unmarked envelope they'll think the package is a bomb and you'll be held as a terrorist."

"Not at all," said Sarah. "I'll mix in with a group of people, walk by the station, pretend I'm admiring the building, climb the stairs, go down, and walk quietly away. The police can test it for explosives and when they do they'll find a pair of broken sunglasses. Then they'll call the U.S. police."

It fell out as Sarah planned. After purchasing a padded mailer and inking "Maine State Police CID: Sergeant George Fitts, Thomaston, Maine, USA, across its front," she parked two blocks from the station, strolled in a leisurely manner behind a family of the ever-present Japanese tourists, climbed the concrete steps leading to the station's front entrance, let the package slide to the ground, and made it back to the car in under ten minutes.

"Hit the road," said Julia as Sarah scrambled into the driver's seat. "This life of espionage is hard on my nerves."

"Not espionage," corrected Sarah. "Simple good citizenship. Now where's Cambridge?"

"The A43 north, then a choice. Scenic or dual-carrigeway?"

"Scenic. Gives us time to think."

"Then head for Bedford and east on the A45. Find a place for lunch along the way."

"I told Alex I'd call him today, so I'll have him alert George about the sunglasses. And maybe there's news about the scarf. If the scarf is bloody, perhaps the glasses are messed up. Little blood cells in the hinges."

🦋

But the scarf was clean. Alex, tracked down in the hospital gave the news. "No blood—not yet anyway. Just dye that runs. But here's an update. The dibble was washed in a liquid soap commonly used in gas station restrooms. This particular soap matches that in an Irving station just south of Portland and in an Exxon station near Westbrook, and Westbrook is, as you know, just outside of Portland."

"Both near the Portland airport?"

"Near enough. And one of the Irving station attendants thinks he remembers someone in a scarf who acted like she was in a hurry. Dropped the restroom key. Then used the ladies' room. Wore a scarf. Slacks or dark trousers. Also wore a plastic sort of raincoat. Dark red slicker."

"She, you said!"

"Or he. Don't jump to conclusions. Slickers can be worn by both sexes. And a scarf makes a good disguise."

"Was she—or he—wearing glasses?"

"As a matter of fact, yes. The attendant thought the person looked like Jackie Kennedy Onasis—you know, the scarf and glasses look. Only a little heavier set. But get this. The Jackie look-alike drove off with the restroom key. Taking the key made the person stick in his mind."

"That's a real lead then."

"Could be. But two Exxon attendants at the other station each say they think they remember several people in head scarves and dark glasses, all with several kids in tow. But no one can remember exactly when."

"Great. Terrific," said Sarah in a tired voice.

"You sound a little ragged. Is Julia getting on your nerves?"

"I think," said Sarah regretfully, "that I'm getting on my own nerves. I want to do something about Ellen and at last count I was sure that at least four of our fellow garden lovers was pretty guilty. Guilty of something, anyway."

"If you feel there's any chance of trouble, I hope you and Julia will get the hell out . . ."

Sarah broke in. "No. It's okay. We'll take precautions. And stay out of trouble." She crossed two sets of fingers and forcing her voice to sound light and carefree, she added, "A few more days and we'll meet you in Italy and hit the pasta. Tonight we'll be at the Hotel Fatima somewhere in Cambridge. Then down to Sissinghurst, and over to France."

"I know when the subject's being changed. You haven't gone sneaking around where you shouldn't have?"

"What," said Sarah, "makes you ask such a stupid question? Listen, I've got to go. Lunchtime. The Barnacle Goose Inn. Ploughman's lunch ordered and a pint of the best. Not to worry." And Sarah replaced the receiver.

"I'm living a life of total deceit," she announced to Julia as she sat down at their table. They sat on a small bricked-paved side terrace under a red and green striped umbrella which offered a fine view of a solicitor's office across the street. "Anyway, that scarf may be a bust because so far the lab hasn't picked up any blood, only dye."

Julia nodded. "Wait and see. Now, let's park somewhere in the center of Cambridge and do the sight-seeing thing. The others will be busy doing the Botanic Garden—Henry said it covers almost forty acres."

"So," Sarah concluded, "all we have to do is avoid the garden until almost closing time. That way we can relax and not have to keep looking over our shoulders to make sure we won't be jumped."

Not for the first time had the two miscalculated. The members of the Garden Club Sarah and Julia had pictured treading the paths of the Botanic Garden turned up instead at every street corner, gazing at the colleges, infesting shops, lingering by the Cam, or in single numbers, in pairs, or in clumps, wandering uncertainly down Drummer Street, pausing on St. John's Street, reversing on Hobson Street, halting on Market Street.

Sandi Ouellette they discovered issuing from a stationer's shop holding a cloth-covered journal. She looked hot, her red cotton skirt was rumpled, and her fair hair tangled.

"I'm so mixed up," exclaimed Sandi. "I've lost Fred and I've been spinning around in circles. I tried to go into some of the colleges, King's and Trinity and Gaius, and some others. I can't remember all their names. But I couldn't. Get in, I mean. Something's going on. Like maybe it's graduation or the end of exams and everyone's going to have some sort of ceremony. Anyway, you can't get into any of the colleges or the gardens. Or the chapels. Barriers all over the place. And besides half the town— the students I mean—are drunk as skunks." Sandi added this last piece of information with some resentment. Drunken undergraduates not being part of her picture of Cambridge.

Sarah made sympathetic noises. She and Julia had both realized that long before they had trudged over the Magdalene Bridge that sight-seeing would have to take a back seat to University goings on.

"You could look around," said Julia. "The architecture is interesting and there's a twelfth-century round church and . . ."

But Sandi brushed architecture aside. "I wanted to get inside the colleges and the chapels," she insisted. "Get the feel."

During the short pause when Sandi stopped for breath, Julia said in a dismissive voice, "We'll be seeing you at dinner, Sandi. Don't give up on Cambridge. How about a graveyard? Graveyards in old cities are very informative."

But Sandi—who was quite possibly feeling a little lonely in her wanderings about town—wasn't ready to give up on familiar company. She held up her journal. "I'm keeping a record," she said. "For a book. I'm going to write a guide for dingbats like me. Like those computer-for-dummies books. But this will be for traveling dummies. No culture hints, just vocabulary and how not to alienate everyone in sight. You know how I said I got in trouble saying 'bum'? Well, there's 'bugger you' and 'sod you,' which aren't nice things to say. And 'pecker.' Did you know that the people actually go around saying 'keep your pecker up?' " Try that in the States and you'll get your bum pinched or worse."

"How about the Botanic Garden, Sandi?" suggested Sarah. "Isn't everyone supposed to be there?"

Sandi shrugged. "Well, I've seen everyone all over town—taking pictures, going into shops. Like it's almost as if they're escaping gardens. Maybe it's burnout. I think only Henry Ruggles and Portia and Carter went right there, but if I have the strength I'll hike over later. I have a map."

"Good idea," said Julia firmly. "You can take a bus. Trumpington Road goes right past the garden. Come on, Sarah, we don't want to be late." And Julia plucked Sarah's shirt and propelled her into forward motion.

"That," said Sarah when they had left Sandi standing some hundred yards to the rear, "was a bit brutal. I think Sandi wanted to hang around."

"She's a grown woman. She can handle being on her own. But you know what I was thinking. It's Fred. I know you say he's cleared but he has one advantage that none of the rest do."

"Which is?"

"A perfect knowledge of anatomy. Where to strike a sharp tool so that it would kill. Maybe you could check back with Alex and see if Fred got loose for just an hour or so on June sixth."

This idea created a heavy silence and the two women strode along without much caring in which direction they went, and it wasn't until they found themselves facing Queens College on the far side of the Cam that Sarah grabbed Julia's elbow and brought her to a halt.

"I think I see another buddy. Or two buddies. Margaret and Edith. Over there. Sitting on the bench. Shall we . . ."

"No," interrupted Julia. "Leave them be. They've probably been hiking all over town and need a rest."

Sarah studied the two sisters for a moment, saw Edith twist around, looking to the left, then the right, and then almost completely about, and meeting Sarah's eyes, gave a visible jump. Then she swiveled back front and center and nudged Margaret.

And Julia watching, nudged Sarah at almost exactly the same moment. "Edith is acting as if she's meeting an illegal bookmaker."

"Shhh," said Sarah. "They'll hear you. And they know we're here. We can't ignore them. Come on." And she walked over to where Edith and Margaret Hopper sat upright on their bench, facing toward the river, exactly, Sarah thought, like a couple of elderly dolls that someone has forgotten to wind up.

Confronted by Julia and Sarah, both sisters gave an entirely unconvincing start.

"Goodness," exclaimed Edith. "Where did you two come from?"

"My," said Margaret. "It's Julia and Sarah. I thought everyone would be going over to the Botanic Garden."

"We thought so, too," said Sarah. "But they aren't."

Edith regrouping, shook her head. "But the whole purpose of the visit was to see the Botanic Garden. Henry said it has a great many specimen trees and shrubs."

"Then," said Julia, "why aren't you there?"

Margaret and Edith spoke at the same time and what came out was jumble about too much walking, fatigue, the excitement of visiting Cambridge, the need to rest on the bench by the Cam and watch the people go by, coupled with the desire to take pictures of the colleges, the churches, the bridges, the river. The whole, in Sarah's opinion, sounding packaged and very poorly rehearsed.

Margaret, as if to emphasize their photographic interest, held up a black compact camera.

"It's an Olympus. With a zoom lens," said Margaret, turning the object over in her hand. "I've never had a zoom lens."

"We hadn't brought our cameras," said Edith. "Because they're only ancient Kodaks. But then we thought we should take some pictures—a sort of record of our trip. And Barbara—she knows a great deal about cameras—helped pick these out. Such a useful size and so easy to use. Mine is a Nikon." And Edith lifted up a black strap that circled her neck and exhibited her camera. "We thought we'd take pictures of the general scene," she added, waving an indecisive hand at the path in front of the bench.

"You won't get any decent pictures here," said Julia. "Much too shady, all these trees. What you need to do," she added, who never took pictures and did not own a camera, "is find an interesting angle with a good light. Any of the colleges or along the river. The punts taken from a bridge would make a good shot." Here she paused seeing no reaction from the two sisters.

"I think," said Edith, fumbling with her camera case, "that this is quite a nice spot and Barbara said the lens would adjust for lack of light."

"Yes," said Margaret. "This is a good place to start. All the children in their school uniforms. So English." She pointed at three small girls in cotton frocks and straw hats who were just then tearing toward a footbridge.

"Here," said Sarah with sudden inspiration. "Give me your cameras. I'll take a picture of you both. Sitting on the bench together in Cambridge. For your family."

"No," said Edith and Margaret in a single voice. And, in an almost single action they clutched their cameras to their respective bosoms and shrank away from Sarah's outstretched hand.

Sarah, surprised, a little affronted, dropped her hand. "Sorry. I thought it was a nice idea."

"Oh it was," cried Edith, recovering. "But we, well we hate having our picture taken. Just what we told Amy. All the wrinkles. I know we're being vain, but we're just two old biddies."

And Sarah and Julia beat a retreat.

"Well," exploded Julia when they were out of ear shot, "what in God's name is going on with those two? They're acting as if they're in an Alfred Hitchcock movie."

"Or have bombs in their cameras," said Sarah. "But it is just possible that they hate having their pictures taken. I know my mother makes a great fuss and talks about looking awful."

"All right," said Julia. "I feel the same way. But this sudden interest in taking pictures under trees of passing schoolchildren. I say, Pooh."

Sarah grinned. "Strong language, Auntie. Do you think we should crouch behind a bush and see if Margaret and Edith are part of a drug drop."

"No," said Julia crossly. "Something's out of kilter, but I don't picture either of the Hoppers with a dibble, and besides you told me Alex said they were cleared for the time of Ellen's death. If they're involved with something funny, I think it's a whole different ballgame. Something to do with that nervous breakdown. Or a so-called nervous breakdown. Or," Julia added, "do you think one of those dear ladies caught us snooping and mugged you last night?"

Sarah shook her head. "Remember we ruled them out. Even both working together I don't think they could have managed it. And, besides, I was only mugged by one person. Margaret and Edith may be a little on the sly side but as lady wrestlers, well, forget it."

Julia looked at her watch. "Past three-thirty. Let's hike back and pick up our car. I think the only place we won't find any of our friends will be the Botanic Garden."

19

THE return walk to their car brought Sarah and Julia sightings of more defectors. Stacy Daniel was espied by the door of the Cambridge University Press, looking particularly lovely in a lemon-colored safari jacket, her figure nicely set off by the white walls of the building. And like Margaret and Edith, she, too, seemed to have been bitten by the photographic bug. Stacy held her large camera to her nose and was aiming it at a confused street scene of automobiles, pedestrians, and bicycles.

Sarah suddenly found this interest in preserving the passing scene contagious. Her own camera was locked in Julia's car, and up to now she had not taken a single picture—her mind being weighted with other things. Well, why not? It might be good to have some memento of the visit; everything mustn't give way to murder and intimidation.

"Let's ask Stacy where to buy film," she suggested to Julia, as they waited for a gap in traffic to let them cross the street.

"I can't stand the woman," said Julia. "Hollow, no center to her at all. Forget Stacy, you can get film at Boots. There's a Boots somewhere along the way. I feel a little, what's the word,

Bertie Wooster uses, 'peckish.' Well, I feel a little peckish. All this walking. We can pick up a snack and film at Boots. They have everything."

"Boots?" said Sarah puzzled.

"You know. Big shopping chain. They're all over Britain and have everything from aspirin to shopping bags to sandwiches."

The word "snack" had had its effect, so after a brief consultation with a passerby, the two women found themselves at the entrance to Boots. And found Amy Lermatov kneeling at the entrance, camera in hand.

"Amy," exclaimed Sarah. "What are you doing?"

"It's the angle," said Amy, twisting around and looking up at Sarah with no particular surprise at seeing a familiar face. "I'm going to have a chase through Cambridge and I need different angles. Not just the stupid pictures of the colleges."

"What chase," demanded Julia. "Have we missed something?"

"My chase," explained Amy. She stood up and slid the cover back on her lens. "I thought Cambridge was going to be a total bore, mother dragging me through the colleges and going on about tradition and the classics and tutors. But we lucked out. Everything's roped off so we've just been walking around and I've been figuring out a chase scene. My murderer will be dodging some people in his group . . ."

"Your murderer is a man?" asked Sarah.

"Or a woman. I haven't decided. Anyway, I'll have him try to escape through the crowds and jump into one of those punts in the river and the detective will jump into another punt and it will make a terrific scene because of all the students in punts and rowboats. I don't know whether or not I'll have anyone drowned or not. Maybe just get pushed in like Henry."

"You don't know that Mr. Ruggles was pushed in," said Julia in her frostiest voice. She had never cared for the way the young referred to their elders by a first name.

"It doesn't matter," said Amy, unabashed by correction. "I'm doing fiction and I need local color. Are you going in this place? Mother's in there getting a snack for both of us because they have a million sandwiches. Weird stuff like scampi and scallions and watercress and mushrooms."

"I'd like a weird sandwich," said Sarah, and she and Julia advanced on the front door as Amy sank to her knees and pointed her camera at several arriving customers.

Doris Lermatov was indeed discovered puzzling over the sandwich collection arrayed in a stretch of glass-fronted cases.

"Think of it," she said. "Such a choice. Not just BLT and egg salad and tuna fish." She reached in and selected a roast beef and chutney number and then added a scampi and cucumber. Pleased, she smiled at the two women. "Did you see Amy out there? She's back on her fiction kick."

"You haven't been to the Botanic Garden?" asked Sarah. This appeared to be the single interesting question of the day. The important horticultural detour promoted by Barbara Baxter had turned into just another tourist visit.

Doris shifted her collection of sandwiches to the market basket at her feet and ran a hand through her hair—her ash brown hair looking like churned up waves on a windy day. "I know," she said. "It's funny. Everyone thought it was a great idea when Barbara first talked it up—even Henry Ruggles didn't fight it too hard—it was spending the whole day he didn't like. But when the bus pulled up at the entrance only Henry and the McClures got out. The rest all said they wanted to see something of Cambridge first."

"Like Aunt Julia and me," said Sarah.

Doris nodded. "You see, I had this crazy idea that some of the cultural ambiance would rub off on Amy. But, wouldn't you know, half the students are cavorting around, drinking up a storm. Not exactly your higher education role models, though Amy's having a great time with cinema verité. Anyway, as soon as we bolt the sandwiches, I guess we'll head for the gardens."

"We'll give you a lift," Julia offered. "We're going there ourselves."

"What I don't understand," persisted Sarah, as the three made for the checkout counter, "is this rage to photograph. I mean, come on, Stacy Daniel taking street scene shots, the Hoppers sitting in the shade with new cameras. Of course, now I want to get in the act so I've picked up some film."

"Not the only people," added Doris when they all had settled on a concrete wall in a cul-de-sac made up of a gravel drive and a few bushes beyond the Boots entrance, "but Justin Rossi's got his camera out."

"I started it all," said Amy. "In the gardens. Taking those people shots for my book."

"No," said Doris thoughtfully. "Stacy and Justin were taking pictures in London. Westminster Abbey, the Tower of London, Houses of Parliament. And Kew Gardens, of course."

"Wrong," said Amy. "I don't think anyone took pictures at Kew Gardens. They just went on about the roses and the greenhouses."

"It's funny about Justin," said Doris. "He said he lived in London for a few years. Why take pictures of Westminster Abbey?"

Julia crumpled up her paper napkin and rose to her feet. "I think this is a lot of babble about nothing. My diagnosis is that everyone is secretly a little sick of the flowers and wanted a change of pace. Now let's get a move on if we're to make the garden by closing time."

"When does it close?" asked Doris.

"I asked Barbara," said Julia, "and she said not until six."

"Well," said Doris, "I don't want to spend too much waking time at our hotel. Have you seen it? Hotel Fatima. It's a sort of seraglio run by these people from—judging from their accents—New Jersey. Some woman from Hoboken married this Middle East type and went into the hotel business. The whole place is filled with brass gongs and pillows with tassels and reeks of incense. What I want to know is where did Barbara find the place? I can't think it's on Whirlaway Tours list of Triple A hotels."

"It's only for one night," said Sarah, "and because someone's from the Mideast doesn't mean they've set up a harem."

"Pink satin sheets and dripping faucets," said Doris. "Anyway, after one look in we all left our luggage on the bus, hoping it would turn out to be a mistake." She shrugged. "Okay, let's hit the Botanic Garden. Amy and I accept the lift with pleasure. As the saying goes, my feet are killing me."

Oddly enough the party of four, after entering at the Bateman Street Gate and working their way to an artificial lake and water garden, ran almost immediately into the garden loyalists. But Carter McClure, Portia, and Henry Ruggles were not engaged in botanical discourse; instead, they faced each other on the path talking loudly. On catching sight of their fellow tour members they broke off and uttered glad cries.

Portia stretched out both hands in welcome. "Well, thank heavens. Henry has been having cat fits, and we've been trying to calm him down. A garden tour and everyone's off pounding the pavement in town. Poor Henry, he's worked so hard getting his lecture ready."

"Poor Henry" stepped to the fore. His wig had been completely refurbished from its Kiftsgate swim and appeared safely settled, but it must have added heat to the top of his head because his round face was red and moisture had accumulated on his brow, necessitating a continuous mopping with a large green silk handkerchief. He greeted the arrivals with a flip of a hand.

"Well, well," he said, in a peevish voice. "At least here are some of you. But it's almost five, and I ask you what IS the point of a SERIOUS garden tour if everyone spends the ENTIRE day goggling at buildings and sodden students. We could have done the Botanic Garden and then visited at least ONE cottage garden late this afternoon. I had counted on Edith and Margaret Hopper at least. As for Barbara Baxter, it was her idea and where is she?"

This appeared to be a rhetorical question for Henry, pausing to mop his brow again, went on. Barbara had moved the entire tour to Cambridge. And for WHAT? So everyone could do the sordid tourist thing. And that dreadful hotel probably run ENTIRELY by terrorists. He, Henry, had given into the scheme because of course the Cambridge University Botanic Garden—Henry, his voice rising, rolled out the full name—did offer the visitor MANY plantings of merit. The Tulipa species collection, the hybrid display, the cedars, the maples, the scented garden.

"However," Henry concluded grumpily, "since you ARE here we might just as well look around since I have indeed prepared a FEW small notes."

Here Amy rolled her eyes heavenward and Henry pounced on her. "You, young lady, might have the absolutely unique experience of learning something by listening to an older person who has a SMALL store of information he is willing to impart."

"Amy," said Doris Lermatov in a dangerous voice. "Pay attention.

With the Lermatovs in tow, Sarah and Julia behind, the Mc-Clures to the rear, Henry led them forth, expounding, indicating with a flourish of a hand which signs to read, which plants to admire, which to hurry past.

And Sarah, following along, as had so frequently happened of late, heard hardly a word. Fortunately, Henry, having found Doris in a docile mood and Amy silenced, concentrated on those two with an occasional nod toward Portia and Carter for confirmation.

Returning to the entry gate, they ran directly into an entering cluster made up of Barbara, Justin, Edith and Margaret Hopper. The last three still wearing a camera around the neck or slung over the shoulder.

"Too late, too late," called out Henry, sounding to Sarah exactly like Alice's White Rabbit.

"Oh dear," said Edith Hopper. "I hope not. We just got carried away. Our new cameras. All the Cambridge sights."

"Oh the garden's still open," said Henry in a sour voice, "but I'm COMPLETELY done in. You're on your own. Entirely. I'm sorry, but that's the way it is. Fortunately, some of your group have seen fit to take advantage of a GUIDED tour."

Justin Rossi smiled down on Henry. "We've been a little thoughtless and I hope you'll forgive us. I suppose the sightseeing pull was too much and we all lost track of the time."

And Barbara, in a most conciliatory tone, took up the plea. "Mr. Ruggles, we do appreciate everything you've been doing for us. We got carried away. Such an interesting city."

"Even with the colleges closed off," put in Margaret. "So many—what do they say—so many photo opportunities."

"And," added Barbara, "we can't wait to get to Sissinghurst and hear what you have to say."

And so Henry, partly mollified, took his departure with his more loyal followers, and left Barbara and company hoisting their cameras and talking about closeup shots.

The tour bus stood at the gate, Joseph, the driver, in a slumbering posture at the wheel. The McClures, the two Lermatovs, and Henry boarded, and Sarah and Julia made for their parked car.

"Why," demanded Sarah, as she pulled out into traffic, "haven't these camera fiends taken pictures at the other gardens. Barnsley House, Hidcote, and Kiftsgate all had spectacular flowers. The Botanic Garden is a little on the dull side."

"Come on," said Julia. "You wanted to buy film, too."

"And I forgot to take any photos, so I suppose it wasn't really a priority."

"Because your priority is other people's business," said Julia. She sounded cross and her face was lined with fatigue, her steel wool gray hair looking more than usually like a bird's nest.

Sarah took a deep breath. "You know why I'm minding other people's business. For a while I put Ellen aside, but now I'm back. I'm minding Ellen's business, and anything that seems out of whack, at least deserves a little thought."

"Frankly, I'd drop this camera kick you're on. Cameras are standard tourist attire. As for me, well, as long as the cameras aren't loaded with gunpowder, I'd say skip it. Now let's hit this Hotel Fatima and see if they can rustle up something to drink." And Julia sighed, closed her eyes, and leaned back against the car seat.

Sarah focused on her driving, keeping to the left, dodging bicycles, inebriated youth, and aged residents who rushed out from behind parked cars and then stood bemused in the middle of the road. This intense concentration prevented her from seeing in advance that the entry from the Lensfield Road into the small street that harbored the Hotel Fatima was entirely blocked.

Blocked by fire engines, police cars, knots of people on the walks, long hoses snaking across the street, hurrying figures in helmets and protective coats, the whole scene fouled by clouds of dark smoke puffing out of a building. Out of the Hotel Fatima.

Sarah slammed on the brake.

Julia opened her eyes and took in the scene. "It's a bomb. Didn't Doris Lermatov say the Middle East?"

"Or New Jersey," said Sarah. "But I'll see what I can find out. Stay here and hold the fort."

She returned almost immediately. "Someone left a burner on and the kitchen went up. And so has half the hotel. They just hope they can keep it from spreading." She climbed back into the driver's seat. "I suppose we should head back to the Botanic Garden and warn the others. No rest tonight for the weary."

"Not at the Hotel Fatima anyway," said Julia grimly. "It's lucky no luggage was left off. And I've been dreaming of a hot bath."

It was Toad Ruggles who saved the day. Or to be accurate, the night. A crisis seemed to be just what Henry's injured ego needed. A chance to regain control, to flaunt his knowledge of the countryside, his possession of friends who could come to the rescue. A telephone call to an old classmate, now holding some sort of post at Trinity, produced the name of a farmhouse bed-and-breakfast at the edge of Grantchester.

"Not many rooms, we may have to double up," said Henry cheerfully. "But it's a pillow for the night and breakfast in the morning. And we can find a pub for dinner. Shake the dust of Cambridge from our feet."

And, with Julia and Sarah following, the garden tour drove to Grantchester. Henry, uplifted by a wave of gratitude, sat by Joseph and dictated the route, all the while extolling the pleasure of being in Grantchester instead of Cambridge, promising a morning sneak look at a cottage garden, calling upon the passengers to remember Rupert Brooke and his poem praising Grantchester.

"Who?" said Amy.

But even Amy could not dampen Henry's spirits. As if presenting a jewel of great price, he turned to her with a knowing smile and recited:

> And of that district I prefer
> The lovely hamlet Grantchester.
> For Cambridge people rarely smile,
> Being urban, squat, and packed with guile.

Margaret and Edith nodded together. Rupert Brooke was a known quantity, close to their generation, and Edith murmured, "If I should die, think only this of me," and Margaret said something about "ye distant spires, ye antique towers," to which Edith said, "Dear, that's Eton College, not Grantchester."

Which remark brought out a number of ill-remembered quotations having to do with towers and spires and spring coming or not coming and then the talk died and the bus rumbled on its way.

Sarah and Julia, driving behind, were also silent. Julia perhaps from fatigue, Sarah, in the early dusk, needing to keep alert for sudden turn-offs and approaching roundabouts. Only once did Julia rouse herself to say plaintively that she thought Newmarket was close to Cambridge and the wholesome sight of horses might be a real tonic. But, receiving no answer from her niece, she subsided, folded her hands in her lap, and dozed.

It was well after ten o'clock of that evening when Sarah, lying on a folding cot crammed in next to Julia's bed in a tiny single room, said that she hadn't called Alex about the change of hotel, and here they were in the wilds of Grantchester with the only farm telephone off limits at night except for an emergency.

"Of course, it isn't an emergency," she said, "and besides I hate to bother him at the hospital." She sighed. "I do miss him, you know. You get so used to someone being there, being close, and it leaves this hollow place."

"And I miss Tom," said Julia. "The hollow place fills in a little after a while, but it's still there."

And Sarah sat up and reached over to her aunt and kissed her cheek lightly.

Julia roused herself. "Now don't get sentimental on me or I shall start acting like Margaret and Edith and go to pieces. Maybe I need a new camera. New cameras seem to have bucked them up."

"Taking stupid pictures under shade trees," said Sarah sleepily.

But Julia had other things on her mind. "You don't suppose, do you, that Henry set fire to the Hotel Fatima? He's happy as a clam to be out of Cambridge, taking charge, with Barbara practically licking his boots."

But Sarah had had turned over to face the wall and closed her eyes against the unpleasant image of Barbara Baxter's tongue lapping at Henry Ruggles's shoes.

❧

Alex, whom Sarah had pictured busy with his patients, was actually hanging up the telephone in another fruitless attempt to trace the registered guests of the Hotel Fatima. The Cambridge police had wanted to be helpful, but the hotel had been reduced to ashes, the records had gone up in smoke, and the fire department had declared the whole place off-limits.

"Was anyone hurt? Anyone caught inside?" Alex had asked urgently.

"No," said the constable. "Just smoke inhalation—two firemen. "The hotel's a total loss," he added helpfully.

With this Alex had to be satisfied, but it made for a restless evening and a night not soothed by Sarah's Irish wolfhound, Patsy, who at three A.M., having intimations of raccoons moving past the bedroom window, rose to bark his head off until Alex collared him and shoved him into the bathroom.

Morning came all too soon and with it Mike Laaka. With news.

"Been in touch," said Mike. "Meet me for breakfast. I'll fill you in. George is mad. He doesn't want anything to slip out of his control. It's bad enough that the Kennebunk police are handling one end of the murder, but add the British police into the stew and George isn't a happy camper. He doesn't like to share."

"What's all that supposed to mean?"

"Details at breakfast. Thomaston Café. Seven-thirty."

At seven-forty Alex demanded details, Mike having taken in the requisite amount of juice and coffee that would allow for coherence. Despite his job, Mike was basically an evening animal and mornings took their toll. Today, his heavy-lidded eyes, his almost white hair newly wetted down and brushed, reminded Alex of an overgrown schoolboy rousted betimes from bed.

Alex sunk his fork into a thick slice of French toast, carried a triangle dripping with syrup to his mouth, chewed, swallowed, put down his fork, and eyed Mike. "Details," he demanded.

Mike blew through his cheeks. "It'd sure be easy if we could wrap the damn thing up Stateside, but looks like we can't."

"Because," prodded Alex.

"Because a pair of smashed sunglasses turned up at the High Roosting police station with a note about sending the things to George Fitts of the Maine State Police CID."

"*The* sunglasses? The ones Sarah found in her bag along with the scarf?"

"What other sunglasses would anyone want sent to George?"

"Sarah brought them to the station?"

"Who knows. The package wasn't signed. No little message like 'wish you were here, love Sarah.' "

Alex frowned. "Sarah told me she'd given the glasses away. To Portia McClure, I think. I told her to try and find them."

"If Sarah didn't, maybe Portia McClure stamped on them and then decided to dump them at the police station care of George. Does Portia McClure even know George Fitts?"

"I have no idea," said Alex. He signaled the waitress for a coffee refill and for a moment both men concentrated on breakfast.

"Seems like Sarah's work," said Mike finally. "Her touch. But why not leave her name? Why not do it in person? Why sneak up on the police station and do a drop with an unmarked package? For Chrissake, it makes her seem like a member of the Iranian secret police."

"You can't be sure it's Sarah," said Alex without conviction.

"Aaah," said Mike. "If you want to bet I think you'll lose."

"So who has the glasses now?"

"Convenience won out. Much against George's better judgment—he hates to leave evidence in any hands but those of his own forensic buddies—he's asked the High Roosting police to send the glasses to their own labs. Which they did. And they have a prelim on them."

"Okay. And they're clean? Like the scarf?"

"Not like the scarf. Blood. Traces in the hinges of the eyepieces."

Alex looked grim. "Go on. I can see you want to lay out one more little item to cheer up our breakfast."

Mike nodded. "Blood. Type B. Rh-negative. Not the most common type, as you know. And they haven't done a DNA job yet.

"But?"

"Ellen Trevino was B-negative."

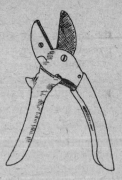

20

ALEX took a long gulp of coffee. Then he put down his cup and confronted Mike.

"B-negatives aren't that rare, but I'm not going to argue it's coincidence. I think it's time to grab this travel group, pack it up, and ship it home. And sit the whole damn lot of them down on a particularly nasty hot seat. I think Sarah's holding out on me. Something about her voice on that last call. I'm not getting the whole story. And, God knows, Julia can be as devious as hell."

"What are they holding back? If Sarah had those sunglasses she was being a good citizen by turning them in."

"Okay, but Sarah and Julia aside, what really matters is that those glasses may be the first hard evidence you've got that Ellen's killer may be on the garden tour."

Mike laid a slab of butter on a cinnamon bagel, considered, scraped off the butter, and took a bite. "My girlfriend's been going on about cholesterol. I told her I'd more likely be killed by some asshole drunk driver than by high cholesterol." Then seeing Alex glaring at him, he shrugged. "So, okay. Ellen's murderer probably flew out of Boston that Tuesday night."

Alex corrected him. "And not any old flight. That scarf and the glasses were shoved into Sarah's shoulder bag when the passengers for her flight piled up during the loading."

"Yeah, but even if the murderer's on that flight, he might not be part of the garden tour. Look, he wants out of the country. Kills Ellen—for reasons unknown, dumps the body, dumps his car, cleans up, and gets himself to Logan. Buys a ticket—or already has one—maybe he planned ahead so he's got his passport. Ends up on the garden tour flight, lands at Heathrow but keeps going. Any direction. Frankfurt, Rome. Calcutta, Beijing."

"Your point?"

"George's point. Nothing has happened on this tour. Not that we know of anyway. No threats, no strangers sneaking around."

"The only people sneaking around," said Alex grimly, "are probably Julia and Sarah. But what do you want, Mike? Another body before you jump in?"

"Well, the glasses with the B-negative blood are making George sit up."

Alex reached for the check. "Here's how I see it. The murderer—who might just be an honored member of the Garden Club—gets queasy about the scarf and the glasses being loose. Can't find the scarf—Sarah's mailed it—but knows Portia McClure now has the glasses so sneaks them away from Portia, smashes them. Someone—Sarah we guess—finds them and drops them at the police station."

Mike stood up, walked with Alex to the door, opened it and said over his shoulder. "Okay, I'll try again and see if George can pull a few wires and drag the whole crew home where they belong."

"You do that," shouted Alex after Mike, the sheriff's deputy, disappeared around the corner of the building.

Twenty minutes later at his office in the Mary Starbox Memorial Hospital, Alex hung up his telephone in exasperation. A call to Whirlaway Tours had netted him nothing more than the information that due to a fire at Hotel Fatima alternative lodging for the tour had been arranged. But Thursday night the schedule called for the group to be bedded down in Kent. The Hagglestone Arms. Near Cranbrook. Very select. Yes, we have the telephone number." Here followed an audible rustling of papers, the number, and the request for him to "have a great day."

❧

"Hagglestone Arms," announced Julia, who had busied herself with the tour itinerary and the road map. "It's by Cranbrook, which is near Sissinghurst. A couple of miles more and you can head south, and scoot right around London on the M25. Piece of cake."

"No one 'scoots' around London," complained Sarah. "You're goosed around by a million lorries and families in caravans and wild men in Jags. You have no idea how I hate being honked and hooted at if I let the speed slip below ninety."

Julia looked at Sarah with reproach. "You're allowing yourself to get tense. If my riders get that way I tell them to forget about having a sixteen-hand, fifteen-hundred-pound horse under them, and simply relax into the saddle, sit properly, keep their heels down, look ahead, and everything else falls in place."

" 'Falls' is right," said Sarah grimly. She leaned forward, and told herself that at least she was not on top of a horse. In celebration she depressed the accelerator more firmly and shot around a startled Volvo. For fifteen or so minutes aunt and niece were silent and then Sarah picked up the familiar thread.

"I've been juggling the pieces in my head and that business about my being roughed up, and I'd say we—or I—just got caught in the crossfire and the tour leaders are really the ones on the endangered species list. First, Lillian; next, Ellen. Then Henry. I'm sure Ellen didn't keep her travel plans a secret. And Henry certainly told everyone that he was mortally afraid of water. Maybe we're in the middle of a tour takeover and Barbara is next."

"I'd say Barbara can take care of herself," said Julia dryly. "She looks as if she could wrestle pythons."

"Barbara," Sarah reminded her, "is already the victim of a room search and she was standing next to me when Henry went into the pool. As for those tour change ideas of hers—London, Cirencester, Cambridge—what if she's afraid of keeping to the schedule? She suspects something and is trying to make it not happen."

"You are reaching."

"Someone has to," said Sarah. "Okay, check the map out for a place to have lunch and then I'll try to call Alex again."

But Alex was out of his hospital office when Sarah called from a small pub in Swanley. "Alex seems worried about you," said his secretary. "Are you okay?"

Sarah replied that yes, she and Julia were fine, and she rejoined her aunt. "Alex and I are just chasing each other by phone all around Robin Hood's barn . . . or the Mulberry Bush." She picked up her ploughman's sandwich—it had become a favorite luncheon choice—this one a slab of bread, ditto of double Gloucester cheese, ham, pickle, onion—and weighed it in her hand. "I suppose I should go out and plough something after eating this."

"You'll get your exercise at Sissinghurst," said Julia. "And, remember, we keep together and look behind us."

Sarah nodded. "And picture Lady Sackville and Vita and Nigel and Violet Trefusis and Virginia Woolf and Leonard all tripping through the roses."

Sarah's idea of conjuring up the former owners and their friends on the paths of Sissinghurst proved a feat beyond her admittedly overheated powers of imagination. The parking area was jammed with cars and tour buses. The Front Courtyard was thick with visitors, a line extended around the corner waiting to climb the Tower stairs, the Long Library was stuffed, and the garden paths were thronged.

Sarah and Julia struggled through several knots of people to the Lime Walk, where the spring flowers had faded, a fact that accounted for the scarcity of visitors. Here in the comparative peace large terra-cotta pots of red impatiens offered the only note of color.

The peace was a short one. Sarah, looking down the length

of the Lime Walk, saw fluttering hands, and members of the Midcoast Garden Club bustled forward, Henry Ruggles leading the way.

It didn't take more than a few minutes for Sarah and Julia to discover that Henry had taken command. He positively bounced. He joked, he gesticulated, he enthused.

With the exception of Carter, to whom smiling was always a chore, the members were all glad deference. Toad Ruggles— early on a rather suspect addition to the tour—was now chief. Barbara Baxter, for one, seemed to have yielded completely to Henry's superior botanical knowledge and, strange as it seemed, to Henry's charm. As they strolled the length of the Lime Walk she listened attentively to his explanations of the proper way to prune lime trees, and when they emerged into the shade of the grove of nut trees she apologized for Cambridge.

"I shouldn't have pushed it," she said to the assembled group. "Henry was right. A few cottage gardens would have been much more rewarding. Cambridge was a mistake. The colleges closed to visitors and then the Hotel Fatima burning."

Henry, today a dapper presence in white flannels and a straw hat, was gracious. "The Cambridge Botanic Garden certainly has merit. Unfortunate," he added with lifted eyebrows, "that so few took advantage of it."

"Oh, and we should have," said Barbara, the olive branch extended even farther.

"Mush, mush," said a voice in Sarah's ear. Sarah was standing a little to the rear of the group.

It was Amy. Amy, still in her black Decomposers T-shirt— or Sarah wondered, did the girl have a suitcase full of them.

"I think Barbara's afraid of being kicked off the team," said Amy. "But the really neat part of Sissinghurst isn't the flowers. It's those guys who lived here and the ones who visited. I got hold of mother's book, *Portrait of a Marriage*. She bought it in Cambridge."

"You mean you read it?" interrupted Julia.

"Actually, I just sort of skimmed. Talk about open marriages. Lovers all over the place. And kinky, you wouldn't believe."

At which point they were joined by Sandi Ouellette. "I read the book, too. Back home when I found out we were going to Sissinghurst, and I said to Fred that the whole scene made me think. I mean a lot of what they were doing, chasing each other around Europe and staying for ages at each others houses, took an awful lot of money and time, but it began to make Fred and me look like a couple of old drones. You know just getting up and going to bed with the same old person."

"I know what you mean," said Amy.

"You do not," said her mother, materializing at her side.

"Anyway," said Sandi, "I think the whole book is very romantic. Harold and Vita really loved each other no matter what."

"People, people." It was Henry. He clapped his hands. "It's almost a quarter of four, and I think we should return to the garden. The crowds will be going into the restaurant for tea, and we'll have a chance to see more. And take pictures," he added looking at Edith and Margaret. "You do have your cameras?" he said.

"Oh, dear," said Edith. She fumbled at the neck and shoulders of her pastel blue cardigan as if to see if she was carrying her new camera. She was not.

"I think," she said apologetically, "I've left it on the bus."

"So have I," said Margaret. "Dear me. It's just that we're not used to having cameras. Taking pictures. What a shame."

"I believe," said Edith, "that we used up all our film in Cambridge."

Henry looked at his group. "Did no one bring a camera? These are some of the most beautiful gardens anywhere. The Rose Garden alone. And with SUCH wonderful literary associations."

Amy held up a small camera. "I brought mine. I can take a group picture and I won't charge much for a copy."

"Amy," said her mother to the others, "will not charge for any pictures you may want."

This exchange gave Sarah the opportunity to check out the day's camera-bearing persons. The Hoppers and Justin Rossi, zero. Doris Lermatov, zero. Stacy Daniel, zero. The McClures, zero. Barbara, zero. Sandi, one (but only a single exposure left), Amy, one. Julia and Sarah, zero—although Sarah regretted she had again left hers in the car. Score: Shutterbugs, 2; non-shutterbugs, 10.

Henry congratulated Amy on her foresight, hoped that a group picture could be arranged, perhaps above that flight of stairs leading to the Moat Walk. They could group themselves around the garden bench designed by Edwin Lutyens. And after that he, Henry, intended to lead them along the Moat Walk. I do not propose," he said in a jovial voice, "to fall in the Moat. I shall be EXTREMELY careful. One unexpected bath is quite enough, thank you."

Henry moving ahead to the flagstones of the Cottage Garden, now identified the overhanging white roses on the cottage wall as *Madame Alfred Carrière*, and, somehow, without actually saying it, Henry let it be known that this was hardly a first visit to Sissinghurst. He had seen the White Garden at night. Something not to be missed.

Sarah joined the party for the group photo and then followed the tour for the walk along the moat—Henry daringly stepping along the water's edge and peering in. Henry was right, she decided. The crowds had thinned and it was possible to examine portions of the gardens, clouds of roses, some just beginning to bud: pinks, reds, magentas, crimsons, all without the distraction of families circling, and chattering, and taking pictures.

And with that thought—they were now rounding a clipped hedge and making their way to the Tower Lawn—Sarah returned to the conundrum of the cameras. Cameras only carried and used in cities or large towns. Cameras left on the bus during visits to distinguished gardens where photo opportunities abounded. Where photographs could give pleasure of remembered warmth and beauty on cold winter nights with the photo album spread out on the lap.

As the group paused, preparing to line up for the visit to the tower and Vita Sackville-West's special room, Sarah grabbed Julia by the sleeve. "Hold it."

Julia turned around and scowled. "Now what?"

"The cameras. Only in cities. Not in gardens. This is supposed to be a garden tour, remember. So listen."

"How can I help it."

"I'm going to try something with Margaret and Edith. I think they're the most vulnerable."

"You sound as if you're going to suck their blood. Do you think they're working for the CIA? Taking pictures of Cambridge suspects? Why not say the cameras are filled with heroin or cocaine. Or uncut emeralds. Edith and Margaret are really Mafia agents and they go into cities to buy—or sell."

Sarah held up a cautionary hand. "Here they come. Down from the tower. Now just go along with me on this."

"I will just for the great pleasure of seeing egg all over your face."

Sarah waved a hand at the two sisters, who walked slowly over, breathing rather hard.

"It was a climb," said Edith. "But worth the effort."

"Imagine," said Margaret. "Vita's own desk with pictures of the Brontë sisters and Virginia Woolf on it. And all Vita's books and the whole room filled with flowers."

Sarah moved in. "Aren't the flowers wonderful? You know I forgot my camera, too. Left it in our car and I'm going to get it. It's a shame not to take a few pictures. And while I'm at it I can pick up yours. And some film at the little gift shop. Thirty-five-millimeter, right?"

Margaret looked at Edith. Edith looked at Margaret. Dismay. Consternation. Then Margaret.

"Oh, no dear. Too much trouble. We're just fine. And you know our hands wobble a bit. We haven't quite got the hang of the new way of taking pictures. All those settings. The lens opening."

"But you said they were automatic."

"Well, yes, but the distance. The light. And there's a bit of a breeze. The flowers will come out all blurry."

"Never mind," said Sarah cheerfully. "You point out what

flowers you want pictures of and I'll shoot them for you. Or set them up so all you have to do is hit the button."

"No," said Edith vehemently. "No. We don't want . . . I mean it's awfully nice of you, but we'd rather not. Really. Quite tired. Up those tower stairs. It's a climb for people our age."

"A nice cup of tea," said Margaret. "That's what we need. And to sit down. And look at the shop afterwards. Postcards. Much better photographs on postcards. Professional photographers." And Margaret gripped Edith's arm, turned, and the two sisters literally scuttled away down the path.

Sarah turned to Julia who had stood entirely silent during the exchange. "Well?"

"Well yourself. Some older people can't handle technology."

"You're older. Can't you handle a simple push-button camera?"

"Yes, but if I were exhausted I might not want to go leaping around the garden doing it."

"Who said anything about leaping. I said I'd help. Come on, auntie. Those cameras are sending up—what did Big Daddy say in *The Cat on the Hot Tin Roof*—a powerful odor of mendacity. I'd like to get my hands on one of those new cameras."

"What a wonderful idea. Perhaps we can search bedrooms tonight when everyone's asleep. Sarah, has experience taught you nothing?"

"It's taught me to be just a tad more careful in the future. Now let me see if Justin Rossi or Stacy will take some pictures of the Rose Garden because my camera's broken."

"It is?"

"It will be. You see the Rose Garden has absolutely ravished me, and I'm going to die unless I have some really wonderful pictures taken. For my memory book."

"Die," said Julia with a grimace, "is probably the operative word.

21

SARAH'S entreaties to have either Stacy Daniel or Justin Rossi take just a few pictures—her own camera being jammed—fell on deaf ears. Stacy shrugged, Justin smiled. Their cameras were put away, back in their cases. Perhaps tomorrow. Right now, some coffee and then hit the gift shop (this from Stacy) or some good brown ale—Hey, join me, Sarah? (from Justin). Sarah put on a disappointed face, which prompted Justin to add that some time he'd take a look at her camera. He was good with cameras. Perhaps she needed a new battery.

And then Amy moved in. "Look, Sarah. Use mine. I just loaded new film. You can pay me by reading what I've written so far." With that Amy thrust the camera into Sarah's hands.

And so Sarah found herself backtracking into the gardens with Amy's camera and taking at random a number of shots of the most colorful displays. "Just to keep it honest," she told Julia who followed shaking her head.

"The word 'honest,'" said Julia, "has no relation to what you're doing."

It was at tea—held at the restaurant next to the National Trust shop—that Henry unveiled his surprise. The White Garden by night. Special permission. He'd made a few phone calls, pulled a few strings, and now they'd all been invited—along with a garden club from Scotland, a delegation from Lyon, and a few of specially anointed friends of Nigel Nicholson's family.

"Connections should not be despised," said Henry complacently. "I've never been a snob, but sometimes it pays to have moved in certain circles—even on the fringe of the circles." He spread a thick layer of strawberry jam on a crumpet and took a large bite, and nodded to the assembled party with satisfaction.

This announcement caused a happy ripple through the assembled party, and Sarah, looking about, saw no further opportunity to detach one member for a debate on the subject of photography.

That evening was notable (from Sarah's point of view) for several untoward events.

The first was the locking up of the cameras. The group arrived post-teatime at the Hagglestone Arms, sought their rooms, freshened for their evening meal, and met in the lower hall. At which Margaret and Edith Hopper, Sandi Ouellette, Justin Rossi, and Stacy Daniel all handed over their cameras to Barbara, who marched the collection to the office for safe keeping.

"What's the matter with keeping cameras locked in your room?" demanded Sarah, who saw her investigative plans for the evening going down the drain.

"Sarah, if you have a camera," said Barbara, "I think you should leave it in the office. Or any other valuables. Jewelry, binoculars. The manager said there have been recent incidents."

"I'm not giving up my camera," said Amy. "It's always with me because you can never tell when something will happen."

"That settles that," grumbled Sarah to Julia as they confronted their first course—beef bouillon.

"I should hope so," returned Julia. "I can hardly come up with another master key."

"I was only planning a few social visits to our friends."

"We're doing the White Garden this evening and then everyone will be going to bed because of the early start for France. No one would have welcomed your little social calls."

Across the table Justin was explaining to Stacy that he was going to skip the evening visit. "I've seen pretty much all I want," he explained, "so I don't need the magic of the evening. You can have the romance; I like to see flowers in daylight."

Stacy concurred. "Me, I want to see more of the area. We're right off the main village road. I think I'll go for a walk."

"You mean a pub crawl," said Justin.

"Another chance to soak up local color." Stacy said smoothly. Tonight she was looking particularly toothsome in a lime and yellow number that clung lovingly to every curve of her body.

"I guess you'll have to count me out, too," said Barbara. She had dressed in her usual plum-colored suit. Odd, Sarah thought, here's Stacy with an endless supply of clothes, and Barbara absolutely lives in that depressing cotton number.

"I'm going to read up on Monet," Barbara went on. "Giverney. I don't want Henry to be ashamed of me." Here Barbara gave Henry a dazzling smile, saying, "You added so much to today's visit that I'm absolutely inspired."

"You'd be more inspired if you come with us tonight," said Henry, detaching himself from a conversation with Fred and Sandi.

"No," said Barbara. "I'm going to do penance for the detour to Cambridge. I want to know all the flowers Monet planted and coordinate the paintings with the ponds, all those lilies."

So it was that an abbreviated tour group returned by evening to Sissinghurst—Sarah and Julia joining the others in the bus. It was, Sarah thought, Henry's finest hour. They were met at the gate by the head under gardener—he introduced himself as Phillips, Arthur Phillips—with orders to indulge the visitors with moonlight views of several of the larger gardens as well as the White Garden. Henry was particularly singled out as a "friend of the family."

Yes, Sarah thought, there was something special about Sissinghurst at night. Even with the others, an animated group from France, the ladies from Scotland, and a few singles and couples from somewhere, there was no feeling of the trampling herd. The cool of the evening, the mist rising out of the shadowy ground—still moist from the recent rain, the muted colors, the heavy scent from the borders of massed flowers, all these combined to convey a sense of the unearthly. A sense that was reinforced by the return of the ghost. Amy Lermatov's ghost.

Amy announced her presence to Julia and Sarah, who, by protective design, had placed themselves in the rear.

"She's back," said Amy in a satisfied voice.

"Who's back?" demanded Julia.

"The ghost. Or my vampire. Suck thy blood?" Amy grinned, her face pale in the rising moonlight, her teeth with the line of silver braces looking positively dangerous.

"Amy," said Sarah, "explain yourself. And make it short. Henry wants to talk about the White Garden. *In* the White Garden. Not hear about vampires."

"You know, the ghost woman. I saw her from my window sitting on a stone wall. At our inn. The Shearing."

And Sarah remembered. The white-haired woman in gray. With the shawl. The one who looked like Alex's mother who walked back from the village after the bodice snatching. Or ripping. She frowned at Amy. "The same woman's here?"

"I saw her over by that hedge. She's with that bunch from Scotland. You can tell they're from Scotland by the way they talk. All those brrrr's and rrrr's and 'weel ye no come back again, Kathleen.' "

"That's Irish," said Julia.

"Whatever," said Amy. "But the ghost is with them. Chatting it up. But she doesn't sound Scotch."

"It's always happening," said Sarah. "You see a person in one place and then they turn up all over the map. She's probably going to Giverney to see Monet's garden."

"I like the ghost idea," said Amy. She bent her head and said in a conspiratorial whisper, "Don't look now, but she's coming this way. Right toward us."

Sarah looked up. There she was. Elspeth McKenzie. White hair, the thin mouth, high cheekbones, a knitted shawl around her shoulders. Like a white-haired Katharine Hepburn who happened to be the one woman to whom Elspeth McKenzie was often compared. In short, a handsome presence.

"We meet again," said the woman. She was tall, almost six feet, and she smiled down at the three. "You were all at the Shearing Inn," she went on. "Such a nice place. Quiet, not completely overrun with American tourists." She had a soft throaty voice that put Sarah immediately in mind of Lauren Bacall doing her thing with Humphrey Bogart.

"You mean American tourists like us?" demanded Julia, never one to gloss over a possible irritation.

"Exactly," said the woman. "After all, the point of traveling isn't to bump into clusters from Kansas and Missouri."

"Maine," said Julia shortly.

"New England," amended Sarah who thought that her aunt was being unusually rude. To make up she extended her hand. "Sarah Deane. And this is Amy Lermatov and my aunt, Julia Clancy."

"Mrs. Thomas Clancy," said Julia, who was not prepared to melt into a state of acceptable civility.

"Jessica," announced the woman. "Jessica Roundtree. I'm from Boston, and really, Mrs. Clancy, I have nothing against people from Kansas and Missouri. My father was born in Kansas and voted for Alf Landon."

"How jolly," said Julia.

"Bleeding Kansas," announced Amy. "We do it in school. Free states or slave states."

"Good," said Jessica, "I'm glad some history has trickled into the schools." She paused. "What a wonderful garden. I'm glad I found a way to see it at night. Joined up with that group from Scotland. One of the women in their party wasn't well and decided to take it easy, so there was room for me in their bus."

"Perhaps," said Julia crisply, "they're looking for you. They may have a timetable and you wouldn't want to miss your bus."

Sarah stifled the urge to throttle her aunt on the spot. Okay, Julia didn't take to strangers butting into her life, but really. "Would you like to see the garden with us?" she asked Jessica.

"I'd love to," said Jessica. She smiled at Julia. "I remember, Mrs. Clancy, you used a cane at the Shearing, so wouldn't you like my arm? Just to be companionable." And before Julia could step back, Jessica had tucked Julia's arm under her own and extended the other to Sarah. "Three musketeers afoot in the Garden of Eden," she announced, and moved forward before Julia regrouped or Sarah could protest.

It is always difficult to detach a portion of one's body from the helpful grasp of another without making a scene or giving the gesture more weight than it deserved. Of course, this Jessica was a total stranger, but she seemed a well-meaning one, so Sarah allowed two circuits of the White Garden before she disengaged herself.

As for Julia, after the initial attempt to shake lose, she permitted Jessica's arm. Not because she had changed her opinion of intruders, but because evening weariness combined with increasing stiffness of joints prompted her to accept the support. Julia, when all was said and done, was practical. Of course, what had really irritated her from the first appearance of this woman was the fact that Jessica, as Sarah had noticed, really did resemble Alex's mother, Elspeth McKenzie. And Elspeth was a woman as opinionated as Julia herself and someone with whom Julia had clashed when the two had met on boards and committees in their roles as elders in a small community.

But Jessica Roundtree, oblivious of the burden of another identity, was going on about the white rosebush.

"Of course," she said, "that central rose—*Rosa longicuspis*—won't come into its own until mid-July."

"Some of the roses are out," said Sarah. "And the other flowers are lovely."

"The *Crambe cordifoli?* So effective against the hostas."

"I like those daisies," said Sarah pointing to a corner. Daisies surely were safe.

Jessica ignored the daisies. "The glory is that central rose. Did you know the family used to plan weddings around its peak blooming. The second Saturday in July."

But Julia had now revived. She removed her arm, braced her feet squarely on the path, and in a firm voice said thank you and that she and Sarah must now join their own party.

Jessica smiled, reached over and patted Julia's withdrawing arm, and said she, too, must rejoin her friends. But it had been fun. Perhaps they would meet again. Another garden.

And Jessica swept her long shawl about her body and floated off into the night.

Sarah turned to her aunt. "If you'd just waited, I was going to ask her if she had any relatives named McKenzie."

"And if she turned out to be a long-lost cousin, what did you plan to do with her?" demanded Julia. "Ask her to share our car?"

"I only want to be civil," Sarah retorted.

"I'm sorry," said Julia. "I just didn't want to be saddled with anyone else and she seemed ready to move in. And don't go on about friendless women who might want a bit of companionship. I grant your point. Anyway, as you said, without any effort on our part we'll probably find her sneaking around Monet's pond."

Knowing her aunt and that this was probably as close to an apology as she was going to come, Sarah herself took Julia's arm and both wandered about the paths of the White Garden until they came upon two middle-aged women, the taller of whom was describing to the other in a scandalized voice one of the more arcane events in the life of Vita Sackville-West.

"I think," said the speaker who spoke in a lowland Scot's accent, "that gardening—all this talk of propagating and fertilizing, do they not bring out the base impulses in very unsteady natures. It's easy to see that in certain of humankind man is truly fallen. Or in some cases, woman. This Jessica Roundbottom or Roundtree is a case in point."

Sarah moved closer.

"You'll be saying she's a wee bit familiar, will you not, Jenny?" said the shorter and stouter of the two.

"Just too forward for my taste, that's all."

230

Sarah moved in, bringing Julia forcibly with her.

"Hello," she said in her most cordial tone. "Such a lovely night. We've just been talking with Jessica Roundtree, too, and I heard you mention her name. Is she with your group?"

The taller woman—Jenny—shook her head—Sarah could see the movement but not the features of the woman. But there was no mistaking the disapproving voice. "Not at all. We had thought she was with you—the American garden tour."

"But you think there's something, well, odd, about her?" persisted Sarah.

"And why do you ask that?" said the shorter woman.

"We wondered ourselves," said Sarah. "My aunt and I were rather surprised when she joined us. A stranger, and my aunt never encourages strangers. Strangers make her extremely nervous." Here Sarah gave Julia's arm a warning squeeze. "You see Miss Roundtree isn't one of our group at all, although we did see her back in High Roosting."

"The woman seemed perfectly harmless and has given us nothing to complain about," said the short one.

"Now, Maggie," said the other, "you know we were a bit put off." Sarah could now hear a warmer tone. This one, Jenny, wanted to unload.

"It's just that one of our friends, one of our group, Mrs. Sinclair—she's from Peebles—actually we're all from Peebles. Well, Mrs. Sinclair, took a nasty fall. Slipped on the wet grass and this Miss Roundtree picked her up."

"And?" encouraged Sarah.

"And Jessica Roundtree picked Mrs. Sinclair right up, right off the ground, and Mrs. Sinclair is a very large woman, almost fourteen stone."

"What my friend is saying," put in Maggie, "that she's afraid that this Jessica is one of those women."

"A lesbian," said Jenny. "Not that I'm prejudiced, but I don't hold with close physical contact between women."

"Not even in helping someone off the ground?" said Sarah.

"Mrs. Sinclair was trying to rise by herself. Of course, I've been reading about Sissinghurst, and you cannot deny that some very strange things went on here," said Jenny, her voice becoming rather shrill. "Perhaps there's something in the air . . ."

"I think," said Maggie in a repressive voice, "that Jenny here is making something out of nothing. A mountain out of a molehill. I certainly don't think that Miss Roundtree was about to drag one of us off into the bushes."

"How very interesting," said Julia, shaking off Sarah's arm. She had been silent during the exchange. "And now my niece and I must join our friends. We've enjoyed meeting you both." And Julia wheeled and set off down past a darkened row of box hedges.

Neither Julia nor Sarah spoke until they had reached the entrance and Sarah had settled Julia and herself on a bench to await the arrival of the others.

"Really," said Julia. "That Jenny. Dour old biddy. John Knox has a lot to answer for. I didn't expect to feel kindly about Jessica, but for heaven's sake, you'd think that someone had been raped and drawn and quartered."

"Leave it," said Sarah in a tired voice. "That Jenny is way off base. My lesbian friends would never dream of accosting strangers."

"Unless the strangers welcomed them with open arms."

"My friends," said Sarah firmly, "are extremely fussy about whose open arms they step into."

At which point they were joined again by Amy Lermatov. Obviously bored, skuffing her feet in the gravel. "I've just about had it with gardens, except," she said, "I did get some details for my story. I've decided to use poison. Get even with garden lovers. I'll poison them all. There's foxglove, which is something called digitalis, and henbane and water hemlock and even lilies of the valley are poison and so are azaleas, and then there's some sort of nightshade. I asked that ghost who has a real name. It's Jessica Round-something. She was really nice and told me all about poisons. She knows a lot about dangerous plants."

"How useful," snapped Julia.

Sarah looked over at her aunt with concern. Under the dim light over the bench she could see Julia's face looking pinched and lined. Time to go home and hit the hay. Tomorrow would be demanding, what with crossing the channel, hiring the new car, driving like mad to Giverney, and probably having language problems. They had not practiced as they had promised themselves.

"Home," said Julia echoing her thoughts. "I'm rather used up."

"Here they all come," said Amy. "I've got to start deciding who I'm going to poison first. Have die in convulsions of agony."

Julia roused herself. "You could," she said, "start with a fourteen-year-old American visitor with red hair.

That night Julia lay in her bed, comforter pulled to her chin because the evening had turned chilly. Beside her lay Sarah, on a mattress dragged in from the adjoining room. Aunt and niece had had an argument on the subject of security, of the need for both to stay together. "You can never be too careful," Julia had said. So now a straight chair was tipped against the outside bedroom door and another such against the communicating door. Julia's cane lay ready at hand by Sarah's pillow.

"You've gone and stirred everyone up about cameras," said Julia. "You may not think you're a target, but I feel a hot spot between my shoulder blades, and I keep looking over my shoulder. You know the saying: Forewarned is forearmed."

"But we're forearmed without the forewarning."

"Honestly, Sarah. What do you want? A knife at your throat or a letter with the Black Spot on it?"

And Sarah subsided and for a moment both lay in the dark. Brains at work. Brains apparently, for once, on the same wave.

"Sarah," said Julia from her bed.

"Aunt Julia," said Sarah from the floor. And then, "You go first. I defer to age and wisdom."

"As you should," said Julia. "I'm thinking about Jessica Roundtree. When we saw her at High Roosting we both thought there was something a bit strange about her. Not just because of looking like Elspeth McKenzie. Or because of Amy Lermatov and her ghost."

"Correct," said Sarah. "My thoughts exactly."

"That report from Sandi Ouellette about the bodice ripper and the woman who heaved the molester out of the WC"

"Right."

"And that perhaps our Scottish friends despite their highly unenlightened and objectionable views of lesbian women . . ."

"May not have been entirely off base when they thought Jessica was unnatural," finished Sarah.

Silence.

Then Julia.

"The whole thing is highly irritating. I think I shall scrub my mind out with soap."

"Good idea," returned Sarah. "Harsh yellow laundry soap." Then after a sigh. "Good night, Aunt Julia."

A long pause, an answering sigh from the bed. Then, *"Bonne nuit, ma chérie."*

22

JULIA in France, was hardly more amiable than she had been the last few days in England. The last-minute packing, the rushed breakfast, her arthritis, the dash to the ferry, the choppy channel crossing threatening mal-de-mer had already darkened her view of the world when she hit the tourist office at Calais. There followed the discovery that the female at the tourist office did not—or would not—speak English, the taxi driver had never heard of Europcar rental, that when this office was discovered, the entirely charming lady in charge spoke only French.

Sarah and Julia finally managed to patch together their rental agreement for the offered Renault, and at last they were on their way, Julia with maps and the automobile's instruction booklet.

"The whole thing is in French," announced Julia as Sarah twisted their way out of Calais and set the Renault's nose in the general direction of Rouen, the city closest to Monsieur Monet's noted pond and garden. She flipped over several pages and frowned. *"Avons-nous plein d'essence?"* she asked.

Sarah peered at the gas gauge. *"Il y a encore* in the tank, I think. At least the little arrow isn't at the bottom. Thank heaven for icons. But we'll have to keep an eye on it."

Julia leaned her head back on the car seat rest and began reviewing those annoying verbs which took the verb *être*—to be—as their auxiliaries. Also it would be useful if she could remember a few telling phrases. *Taisez-vous* and *allez-vous en*—"be quiet" and "go away"—ought to come in handy.

Sarah, however, was not wrestling with language but with scenery. She was puzzled by the rural character of the roads. Didn't they have superhighways in France? Of course, the woods, the fields blanketed with poppies, the cows meandering down to small streams, hawks soaring in a cloudless blue sky, all these were charming, but they weren't making very good time. In particular, Julia was routing them through endless small villages whose speed was set at a snail's pace and Sarah had been warned about exceeding the limit. The French police loved to nail feckless American tourists. "What," she demanded of her aunt, "does your map say about main roads? We won't be in Vernon until midnight at this rate."

Julia bent over her map, traced a line with her finger and said that all seemed to be well. "It's a good map. Little bits of French history printed on the side. For instance did you know that *pour perfectionner le français le cardinal Richelieu . . .*"

"Give me that map," said Sarah, reaching over and snatching it from Julia. Driving with her left hand she frowned at it and then exploded. *"Merde!* By which I mean 'shit!' Your map is at least twenty years old. My God. When you said you had French and Italian maps I thought you had something printed after the invention of the automobile."

Julia contrived to look apologetic. "I was saving money. I have all these maps left over from old trips. Tom and I had a wonderful time driving across France back in the seventies. Or was it the sixties? After the war, anyway. Through the Loire Valley and then into Italy. Venice, Florence, and on to Lake Lugano."

"Damnation," said Sarah. "We're creeping along reading a map probably used by General Eisenhower. Let's stop and find something printed in the nineties. We can get gas then or *essance* and you can be very humble for the next hundred miles."

They reached Vernon at twilight unfortified by not much more than a couple of croissants and at a highway pit stop. The waitress, annoyed at their arrival just as the luncheon period ended had slammed down their plates with a surly *"bon appétit."*

Sarah and Julia found their party gathered around two tables on a little paved area in the front courtyard of the Hotel Fontaine. Everyone seemed to be in fine fettle raising glasses of wine, or in Amy's case, the always available Orangina. The bus trip, Sarah reflected, had allowed them all to sit back and be whizzed—via super highways—to Vernon stopping en route at a restaurant with two Michelin stars for their *déjeuner*. Really, there was a great deal to be said for bus tour travel; she and Julia were hot, dusty, and hungry.

The spirits of Margaret and Edith seemed to have revived, so that they were able to dip into their memory book and talk of a walk taken along the Seine, of a picnic taken on a ridge above Giverny, of a memorable visit to the Château de Bizy. Carter McClure, unusually amiable—he had slept for most of the bus trip—described to anyone who would listen the details of a remarkable *civet de lapin*. Sandi and Fred Ouellette were in a flourishing state, speaking French at every opportunity, Fred announcing that he was very anxious to meet with a local undertaker—*le entrepreneur de pomps funèbres*. Perhaps he and Sandi could pay a visit after dinner. As for the rest, Doris Lermatov and Portia were deep into a discussion of Monet— haystacks versus lily ponds—while Justin Rossi and Stacy Daniel argued about wines and vintages. Wines of the Loire and the Médoc. The virtues of a *vin de la maison* compared to the high price of a *vin de cru*.

Sarah looking around the familiar faces decided that a change had come over them all. It was as if the arrival on French soil had altered not only their spirits but their whole appearance. Everyone looked, well, smarter. Stylish. In some cases, positively chic. In England, attention had been paid to comfort. To serviceable clothes and sturdy shoes. Only Stacy Daniel had maintained a fashion profile, the others settling for being simply decent, and in Carter McClure's case, what with his rumpled jackets and cowboy boots, raffish. Now only Amy Lermatov in her jeans and T-shirt looked the same.

Here sat the Hoppers, who had added long scarves tossed dashingly over the shoulder to their usual navy blue dinner attire. Doris Lermatov wore a black float with drippy silver earrings, Carter McClure sported a white linen jacket and had a Panama hat on his knees; Justin Rossi, handsome in a blazer and an open-collared shirt, now raised his glass to Portia McClure, clad in a rust-and-black-striped caftan. Sandi, in heavy-duty eye make-up, wore an above-the-knee black number, and husband Fred had dressed up his olive sport jacket with a purple and yellow flowered tie.

But Henry Ruggles had outdone them all. A beret encased his wig, he wore a pinstriped suit with a boutonnière in his buttonhole, and the whole effect was such that Sarah would not have been surprised to have him leap to his feet and start singing, "Thank heaven, thank heaven for little girls." All in all, she thought, the group had managed to reduce Aunt Julia and herself to a pair of sordid, dirt-splotched interlopers.

Only Barbara Baxter in her cotton travel suit seemed untouched by the festive atmosphere. Preoccupied, she looked at her watch and frowned as each new car arrived at the hotel and pulled to a stop.

This behavior did not pass unnoticed.

"Looking for someone, Barbara," demanded Carter McClure. "You have a secret rendezvous?"

"Aha," said Fred. "A Claude or Jean-Philippe or André?"

"Who is *très charmant* and twirls his mustache," put in Sandi.

"Or a spy who is carrying a secret message for NATO which must be delivered by a woman at midnight at the entrance to the Louvre," said Henry.

Amy grinned. "You're meeting a representative from Columbia. A drug lord. He has the cocaine trade in his control and he wants to make a big buy. Lots of kilos hidden in gift paper which you had wrapped up in England."

Barbara gave Amy a hard look. "My brother. Greg. Short for Gregory. He's going to be in Paris on business and we set this up as a meeting place. To have dinner. I don't see him very often. He lives in South Carolina and travels a lot." She looked around at the interested faces. "I thought this would be a good time because it won't interfere with the gardens and the trip. Tonight everyone will be going out for dinner. Won't you? I mean . . ."

"Relax," said Carter. "You can meet your brother."

Julia smiled—it was an expression Sarah knew well. "No explanations necessary." And to Sarah in *sotto voce*—they sat at a distance from Barbara—"too many explanations."

"Don't pay attention to my evil-minded daughter," said Doris to Barbara. "Enjoy yourself. It's too bad you can't go off to Paris with him for a whole day."

"I would never do that," said Barbara. "No, this is just a quickie. To catch up on family news."

"Well, family is always important. What does your brother do?" asked Portia. Portia usually managed to restore equilibrium, but Barbara had now pulled herself together. "I don't want anyone to think I'm taking off in the middle of the trip. I didn't mention my brother turning up because, well, I like to be professional and not mix my personal life with my business life."

"Well," said Sandi good-naturedly, "we're all friends by now. Tell your brother to join us for a drink."

"We never mind," said Julia, "hearing about each others' private lives. Their special interests. Hobbies. For instance, I had no idea so many of you were interested in photography. I think knowing these things about each other makes us all seem a little more human." Julia looked up and bestowed a benevolent gaze on the gathering.

"Oh, yes," said Sandi. "Although," she added, "I'm not sure you want to hear all the details of what Fred does. I mean his life simply revolves around dead bodies."

"My brother," said Barbara, "is a sales representative. Southern crafts. He goes around the southern U.S. looking for hand-made things to sell all over the world. Especially in Europe. That's why he's in Paris." She paused and then looked directly at Amy. "Sorry to disappoint you, Amy, but Greg and I are not about to pass kilos of cocaine back and forth."

Amy blinked. And then revived. "You couldn't," she said. "They have dogs now who sniff out the drugs and you get nailed at the airport. Even if you've got drugs sewed into your under-wear. Or into your body. Did you know that some people take little packages filled with drugs like cocaine and shove them right up . . ."

"Quiet, Amy," said her mother. "And Barbara, we hope you have a lovely evening. The temperature is perfect. Your first night in France."

"Actually," said Barbara, "I've been in France before. But never right here. I've never been to see Monet's place."

"She makes it sound like a bar," sniffed Julia to Sarah.

Sarah turned on her aunt and positively hissed. "Shhhh. Be-have yourself." She raised her voice. "Where are you going for dinner? Have you any recommendations? I've never been to Ver-non either."

Barbara gave her a grateful look. "The hotel made lists for us. Five or six places—all quite simple and not far away and not too expensive. You can walk to all but one of them."

At that there was a scraping back of chairs, a reaching for the restaurant lists, a buzz of discussion, and then the group frag-mented, some to make further preparations, some to take off and explore. Barbara to wait for her brother at the entrance. Julia to wash and change.

But Sarah lingered at the table.

Julia stopped at the hotel threshold. "Sarah? You coming?"

"Go along. I'll catch up in a minute. There's something I need to check. My passport. Some traveler's checks."

Julia returned and faced her. "Out here, on the terrace?"

"Not exactly," said Sarah. "Please, Aunt Julia. Go on up to your room. Trust me. I'm not doing anything I shouldn't. Just a little bit of evening air. I'm safely surrounded by at least twenty other hotel guests." She gestured toward a phalanx of tables.

And Julia retreated. Passing Barbara she wished her *"bonsoir,"* a message Barbara graciously received and wished her the same.

Sarah in her turn retreated. Quickly, with a sort of step, jump, she sidled into the shade of a series of clipped hedges that marked the border between table area and a small front garden. Here she found a bench upon which she knelt, finding that she could just see over the hedge and so had an excellent view of arriving and departing vehicles.

Not long to wait. Some seven or eight minutes later a gray Peugeot glided into place and came to rest under the street lamp. Barbara, who had been lingering by the front door, walked swiftly down the walk to the curb, pulled open the passenger door, climbed in, the car accelerated, took a sharp left and was gone.

And Sarah, watching, did not think in the lamp-illuminated moment that she saw anything like a brotherly-sisterly embrace. But was that significant? There were times when she, herself, felt more like kicking her own brother, Tony, than kissing him.

In Julia's room she found her aunt dressed and fortifying herself with a few inches of scotch in the hotel glass. "What," demanded Julia, "were you doing down there? I thought we were going to keep an eye on each other."

"We are," said Sarah. "Until the end of time, or at least until Alex meets us in Bologna and then we can be a threesome. And don't say 'how jolly' again. Alex has a protective streak a yard wide. I'll be ready in minute. Just let me wash up and change."

"I've been looking over the restaurant list," called Julia to Sarah now splashing vigorously in their shared bathroom. "There's one called L'Auberge du Dragon only a few blocks away. It's marked 'charming and quiet.' And on the same street, Le Petit Monarque with a walled garden and marked 'budget.' "

Sarah put her head around the door. "I have something else in mind, but we'll have to drive around to find it."

"Why on earth? We've been driving all day."

"Trust me."

"If you say that again I'll scream and call for *La Sûreté*—or *les gendarmes*."

Sarah rejoined her aunt clad soberly in a dark gray shirt and a black skirt. Her dark hair was wet and neatly brushed back from her face.

"You look a bit funereal," remarked Julia, eyeing her.

"Being inconspicuous is my game and yours, Aunt Julia. Take off that yellow chiffon scarf thing. We're going to eat with—no, not with—but near Barbara Baxter and her brother, Gregory." Sarah held up a warning hand. "Not a word. We haven't that much time. We want to get to the restaurant right after they've been settled in so as not to miss too much. We can slip in and take a seat and if we're lucky they won't notice us immediately. When they do it will be too awkward for them to leave. We'll make it clear we don't want to join them, that we just wanted to be away from the others. We've already established that you're something of a crank . . ."

"Thank you."

"And cranks like to eat alone. Or with long-suffering nieces. All right, I'm ready."

"I suppose," said Julia in a resigned voice as she climbed into the passenger seat of the Renault, "this all has to do with the fact that the lady hath protested too much."

Sarah busy with starting the car didn't answer immediately, but after she had maneuvered the Renault out of the precinct of Hôtel Fontaine, she nodded. "I have this feeling. Barbara wasn't happy about having us know about Greg. Why? It's perfectly natural to want to have dinner with your brother, but I don't buy that bit about it not being professional to mention it. So keep your eye out for a gray Peugeot. I'll swing round the block." And Sarah slowed the Renault by the awning of L'Auberge du Chat Noir. "Why," demanded Julia, "do we want a gray Peugeot?"

"It's the key to our dinner," said Sarah. "But I don't see it at the Black Cat. Look, I'm going to take a guess. What's the name of the restaurant not in walking distance from our hotel?"

Julia drew her finger down the list. "L'Auberge sur le Pont, so I suppose it just might be on a bridge. Or near one. Turn here, then take a right on rue Ambroise Bully, and a block after the traffic circle, a left to a bridge crossing the Seine. And while you drive I'll try and figure out why we're going to be hanging around Barbara Baxter's dinner with her brother."

"Nothing ventured, nothing gained," said Sarah.

The dinner scenario worked out as she had predicted. The Peugeot was discovered in the parking lot, the two women entered, saw Barbara and brother Gregory at a far table heads bent in conversation. The two women slid into a table in the general vicinity, nodded and smiled when they were discovered. Sarah thought that Barbara had handled their appearance rather well, waving a cheerful hello and then returning to her conversation. No attempt was made, however, to introduce the brother.

"It's just a matter of our pretending to talk," said Sarah. There aren't many people in here and after a while Barbara will forget we're here and we can pick up little pieces of conversation.

"To make a quilt," said Julia who seemed to be backsliding into her crank mode.

"Mesdames?"

It was the waiter and after a certain amount of dithering, Sarah went for the *magret de canard* and Julia opted for a *feuilleté de foie et de poulet*, both to be washed down with a recommended *graves*.

And then industrious and silent eating—the food was splendid. Finally, when Sarah was beginning to have qualms in view of the fact that the prices noted on their list were marked "high"—small scraps of talk began to become audible. Nothing made much sense and Julia's analogy to the quilt seemed rather apt.

First, Sarah heard Barbara make a reference to Hawaii. The prices there. Nothing unusual about that, since she was, after all, in the travel business. Then Gregory responded and Sarah caught the words "steam service" and then "Liliuokalani" and the date "1891." The two seemed to be caught up in Hawaiian nineteenth-century history. Perhaps Gregory sold U.S. southern crafts to Hawaii and Barbara arranged tours there. If she had it would be incumbent on her to be knowledgeable about the islands.

Then for a space of time lowered voices and then Gregory came out loud and clear: "Two million. Can you believe it. Jesus." And Barbara's lower, "Well, you thought it might." And then mumble, mumble, the words "ten percent buyer's commission," followed by a talk of cancelation and a museum offer.

"I think selling southern crafts must be good business," whispered Julia during the rattle of coffee cups being placed on the table. Julia had the hearing, when she wished, of a nosy teenager.

"Nothing to do with cameras," said Sarah.

"Two million spells jewelry to me," said Julia. "Or uranium."

"Be quiet," whispered Sarah.

But nothing more than a few random and absolutely incomprehensible words followed. A reference to the "rotary" or "a rotary," something about a "black inverted center," and several remarks about Poly Pro film and an upcoming Canadian auction.

Further information came, in fact was delivered by Gregory Baxter, a tall fair-haired man with the impressive shoulders of a linebacker, a cleft chin, rather startling brown eyes, emphasized by his wire-rimmed glasses. Brother and sister had risen, walked over to Julia and Sarah's table, and Barbara had introduced her brother.

"We've been talking over old times," said Barbara.

"All those trips to Hawaii," added Greg. "When we were kids. Our mother was born in Honolulu."

Sarah saw no reason to lose the opportunity to ferret out more information. "Barbara said you market crafts. Things from the south. How interesting. What sort of things? I mean if you have buyers in France you must have to know what French dealers want."

"And British and Italian and Scandinavian dealers. Greek dealers. Spanish dealers and ones in Bombay and Yokohama. Jakarta, Bangkok. All over the whole blessed world, in fact. I travel a lot and, of course, Barbara, here, can eyeball possibilities when she's on one of her tours."

"That's enough, Greg," said Barbara. "They don't want to hear all that. Besides it's getting late. We've had a long day. Haven't we?" This last addressed to Julia and Sarah.

"Yes," said Sarah quickly, "but I love to know what other people do. Teaching English is really boring. Static. And I never travel. What kind of crafts do you sell?"

"I don't actually 'sell.' I work with agents and dealers. As for crafts—I don't know what Barbara told you, but not things like salt and pepper shakers made out of walnuts or hand-carved salad forks. Unless they're old. Our things are what you'd call 'folk craft.' Dolls, drawings, small toys. Hand-made religious items."

"Jewelry," said Julia in a hopeful voice.

"Simple jewelry made from seashells, nutshells, stuff like that. Pictures, too. Sketches. Small paintings—done with herbal dyes, tempera, ink. And we do a lot with paper artifacts. In as mint condition as possible. Perfect condition counts for a lot. From the south. And Hawaii. Those are our special areas."

"You mean antiques?" demanded Julia picking up on the "old."

"You could say that," said Greg. "I don't use that description but some of our things are pre-Civil War. Or made during the Confederacy. Believe it or not there are galleries and agents and auction houses who have customers panting for the stuff. Baxter Enterprises aims to please. And provide."

Barbara pulled at Greg's sleeve. "Greg, I'm tired even if Sarah and Julia aren't. And the waiter's over there with our check."

Greg stepped over to the waiter, took a slip of paper from the small tray, frowned, fished for his wallet, and began slowly to count out franc notes.

"I hope you don't mind Greg," said Barbara. "He gets wound up about his job. All the details you never want to hear."

"But I love details," said Sarah. "They make everything seem more real. I tell my students, go for it, pile on those details."

"Pirates," said Greg, returning to the group. "But I never argue about food prices. Anyway, to finish up, I'm over here—Paris, then Amsterdam. To deal personally. Trouble is we used to mail our things but the damn U.S. Postal Service won't insure registered mail to Europe, so we've had to use Lloyds."

"Of London?" asked Sarah.

"Is there another Lloyds? You see a really valuable shipment on the way to Germany was heisted and so now even Lloyds won't insure our mailings anymore." He grinned, looking from Sarah to Julia. "You can't trust anyone anymore."

"I suppose," said Julia when they reached their car, "that they knew we'd been trying to overhear what they said during dinner, so Gregory decided to bring it all out in the open. She fastened her seatbelt and sighed. "A lot of trouble over nothing."

"Not so," said Sarah. "We've got a whole bag of odd references, and later Barbara didn't want Greg to go rattling on and when he mentioned not trusting anyone she stepped on his foot."

"I'd hate to take that into a court of law," said Julia.

"I'm beginning to think about Hawaiian gemstones being hidden in a bunch of old carved southern crafts," said Sarah. "But what kind of crafts do you suppose?"

"Crafts shrunk down to fit into cameras," said Julia.

"And sold in English and French gardens?"

"Or in Cambridge and Circencester and London. Those little side trips. With support from the Hoppers and the rest. Now I think we'd better scratch this particular line."

"I do not believe in scratching," said Sarah in a firm voice. "Tonight, or tomorrow at the very latest, I'm going to get my hooks on a camera or two. Preferably belonging to Margaret and Edith. By stealth or by outright bullying. I think they can be bullied."

"As I said, Sarah, you're beginning to sound a lot like me. It's in the blood. Now there's the train station. Take the next left and we're almost back."

"I don't think," said Sarah thoughtfully, "that you'd better talk to Alex about this genetic compatibility. He's already detected signs of it and it makes him extremely irritable. Remember, that my dearest Alex is an ordinary mortal who only wants to get his excitement from the Celtics and the Red Sox."

As if conjured by the reference to his name, there was on their return to the hotel a fax waiting for Sarah. From Alex. It was short and to the point: Cut loose and get out. I've changed plans and am flying Alitalia to Milan. I'll meet you there in two days. The train station between noon and three. Love, Alex.

"I think," said Julia dryly when Sarah showed her the sheet, "that Alex has more on his mind than the Celtics and the Red Sox."

23

SARAH did not make a preemptive strike on the Midcoast Garden Club's cameras for the simple reason that Madame at the desk—a black-browed Madame Defarge character busily knitting between guest arrivals and departures—informed Sarah that all such were under the hotel lock and key for reasons of security.

"Toujours," said Madame, holding up a needle, *"prenez garde."*

"I'm going to have to trap the Hoppers at Giverny," Sarah reported. "And forcibly snatch one of the damn things." She and Julia were preparing for bed after having activated their own security system of locks, bolts, and tipped chairs.

"Giverny!" exclaimed Julia. "We're heading for Milan. I've been looking over the map. Drive to Lyon, turn in the car, take the train for Turin, change for Milan. As we planned to do, only quicker. No stops for a château."

"After Giverny," said Sarah, who was kneeling on the floor wrestling with the strap on the hated wheeled suitcase. She had meant to dump it long ago.

"Of course," said Julia, "it's a pity to miss Monet's garden. I've never been there."

"We aren't going to miss it," said Sarah, standing up.

"What?"

"Not—going—to—miss—it. We'll go to Giverny in our car, park safely with thousands of others, and see what develops. "Develop"—as in film in a camera. Or no film but a little cache of something. Tiny handcrafted items made by Hawaiian missionaries or Créole children or loyal Confederate women back on the old plantation."

"But Sarah . . . ," began Julia.

"But me no buts. I'm absolutely determined to follow this one to the end. All we have to do is exercise sensible caution."

Julia shook her head. "Alex must have had good reason to scrap his own plans. That Lyme Disease Conference. Why don't you call him and see what's up?"

"I'm sure he expects me to call and protest, and then he'll give me fifty reasons for leaving the group and we'll end up wrangling, which will do nothing to cement our marriage. Because I'll say no."

"Alex probably wants a live wife. Even a live Julia Clancy."

"Alex knew what I was like before we got married."

"He probably knew he was marrying an independently minded English teacher but not a candidate for the morgue."

"No more talk. It's bedtime. Keep the door open between us and think about lilies floating under a bridge."

Julia did not stop to reply but retreated to her own bed, pulled up the pink cotton blanket to her chin, turned over and gazed fixedly at the wall. Unfortunately the wallpaper featured a pattern of morning glories twined about a lattice. I can't get away from gardens and I've lost my grip on Sarah, she told herself. I've met my match. My own flesh and blood. She reached over and turned off the light but her brain, though sluggish, was still circling.

If only, she told herself sleepily, we had some sort of weapon. A pocketknife. A folding bread knife. Did they make folding bread knives? Or better, just an automatic revolver. A tiny automatic revolver. Travel size. Or a stiletto. An icepick. And for a time a parade of desirable weapons floated across Julia's inner eye, and then reaching for the handle of a miniature dibble, she fell into a troubled sleep.

Sarah, on the other hand, closed her eyes in five minutes' time and slept the sleep of the virtuous person who has not hesitated nor been swayed by wiser heads and sane counsel.

❧

The next day, June the nineteenth, in the midcoast area of Maine, Alex reviewed again the fifty urgent reasons for Sarah and Julia to remove themselves immediately from the garden club's tour and to hit the road. Because as surely as night followed day, Sarah would call and he, Alex, would have to persuade. She would resist but he, with logic and sense on his side, would prevail. And if this approach failed, he was prepared to play the fear-and-love card: I love you and remember what happened to Ellen Trevino.

After all, things were racheting up. The Maine State Police in the person of George Fitts had called Alex the day before and said that at last the DA's office had okayed a plan to try and reel in the Garden Club. A message was to go out to the tour's next planned stop—they were booked for the night in a Paris hotel before they flew out the next morning to Italy. The message would be delivered courtesy of the Parisian police and would inform the garden lovers that they were all urgently wanted back in Maine for questioning in matters pertaining to the death of Ellen Trevino.

"We can't force them," Mike Laaka told Alex early that morning at their common meeting place: the hospital cafeteria. "Practically our club," Mike said, as the two men settled down over cups of coffee and cinnamon doughnuts. "I mean," he went on, "we'd have to go through the whole legal song and dance—show just cause—pull in the French police and Interpol to manage the extradition. But we can't and so they wouldn't. But what we can do, George thinks, is put the fear of God—or the fear of the Maine CID—into them. Suggest ever so delicately that delay in returning might be construed as an obstruction of justice or a withholding of evidence or some such garbage."

"I've put a firecracker under Sarah and Julia," Alex told him. "Sent a fax telling them to hit the road and meet me in Milan."

Mike dumped a second plastic cup of cream into his coffee and shook his head. "You're sure Sarah will jump when you whistle."

"I'm just making a reasonable request," said Alex crossly.

"I don't think reason figures in," said Mike, "Besides, Sarah's traveling with an unreasonable person called Julia."

Alex shook his fist at Mike. "You're a troublemaker. Sarah will listen and I know Julia. Her bark is worse than her bite."

"We're not talking about bites, we're talking about a woman who once decided to steal three horses on Christmas Eve. Assisted by Sarah."

"Good-bye, Mike."

Mike held up a restraining hand. "Relax. I've got other news. We've run bios and work profiles on the whole tour group."

"And?"

"About Stacy Daniel—only that isn't her name."

"You said she's done modeling. Maybe her own name wasn't very fashionable."

"Previous name was Sherri Norton."

"Which wasn't real either?"

"Apparently not. We're looking and so far have come up with a stepmother in a nursing home called Janice Hirschenburgh. Not much help there, she has Alzheimer's."

"Dead end?"

"Not yet. We'll keep trying. And something funny has turned up about Margaret and Edith Hopper, but we bumped into a stonewall when we tried to run it through the system. Sealed documents or case dropped, that sort of thing. Intervention by judge. George is trying to get the DA's office to do some digging."

"If Edith and Margaret Hopper are candidates for anything other than sainthood, then I'm a monkey's uncle."

Mike grinned. "I'll try to hurry that part of the investigation."

"No other stupid red herrings?"

"More sealed briefs because he was a minor at the time. But it looks like our legal eagle Justin Rossi was arrested one Halloween in Cambridge. Sixteen at the time."

"You can break into those records?"

"If we can show justification, the need to gather evidence—but evidence of what? Hell, half the teenagers in New England have probably been in police trouble on Halloween."

"I was picked up for throwing raw eggs," Alex admitted. "I hit the dean of the medical school in the back of the neck."

"You see," said Mike. "And the law has protected your youthful reputation by sealing the record."

"Actually," said Alex, "I wasn't that youthful. I was a first-year med student at the time."

That June morning in Vernon was again clear, sun-filled, with balmy currents rustling the roadside poplars and featuring a kindly temperature in the mid-seventies. It was the sort of day, Sarah thought, that said "Get thee to a garden." Sniff the roses, wander down paths, and linger in bowers. It was not the sort of day, she told Julia as they walked down the stairs for breakfast, to be cowed by forebodings, or the apprehensions of an absent husband. Giverny and Claude Monet beckoned.

These sentiments seemed to be shared by Aunt Julia, who had awakened in good humor. "I'm with you," she announced. "Loaded for bear."

Arriving at the breakfast for the shared *petit déjeuner*, they found that the group's good humor of the previous night had blossomed into a tangible excitement. There at a long round table set with a snowy cloth and carafes of coffee and silver pots of chocolate, with baskets of hot croissants, apricot and blackberry confiture on the side, they rehearsed the pleasures of the day to come. Presiding over the whole was Henry Ruggles. Monet was apparently his "thing," if an eminent artist can be so styled. Henry, Sarah thought, spoke of Giverny as if he personally had helped the artist buy the place, arranged the placement of the Japanese bridge, and laid out the flowerbeds. Henry, a croissant in hand, waxed eloquent on the subject of color expanding in the air to vanquish figurative form, the dialectic harmony between still water surfaces and the embedded water lilies, the decomposition of substance, the triumph of sensation over visual fact.

"I don't quite get it," Sandi Ouellette whispered to Julia. "Maybe we should buy a guide when we get there. I read up on Monet before we came, but I didn't know he vanquished figurative forms."

"Don't fight it," advised Fred. "And don't get hung up with art criticism. Enjoy."

"You might want to read Kandinsky," put in Justin Rossi in a kindly tone. "He's really quite good on Monet." Justin, too, seemed infected by the general atmosphere of pleasantness, along with the usually aloof Stacy Daniel, who was making an effort at conversation with Margaret and Edith Hopper, asking them details of Monet's life, a subject on which they seemed quite knowledgeable.

Sarah, who was sitting next to Barbara Baxter at a far remove from Henry's sphere of influence, decided that Monet and Giverny could, for the moment, take a back seat, inquired after her brother, Gregory.

"He should have joined us for breakfast," said Sarah. "I'd have loved to hear more about those craft objects. For instance, I never imagined that so many people in the Confederate States, in the middle of a horrible war, were busily carving or painting miniature pictures."

"Life did go on," said Barbara. "On the southern homefront it wasn't all war and burying the silver and making clothes out of curtains and worrying about escaping slaves. And a lot of Gregory's objects were actually made on the plantations. Items that are very collectible, very marketable, you know."

"So were the enslaved," said Portia McClure, giving Barbara a steely look. "My great-great-grandmother was collected and marketed."

Barbara paused, put her hand to her mouth. "I didn't mean . . ."

"I don't suppose you did," said Portia crisply.

Amy broke in. "That's sort of exciting. Having a great-great grandmother as a slave. Have you written a book about her?"

Portia eyed the girl. "Not everyone is a subject for fiction, and I doubt if my great-great-grandmother found being in bondage on a plantation exactly exciting."

Amy flushed and looked chastened. "I'm sorry," she said in a low voice.

Sarah, turning back to Barbara with the hope of grilling her further on the subject of Gregory's business interests, found her now deep into conversation with Justin Rossi. Never mind, she told herself, there are the cameras. She looked around the table noting the empty bread baskets, the drained coffee cups. "I suppose, we're about ready to take off," she announced to the party in general. "I'm all packed because Aunt Julia and I will be leaving from Giverny in our own car. So why don't I get all your cameras out of the safe. Save you all one more step."

The Hopper sisters rose in their seats like a pair of scalded cats. Both with an emphatic and high-pitched "No!"

And Justin Rossi turned and gave a little shake of the head. "Thanks, but I'll pick mine up on the way out."

Here Barbara intervened. "Actually, I have the receipts for the cameras. Except yours, Sarah," she added reproachfully. "So I'm the one to retrieve them. But thanks anyway."

"Well, you struck out again," said Julia as she and Sarah mounted the stairs on their way to pick up their luggage.

"Never mind. I'll snatch one of those cameras by force if I have to."

"Knock the Hoppers into the pond, hurl them into the rose-bushes."

"Something like that," admitted Sarah.

"I can hardly wait," said Julia. "And when you are hauled off by the local police I will say that *vous êtes une femme que je n'ai jamais vue* in my whole life."

———

The single fact to register on every member of the Midcoast tour when they arrived at the car park at Giverny was that the entire population of the known world had decided on that day to pay their respects to the artistry and the home of Claude Monet. Even after crossing the road leading to the farm house and studio, the group found that a long line had formed by the ticket door.

"Merde," said Julia with feeling. "This is going to be worse than Sissinghurst. We'll be lucky if we even see a garden path let alone a garden. Or be able to hear Henry."

At which Henry bustled forward, his arm outspread as if to embrace the whole group. "Now everyone, you don't want to hear ME nattering away for the whole day. I suggest that I do what you Americans call a show and tell at the house, the gardens, across to the ponds. Then lunch and you're on your own to take in Giverny for yourself. To IMAGINE yourself with a canvas. Try to see and feel the colors, the light. The provocative magnificent light. You by the pond. You are MOTIONLESS but the breeze moves, the water breathes, images wave under the surface of the water. The light changes. Or as Monet said, 'The light that fades and is reborn.'"

For a moment the group remained respectfully silent, and then Carter McClure, always impatient, said, "Well put, Henry. Now let's get on with it. There's another bus pulling in and we want to get ahead of the stampede."

But Henry was not finished. "I've talked to our good driver, Joseph. He'll have the bus ready at four. I have a little idea that deviates just a trifle from the master plan. I know we're are all going to fly from Paris tomorrow. Straight to Milan. And then off north to Lake Como and WONDERFUL Bellagio and two or three last MARVELOUS gardens. Now, I'm proposing that we take a later flight—I've called the airport and there's room on Air France—and come back here at dawn. We can walk along the hills with a view of the Seine, we can sit quietly by the little Epte River that feeds the ponds. We can be closer to the SPIRIT of Monet than we will with these crowds. Barbara, will you go along with this? You are our faithful tour director."

Sarah looked quickly over at Barbara, but her face had set into a listening smile. And then she shrugged and turned to the others. "What do you all think? It means getting to Milan later, but . . ."

"Sounds like a fine idea," said Fred. "I like getting the feel of a place. And I'm always up for a morning hike."

Barbara nodded. "All right, but I'll have to see if there's room at the Fontaine for another night."

"There isn't," said Henry, "but the Fontaine has found us rooms in the area. A little pension."

"I'll tell Henry no rooms for us," said Julia to Sarah, as the queue shuffled forward and Barbara began the negotiations for the entrance tickets.

"Well," said Sarah, doubtfully. "Maybe we should hang in . . ."

"Sarah, do not push it. Alex is meeting us in Milan."

"Okay, but only if I can get hold of a camera."

And so, along with the throngs of tourists and garden lovers and art appreciators, Henry and Barbara's charges moved ahead to enter the world of Monet, Henry flushed with excitement, a man in love with every word he spoke.

And Sarah half listened to Henry—he was going on about aesthetic principles as they applied to the plantings of columbine, foxglove, nasturtiums, gentians, sweet peas—how their colors rioted and quieted, how they persuaded, transformed, and retreated. The other half of Sarah's attention centered on the cameras. The very sight of them hanging from Edith and Margaret's shoulders acted like a magnet. She dogged their footsteps, exclaimed over the flowers at which they lingered and again offered to take pictures of the two on a bench, by the bridge, but to no avail. Nor were the suggestions that one or the other take pictures of Sarah herself at some memorable spot since her own camera was still ailing. "I thought," said Sarah in a pensive voice, "that Alex—and my mother and father—might like a shot of me at Giverny."

It was a suggestion that cut no ice; Margaret fidgeted, and Edith finally told Sarah irritably that she was making them very nervous and please go away.

Sarah retreated.

"And you're making me nervous, too," said Julia who had been tagging along several steps behind Sarah.

"Okay, so it's time to get physical. A little push and shove can accomplish wonders."

"Like a broken hip."

"As Madame at the desk said, I will take care."

But opportunities for upending either of the Hopper sisters were nonexistent. Henry kept a tight hold on the flock and the streams of visitors up and down the paths, lining up to get into the farmhouse, crowding into the kitchen, the yellow dining room, the bedrooms, circling the studio, thronging the tunnel to the ponds—all these confounded assault on the Hopper equilibrium.

At the café outside the farmhouse, Sarah turned to Julia and shook her head. "It's harder than I expected."

"What is?"

It was the ubiquitous Amy holding a basin of stew. Amy, who was possessed with the sensitivity of radar. "I know," she said. "You're investigating. Is it about Barbara's brother?"

"What!" exclaimed Julia and Sarah in one voice.

"I'll whisper," whispered Amy. "I'll bet you've found out about something about her brother, Gregory. Do you know that this morning he stopped by to say good-bye and she gave him her big suitcase and told him to get rid of it. It was too big. She said you should get rid of yours, too. And I think Gregory's a sinister name. It's Russian, isn't it? Grigori. We did Russia in Social Studies this year and there were a lot of them. That crazy man, Rasputin, his first name was Grigori."

"Amy," said Sarah in a voice usually reserved for freshman who are handing in late term papers. "You can join us at our table if you'll stop pretending we're all on the Orient Express with a corpse hidden in the lower berth."

"Or hidden in Barbara's and your suitcases," giggled Amy. "But how about the cameras?"

"Cameras!" said Sarah, a little too loudly. "What do you mean cameras?"

"Sarah, you can't be as dense as you pretend. Those two Hoppers don't know one end of their cameras from another. I saw Margaret trying to take a picture with the shutter closed. And Stacy Daniel. She just aims at anything. People's feet, the tops of trees, the backsides of buildings."

Julia put down her fork. "Amy, have you looked carefully at Monet's collection of Japanese engravings? The pearl divers, for instance. Naked from the waist up. By Chikanobu Yōshu. Very distinctive. And the woman breastfeeding her baby. By Utamaro Kitagawa. Late eighteenth century, I think. You might be able to find copies at the gift shop. Souvenirs of the trip. You could take them to school next year. For your homeroom bulletin board."

Amy showed her braces. "*D'accord. Mais oui.* Mrs. Clancy, I know you're trying to distract me but it's kind of a neat idea. And I've had it with this stew thing." Here Amy looked disdainfully at her bowl of now congealed meat and vegetables. "What I'm really dying for is what the French people call a 'ahm-boorgaire.' I want one with fries and catsup and relish and mustard. I have withdrawal symptoms."

"Hurry up to the gift shop before all the Japanese engraving copies are sold out," said Julia putting spur to the moment.

And Amy departed.

Sarah was admiring. "Brilliant. But how in God's name did you know the names of the Japanese artists?"

"Simple, my dear Watson. Tom had a collection of Japanese engravings—many rather graphic. We sold them at auction and bought a Hanoverian stallion with the money." Julia put down her napkin. "And now I suppose we're ready to wander about and discover Monet each in our own way."

"Discover the Hoppers," said Sarah. "Preferably alone by a large thicket of lilacs. But I don't want you to get too tired traipsing after me."

Julia squared her shoulders, almost, Sarah thought, flexing her biceps. "I am an old workhorse. If Claude Monet could ramble around the place in his eighties, a New England woman of seventy should be able to handle it. We said we'd keep an eye on each other, so I'm going to dog your every footstep."

But she couldn't. A restless night had taken its toll, and after a short time, Sarah left her on a bench under a willow at some distance from the stream of visitors.

And now where were Margaret and Edith Hopper? Sarah fell in behind a group of visitors and followed them around the ponds, through the tunnel to the farmhouse, the studio, back to the café. Then back to the lily ponds. Only Stacy Daniel (taking the sun in a clearing) and Doris Lermatov with Portia McClure (on the Japanese bridge) had been encountered. Sarah, feeling cheated of her prey, decided to linger by the far margins of the pond where the less populated areas might lure purists like the Hoppers. She remembered that Edith had remarked rather tartly that the true spirit of Monet and the understanding of his vision certainly couldn't be found in a crowd.

After walking back and forth for a time, she decided to work her way toward the water that fed the ponds—the little River Epte. Here, too, she drew a blank, and just when her watch told her it was time to give it up, pick up Julia and leave, perhaps grabbing at Stacy Daniel's camera as she rushed out—an unlikely scenario at best—Margaret and Edith, one after the other, stepped cautiously across a moist patch of ground and coming out of the shadows, paused blinking in a patch of sunlight.

Sarah, shrinking back behind a heavy growth of vines, took a deep breath. It was all very well to talk briskly about giving a hearty push, seizing a camera, and speeding off into the underbrush, but now faced with the two elderly women—two people who had always seemed the epitome of gentleness and kindness—well, it wasn't so easy.

She was saved the trouble.

There was a distant splash, a gurgling noise and sort of yelp. Thrashing. Another cry. A choking noise. Running footsteps. A long pause. Then another splash. Another pause. Then a series of heavy sodden thuds.

And Sarah was in motion. But the sounds apparently came

from off the beaten path, and, desperately, she had to double back, begin a short climb, come down and then found herself at the edge of the stream.

On the banks of which knelt Barbara Baxter, soaked to the waist, giving CPR to a body.

24

SARAH plunged down the bank and stopped. The body, soaked, the eyes closed, the bald head. Sarah saw it all again even as she knelt beside Barbara. The sodden lumpish body being hauled out of the Kiftsgate swimming pool. The wig afloat. Henry. Henry Ruggles.

Barbara, without stopping her efforts, jerked her head to the side, saw Sarah and shouted, "Get help. Anyone. See if there's a doctor. Call an ambulance."

Sarah rose to her feet and found she had been joined. Margaret and Edith Hopper and two men and a woman all hastening forward. And then a troop pushing through the brush. A man in a striped shirt and shorts shoving people aside.

"*Je suis médicin,*" he announced. "*Alors. Permittez-moi?*"

Barbara yielded and, without missing a stroke, the doctor took over, Barbara sitting back on her heels, quite red in the face and breathing hard from her exertions.

And now, summoned by the cries, the splashing, a swarm of visitors, what appeared to be the entire complement of the Garden Club, another physician, and a woman who announced in a Texan accent that she was an emergency technician.

For what seemed an interminable period the doctor continued his exertions, and then suddenly Henry opened his eyes and struggled to sit up. And was gently forced down. And over on to his side. At which he coughed, vomited, coughed again, sighed deeply. And closed his eyes.

And then Portia McClure pushed through the crowd and sank to her knees on the damp ground beside the doctor. "Henry. Henry," she repeated. "What have you done?"

Henry opened his eyes. "I'm shhick," he said in a slurred voice.

The doctor shook his head. *"Eh bien, monsieur. Restez tranquille. Içi. Sur la terre. Vous comprenez?"* He reached for Henry's wrist, felt for the pulse, shook his head again. *"Un peu rapide. Et vous avez froid."* He looked up at the assembled crowd. *"Un couverture, un manteau? Vous, monsieur?"* pointing at Carter McClure, who had stepped forward and was now bending over the top half of Henry.

Carter stripped off a light cotton sweater and several others followed so that soon Henry was covered with a colorful array of jackets, cardigans, pullovers.

"He's English," Carter told the doctor. "Do you want me to translate for you?"

"Eh? No. I speak English. Not so good, but a little." The doctor addressed Henry, speaking directly into his ear. "Stay quiet. Okay? You will feel better soon, I think."

"Better now," said Henry in the same thick voice. "Want to go home. Soon as possible."

"But no. We will check you in my hospital, your vital signs," said the doctor. "You will go on—what is the word—a litter, a stretcher. *D'accord?* Not *à pied*, not walking. Then, if everything is how you say 'go,' okay, you may leave. To England, is it?"

"We'll come with you," announced Portia. She looked at her husband. "Won't we, Carter?"

And Carter—who looked, Sarah thought, genuinely

shaken—nodded vigorously. *"Nous sommes les amis de Monsieur Ruggles,"* he said. "We will take care of him."

"An ambulance has been called," said a voice from the crowd.

"Bien," said the doctor. He looked up and around at the throng. "Okay, give him air. The two friends may stay. The rest, all of you, go away. *Allez-vous en. Abgehen Sie, bitte."*

A faint smile crossed Henry's gray face. *"Merci. Dankeshön. Gracias."*

"Ah, you see, Monsieur Ruggles," said the doctor, smiling down on him. *"Vous n'êtes pas mort. C'est bon."*

Henry managed a weak grimace. "Not yet. *Pas encore."*

"Come on, Sarah." It was Aunt Julia plucking at her sleeve.

"But Henry."

"Henry is in good hands. The doctor. And Carter and Portia. There's nothing we can do."

"But we can't just leave him here."

"They're taking Henry to the hospital. Then he'll go home. Or stay if he wants. But we have to get out, get to Milan. If I thought we could be of any use here, we'd stay."

And now Sarah and Julia, fully caught up with the retreating crowd, found themselves pushed away from the riverbank, back toward the ponds, and there, by the side of the beaten down path, spied two most sought after objects.

Two cameras.

Sarah with a quick glance left and right, scooped the two up, thrust one down her shirt where it sank to waist level creating an awkward midriff lump. The other she shoved at Julia who for once didn't stop to argue but stuffed it into her large handbag.

"Hurry up," said Sarah. "Margaret and Edith must be behind us. They were around just before Henry went into the water."

"How do you know these cameras belong the Hoppers?"

"An informed guess. Here's the bridge. Hurry, we can beat them to the exit."

"And if the cameras belong to the Japanese ambassador or the German High Command?"

"I'll mail 'em back here with an apologetic anonymous note."

Sarah looked anxiously behind her. Margaret and Edith might any second raise the cry. She could hear it now: Thief, stop thief. There she is. She's been after our cameras for days. "Come on," she said, "let's get out of here." And she grabbed Julia's arm, dragged her to the exit, across the road, and then pushed her into the Renault. And then, over her shoulder, she saw them. An ambulance, lights blinking, slowed by the entrance and a police car, siren yelping, roared down the road.

"Give me the camera," demanded Sarah. She seized Julia's handbag, emptied it, unearthed the other camera from her shirt and threw both onto the back seat and covered them with a jacket. Then started the car, and with the greatest decorum, brought the Renault out of the car park and turned its nose in the general direction of Italy.

"What I think," said Sarah, "is that Margaret and Edith dropped the cameras when they heard Henry go into the water."

"You mean when Henry was pushed into the water."

"Of course. You can't tell me that two dunkings of a man that everyone knew couldn't swim a stroke are anything but homicidal."

"Not an efficient push. After all he's not dead yet."

"It was close. The water in that river may not have been over his head, but he panics in water. So he was damn lucky."

"Or unlucky. Depending how you look at it."

Sarah slowed the car. "The way I'm looking at it is we're a couple of rats deserting a sinking ship."

Julia made a face. "Change that around. We're a couple of ships deserting the rats. Because as sure as my name is Clancy there are rats we've left back there."

"I still feel guilty."

"And I have the cure. Where are those cameras?"

"I threw them in the back. Under my jacket."

Julia hit her seat-belt button, swiveled about, and returned, a camera in each hand. She laid them carefully on her lap and rebuckled her belt. "One Olympus and one Nikon."

"Be careful. They may have film in them."

Julia peered at the camera, pushed the slide to "On" and

shook her head. "The battery sign is blinking and there's no film number. So I can open. Presto." There was a long pause and Julia said in a disappointed voice. "Nothing. The thing is empty."

"You mean out of film. You already knew that."

"No, it's completely empty." Julia looked over at her niece. "I suppose you expected diamonds or white powder packets?"

"Something at least," Sarah admitted. "Try the other one."

Julia turned the second camera over in her hand and examined it. And frowned. "Empty."

Sarah, looking ahead, spied a gravel indentation that led down an embankment to a widening river. "I'm going to pull in over there. If these cameras are innocent, then we're a couple of thieves . . ."

"One thief. You."

"You're an accessory. And poor Margaret and Edith have lost their new cameras. And the fuss they made about my borrowing them might have been perfectly natural. They didn't want me fooling with their new toys. So if these are on the level, I'm driving back and return them."

She turned the car and pulled it under a sheltering oak. "Okay, let's have a look." Sarah opened the two cameras, compared one with the other, and slid her fingers around the interior of both instruments. Then, turning to Julia, she said, "These little buggers are about as innocent as an empty syringe."

"But I said they were empty."

"They're empty all right, but they're hollow. There's no place for film and no spool to wind the film on. The only difference is a piece of loose plastic at bottom of the Nikon. But, the things are dummies. They may have started life as cameras but now they're containers."

"Containers for what?"

"God knows. Certainly not little Hawaiian and Confederate handcrafts. Even miniatures. We've got to think very small."

"Diamonds. Or emeralds. I thought so all along. Or drugs."

Sarah turned on the ignition. "Wait and see. Okay, we're off." And they drove, on through the countryside, farmhouses, cows, more poppy fields, the Seine, mist rising, on their right hand, distant villages, the Loire Valley speeding by. Once Julia pointed to a distant spire. "Café, tea?" she said plaintively.

Sarah accelerated. "No time. Let's get this trip over with. I've got a nasty feeling that we're being followed. There's a car that's stayed behind me for the last hour. I keep asking why it hasn't passed me. No French driver stays behind anyone."

"Of course not. It's national pride," said Julia. "It's called *èlan.* But do you recognize the car? It's not that gray Peugeot?"

"Barbara's brother? God, wouldn't that be interesting. But I can't tell the make. There's a ground fog coming up. It's just a gut reaction I'm having."

Julia turned an anxious face toward her niece. "So move it."

"Okay, hold your hat. And when it gets dark we'll try and find a B&B off the beaten track. A place to crash tonight."

"Don't use the word 'crash.' "

"Listen, Aunt Julia. You check behind us and keep an eye out for the police at the same time. I'll drive like fury and try not to think what I'm going to do to certain lousy no-good people belonging to the Midcoast Garden Club Tour."

"Tough Ms. Deane."

"Angry Ms. Deane."

Sarah, as promised, drove like fury. They shot past villages, sped around astonished drivers, and then when the fog had thickened and the shadows had lengthened over the Loire Valley, Sarah, with one hasty glance in the back mirror, wrenched the wheel around and plunged down a gravel road, took a left, a right, and by some sort of Gallic miracle pulled screeching into the outskirts of the tiny town of La Verdière, and after two rights and a left stopped before an iron gate in a small street, Rue St-Simon. On the gate, written in curling gold letters, "Hostellerie: La Maison de Celeste." Julia took a long breath and unfastened her seat belt. "My Lord, Sarah, you deserve the Croix de Guerre."

Sarah let her body slump. "We've lost it. The car. I haven't seen hide nor hair of it since we turned off."

"I think," said Julia slowly, "that we should find a church and light a candle. For heavenly favors received. It's enough to make me turn Catholic."

What Julia referred to as the "mystery car" did not reappear, and the remainder of the trip took on the aspect of a bad comic movie. Or as Sarah remarked as they spun in and around Lyon, down one ramp, reversing, and up another it was more like a daytime nightmare. The most positive thing that could be said about the hit-and-run visit to one of France's most bustling cities is that after the Renault had been turned in, Sarah, encased in a vault-like room high up in the Pullman Part Dieu Hotel made the heroic decision to scuttle her oversized suitcase by shoving it under her bed, and then deliver half of her wardrobe to the tender mercies of the French postal system for mailing to Maine.

"If Barbara could do it, I can too," Sarah remarked as, clutching only a shoulder bag, she pushed her way with Julia through the station crowds into a second-class coach bound for Turin. "You know," she added, "for a while I considered that Barbara's big suitcase was something sinister. But when we searched her room the thing was completely empty."

But Julia was not listening. She was wearing her half-glasses and held up a small volume. "I'm studying up. Learning to ask for tickets for Milan when we hit Turin. '*Due biglietti per Turin. Seconda class, per favore.*'"

"You say *Milano*," Sarah corrected her. "And Florence is *Firenze.*"

"We're not going to Florence," said Julia. "But what a lovely language. It has a real swing." She held the book up to the light. "*A che ora parte il primo autobus per Villa Adriana?*"

"What!"

"What time is the first bus to Hadrian's Villa? You never know when you'll want to say something like that. And how do you like, '*Da dove parte l'aliscafo per Lugano?*' which means, 'From where does the hydrofoil for Lugano leave?'"

Sarah sighed. "Lugano sounds peaceful. Away from our group and if we were lucky there wouldn't be a garden in sight."

Turin proved another scramble, fumbling for passports and puzzling over the Italian lira numbered in millions, the only refreshment being the view of a long stretch of the distant Alps seen through a smutty train window. But at last, Milan. Or Milano.

And Alex. Looking a little disordered, dark hair rumpled, shirt wrinkled, jacket slung over his shoulder.

He kissed Sarah soundly and embraced Julia.

And then he took a second hard look at Sarah. Saw her face, the bruises on her forehead and cheekbones now an interesting mix of yellow and fading purple.

"Sarah! In God's name what happened? Are you all right? Why didn't you tell me?" He stopped and ran a professional and concerned eye over her face. "Your nose seems okay. But you cut your lip, didn't you? Sarah, love of my life, what in hell have you been up to?"

Sarah lifted her face. "I'm okay. Really. A minor accident. A little miscalculation at the Shearing Inn. The floors are very uneven and I wasn't watching where I was going." Or who was following me, she added to herself. Avoiding Alex's direct gaze, she said, "It happened days ago. I'm fine now. Not to worry. But you look tired. That long flight."

Alex shook his head with resignation. "You're changing the subject, my beloved. I know you're lying through your teeth. But I won't torment you about it. Not yet. Meanwhile, let's get out of here." He looked at his watch. "Not bad timing. You made it with an hour to spare."

Sarah grinned at him. "And thank God for someone who isn't carrying an empty camera or sunglasses and doesn't know a dibble from a donkey."

Alex made a rueful face. "I know more than I want about dibbles. So let's get out of here. The airport, right?"

Sarah put a hand over his mouth. "Not now. Let's find a lunch place, dig into some pasta, and talk about the next phase."

Alex removed her hand. "The next phase is called airport. I've got our reservations. Milan to Heathrow to Logan. And home."

Sarah scowled. "Reservations can be cancelled because Julia and I have other ideas. We can't talk here." She waved a hand at the waiting room packed to the gills with the people—students, children, pilgrims, the clergy, the aged, the tour groups, the cacophony sounding like opening day at Fenway Park.

Alex ran his eyes over Sarah again, took in not only her bruises but the shadows of fatigue under her eyes, her hands gripping the strap of her shoulder bag, saw Julia drooping, and decided that Sarah was right about one thing: the airport discussion should take place after the intake by all travelers of a quantity of protein topped by some friendly carbohydrates.

Alex led the two women to a white rental Fiat, and after the three had settled themselves, brought the two women up to date.

"George is going to call the rest of the group at their hotel tonight in Paris. Hit them with a lot of ambiguous legal language and hope they'll pack up and come home and cooperate with the forces of law and order. Skip the Italian leg of the trip."

"I have news for George," said Sarah. "Henry Ruggles made other hotel arrangements, but then Henry almost drowned at Giverny, so God only knows where they all are."

Alex stared at her. "Whoa, back up. What do you mean, Henry Ruggles almost drowned? Do I know about Henry Ruggles?"

"I told you. I'm sure I did. The little man with the wig."

"If I knew, the name has gone. Blame it on sitting up all night with a crying baby in the seat behind me. Bring me up to speed."

"Sarah did tell you about our ghost, didn't she?" demanded Julia. "Or about Edith and Margaret's new cameras. Sarah had to steal them. And guess what? Completely hollow."

Alex visibly braced himself and took a long breath. "I'm going to drive out of town in the general direction of the airport, and you will both speak very slowly and enunciate clearly and tell me what the hell is going on. Me, I've just been in Maine worrying about Ellen Trevino and bloodstained sunglasses while you've obviously been consorting with the powers of darkness."

"It's like this," Sarah began, and launched into a not-entirely-sequential description of events, a narration addled by remarks from Julia on the personalities involved, her opinion of fourteen-year-old mystery writers, and of dubious women who roam gardens at night.

"Actually," said Sarah, "Jessica Roundtree—that's her name—was impersonating your mother, Alex. Just like her, the hawk look, you know. But not Elspeth's hooded eyes."

"Shall I let Mother know you've been thinking of her?"

"I'm serious. Do you have any stray relatives slinking about gardens this month?"

"That much of a resemblance, was it?"

"Striking in a way," put in Julia. "But there was another McKenzie look-alike. Justin Rossi. Looks like you. Sarah was quite taken."

Sarah made a face. "Honestly, Aunt Julia. Justin has his points, but he's a poor replica of the original."

"This Jessica turned up twice, you say," Alex persisted. They were now fairly well out of the city, and Alex turned off the multilane highway and swung the Fiat in the direction of a small group of stores: a *farmacia*, a *trattoria*, and a *gelateria*. "Have you considered," he added, "that this resemblance—not just to the McKenzie clan—might be legitimate. That Justin Rossi and this Jessica might be related. Mother and son. Or aunt."

"You mean," said Sarah, "some relative who's following Justin around England for some nefarious reason."

Alex pulled into the parking lot of the tiny *trattoria* with a red-striped awning that sat between a small settlement of houses. "This looks okay. Let's hope it's open." He twisted about to face Sarah and Julia. "This tour group of yours. It's as if there are partners. Two by two. Noah's Ark."

Sarah looked puzzled. "I don't get it. You mean people like Sandi and Fred Ouellette."

"Those two are natural partners. I mean if there's something odd going on, there seem to be teams. Carter McClure and this Henry Ruggles. Barbara and brother Gregory. The Hopper sisters acting like two spies in an old movie. And now this Justin Rossi and his look-alike mother—or whoever." Alex cut the engine and opened the car door. My theory," he said, "is still in the planning stage."

It is amazing what food can do—especially simple food well spiced and pleasantly served by cheerful people. The little restaurant was off the beaten tourist track, and Maria, Carlo, and daughter, Flora, owners of the Caffé Allegro, had apparently not grown hardened to travelers from foreign parts, and the meal was attended with a good deal of jollity in the matter of selecting and ordering a variety of fish and fowl with pasta on the side.

Alcohol and coffee also did their part. Julia, finishing her second glass of *vino bianco*, declared her arthritis in remission, Alex relaxed with draught beer *(birra alla spina)* and listened to Sarah's plan, while Sarah, warmed by *cappuccino*, gave her arguments for staying in Italy in a reasonable manner—when before lunch she had been planning to browbeat Alex into submission.

"You see," said Sarah, putting down her coffee cup, "it's not just Ellen's murder—the police are dealing with that, the evidence, the forensics angle. I want to tie together all the things that have happened on our trip. And if it means seeing Margaret and Edith Hopper behind bars and Justin Rossi and Barbara Baxter and Stacy Daniel hanging by their thumbs, well, so be it. To me it seems obvious that there's been this ongoing crazy plan to get rid of tour leaders.

"Barbara's still going strong, isn't she?" asked Alex.

"Maybe she's next. Or maybe she's behind it, but I don't think so. Her room was searched when mine was and she didn't push Henry in the pool at Kiftsgate. And, from what I saw, she probably saved his life at Giverny. We've really drawn a blank on what's going on. Lots of theories. No conclusions."

"And poor Sarah," said Julia, "her searching of everyone's room only ended in her being mugged." Julia always enjoyed stirring up the waters, but in this case Alex was only too ready to jump into the subject; it had been with great difficulty that for the past hour he had stopped himself from pressing Sarah on the subject. Now he pointed accusingly at her face.

Well, it was time to come clean since Alex was now imitating some sort of animal glowering at the mouth of its den. Sarah grimaced and admitted to breaking, entering, and being caught in the act. "Not a big deal, really. It could have been much worse. Though I do wish I'd spent more time learning self-defense." Then, she added that she hoped it was all settled. They would not go to the airport but would join the tour group—as planned—at the hotel in Bellagio and see what developed. They would exercise extreme caution, stay together.

Alex hesitated, frowning.

"We'll regret it if we don't."

"I'm afraid we'll regret it if we do."

It was Julia who put the objections to rest. "We must stay and find out about those hollow cameras. Besides, I have another job. Margaret and Edith. Please, leave them to me. Those two are my generation. I will take them aside—away from all of you because you'll only make them more nervous than they already are, and I will talk to them. Gently. Firmly. It's like horses, you know. Be calm. Be kind but don't give in, don't allow for distractions, and after a while the animal comes around. Knows there's no choice."

Alex grinned a resigned grin. "When you put it that way, Julia, it's absolutely irresistible. Did you bring your saddle?"

25

THEY drove north on a large highway, Alex assuring the two women that he wanted to drive and would not fall asleep at the wheel. Why didn't they talk to him? For instance, why was everyone going to Bellagio anyway? Weren't there gardens enough in France?

"I think," said Sarah, "the idea was to give us a taste of three countries. Bellagio is supposed to be the grand finale. Lake Como, cobbled streets, ancient ambiance, plus super gardens. The hotel—Albergo Nuovo—has a swimming pool . . ."

"The better to push someone into . . . ," observed Julia dryly.

"And shopping might even be allowed. Especially since Portia and Carter McClure—he fought shopping all the way—are taking Henry back to England. Anyway, Alex, I'll buy you an Italian silk tie. A tie to kill for."

"See," said Julia, "that's all she can think of. Crime on the brain. Well, I'm going to bring a little culture into your lives. I've got the Bellagio guide." Julia leaned forward from the backseat and informed them that Bellagio was already a going concern between the seventh and fifth centuries B.C., that Celts and

Gauls, assorted Teutons, sundry Roman consuls, and a bunch of Germanic tribes had been at each others throats over the centuries.

"Goths, Visigoths, Ostrogoths," said Alex.

"Then those city-states," said Sarah. "The Guelphs and the Ghibellines. Dante was mixed up in all those wars. Aunt Julia, we should read Dante while we're here."

"I have several circles in hell ready and waiting," said Julia, turning the pages of the guide. "Now let's see, we have the Sforzas and Viscontis. And the Medici. They were a tricky bunch and Gian Giacomo Medici seems to have caused a lot of trouble."

Alex turned to Sarah. "Can you possibly believe that Edith and Margaret Hopper are involved in a criminal conspiracy?"

"Well, why were they waltzing around Cambridge pretending to take pictures with fake cameras?"

"Where did they get the cameras?"

"In Cambridge," said Sarah. "It was Barbara Baxter's idea."

"Bellagio, along with the rest of Lombardy, became subject to Spanish rule in 1519," announced Julia.

"So Barbara Baxter is behind the camera buying," said Alex. "That should make you think. Unless—and this is reaching—some sleazy camera dealer in Cambridge was trying to unload a couple of dummies. Cameras they use in display cases. And along came these stupid Americans. Perfect dupes."

"Maximilian of Austria in 1493 went along Lake Como, leaving destruction and death behind him," read Julia.

"If Edith and Margaret found their cameras were dummies they'd have made a fuss," said Sarah. "I have the feeling money's pretty tight. I think they're a working part of some scheme—or scam."

"Connected to Barbara? Her brother Gregory? Who?"

"Shall I skip to Garibaldi?" asked Julia. "Or how about Liszt? He sneaked off with someone's wife—her name was Marie—and they holed up in Bellagio."

"I can't think," Alex went on, "that Barbara Baxter—who

from all accounts is a practical female—would actually choose Edith and Margaret Hopper to help pull off some scam."

"But," objected Sarah, "if the Hoppers don't fit the bill, who've you got left? Justin Rossi and Stacy Daniel."

"Of course," said Julia, "there's no mention in the pamphlet of Mussolini. I suppose he's an embarrassment. The pamphlet just goes on about fishing and gardens and churches. And all sorts of boutiques and *pasticceria* and *gelaterie*. And bars."

"*Gelaterie*," exclaimed Sarah. "I feel like ice cream. Let's find a place, okay?" She consulted the map. "We'll be turning off the big road and heading for Lake Como in a few miles."

Fifty minutes later Alex and Julia and Sarah, each armed with the ice cream cone of their choice, stood at the edge of the Via Pescallo. Each felt for that brief span of time that an Italian lake in June was the proper place to be. The sun shone but not too hotly, the breeze blew but not too fiercely, some unidentified bird chirped and fluttered in a nearby unidentified bush, and even Alex, serious birdwatcher, did not reach for his binoculars, but was content just to sit on the edge of a boulder and work his way slowly through a ginger cone. Sarah by his side ran her tongue around a pyramidal lump of strawberry, and Julia, leaning against what might or might not have been an oak tree took satisfying bites of her vanilla.

And then it was on to Bellagio, that ancient little jewel of a town that raised its turtle-shaped head between the misty waters of Lago di Como and the Lago di Lecco.

The Albergo Nuovo proved a recently constructed complex that sat to one side of the Via Roncati well above the tangle of narrow cobblestone streets and buildings, and piazzas that made up that part of Bellagio called the Borgo. The hotel itself boasted a small garden and a most welcome swimming pool; an item that had much refreshed the rather frazzled automobile party of Julia, Alex, and Sarah. Each had spent a reviving hour in the pool, even Julia, wearing an ancient full-skirted navy blue bathing costume—Sarah told Alex there was no other term for the outfit—had spent a placid period doing a stately breaststroke up and down the length of the pool.

And now at six o'clock on the evening of Wednesday, June the twenty-first, the members of the Midcoast Garden Club had gathered on the patio that overlooked the terraced garden and the pool. Even with the welcome news that Henry Ruggles, although fragile, was now safely back in England, the group in Sarah's opinion was sadly fragmented. Each person seemed somehow detached from the others as if the threads that in Gloucestershire had made for cohesiveness had been severed—severed when Henry lay on the bank of the River Epte gasping for breath. Perhaps that was it; the enthusiastic Henry, the peppery Carter McClure, the soothing Portia—had taken with them some of the glue that had held the group together.

Sandi Ouellette, usually bubbling about a new visit, remarked only that she missed Henry, he added so much. And then fell silent, bent over a list of museums to be found in the village. Justin Rossi sat somewhat apart, nursing a carafe of red wine and jotting in a notebook. "A case coming up when I get back," he explained. Doris Lermatov and Amy argued about a book report that Amy had due when she returned to school in the fall, and Stacy Daniel, as beautifully draped as usual, oblivious of anyone around her, occupied herself with making a list of the dress shops in the town.

As for the Hoppers, Sarah saw them with increasing concern. They seemed to have shrunk inside their navy travel dresses and their white cardigans. Their faces were lined and pale, Edith's hair had lost its careful wave, Margaret's hairnet was torn, and they had both abandoned the modest efforts at make-up employed at the beginning of the trip. Sarah looked over at Julia and saw her aunt studying the sisters, planning no doubt the attack on what was left of the Hopper peace of mind.

Only Barbara Baxter and Fred Ouellette presented facades of good cheer. Fred—apparently impervious to emotional undertones—had cornered Alex and launched into an enthusiastic plan for visiting the remains of a necropolis discovered in the area. Burial vaults and cemeteries, Fred told Alex. "I thought," he said, "that Bellagio would just be more gardens. But I've lucked out."

As for Barbara, she seemed determined to make a success of the Italian phase of the trip. To this end she had studied the Bellagio guides and now spoke glowingly of the famous gardens. Should they try Villa Serbelloni first with its hedges of yew and box, its cypresses, its bay trees? What did everyone think?

The question hung unanswered until Barbara, ignoring community apathy, switched gardens and began a confused description of the wonders of the Villa Melzi. Grottos, goldfish, camellias, a cedar of Lebanon a cedar of the Himalayans, a sequoia, a chapel—all these Barbara brandished before the group.

Then, as she was running out of steam, Justin Rossi, picked up the thread and admitted if you liked villas and gardens and goldfish, well the Villa Melzi might be as good a place as any to see them. Seconded by a nod from Stacy Daniel.

But Barbara, as if possessed by some Spirit of Tourism, got her second wind. Churches and museums opened their doors to evening visitors, as did the many specialty shops. And a ride on the lake, a walk along the shore would be fun.

"And," added Barbara, "I think Margaret and Edith might find a store selling new cameras." She turned to Alex and Julia and Sarah. "They've been so depressed. It's as if you can't trust anyone. Their new cameras were stolen at Giverny. Of all places. You'd think a famous garden like that would be safe."

Alex looked over at Margaret and Edith. It might be a good idea to find out exactly what the two sisters thought about the disappearance of cameras. "Were they snatched?" he asked. "Were you held up?"

"Oh no," faltered Margaret. "We were so careless. When we heard the shouting—it was Henry when he'd gone into the river—we just dropped our cameras . . ."

"And I dropped my purse," said Edith.

"And we ran. To help if we could, but, of course, Barbara had already pulled Henry out, and with all the excitement we forgot the cameras, what with Henry being so terribly sick."

"We left," said Edith, "because the doctor didn't want us crowding around, and then I remembered the cameras and my purse. But when we went back . . ."

"Only Edith's purse," said Margaret. "The cameras were gone."

"How dreadful," said Sarah, feeling it was time to join the chorus. "And you'd only had them a day or so. But, then," she added, "you didn't seem to want to use them."

"Nonsense," said Barbara stoutly. "Everyone wants to take pictures of the places they've been. And I feel very sorry that it all happened on—what's the term—my watch. So Margaret and Edith, Whirlaway Tours is going to buy you two new cameras. Right here in Bellagio. There's bound to be a photography shop. We'll use my VISA. Go down into town and look. Even if the ones you find are a little more expensive, I want you to buy them."

"We're to choose them?" faltered Margaret.

"Of course. I only helped find the others because you weren't sure about new models. Whirlaway Tours wants you both to have two nice cameras. Let's say about two hundred each for replacements." Barbara's confident smile gathered everyone to her. "Face it. It's good PR for us, too. We can't have Margaret and Edith going home and saying Whirlaway runs a loose ship."

"I think," said Julia, later that evening after dinner, "that Whirlaway—or Barbara—runs a very tight ship indeed."

Julia, with Alex and Sarah, was on her way down one of the steep, narrow cobblestone streets that snaked its way down to Piazza Mazzini and the waterfront.

Alex paused in front of a crowded pizzeria. "I stopped Margaret and Edith after drinks—and I may say both seem like candidates for Prozac—and ferreted out the information that yes, Barbara produced two compact cameras from some store in Cambridge. An Olympus and a Nikon."

"Name of store, name of street?" demanded Sarah.

"They can't remember. And no sales slips."

"Just like that. Barbara turns up with hollow cameras from a legitimate store."

"So," said Julia, "the store may front a smuggling operation run by a camera store and they dumped the cameras on Barbara.

Anyway, tomorrow will reveal all. I told you I have a plan. The Hoppers are my babies."

"As long as your plan involves no strong-arm business and is done in broad daylight surrounded by two loved ones," said Alex.

Julia nodded and the three set off again and the rest of the evening was spent ducking in and out of small stores, the purchasing of a striped shirt and checkered tie for Alex, a journal covered with handmade paper by Sarah, and a carved letter opener by Julia. "In case I need a personal weapon," she explained with a sidelong glance at Alex.

Their tour of the town proved to be refreshingly clear of members of the Garden Club, although Sarah admitted to missing Henry. "He really enjoyed what he was doing and when he'd been pulled out of the river he looked so forlorn, like an old doll that had lost its hair."

They stood at the waterfront looking into the mist that hung over the lake, each silent with his or her own thoughts. And then, just as Sarah was rejoicing in the absolute tranquillity, Amy appeared. A somewhat subdued Amy.

"It's the whole place," admitted Amy. "I couldn't have imagined it. Lake Como, all it needs is the Loch Ness monster. And the winding stairs and the narrow streets. And people sticking their heads out of overhead windows and all the niches in those high walls where you can leave messages or poison or something." Amy stopped and shook her head. She sounded, Sarah thought, for the first time on the trip, genuinely awed by her surroundings.

But then Doris Lermatov loomed and, taking Amy by the arm, drew her away, saying that she wasn't to go around by herself because some Italian men—just some—find redheaded girls particularly interesting.

"You mean sex objects," said Amy, at which her mother suggested a gelato and the two went their way.

Julia had just said she was going to start climbing back up the stairs to their hotel when Sarah jabbed her elbow into her aunt's side. "Look over there. Alex, there she is. Our ghost. The one like your mother. Down by the entrance to the Hotel du Lac. Quick, or you'll miss her."

There indeed she was. The gray draperies, the shawl, the abundant white hair. She walked along slowly, stopping to look into store windows, and then she disappeared into a dress shop bordering the hotel.

"Your mother?" asked Julia of Alex.

"Something like," said Alex. "There's sort of an aura."

Sarah didn't answer. In fact couldn't because two images— no four images—had begun to mass in her brain, joining, separating, rejoining, reforming. But she couldn't quite make the final fusion.

Alex was also thinking. His mind was busy rebutting the idea that this Jessica Roundtree was pursuing them for some unknown purpose. "I think you have to credit coincidence. People on trips do keep bumping into the same people."

"Yes, they do," said Sarah, "but I don't think this is any coincidence. And I'm not one hundred percent sure but I may have the answer to this particular puzzle."

"You're going to let me participate in your brainstorm?"

"You can even help. I need basic research. Now let's float up these stairs and think beautiful Italian thoughts. Listen, it's a wonderful language. *Da dove parte l'aliscafo per Lugano?*"

"Which means?"

"Translation ruins it. But if you must know, it means, 'From where does the hydrofoil for Lugano leave?'"

"I think you can forget Lugano. Bellagio is enough of a challenge."

And the two caught up with Julia, who was just starting the long climb to the top of the stairs. Alex offered his arm and Julia without protest gratefully accepted.

They reached their hotel floor and were about to part for the night, when Julia stopped Alex. "I need your car keys. I've left my needlepoint in the Fiat and I've been neglecting it terribly."

"Let me get it for you," Sarah offered.

"Nonsense," said Julia. "I'm feeling quite brisk again."

"I'll go with you," said Sarah. "Remember we're going to keep an eye on each other."

"Certainly not," said Julia. "No one has the slightest idea where anyone is. Besides the parking lot is lighted and there's an attendant standing right there by the lamp post. So stay put and I'll see you in the morning."

Morning came and when Alex opened the bedroom door he found a folded sheet of hotel stationery on the threshold. He confronted Sarah, who was pulling on her shorts, ready for a morning run.

"Julia has written us," he said grimly.

"She has what!"

"She says she's very sorry about taking the car keys but she needs them to start the car. Make her apologies to the group and tell them she had a wonderful chance to visit a private garden with two old friends. And for us not to worry because everything will work out and she'll be in touch."

"That's it?"

"That's it. Wait here a minute." And Alex flung the door open, sprinted down the hall and out. And returned almost immediately. "She's right. No car," he said.

Sarah stood in the middle of the room, red-faced and looking as if she wanted to bite someone. "What old friends," she demanded. "Let me see the note."

"She doesn't say," said Alex as he handed over the note.

"Well, I have a damn good idea," said Sarah. "She's gone and kidnapped Margaret and Edith Hopper."

"In our car," added Alex ruefully.

Sarah pulled a T-shirt over her head. "Okay, before I start spitting nails and throwing furniture, let's run a check on the two old friends.

Twenty minutes later, after a joint check of the grounds of Albergo Nuovo, they gave it up.

"Now what," demanded Sarah. "Any bright ideas?"

"Yes," said Alex. "It's a beautiful day, so let's run a mile or so and then have a swim. To hell with Julia. At least for the next half hour."

"And then?"

"We will telephone Signore Hertz or Signore Avis or Signore Budget and find a car and then consider whether we can speak Italian well enough to call on the Carabinieri or the polizia."

"I think I can handle that. More or less. *Mi scusi, per favore. Mia zia mi ha rubato mia macchina.*"

"Which means?"

"Excuse me please. My aunt has stolen my car."

26

AT home in Maine, when alone in her car, Julia Clancy drove with abandon; however, with passengers—often these were horses tethered in a trailer behind her truck—she exercised the greatest care. Today she kept a conservative foot on the accelerator.

It was four A.M. and Julia didn't like driving before it was light. But really, there was no help for it. Her plans had been laid with care and they depended on a predawn departure. All the way on the still dark road that had led from Bellagio to Como and then turned north, she had kept up, for her passengers, a soothing stream of comment on the beauties of the Italian hills and the magical quality of the Italian lakes.

These passengers, unfortunately, remained resistant to comfort. They had been aroused by telephone in the small hours of the morning, told to pack up, bring their passports, and by stealth to join Julia in the parking lot because it was a matter of life and death. Now, almost two hours later with the town of Como well behind them both Margaret Hopper, in the front passenger seat, and Edith in the rear, teetered on the edge of collapse.

Julia, regretted using the threat of "life and death," but had felt that no other phrase would move the two. Now she kept up her efforts to calm her passengers. No need—as yet—to pounce. Finesse, though never Julia's strong point—was the way to go.

"Not quite life and death," she told the sisters. "But almost. You were in real danger. And I had to try and do something. Please just sit back and rest. Take deep breaths." She indicated a faint lightening of the sky. "It's going to be a beautiful day, we'll be able to see for miles. Like a Bellini painting."

Margaret Hopper coughed. "I don't think Bellini painted around here; he was a Venetian. And Julia, you are making a terrible mistake. We should have stayed in Bellagio. With our friends."

Margaret seemed to be rallying, so Julia decided to skip the finesse. "Stuff and nonsense. What friends? I'm your friend and I and no one else understands about your situation. And the danger."

Margaret turned a frowning face. "You keep saying danger, Julia, but I don't know what you mean. And by what possible right are you forcing us . . ."

"Not forcing," said Julia with some irritation. "It's called—what's the expression—crisis intervention." She slowed the car, pulled to the right, and allowed an irate Maserati—coming out of nowhere—to gun past. Returning to the road, she checked a sign announcing Capolago, and nodded with satisfaction. "I did some research at the hotel desk yesterday and they came up with a nice quiet little *penzione*." Here Julia accelerated and swung past a road sign announcing *Curva Pericolosa*.

"That sign says 'Dangerous Curve,' " said Edith sharply, and Julia was pleased to hear a measure of energy in her voice. Both women were recovering. It was time for the medicine. At least a small dose. She took a deep breath.

"You two ladies are not spy material and you're in danger because you're trying to pull off an act for which you are very ill-equipped. You're completely out of your depth."

"What are you talking about," demanded Margaret with a brave show of anger.

Julia waved her into silence. "Please. Hear me out. In the first place neither of you has any notion of how to conceal your feelings. You've been in terrible state since High Roosting and everyone has noticed it. Sooner or later you were going to be seen as a pair of god-awful liabilities. And suffer the consequences."

"What do you mean, 'consequences,'" said Edith. "We haven't done anything except cooperate with everyone." It was a poor effort at best and Julia ignored it.

"Margaret and Edith, we all go back a long ways. School, summer camp. You were always older and wiser, always on the honor roll. You went in for education, and I was the ragtail tomboy who lived in a horse barn. But now, all of us, we're part of the old guard. So I want to help you and you have to let me."

"We have always taken care of ourselves," began Edith.

"Let me finish," said Julia, trying to keep her voice from it's usual sharpness. "If you go back to Bellagio you may end up like Henry Ruggles, only there may be no one around to pull you out of the lake. Or if you survive Bellagio, you'll go home to sizzle on Sergeant George Fitts's hot seat, and it will be very public and very nasty. I think I can make it easier for you. Now here's the turn-off I'm looking for. South of Lanzo. It's a nice family place, quiet and peaceful. La Pensione Vittoria."

Julia drove carefully the last few miles, peering at signs and then pulled in front of a small tiled-roof stucco building snugged into the hillside. The Pensione Vittoria was indeed small and peaceful, and the sun coming up gave a sparkle to its small casement windows. All in all, Julia decided, it was exactly what the doctor had ordered. One night in a new place can make all the difference.

They were greeted by the son of the establishment, a wiry youth called Roberto, who seized the Hopper suitcases and led them up the stairs. Julia, prodding the reluctant Hoppers, saw them into their room. It was a cheerful chamber with white-washed walls, and beds, chairs, and bureaus all painted a bright blue. She gave the sisters—who had ceased to resist—orders for an hour's rest to be followed by a meeting outside. Lunch with a view of the Lake Lugano and the mountains.

Seventy minutes later Julia ushered her reluctant guests to a table on a paved terrace. The table faced a tiny garden set about with pieces of statuary, including a donkey and cart, a cherub with a broken arm, and a pair of griffins, all looked over by a solemn St. Francis holding a birdbath and a Virgin Mary in a blue coat, her arms outspread. An ideal setting, Julia decided, for the telling of truth and the unburdening of the soul.

The setting was completed by the table on which several white roses stuck out of an earthenware pot and a bottle of *vino bianco* sat next to a serving platter of *cannelloni al forno*. Edith Hopper had asked wistfully for tea—but Julia had voted this down. Courage—even if it came in a bottle—was the order of the day.

"Now," said Julia, when the first glasses of wine had gone down the Hopper throats, "tell me what has been going on?" And Julia reached for a pack of tissues—she had come prepared—and put it in front of the sisters. There was a long pause, and then:

"It started," said Margaret in a shaky voice, "a long time ago. Edith was nine and I was almost eleven."

"About a week before your birthday," said Edith."

❧

"Are we going to try and trace Aunt Julia?" demanded Sarah. "Get the police into the act. Or just hope for the best?"

She and Alex, after a demanding run and serious lapwork in the pool, were now settled at eight o'clock at a tiled table having breakfast. Sarah wore her tourist jumper of blue denim.

Alex buttered a chunky piece of toast, dribbled honey across its surface, and took a bite. He was, Sarah thought, looking less haggard than he had on arrival. The run had given him color and his new green and red striped shirt gave him a rakish look—a look at variance to Alex's ironic and usually realistic approach to life.

"You fit in," said Sarah approvingly. "Almost Italian. You can go out on the town after breakfast and mix with the natives. Anyway, I'd say let Julia get on with what she's doing, which I suppose is pumping the poor Hoppers. I just hope she doesn't scare them into a total breakdown."

"Come on. Julia won't hit them with rubber hoses and put lighted matches under their fingernails. I say hold it for now."

"Agreed. Now, as I've said, I have a research job for you."

"You mean as your back-up? I ride shotgun and you head for the border?"

"No, listen. It's research worthy of your talents. The Garden Club is supposed to do the Melzi Gardens this morning. The bus loads up at ten, so you've got about two hours. You'll have to table-hop during breakfast or lurk on the terrace. You're the new face and everyone will probably chat it up."

"This is a worthy cause? It ties in directly with Ellen?"

"No," admitted Sarah. "This is peripheral. But it may lead to Ellen. What did the man say, by indirections find directions out. Well, I'm going the long way round because I need to be very sure about someone. And something."

"You want to share?"

"I don't want to taint your objectivity. As follows. Please cozy up to Sandi Ouellette, which ought to be easy because she's friendly—and a gossip. Ask if she can give you any new details about the woman who bounced the molester out of the Hound and Hare pub back at High Roosting. All we know so far is that the woman was tall and that she must have been strong to pull off the bouncing act. And here on deck we've got two tall strong women and one shorter strong woman, and we need to do some weeding out."

"Okay, I'll work on Sandi. I rather take to her. She says what she thinks and doesn't bother about impressing people."

"You're right. I'm growing very fond of Sandi. Okay, next job. Take a notebook because you're doing research on pubs."

"I'm what?"

"On pubs. English pubs. French and Italian pubs. It's a long-standing interest of yours. Throw in some medical angle if you want, like the therapeutic value of draught beer. Whatever. You're writing a monograph. No, make it a guidebook. And you've missed out on some of the Cotswold pubs. Particularly High Roosting area pubs. Move in on Stacy Daniel and ask some questions."

"She's a pub expert?"

"Pub crawler. Everyone says that at night she takes off. Never hangs around with any of the rest of the group. Justin Rossi doesn't either, but I'm leaving him until later."

"Good," said Alex. "I'm not crazy about doppelgängers."

"You said things were happening by twos," Sarah reminded him. "Anyway, find out if Stacy's ever been to the Hound and Hare in High Roosting. Say you need a critique of the place. And ask about the other town pubs just to be legitimate. One's called the Black Badger and I can't remember the name of the other one."

"There's no such thing as a black badger."

"For God's sake, Alex, it doesn't matter. Some fool in the sixteenth century thought there was and named the place."

"This is important?"

Sarah reached for a last roll and spread it with apricot jam and faced her husband. "You can bet your life—or mine—it's important. And one last thing. When you finish covering the breakfast scene, look over this list." Sarah fished in her pocket. "This has the items mentioned by Gregory Baxter and sister Barbara when Julia and I had dinner next to them."

"Dinner, as in eavesdropping."

"That was the point of being there."

Alex examined the list. "Something rings a bell. But I don't know if any of it ties into those hollow cameras. And, by the way, where are they?"

Sarah made a face. "They're in the Fiat. Julia may be sticking them in Edith and Margaret's faces as we speak. But the only thing I found was that piece of clear plastic in one of them."

Alex put down his napkin and stood up. "All right. I'll hit the breakfast crowd. You stay put in our bedroom until bus time. Door locked, okay?"

Sarah nodded and then added, "A tip. Stacy Daniel, as you may have noticed, is absolutely gorgeous. She reminds me of a lioness stalking through the veldt. I never can picture her locked up in a bank job. So let her know you're taken with her."

Alex grinned. "No problem."

Exactly one hour and fifty minutes later, Alex escorted Sarah to the meeting place for the tour bus.

"I've worked on my notes. For my guide to pubs of the world."

"And?"

"Sandi remembers nothing new about the lady bouncer except she didn't think she was young, but Stacy was crazy about the Black Badger because you can meet people there and have a great evening—whatever that means, although I can guess. Stacy said she wouldn't be caught dead at the Hound and Hare. She'd heard the place was a mob scene and some football club practically lived in it. And," Alex added, "she's glad she's met me and perhaps we can hit the local pubs some night. La Grotta, or better Il Tiglio, which is a pub and restaurant. She was sure you wouldn't want to come because, and I quote, 'Sarah is the home type.'"

Before Sarah could express her feelings on that score, Alex held up his hand. "Here come the others. Does my report make the whole mess a little clearer now? To you anyway?"

"Some clear parts, some clear like mud," said Sarah.

"Can't you skip this Melzi Garden visit?

"No. It just might clear some of the mud."

"Don't get yourself off in a corner with anyone even if it's Mother Teresa. Buddy up with Sandi and Fred. Or Doris Lermatov. I'll see you here at the hotel when you get back."

But Alex didn't find Sarah at the hotel, and, in fact, by noon of that Thursday, the twenty-second of June, the Midcoast Garden Club had ceased to function as a tour group.

———

It resembled—this last trip to the gardens of the Villa Melzi, the last trip to any garden—other trips taken by the club. Because, even in its sadly diminished form, some small degree of excitement remained. Here was all the usual paraphernalia: the notebooks, the Bellagio guides, the flower identification books, and, in the case of Amy and Sandi, cameras (genuine ones, Sarah hoped). Stacy wore her straw hat with the wide brim and the flame-colored ribbon, Doris and Sandi had canvas hats of the boating variety, Amy wore a genuine Pittsburgh Pirates baseball cap pulled over her eyes, and Barbara sported a tennis visor. Sarah had explained to everyone that Julia had taken Margaret and Edith Hopper for a drive into the hills, and this was accepted without much comment. Julia, often an irascible presence, would not be much missed and the Hoppers had become mere traveling shadows.

Of all the gardens Sarah had visited, those of the Villa Melzi had the distinction of receiving her full attention. Actually, she had little choice; no opportunity offered for private talk, and there was no Julia with whom to argue or plot. The diminished group—only eight of the original fourteen—clung together, and leader Barbara, relentless in the pursuit of the advertised specialties of the garden, was alert for stragglers. The moment anyone slowed their steps on a path or lingered too long over a planting, she halted the group and waited until he or she caught up.

"If we'd all stayed together at Giverny," Barbara explained, "poor Henry would be with us today."

"Maybe, but staying together wouldn't have helped Margaret and Edith," said Sandi. "I just don't think we cared enough about what was wrong with them." She turned to Sarah almost accusingly. "And now your Aunt Julia has driven off with them. I'll bet she's trying to browbeat them into telling some awful family secret when it's none of her business."

This was so close to the actual truth that Sarah for a moment had to scramble for an answer. She was only able to come up with the feeble remark that Julia was concerned for their happiness. To which Sandi gave an unbelieving, "Sure. Right."

But Barbara had held up her hands again. It was as if she was possessed of the wish to be the most informed, the most attentive, the most energetic tour leader in all Italy.

"She's trying to win Camp Spirit," whispered Sandi to Fred.

"Sandi," said Barbara. "Did you know Napoleon visited the Villa? And had his portrait painted? And Liszt came here. And the gardens have wonderful ponds and vistas and a grotto. Some really interesting tropical plants." Here Barbara glanced down at her guidebook. "It says here that these grounds were the very first example of English gardens in the whole area."

"Then why," demanded Stacy Daniel, "are we here? We've already done English gardens."

But Barbara didn't blink. "These are Italian gardens with an English flavor," she said. "There's all the difference. Now let's walk around the pond. You can see the goldfish from the bridge."

But Fred rebelled. The Grotto—the one by the gate—well, he'd read that it held a cinerary urn brought from the tomb of the Scipioni family in Rome. He wondered if it was visible. On display. Perhaps there was special information to be had at the ticket office about Roman habits of ash disposal. And Fred marched off in the direction of the gate.

Barbara, torn in two directions, hesitated. And then decided to chase the stray sheep. "Stay right here. Please," she ordered and took off after Fred.

"She needs a Border Collie," observed Justin to Sarah. Both had climbed onto the little bridge while the others gathered at the bank.

Sarah gazed down into the pond, spiked by reeds and an occasional floating lily pad, and saw—as advertised—a number of large goldfish lazily circling in and out of the shadows. A large, deeper-hued one was making persistent runs at two smaller fish. Then these two wriggled themselves into pursuit of even smaller, less brilliantly colored ones. Just like the English Department, she thought.

Justin, too, was looking down into the pond. "Poor old Henry," he said. "This is only a few feet deep, but even that would be too much for him if he went in. He'd have panicked, sunk to the bottom, and just lain there until someone fished him out again."

Sarah looked at him quizzically. "Are you saying Henry has gone through life falling into ponds and being rescued?"

But before Justin could answer, Doris Lermatov, waiting on the bank, called out in an anxious voice, "Amy. Has anyone seen Amy?"

Everyone turned to everyone else, Barbara came bustling up with an apologetic Fred in tow, and, after a certain amount of circling and calling it became clear that Amy had departed.

"Or," said Doris, her voice rising, "she's been taken."

"Don't be silly," said Barbara. "Amy's done it on purpose. To drive us all crazy. She's never enjoyed the gardens."

"Which is putting it mildly," said Justin to Sarah. He raised his voice. "Look, Doris, I'm finished with the Melzi Gardens. I'm going back to the hotel so I'll keep an eye out for her. Don't worry, Amy is a smart girl. She just has had it with the tour scene." And, with long strides and without looking back, Justin stepped off the bridge and headed for the gate.

"Well, I'm going to start looking," said Doris. "I think she'd go into the town. I'll head that way."

"Wait," said Sandi. "We might as well be systematic. No point in everyone looking in the same place. I'll take the lake side and the cafés and Doris can do the stores and hotels facing the waterfront. She pulled out her guide. "It's called the Piazza Mazzini."

Here we have, thought Sarah, a person who teaches lifesaving. She stepped down from the bridge and went up to Doris. "Amy was with us just a few minutes ago, so she can't have gotten far.

"I'm sure," said Fred, "she's just gone off to look at the shops. She said at breakfast she wanted to explore the whole town."

"She didn't tell me that," said Doris in an injured voice.

"Because," Sandi pointed out, "you wouldn't have let her go."

"I think we need to organize," said Barbara belatedly.

"Sandi already has," said Fred. "She's good at it."

It was decided. They would go back along the promenade to the town center and then split. Sandi and Doris as assigned, Sarah, Fred, and Barbara checking the narrow shop-lined roads and the steep little stairways that led to the upper levels. Stacy Daniel would explore the full range of the Villa Melzi gardens and then head for the main road and the hotel.

"I think we're overreacting," said Fred, as five members of the search party hustled along the promenade. "Teenagers never stay put. It's a wonder she didn't get loose sooner."

"I know," puffed Doris, who was having a hard time keeping up with Fred's long striding walk. "I know she's been bored, and I usually don't go into a fit over something like this. It's only that it's a strange place and a strange country and with everything that's happened . . . well, I feel better trying to track her down."

Amen, thought Sarah. She was entertaining a familiar sinking sensation. Amy loose on the town. Amy with her notebook asking all those questions about ghosts and murder mysteries. Amy might have been asking for it. It? Oh hell, Sarah told herself and quickened her stride.

Then, as the group approached the Piazza Mazzini, she asked herself a crucial question. Should she sound an alert, point a finger. But at whom? She knew Barbara Baxter was probably dealing in hollow cameras but to what end? And yesterday she and Julia may—or may not—have been pursued by the gray Peugeot. Or an unknown car. But none of this seemed directly life-threatening. She didn't know who tipped Henry into the Kiftsgate pool and later into the river. And, damnation, she didn't know who had killed Ellen Trevino.

Biting her lip, Sarah walked on without speaking. And following Sandi's direction, she began climbing the nearest stairs leading toward the top of the town, while Barbara and Fred split and each set off on other routes.

But spotting Amy among the throngs that pushed in and out of the *pizzerie*, *ristoranti*, *gelaterie*, the grills, bars, clothing stores, and trinket shops was just about hopeless. Sarah dodged in and out, shop after shop, up the stairs, down again, up again. More and more anxious. Spotting a frizzy redhead here, there, in a doorway. On a stair. But never the right redhead.

It was now long past noon, almost one o'clock, and the sun was burning hot, but there was a heaviness to the air and some thick looking clouds hanging low over the mountains that promised a later storm. Panting, holding her side, Sarah had stopped on the upper reaches of one of the narrow steep stairways—a *salita* it was called, she remembered. I've got to get my breath, she told herself. If I pass out it won't help find Amy. And they should have arranged for a meeting place, or a signal if she were found. Now they all might be doomed to spend the day scrabbling around Bellagio while Amy would be taking her ease with a gelato on some distant park bench.

At least this particular stairway was not a popular tourist route and no one was in sight. There were other, easier climbs. Sarah leaned gratefully against a rough stone wall and wiped her forehead with her sleeve. She'd take five minutes' rest and then start hunting again. And, wouldn't you know, Amy hadn't worn her distinctive black Decomposers T-shirt today, a shirt Sarah might have spotted in a crowd. No, she was in a plain white number with an Italian flag on its back. Just like millions of others. "Damn," she said aloud.

"Damn is right," said a woman's voice above her, behind the curve of the wall. Sarah whipped around.

"You're alone," said the voice. "Good. So, okay, where are those cameras?"

Sarah found her voice. It felt thick in her throat. "What cameras?" she managed.

"Don't give me that shit. Margaret and Edith Hopper may think they're stolen—the dear old things would never think ill of a friend. I know better. You've been after them for days. So, where are they?"

Sarah braced her back against the wall, only too aware that the two of them were completely alone. "I don't have," she said slowly, "any cameras." String this out, she told herself. Someone's bound to come.

The woman inched closer and now stood on the step above her. "I've had it with you. You've pushed it too far. You'd think that after everything that's happened, you'd get the idea. Kept your nose clean. Now listen, someone will be along any minute so I can't fool around. Where are the cameras?"

Keep stalling, Sarah ordered herself. "What have cameras to do with this tour?" she asked in what she hoped was a calm and reasonable voice.

"Bloody hell. For the last time tell me where you've put those fucking cameras or I'll blow your head off. And, no one in this fucking town will think a thing about it. It happens all the time in this country. Just like home."

"Oh, come on," said Sarah. "You're not making sense. You haven't got a gun. Let's go on down and work this out." Sarah lifted her head and ran an eye over the woman. Her face was almost raspberry from anger—or exertion. Her shirt was sweat-stained and she was hanging over Sarah as if she meant any moment to hurl herself into Sarah's midriff. But no telltale revolver–like bulge showed in her skirt pockets.

"I'm going to count," said the woman, and Sarah knew from the lower register of her voice that she'd heard it before. Heard it in the hallway of the Shearing Inn.

"Hey, wait, hold it." And Sarah took one step down the stairs and moved toward the center of the stairs. The idea of being rammed into the wall was not appealing. But neither was falling hundreds of feet into the piazza. "How about meeting back at the hotel?" she said softly. "See if we can figure out where those cameras have gone." She tilted her head slightly. Footsteps. Heels. High heels. Someone coming down the stairs. Thank God. Only another minute to hang on.

But her companion had ears, too. And she didn't have another minute. She reared back, lowered her head like a bull about to charge, put both fists in front of her body, and rose on her toes and launched herself at Sarah.

And Sarah had only time to dodge aside one step and then she found herself grabbed and flung violently back against the wall.

And saw the woman in her full-attack posture become airborne, and hands still clenched, plunge through the space where Sarah had just been. And then down. Down.

Down the steep, cobbled steps. Head-first she plummeted. Step after steep step, one after the other. And now the whole body bunched itself and curled into a grotesque somersault, head bent, it turned over, banged against the wall, hit the next step, thudded into the next one, and rolled heavily to rest at a small paved landing some fifty feet below. And like the sack of laundry clothes it so now much resembled, it did not move.

Sarah turned away gasping. And looked straight into the face of the person whose arm had flung her aside. Whose arm had saved her from the fall she had just watched.

The face and the arm of Jessica Roundtree.

27

ALEX had no sooner seen Sarah climb aboard the bus bound for the Villa Melzi Gardens than qualms set in. He tried to settle to the study of European birds in his field guide, but time passed slowly. Even in the face of Sarah's assurances that she would cling like a limpet to the certified "safe" tour members he felt his qualms deserved more attention than he was giving them. At last he stood up and unfolded the map of Bellagio. Where were these gardens, anyway? Why not just stroll down in that direction?

This moment of indecision was broken by the desk clerk arriving at his table. A call for S. Deane or A. McKenzie.

Alex took the phone in the hall just off the main lobby.

"Hello, Sarah? Alex?" croaked an electronic voice. "This is a terrible telephone. I think it belonged to Marconi. Or do I mean Alexander Graham Bell?"

"Julia! Is that you? If it is, get back here. With Margaret and Edith in one piece. And the car."

"You sound like Mussolini. It must be the Italian male thing. Testosterone in the air. Listen, Alex. Be grateful. Edith and Margaret have explained the whole affair. A lot of tears but now they're feeling better. And they'll fly home tomorrow."

Alex resisted the impulse to pull the telephone out by its roots. Between clenched teeth, he said, "From what airport?"

"I won't say because you and Sarah will come charging down like a couple of bulls in a china shop and upset things. It's all arranged and I've talked to their families."

"For Christ's sake, Julia."

"Don't swear. They'll be met in Boston and driven straight home. I've got to go now. And you should have that Fiat checked. The frame shudders and it's leaking oil."

Alex tried again. "What did Margaret and Edith tell you? It's important, for God's sake."

"I'll tell you when I see you. The poor dears were in her clutches. Blackmail. Good-bye, Alex. You and Sarah be careful."

"Julia!" But the line was dead.

Alex, in a high state of exasperation, returned to his table, drained his cold cup of coffee and picked up his Bellagio map. To hell with being circumspect. He'd just march down and join that blasted tour. Perhaps even announce that Margaret and Edith had confessed everything—since they were safely out of reach—and watch reactions. Let chips fall where they may.

But these heady thoughts were throttled by the entirely too familiar voice calling out *"Buon giorno.* And then, in guidebook Italian, *"Come sta?"*

And next like an apparition from another planet, complete with flowered shirt, navy shorts, gleaming white new Nikes, the broad-shouldered Nordic presence of Mike Laaka.

Alex stared, unbelieving.

Mike, an enormous smile spread over his face, sat down at Alex's table. *"Buon giorno, Alessandro. L'Italia e molto bella."*

Alex confronted the still grinning Mike. "What the hell! You here? Who let you loose? Not George, I'll bet. And make it fast. I want to track down Sarah."

"You haven't let her off by herself, have you?"

"She's with the garden group. She thinks she's got an answer to one of the puzzles and wants to check it out."

"With a Beretta in her hand?"

"It's a safe scenario, believe me. But even so I'd like to be around. Now explain yourself while we head for the tour group." And Alex stood up and headed for the road leading to the town center. Followed by Mike, who was shaking his head.

"No word of welcome for old Mike? Okay, why am I here? Answer, Ellen Trevino's stepfather finally surfaced. Big timber man, lots of cash. We put him in the picture and met with some of the other tour families. The upshot is I've been sent to persuade the whole bunch to move it and then escort them home."

"The sheriff's department has paid your way to Italy?"

"God, no. They wouldn't pay me to go ten miles. Nor would the state police. It's Kevin Webster—Ellen Trevino's stepfather. He didn't see much of Ellen, but apparently was crazy about her. He's in a rage about her being killed. He paid for my ticket after George flunked the job of trying to haul the tour back from France. So here I am. How do you like the outfit? Do I look Italian?"

"You look like an American tourist who got lost on the way to Hawaii. Listen, a lot's been happening. The tour group has shrunk, one of the leaders almost drowned, and Julia's been putting the squeeze on two Hoppers, with the result that they're flying to the States tomorrow. Come on, Mike, step on it." This as Mike stopped to admire the display of baked goods in a *pasticceria.*

And Alex began a downhill jog, followed by Mike, both ducking around clumps of slow-moving tourists, dodging the occasional motor scooter, and reaching the shopping mecca of the Piazza Mazzini.

And running smack into Amy Lermatov.

Or to be accurate Amy ran into them. From a dead run she stopped almost under Alex's chin. Her hair, wilder than usual, her face bright red, her eyes wide and scared.

"Dr. McKenzie. Dr. McKenzie. You've got to come."

"Take it easy, Amy. What's the matter?"

"Down the stairs. The whole way. Or almost. And she's dead. Or she looks dead. And there's blood all over the place and her teeth are sticking through her lip and her legs are bent in a funny way." And suddenly Amy—Amy the tough junior writer of murder mysteries—burst into tears and became a frightened fourteen-year-old girl.

"WHO!" Alex and Mike shouted together.

Amy lifted a tear stained face. "They're all there. Sarah and the ghost woman, Jessica, and Barbara."

Alex grabbed Amy's shoulders with both hands. "WHO FELL DOWN THE STAIRS?"

"Barbara Baxter. She fell almost the whole way. I was down here by myself looking at the shops because I couldn't stand any more gardens. Then I started to climb the steps to go back to the hotel and she almost landed at my feet. And she looked dead, and Sarah and this Jessica came running down, so I thought I'd better tell someone. And get help."

"Show us where," commanded Mike, as Alex broke into a run heading for a sizable crowd at the foot of one of the narrow stairways.

Barbara Baxter was not dead. But she was injured. Badly. And in shock. Sarah had not left the crumpled body. Still in horrified astonishment at the attack, her rescue, and Barbara's fall, she could think of nothing more to do than to grab Jessica Roundtree's shawl, cover Barbara, call out for a doctor and, then sit holding one bloody broken hand between her own two hands.

Jessica Roundtree, her long skirts torn, her white hair unraveled, knelt down on the other side of Barbara, checking her pulse, listening to gurgled respirations, but with the arrival of a vacationing Swiss doctor, a Swedish dentist, then Alex, Jessica stood up, stepped to one side, and disappeared into the crowd.

Alex did not immediately reappear at the Albergo Nuovo; he and Mike had followed—in Mike's blue rental Fiat—the ambulance to the hospital in nearby Lecco. Sarah had joined the remnants of the garden tour in an entirely silent lunch. And then everyone had risen and scattered to their rooms. Or went to sit on the terrace and stare at a sky weighted with cumulus clouds and at flashes of lightening that burst over the darkened mountains.

Sarah moved by herself to a cluster of chairs placed under an olive tree. She was certain she would be followed.

She was.

Justin Rossi, in immaculate khaki shorts and a blue tennis shirt. Freshly shaved, a look of resignation on his face. He took a seat beside her. "How long have you known?"

"I'm not sure," Sarah said slowly. "I think it started with Amy. Going on about the ghost in the garden. Before that she said you looked suspicious. Thought you wore a wig. But I looked you over and decided you didn't."

"We all make mistakes," said Justin. "And I think Amy Lermatov should have been at summer camp learning how to pitch a tent."

"Amy's just had a nasty close-up look at the real world. She's quite subdued. But I think it's the McKenzie look-alike business that really got to me. Jessica Roundtree looked so like my mother-in-law, Elspeth, that it sent shivers up my back."

"Mothers-in-law often have that effect," Justin observed.

Sarah ignored this. "Of course, you look like Alex, and Alex looks like his mother, and it seemed unlikely that two McKenzie types would turn up at the Shearing Inn, and then at Sissinghurst giving nervous fits to those ladies from Scotland."

"Go on."

"And then turning up in Bellagio last night in the piazza."

"Three appearances by Elspeth McKenzie."

"Yes, and, of course, Aunt Julia and I were worried because of Ellen being killed, and the Hoppers falling apart and Henry being pushed into pools. We wondered which of you was behind all of it. But I found out Jessica Roundtree was safe. And so was Justin Rossi."

"Detective Inspector Deane?"

"It didn't take much detecting. A tall strong-armed older woman had tossed that Jack the Slitter into the pub room of the

Hound and Hare. Stacy Daniel is strong—all that power walking and aerobics—but she never went near that pub. Preferred the Black Badger. And Barbara Baxter isn't what you call tall. But Justin Rossi had been to the Hound and Hare because he mentioned the smoke-filled air. Anyway, Jessica fit the strong older woman description. And today she did another good deed or I'd have probably been in that ambulance on it's way to Lecco. If I happened to be so lucky. End of story, I guess. Except"—Sarah turned to Justin who turned his head slightly away from her—"I do thank you." She touched his hand lightly and smiled.

For a moment both were quiet and then Justin indicated the sky. "We're going to have one hell of a storm tonight."

"Why did you go out in the daytime? Take a chance?"

"I'd seen enough of the Melzi Gardens, and all at once I'd about had enough of Barbara and her thumbscrews. I was going out in the daytime and to hell with it. I wanted to show her that I just didn't give a damn any more, and if it meant I couldn't practice law—at least not in that stuffed shirt law firm, or maybe in any law firm, well, so be it."

"So she caught you dressed and blackmailed you into carrying hollow cameras around Europe. And the Hoppers. And Stacy Daniel."

"Me, she did. I don't have a clue about what she had on Margaret or Edith. Or on Stacy—unless it was that Stacy can be such a bitch."

"Except Stacy liked Henry—a redeeming quality. But who pushed Henry into the Kiftsgate pool? Into the Epte River at Giverny? Not Barbara. Not Stacy. Did you?"

"God, no. I wouldn't do that. I liked old Toad Ruggles."

"And the real question. Who killed Ellen Trevino?"

Justin ran his fingers through his short black hair—the Alex gesture that had unnerved Sarah. "I did not. And I don't have the least idea who did. Barbara never told me exactly what she was up to. Just be in certain towns and certain places and hand over the camera to some designated person. Who would take something out of it. Believe me I never looked into the camera. I didn't want to know what I was passing around. Just hoped to hell it wasn't drugs. Call me an ostrich. Or a bloody coward."

Sarah thought of the mugging scene. Had Stacy been involved, perhaps keeping watch in the hall? "Did Stacy work with Barbara?"

"Could be. I just don't know. I'd say ask her, but I'm not sure it's safe to mess with Stacy."

Sarah nodded. She listened to another rumble of thunder and saw another streak of lightning knife across the mountain tops. Then she returned to Justin. "I've got two more questions. Do you have a mother and a sister? And do you buy clothes for them?"

"A devoted mother. No sister. I buy clothes for Jessica. Not Mother. She's only a size eight."

Sarah smiled over at him. "And are you by any wild chance related to any McKenzies?"

Justin gave her an answering smile. A wry one. "We're all related, aren't we? Down from Adam. Or," he added, "from Eve."

It was late afternoon and the sky had gone from being slightly threatening to distinctly ominous. Mike and Alex, having grabbed a quick lunch after leaving Barbara Baxter in an intensive care unit at the hospital in Lecco, were now headed back to Bellagio to tie up the last loose ends.

"Too many loose ends," complained Mike.

"I think she'll make it," said Alex. "Internal bleeding is under control. In fact, after they stabilize her, set the fractures, she should be able to travel in a few weeks."

"With a serious escort," said Mike. "George will probably try to have her extradited."

"On a charge of murder?"

"For assault—to begin with. But Barbara qualifies—time and opportunity—for the murder. And the police have finally tracked down the car Barbara rented—the one that was wrecked and sold for parts. The lab's found fiber and hair matches on the upholstery."

"But motive? Did she attack the other tour leaders—Ellen

and Henry, and possibly Lillian Garth—in order to change the tour schedule to hit designated cities and sell some mystery contraband in hollow cameras? With the help of brother Gregory?"

"Gregory's got to be the key. You said you had a list of things Sarah and Julia overheard at that dinner and some of it rang a bell. Run through it for me. Maybe a bell will ring for me."

Alex reached into his pocket and pulled out the sheet of paper. "I swear I associate some of this with an old uncle of mine and a magnifying glass sitting at a desk. But he died when I was five or six and it's just one of those shadow memories."

"Read it," urged Mike.

And Alex read. Hawaii, handcrafts, Confederate states, auction. Big bucks, no postal insurance. Lloyds canceled. Theft. Rotary, black inverted center, perfect condition PolyPro film . . ."

"Hold it," yelled Mike. "Did you say inverted center, rotary? Hey, buddy, I've got it. Hear that? I've got it. What stupid shitheads we are. Or you and Sarah are. And Julia. Jesus, isn't that a cute little operation. Big bucks is right. Hey, Alex, I've gone and beat you on this one. You just didn't have a proper boyhood. And I did. I got a Boy Scout badge for it."

"Okay, okay, spit it out. And does my uncle's magnifying glass fit in?"

"Does it ever." Mike stamped on the gas, whirled into the road for Bellagio and chortled. "Stamps, you idiot. Itty-bitty stamps that are so valuable, so easy to hide, and so easily swiped that even registered mail isn't safe. Lloyd's paid up once too often and doesn't want to insure the stuff any more. Stamps are great big bucks. A Hawaiian envelope with two U.S. stamps and two Hawaiian Missionary stamps went for over two million. An auction in New York at the Robert A. Siegel Galleries. Besides, I get this stamp magazine, *Linn's Stamp News* and you should read about the stealing that goes on. Listen, I still collect stamps. Nothing very valuable, mostly U.S. stuff, but I've some nice old stamps from Finland."

"And I thought horse racing was your thing."

"That's my outdoor love. I do stamps on cold winter nights with the snow raging outside my window. I'm versatile. Every-one has these secret things. Julia plays the piano and Sarah snoops and you chase after birds." Suddenly Mike twisted his head around as a rather battered limousine with the inscription AEROPORTO writ large on its flank, slowed and crowded the blue Fiat.

"Bugger," said Mike turning his car toward the road's edge.

"Not bugger," said Alex peering at the faces behind the glass. "Stacy Daniel. I think. Beautiful woman, one of a kind."

"Hey," shouted Mike, slowing the car, "we want her."

"I don't think you can do a thing about her now. Just get to the hotel, call, and try to block her at the airport."

Mike sighed. "I don't have any authority for that. And I doubt George can crank up the international machinery in time."

The telephone call, as Mike predicted, produced nothing of substance. George Fitts, a man not given to four-letter words, used several to no avail.

Mike did not return immediately to Alex, who was left prowl-ing about the lobby. But when he did he wore a wide smile that radiated satisfaction. "Good news and bad news," he announced.

Alex gave him a sour look. "I can only imagine bad news and bad news."

"Come on out on the terrace," commanded Mike. "Away from flapping ears."

Settled in a far corner of the terrace surrounded only by empty chairs and a trellis laden with small yellow roses, Mike unburdened himself. "Bad news. We can't nail Stacy Daniel. Not yet. She can't be charged with anything so far and even George back in the States can't pull off one of those airport scenes you see in the movies."

"You can find out what flight, where it's going, can't you?"

"We can and we will. Now, you want the good news? Stamps is it. What I said."

"How do you know? You've just been guessing."

"Listen to Detective Laaka. He's been working hard. While we were at the hospital and you were playing doctor, I took a look at Barbara's clothes. They were dumped in a heap on a chair outside the ER. Found a key in her skirt pocket and, since it had a number and the hotel name on it, I decided to keep it. Not that I don't trust the Italian police but this is a hometown matter."

"Go on," growled Alex. "So you went up to her room just now."

"Making sure the management had its head turned. And you guessed it, I found stamps."

"In a camera!" exclaimed Alex.

"Keep your voice down," said Mike. "Not in a camera, fitted into Barbara's writing case. Tucked into lined envelopes— between the lining and the outer paper. A nice selection of Confederate States issues. Nashville and New Orleans. And a couple of cuties from Hawaii and Guam, plus a couple of beautiful mint-condition Columbian issues. Something for every budget. And we're talking budgets well over a thousand bucks."

"God, what did you do with them? The stamps, I mean?"

"Put 'em in the hotel safe. Under my name. Soon to be flown home and handed over to George Fitts and his merry men." Mike rose from his chair and stretched. And yawned. "Busy day," he remarked. "Okay, is Sarah joining us? A night on the town before I gather up the garden lovers and take them home."

"Under lock and key?"

"If only. But when we make it home the DA is going to hit at least two of them—no, add the Hoppers, that makes four— with being accessories to fraud, robbery, and God knows what else."

"Accessory to murder?" Alex asked quietly.

Mike shrugged. "We'll see, but I'm sorry Stacy's off into the wild blue yonder. She's got quite a background. Did I tell you?"

"Tell him what?" It was Sarah. As if prepared for a party: dark hair brushed smoothly, small gold shell-shaped earrings in her ears, wearing her green silk dress.

Alex eyed her. "New?"

Sarah touched her ears. "A prescription for depression. I feel like the weather—about to blow up. Or come down. Spending a little money seemed to help. After I'd talked to Justin I decided to walk around town, look into shops. See Bellagio as a place to visit, not the scene of a crime. Also I bought these." Sarah reached into her handbag, produced a narrow white box and drew out a chain made from twisted strands of gold.

"It's for your mother," she told Alex. "Somehow I feel I owe her something, although I can't exactly say why."

"Nice," said Alex. "But don't ever try and explain it to her."

"So, okay," said Mike. "Tell us about this guy, Justin. What has the Legal Eagle been up to? Is he part of the camera scam? I only know the Hoppers were in on it and so was Stacy."

"At dinner," said Sarah. "At some little *ristorante* with a large menu and a view of the lake. Let's go before the storm hits. And I've had a call from Aunt Julia. She's not coming back here and wants to meet us in Milan tomorrow. I'm to pack her things. But she did squeeze it out about the Hoppers." She shook her head. "It's quite sad, but I'm hoping that someone—the Maine police or some kindly old judge—will have a little mercy."

"So what is it?" demanded Alex. "Julia wouldn't tell me."

"Give," said Mike.

"Over the antipasto, I will," said Sarah and headed for the door.

28

THE Ristorante Angelica, standing two-thirds of the way down the winding stone stairs of the Salita Serbelloni, was an establishment whose best feature was a roofed terrace giving a wide view of Lake Como. And because a rising wind had ruffled the now gray lake into whitecaps and thunder growled at the very gates of the town, the terrace was almost deserted.

"Privacy," announced Sarah. She indicated the roof overhung by a profusion of red flowers. "And we won't get entirely wet."

"Only struck by lightening," said Mike, unfolding his napkin.

There followed the serious business of ordering in a mixture of confused Italian, shreds of French with a base of English: Mike chose the *lasagne verdi* because the name was familiar; Alex, crab with cheese; and Sarah, chicken with asparagus tips. All begun with antipasti and the recommended table wine—*vino da tavola*. "At least," Sarah had said, "I guess the waiter's recommending it. He keeps sticking that carafe in our faces."

"His brother probably owns the vineyard," said Mike. "That's the way it works back home. Family backscratching."

After early hunger had been satisfied, and the storm had for the moment settled into a low snarling, Sarah put down her fork and returned to the subject of Stacy Daniel—for her, the least loved member of the tour party—Barbara Baxter excepted.

"Stacy," said Mike, "wasn't Stacy. That was about name number five. George worked through a heap of names, jobs, identities. Had to go out of state and dig around."

"And," prompted Sarah.

"Stacy was a sort of child crime prodigy. Drugs, rehab, kid hooker, junior pimp for a teenage prostitution ring. But she was pretty sharp at getting out of things. Youth home, couple of suspended sentences, assault charges dropped because not enough evidence. Name changes when necessary. But then, about six years ago, when she was about twenty-two, she pulls up her socks and enrolls in a community college."

"She found God?" queried Alex. "Or a good man?"

"Or a good woman?" put in Sarah. "Never underestimate the influence of a good woman."

"Actually, a good job," said Mike. "Modeling. She is, as you've noticed, quite a dish. Well, she pulled herself together, picked up a few contracts for sports ads and women's catalogues. Then hit the magazine covers. Made enough money to fund college tuition. Business major—accounting and personnel management. Honors degree. Then a year of grad school. A few years go by, and bingo, there's Stacy Daniel, publicity director for Back Bay City Bank, which has a bunch of branches in and around Boston."

Sarah put down her empty wineglass and Mike reached over and filled it. "And Barbara knew all this about Stacy?" she asked.

"That's Barbara's specialty," said Mike. "To know things about people. Dig dirty secrets out of the woodwork."

Alex nodded. "This is one case that doesn't make sense if you try to start with Ellen's murder."

"Yeah," Mike agreed. "Usually you begin with the homicide and branch out from there. But poor Ellen Trevino was just one obstacle—another wrench in the works. Barbara's works."

"What works, for heaven's sake," demanded Sarah.

"First," said Mike, "you tell us about Justin Rossi—Alex's rival—and about the Hoppers. Then I'll put it together for you. Though you did it yourself when you and Julia listened in on the Gregory–Barbara dinner scene. No, wait"—this as Sarah seemed about to explode—"George isn't here to force us to be logical, so I'm taking his place. I feel very George-like. So what did Barbara have on Rossi?"

"She caught him dressed up."

"Dressed up? Like for a party? You mean undressed?"

"Dressed. In a dress. He cross-dresses. It's what he does. His quirk, his hobby. What makes him feel good. He brought some women's clothes in store boxes and added to the wardrobe in High Roosting. In fact, I helped him buy some of the things. For his sister, he said. Only he hasn't got one. But Barbara found out a few years ago. He went on one of her art tours to Hawaii—the tours are legitimate, but I suppose they're also a part of Barbara's operation—the operation you're going to tell me about. Anyway, she caught him in drag—maybe in a grass skirt for all I know. Well, he was a great target for blackmail. A lawyer who's a member of a super-conservative Boston law firm, a lawyer whose specialty is family law. He swears he didn't know, didn't want to know what he was passing around in those cameras. And he says he had nothing to do with killing Ellen or dunking Henry. I really believe him. He's the woman who took care of Jack-the-Slitter at the Hound and Hare back in High Roosting—judging from the description of her. Besides, he saved my life—or my bones today," said Sarah. She grinned at her husband. "And anyone who looks like Alex must have redeeming qualities, even if he's been dealing in hollow cameras."

"Thank you," said Alex. "Saying nice things like that is what warms a marriage. Now the Hoppers. I could have wrung Julia's neck for not telling me."

"Julia took Edith and Margaret off to this little B&B overlooking Lake Lugano and calmed them down. I give her full credit for once in her life not acting like a Tyrannosaurus."

"Does this tie in with the information the police dug up about some sealed records pertaining to the Hoppers?" asked Mike.

Sarah nodded. "The first thing to know is that the Hoppers have never had much money. Their parents struggled and times were tough. So one day before Margaret's eleventh birthday when their parents had told her not to expect much in the way of presents, they went shopping. And Margaret came home with a new watch. And that began it. The sisters worked as a team and every now and then simply lifted little tidbits. Gloves, junk jewelry, handbags, perfume, cosmetics—they adore Lancôme products. They didn't do it too often, never at the same store twice in a row."

"Kleptomaniacs?" asked Mike.

"No. Not compulsion. They liked nice things and didn't have the money to buy them. They only got caught once, but the judge was friendly, the evidence wasn't clear—they'd dumped the stuff—and they were such upstanding members of the community that the charges evaporated and the records were ordered sealed. That's it. Until Barbara Baxter—who has the eye of a raptor—saw Margaret lifting a pair of gloves in Cirencester. And added the Hoppers to the camera distribution team."

"Something I'll bet Barbara regretted," said Mike.

"Two worse operators I can't imagine," said Sarah. "Just because they were good at shoplifting didn't mean they were ready for the big time. And they were so humiliated at being caught and so afraid of it all coming out and so nervous about pretending to take pictures and meeting agents that they simply went to pieces."

"They're well over seventy," said Alex. "What's their future?"

Mike shrugged. "Depends on a lot of things. Good defense lawyer, mitigating circumstances, willingness to cooperate with the DA's office and testify about Barbara. If it comes to trial those two ladies would look pretty pathetic on a witness stand. They'd have the jury in tears. I'll bet they end up with some sort of suspended sentence. Rossi might not fare so well, but then he's a lawyer himself. He may find a loophole."

The waiter arrived with three little dishes of strawberries covered with cream and looked meaningfully at the waterfront. *"Tempesta,"* he announced.

Sarah following his glance saw that the lake surface had gone from gray to dark slate. "Five more minutes and then I think we'll have to evacuate. Or find an ark. So, go on, Mike. You're driving me crazy. What *was* in those cameras? I've thought of everything from cocaine to radioactive diamonds. Or miniature folk art made entirely of eighteen-caret gold."

"None of you had the proper childhood hobbies," said Mike. "It was stamps. Valuable rare stamps. The sort that are impossible to find unless you're a millionaire or you steal 'em."

"Stamps?" repeated Sarah stupidly.

"Alex told me Gregory dealt in southern crafts. That was his cover. Baxter Enterprises. But he was dealing in stamps. Moving them out of the country, passing them to agents all over the map, I suppose. Confederate stamps are very desirable if they're in good condition. And if he'd got his mitts on a collection of Hawaiian missionary stamps, well, the prices for those have gone through the ceiling. As have the prices for early U.S. issues. We're talking thousands and thousands of bucks. As soon as Alex said 'off center' and 'PolyPro film'—that's the stuff used to protect them—I was pretty sure what Gregory and sister Barbara were up to."

Sarah's eyes widened. Suddenly she remembered Gregory after dinner. Talking about his business. Smiling his smooth, deep voice explaining, "We do a lot with paper artifacts. In as mint condition as possible. Perfect condition counts for a lot. From the south. And Hawaii." And that those were his special areas.

"What a slime!" exclaimed Sarah. "He told us right to our faces." She looked up into Mike's face. "You've got proof?" she asked.

"Genuine proof. Made a little visit to Barbara's hotel room a while ago and looked in her writing case. Beautiful stamps tucked into the lining of the envelopes. Made my eyes bulge."

"Her Crane writing paper!" exclaimed Sarah. "And I only thought she liked to write expensive letters."

"The rest of her so-called helpers used cameras," said Mike. "You don't need a lot of space for stamps. Just a safe container.

Gregory or Barbara probably picked up cheap or used cameras and gutted them."

Sarah speared a strawberry with an angry thrust. "I never guessed. And old cameras are everywhere. The Good Will shops. Yard sales. Everyone wants new models and they dump the old ones."

"Harmless-looking tourist types traveling with a camera," said Mike, "aren't questioned by airlines. Put those cameras through X-ray, let 'em be sniffed by dogs and they're clean. Tourists *without* cameras are conspicuous. As for the others on the trip, Barbara probably recruited them to carry the stuff. Help with the distribution."

"Not just to carry stamps in cameras," put in Sarah. "Those assistants acted as a back-up chorus. All those tour changes Barbara suggested—London, Cirencester, Cambridge—her assistants, Stacy, Justin, and later the Hoppers supported her. Of course, Sandi and Fred helped out innocently because they were always up for a side trip. Both Ouellettes are more tourists than garden lovers. But some of those assistants were less than ideal help. Justin floated around at night in drag—Julia said Barbara chewed him out once, so maybe she caught him as Jessica Roundtree. Then there were Margaret and Edith red-eyed and trembling like leaves."

Mike grinned. "You just can't get proper help these days."

"Of course," Sarah added, "I noticed that Justin and Stacy didn't take pictures in the gardens. Only in the cities, where I suppose they met their assigned contact. And, of course, Margaret and Edith were hopeless. That scene on the bench in Cambridge, pretending to take pictures of trees. Really. But the Hopper cameras were new, weren't they? Not old yard-sale models."

"Barbara just said the cameras were new. Margaret and Edith wouldn't know what a state-of-the-art camera looked like. They'd been using twenty-year-old Kodaks," said Mike. "The cameras probably all looked okay."

"Margaret and Edith," repeated Sarah. "The poor dears."

"Those poor dears," said Mike with a noticeable lack of sympathy, "have apparently been operating on the wrong side of the law for years." He raised his wineglass. "Now, let's skip the rest of the crap and have a good time. Here's to a terrific dinner."

"No, wait," said Sarah. "What about Ellen? And Henry?"

"Come on," said Mike, "you can figure that one out."

But before Sarah could answer lightning split the skies, the thunder crashed, the wind swept down on the town, on the streets, the houses, the shops, the restaurants, café umbrellas down along the piazza folded, the rain spattered on the terrace roof and blew through the open sides over the dinner table. The candles flickered and expired and for a moment time stood still.

Sarah, Alex, and Mike moved back against the far wall and watched the storm work its will. Watched tree branches thrash, vines tremble, and, most wonderful of all, saw lightning in double and triple streaks play across the mountains, strike into the lake, zigzag back over the rooftops, and skewer a distant clump of trees.

And then, grumbling, muttering as if in high dudgeon at being recalled, the storm retired again behind the mountains. The rain shrank to a small patter and the wind softened and turned away.

And somehow, the storm had not only cleansed the heavy air, it had cleared away the patches of fog in Sarah's brain.

The three found the waiter, paid the bill—"millions and millions of lira," marveled Mike—and began the climb up the wet cobblestones of the Selita Serbelloni toward their hotel.

"It's all coming together," said Sarah. "Poor Ellen was killed because garden tours aren't like ordinary tourist tours. The kind Barbara had been leading. The kind where she was the boss. She could do what she wanted with her own groups."

"That's right," said Mike. "Up to this Midcoast Garden Club thing, she handled all tour details. Set the convenient—convenient to her—itinerary, changed reservations en route if she had to, and no one argued with her about where to stay, when to leave. She knew enough about art galleries and museums, the southern states, about Hawaii—she was born there—to give satisfaction. Knew her way around South America. So the tours must have have worked on two levels: legitimate sight-seeing and undercover to move stolen stamps to agents and dealers who had clients salivating for certain issues. Gregory was chief, Barbara his field commander."

"And then," said Sarah, "Barbara comes smack against a tough co-leader, Lillian Garth, who adds another strong-minded expert—Ellen Trevino. Later, of course, Carter fills the gap with another expert, Henry Ruggles."

"So," said Alex, "Barbara pushes Lillian down the cellar stairs—by turning off the light—if she did. You may never prove it because Lillian doesn't remember. Typical for head traumas."

"But next," said Mike, "there's Ellen. Barbara saw her three days before the trip and Barbara undoubtedly found that Ellen had a mind of her own."

"Yes," said Sarah. "Barbara would find out fast what Ellen told me. The trip was entirely serious and there weren't going to be any tourist deviations. No fancy restaurants, no shopping excursions, no daytime pub visiting. The schedule was sacred."

"Remember," Mike pointed out, "Ellen mentioned to Mrs. Epple, her neighbor, about a meeting, seeing a friend, going to check on something. Well, it looks like Barbara was ready for her. Either by prearrangement, or she trailed Ellen into a turnpike rest stop. Came prepared to kill and covered the rental car seats with a plastic tarp. Maybe brought a gun but then found the dibble among Ellen's gardening tools. Wore a slicker to protect against blood spattering and put on that head scarf and the dark glasses so no passing tourist will get a good look at her."

"So," said Alex, "since Ellen is a trusting soul, Barbara, at some point, talks her into sharing the ride to Logan. Maybe Barbara goes to a phone booth to make a fake call and then tells Ellen she's arranged to have her car picked up and so they can travel in her rental."

"So," put in Mike, "Barbara loads Ellen's luggage into her car. But we haven't found the car or the luggage."

"Wait up," shouted Sarah. She came to a halt in front of a shop announcing "La Lanterna—Snack Bar." A great light had suddenly broken. "Barbara brought that big suitcase. She tells us to travel light, then there she is at the Logan with this monster. Like mine. I thought hers must be filled with her tour stuff, guidebooks, and garden folders. But then she dumps it in Vernon and has the gall to say I should dump mine, too. But I did notice that even with a big suitcase she only seemed to have a few changes of clothes. Always in that plum cotton thing. Because—"

"Because," broke in Alex, "her suitcase didn't hold clothes, it held Ellen Trevino's luggage. Ellen probably did travel light. A carry-on and a briefcase. And Barbara could just fit them in a big suitcase along with a few of her own personal things and the suitcase flies to Heathrow on Barbara's ticket."

"If I were pulling this off," said Mike, "I'd empty out Ellen's stuff as soon as possible. Put it in storage. Or deep-six it. In London, maybe? Barbara wouldn't want to take the chance of someone opening her big suitcase. Someone like Sarah."

"Who went snooping into everyone's room at the Shearing Inn," said Alex in a disapproving voice.

"The big suitcase was in her room," said Sarah. "I unzipped it and it was empty. And Barbara's clothes were in her bureau."

"Okay, she must have dumped Ellen's things by then," said Mike. "George can ask the Metropolitan Police in London to check out storage units. The hotel the group stayed at. Bus stations, train stations. Heathrow."

"Or the Thames," added Sarah. She resumed the walk and then, as they reached the glistening wet pavement of the Via Garibaldi, stopped a second time and faced the two men. "Some other things don't make sense. Why was Barbara's room ransacked at the same time mine was? And who pushed Henry in the Kiftsgate swimming pool? Not Barbara. Or even Stacy. And last, why did Barbara give Henry CPR at Giverny when he was one of the tour people she was trying to get rid of?"

"Think. Both of you," said Alex.

"Well, I don't get that part at all," admitted Mike.

But Sarah was remembering. She returned to her ravaged bedroom at the Shearing. Listened again to Barbara's voice saying, "You, too." Then heard Barbara insisting that Sarah and

Julia inspect her own room. That perhaps the same person had ransacked both.

"We were set up, she wrecked her own room," said Sarah, shaking her head. She walked ahead a few steps, turning her thoughts to Henry. Excitable, talkative Henry. Never looking where he was going. Who stumbled. Tripped over his own feet. "I suppose," she said, reluctantly, "that Henry simply fell in the Kiftsgate pool. A genuine, honest-to-goodness accident."

"Which gave Barbara the idea," said Mike.

"But," protested Sarah, "what about resuscitating Henry? There she was giving him CPR, really working him over."

"How hard do you suppose she would have worked if you hadn't shown up and then the French doctor?" said Alex. "And it's possible that she didn't have to drown him, just waterlog him, damage him. See that he quit the group. Which is just what happened."

They had reached the gate of the terraced garden of Albergo Nuovo. And, as if by agreement, the three friends walked down to the lower level and stood facing the lake—now a dim wrinkled expanse set under the dark outlines of the mountains.

"My first night in Italy," said Mike. "And my last night, too. So much for foreign travel. Well, it hasn't been dull."

"I suppose," said Sarah, "I'll look back on some of the trip as not being entirely awful. There were moments."

"Like tonight," Alex reminded her. "The storm."

"And some of the gardens, the roses, the wisteria, the red valerian, Sissinghurst at night. Monet's farmhouse and the lily pond. The drive to Bellagio. I'd like to come back."

"So let's," said Alex.

Mike yawned. "What do they call it when you go through a lot of time zones? I feel a little groggy."

"You'll feel worse back home tomorrow night," said Alex cheerfully. "It's called double jet lag."

"Hey," said a voice. A remembered voice, one noted for breaking into moments of quietness and peace.

"It's me, Amy," said Amy materializing from behind a clipped hedge. "Mother said I could stay up late because it's my last night here. As long as I stayed here in the garden. And, Sarah, I have this new idea for a book. Not a modern murder mystery. Those are gross. This is going to be an Italian romance thing. Here in Bellagio back in the sixteenth century with poisoned wine, and someone being killed because he owes moneylenders, and lovers hanging over balconies, and families having feuds and duels and ghosts of dead fathers haunting their sons."

Alex walked over to Amy, took her by the shoulder and pointed her toward the hotel terrace. "Good night, Amy. *Arrivederci. Ciao.* Go to bed. Your story has already been written. It's called *Romeo, the Merchant of Hamlet.*

Afterword

ENGLISH teachers who are both mystery novel addicts and fans of the nineteenth-century novel appreciate an ending. Or closure, as it is popularly called. Sarah Deane was no exception, so five days after the evening of the Bellagio storm, she and Julia Clancy and Alex, forces joined, sat together on a soft June evening on several lawn chairs over looking a distant pasture. The pasture belonged to the Dodgeson Farm, the very place where the Clancy–Deane English experience had begun. Where Julia had considered adding Suffolk Punch to her stable. Where Sarah had become agitated about an alien scarf and a pair of sunglasses. And where Julia today had chosen as a place for the three to decompress before they had to take up everyday life.

The three, however, had been busy communicating with the world at large and with the police world in particular. Barbara Baxter, Alex informed them, would be ready to be flown home under guard and, although she had not admitted to murder, she had talked at length about the business of transporting stamps in innocent-looking containers. She had balked at first, but it had been pointed out that her best interests lay on the side of the truth. Further, her cooperation was motivated by her fury when she found out that brother Gregory had taken off from Bellagio and . . .

"Hold it," said Sarah. "How did he get to Bellagio? And how did he know Barbara had been hurt?"

"Gregory," said Alex, "along with Barbara, got the wind up when you and Julia turned up to sit in on their restaurant dinner in Vernon. He decided to trail you to Giverny and follow you across France. See if he could ditch you or, worse, get rid of you."

Sarah turned pale. "The gray Peugeot."

"Since he didn't catch you, you must have been driving like fiends from hell." Alex looked at the two women with lifted eyebrows. "Then," he went on, "Gregory made for Bellagio to check on Barbara, found she was in the hospital, and took off for points unknown, leaving her—in gang-talk—to take the rap. Barbara claims that Gregory planned everything, including the elimination of strong-minded tour leaders. She blames him for Ellen's murder and said he masterminded the disposal of Ellen Trevino's body at the Biddeford Maine Turnpike exit. That she, Barbara, was horrified, and was just along for the ride."

Sarah shook her head, her expression grim. "There was no Gregory around when Lillian Garth fell down the cellar stairs or when Henry went into the river at Giverny. And judging from her expression when she came at me on the steps at Bellagio, she was more than capable of driving a dibble into poor Ellen Trevino."

"Barbara's trying to sing. Or squeal. Isn't that what gangsters do?" asked Julia. She had returned to her equestrian scene needlepoint with renewed vigor and was engaged in driving her needle back and forth through the knee of a rider.

"They don't sing anymore," said Sarah. "That's passé. Now I think they rat on each other. In this case I think we have two large rats and some lesser ones."

But Julia had other news. "I talked to Portia McClure. The McClures are back home, but they left Toad Ruggles doing well. He had a touch of pneumonia but he's better and is staying with

Leslie and Harold to recuperate. Remember Thalia Cottage, Sarah?"

"How could I forget? Calpurnia and Julius Caesar."

"Portia reports that Leslie and Harold are being very attentive, and she hopes Henry doesn't drive them crazy making suggestions about their garden."

"How about Margaret and Edith?" asked Sarah, turning to Alex, who had just finished a long call to Maine.

"In good hands. A family lawyer and plea bargains in the works. They may be able to keep their past activities fairly quiet because Ellen's murder and the Baxter Enterprise scam are really the attention getters."

Julia looked up from her needlepoint. "What about that unpleasant Stacy Daniel? You and Mike saw her heading out in an airport limo?"

Alex nodded. "She beat it out of Italy, flew to Lisbon, and jumped on a flight to Amsterdam, where she was met by the local police. Which, in due course, is what will happen to Gregory. He's said to be holed up in Switzerland. And Ellen's luggage has finally turned up. Her passport, her wallet, and any other I.D. had been dumped somewhere, but the duffel and briefcase came to light in a utility closet in that hotel on Ebury Street—you know, where the group stayed the first night in London.

"But why the delay?" demanded Sarah. "Why didn't the hotel people call the police right away when they found the luggage?"

"Because," said Alex, "when she got to London Barbara made out new luggage tags for Ellen's bags, and since Ellen's briefcase had the initials E.T. stamped on it, she had to come up with a matching name."

"Are you going to tell me the hotel people thought they were entertaining an extraterrestrial visitor?" asked Julia.

Alex grinned and shook his head. "You won't believe this but Barbara came up with one name that stopped the hotel cold."

"I'll bite," said Julia, pulling her wool too tight and bunching the stitches on a rider's head.

"Elizabeth Taylor," said Alex with satisfaction. "When the luggage was found, the hotel people had a sort of collective seizure, but because no one had reported Miss Taylor missing, the manager decided she'd been staying incognito at the hotel and wouldn't be pleased to have the police called."

This information was sufficient to bring about total silence, and for a few moments the three sat quietly watching the pasture scene. Sarah saw that the two chestnut horses—the Suffolk Punch—were moving toward the gate. It must be feeding time. She and Julia had really come full circle. Tomorrow they'd have to drive to Heathrow and fly home. Full circle was right. The airborne panic, sweaty palms, and having to recite Dan McGrew.

"Alex," she said. "Don't you have a real knock-out pill? So I'm completely out of it until we're back on the ground."

Julia smiled her all-knowing smile. "Sarah, calm yourself. I have solved your flying problem. You may rest easy tonight."

Sarah looked at her aunt doubtfully. "You have?"

"Yes. I have talked to the DA's office and we've a period of grace for our depositions. And Alex had already cleared the rest of this week and his back-up agrees to cover for a few more days."

"Aunt Julia, you're not making sense."

"Don't interrupt. You and I and Alex will not be going to Heathrow. I'm giving myself a seventy-first birthday present ahead of time. We will drive to Southampton and there climb aboard *The Queen Victoria*—that new Cunard cruise ship. Sister to the *QEII*. On it we will cross the Atlantic, not fly over it."

"You mean we're going by boat?"

"Or a ship. Ship is the preferred word."

Sarah got up and threw her arms around her aunt's neck. "Hallelujah. We don't have to take off and look down from thirty thousand feet and then circle over Boston for hours. You've made me very happy."

"And," added Julia, with a sidelong glance at her niece, "only a few icebergs have been reported on our route."